Becoming NADIA

Cyrus Keith

MuseItUp Publishing
www.museituppublishing.com

Becoming NADIA © 2012 by Cyrus Keith

MuseItUp Publishing
14878 James, Pierrefonds, Quebec, Canada, H9H 1P5
http://www.museituppublishing.com

Cover Art © 2010 by Delilah K. Stephens
Edited by Fiona Young-Brown
Copyedited by Greta Gunselman
Layout and Book Production by Lea Schizas

Print ISBN: 978-1-77127-181-3
eBook ISBN: 978-1-926931-54-8

Production by MuseItUp Publishing

Becoming NADIA

♦

Book One in
The NADIA Project

Epic Award-Winning Novel

♦

Cyrus Keith

For Dad, who taught me how to dream.

Acknowledgements

To my family, who sacrificed so much of me to make this a reality. I love you all. To my God, who makes old men dream dreams, and young men see visions.

Author's Note: Irving's account of the opening days of the Korean conflict are taken from General William Dean's citation for the Medal of Honor he received from his and his unit's actions at Taejon. In honor of all who place themselves between Evil and the Innocent.

"This book is an excellent thriller with impeccable pacing and believable characters."
—Zellakate's Reviews

"Nadia may be missing her memory, but this is one story you will never forget!"
—Rachel DiMaggio, Freelance and Fiction.weebly

Chapter One

She had no memory of her own from before the Darkness. She had no feeling, no taste, no perception at all. All was formless and void, the silent bliss of the Nothing. The Darkness was complete, and she floated in blank oblivion, a peace so total that no care existed to interrupt her sleep. She felt nothing, saw nothing, heard and thought nothing, and was at peace.

There came a moment when she began to sense there was more than her in this world, the beginnings of a farther consciousness. Awareness awoke in her. Perceptions came. Noises invaded, small and gentle but persistent. More and more, they infiltrated her senses. Hums, beeps, ticks, and tocks washed over her mind in waves that carried away the Nothing, replacing it piece by piece with her surroundings.

Hearing: "Nadia? Nadia, I need you to open your eyes for me, please." The gentle male voice sounded alien to her ears, as if from a great distance. *Who's Nadia?*

Comprehension: She understood someone was talking to someone named...Nadia.

Sensation: A gentle touch registered on her arm as the voice spoke again. "Nadia? Open your eyes, dear."

Identity: She was Nadia. There was something in her mind, a nagging feeling that it wasn't right, *couldn't* be right. But the man insisted. "Open your eyes, Nadia."

Awareness.

Nadia complied, though with some effort. The lids were stiff, unresponsive at first. She had to *think* about moving them, and finally she forced them open. After a few more experimental blinks, a small but intense white light pierced into her eyes. She blinked shut again in irritation and the same voice droned in her ears. "I'm sorry, Nadia, but I have to see into your eyes."

"Why?" Her own voice sounded like a harsh croak. It hurt to speak. "Where am I?" She left her eyes closed. If someone was going to shine a light into her eyes, he'd better have a damned good reason, and she was in no mood to put up with any foolishness. It was hard enough just to talk. Her lips felt dry, swollen; her throat was parched.

The man's response was good-natured, but insistent. "You're in hospital in Twin Oaks. Come, now. Let us see your eyes, please."

From somewhere in the shadows of her mind came concepts and images she could grasp, even though she couldn't remember having experienced them before. The doctor spoke with a heavy, European accent — German? Danish, maybe. Something else flashed in her mind. "Where's Phillip? And why am I in a hospital?"

A woman chuckled in the far corner of the room. "Always the good reporter, full of questions. All in good time, dear. Let the doctor examine you. You've been through a lot."

"What *have* I been through?"

"Later," said the doctor. "I can only help you if you cooperate with me. Now, if you please...."

Nadia reluctantly opened her eyes and let the doctor pull down on her bottom eyelid while he shined that irritating light into her eyes again. After several seconds, she heard a satisfied grunt and the light source diminished, but a shapeless gray blob obscured her vision for several frustrating seconds.

She heard the sharp clank of metal scraping on a tray. The doctor took her forearm in his hand. "Just a few taps to test your reflexes, now." The rubber mallet struck the inside of her elbow. Her arm twitched, and a shock of pain flared up her arm. She moaned in response and the doctor hastily apologized as he moved on to her other elbow, then each knee, and each ankle. Finally, he was done. *About damned time.*

Her vision slowly cleared, and now she could focus on her surroundings. She was indeed in a hospital bed, in a hospital room, but what a room! It was large, lit by several panels in the ceiling. Cable tracks supported wiring bundles that routed signals between a half-dozen different computers and a motley collection of equipment cabinets that lined the walls. More boxes were stacked on top of the cabinets so the equipment obscured the walls and any windows that may have existed. Display screens, knobs, dials, and keypads filled the front panels of all those cabinets and boxes, and lines, numbers, and strange patterns filled the screens. Had the ceiling lights been turned off, the glow from all those screens and illuminated switches would still have lighted the room.

Nadia was hooked up to three different intravenous tubes. Wires led from at least a dozen places on her head and body to that strange array of gadgets.

In addition to the doctor, there were six others inside with her, standing or sitting around, with various expressions of concern or interest on their faces. The doctor and two of the women wore identical sets of purple scrubs with bouffant caps. Three men stood by in jeans and casual shirts, next to another woman who wore khaki slacks and a simple blue blouse. Slim, brunette, and beautiful, she smiled warmly at Nadia as their eyes met. Nadia did not return the smile. She was still as confused as when she first opened her eyes.

Nadia tried to sit up. She felt weak, nearly unable even to raise her arms to grasp the side rails. The pain in her limbs was nearly unbearable, but she had to try. "Where's Phillip, what's happened—?" A gentle hand pushed against her chest. She fell back, unable to resist.

"Not just yet, please, we still have to make sure you're all right." The doctor whispered to one of the women in scrubs, who turned to one of the pieces of electronic gear that filled the walls and turned a couple of dials. Then she entered a code into a keypad. Nadia heard a "beep" as the command was entered, and suddenly she couldn't remember whom she was so concerned about before. A warm, slick feeling spread slowly in her mind and she was sleepy again. "Now how do you feel, Nadia?"

"Kind of tired," she slurred. "A little weak. Like I forgot how to blink."

A slight chuckle was suddenly stifled, and then the doctor spoke again. "And who were you so concerned about?"

"I—" Nadia tried to glean the memory, but it was as if she'd put it down somewhere in her mind and lost it; it just wasn't where she thought it was. She searched her mind again, but it was gone. "I...don't know. What were you saying again?"

"What about pain? On a scale of one to ten, how is the pain?"

The drugged feeling was leaving her mind, but only slowly. Her words staggered out in a slow slur. "I don't feel any pain until I move. Then, it's pretty bad. About a seven."

The doctor smiled and leaned closer. "All right. We can help you soon with the pain. Now, what do you remember about the incident?"

7

Incident? There was an incident? *So that's why I'm here.* "I—" Nadia struggled with her memories, trying to retrieve something about what, or who…it just wasn't coming. Very little of anything was coming. "I… remember…I'm sorry, I can't remember anything about it." Did Nadia imagine it, or did a collective sigh of relief fill the room?

"Well," he said, standing, "At least you seem to be in good physical shape. I'd say we're out of the woods, here. Welcome back, Miss Velasquez." He grinned and reached out, taking her hand gently in both of his. "I'm Doctor Petr Hamund, and these are all friends." He indicated the taller woman in scrubs with a casual wave. "This is Doctor Spielberg, my assistant, and this," he said, pointing to the woman in khaki's, "is Doctor Mitchell. I believe you may already know Mr. Olsen, Mr. Hicks, and Mr. Glass. These gentlemen are all team members at your studio and Miss Paine here is your physical therapist, all concerned for you. You were a very lucky woman."

"I'm sorry, I don't remember any of you. What happened to me?"

"I believe we need to leave you alone with Dr. Mitchell and she can explain some things to you." Dr. Hamund waved the others out and followed them after turning once more to smile at Nadia. "I'll be back in a while to see how you are doing and to give you something for your pain."

For some time after everyone had left, Nadia lay still while Dr. Mitchell sat on the bedside stool, quietly watching her.

Nadia still felt drowsy, but she was more bothered from not knowing or remembering anything than from being tired. She was steeling herself to ask questions for which she wasn't sure she wanted to know the answers. *Ah, well... let's get to it, shall we?* "Okay, Doc, give it to me straight. Why did they leave you here? Was there a vote and you lost, or something?"

The doctor smiled. "No, there wasn't a vote. And you can call me Becca, okay? I'm your psychiatrist; I'm here to help you ease back into your life."

"Okay, then." Nadia took a deep breath, and let it out. *A psychiatrist. Great. Does someone think I'm crazy?* "I'm not sure I really need a psychiatrist—"

"Who's Phillip?" Becca leaned closer and looked into Nadia's eyes. She had dark brown eyes that seemed to penetrate into Nadia's soul, probing gently but firmly for some hidden truth.

"Is this some kind of test?" Nadia snipped. "Look, Becca, I think you mean well, but don't even think about playing head games with me. In case you haven't noticed, I'm not in the best shape of my life right now—"

"You asked about someone named Phillip," said Becca, her voice even and smooth. "I was wondering what you could remember."

Nadia looked away, uncomfortable. She couldn't stay angry with someone so damned *calm*. The room was silent save for the sounds made by the medical equipment surrounding her: the whirrs and buzzes from the IV pumps, beep-beeps from the monitors. A kind of thrumming, pulsing power hum made a sonic background that was somehow strangely comforting. But try as she might, she just couldn't find that memory. Was it even there at all? "I can't remember. Do I know a Phillip?"

"I don't recall there being one mentioned in your file. Is there anyone you need us to contact?"

"Why can't I remember?"

Becca paused before answering. "Sometimes a head trauma like you experienced can affect the memory centers of the brain—"

"What 'head trauma'? What happened to me?"

"One thing at a time, dear. I'll get to that in a moment." The doctor retrieved a folder and opened it, carefully leafing through the contents.

Nadia caught glimpses of forms and notes, but couldn't read what was in the folder from her angle.

"Nadia, it says here that both your parents were killed in an auto accident some years ago. You don't have any brothers or sisters. Is there someone else we can call for you?"

Mom and Dad? Dead? Where in hell was I? Nadia felt a dread rising in her soul. She fought it back and tried to think of an answer to the question at hand. "I can't think of anyone. Maybe Phillip was in a dream or something."

"Maybe so."

Nadia's fingers worried at the hem of her blanket. She watched her hands work for a few seconds, as if they were something she'd never seen before. Before fear froze the question on her lips, she asked, "I've been unconscious, haven't I?"

"Yes, you were in an extended coma," answered the doctor.

"How long?"

There was a long pause. "Three years, seven months and thirteen days."

Nadia felt a sudden flush wash over her face like an icy splash. Tears formed at the corners of her eyes. Her hands began to tremble and she knitted her fingers together to steady them. It didn't work. She looked down at her arms. Three IV tubes pushed fluids into her. She raised her hands to her head and felt a tangle of filaments. She followed the snarl with her fingers until she could see what it was. A hydra of tiny, multicolored wires led away from her scalp to join into a harness running to a machine that drew a series of scraggly lines across a monitor screen.

The fear was stronger now, almost overpowering. Her voice shook as she asked, "Wh-what happened?"

"You were interviewing the President of Nigeria. There was an assassination attempt; someone planted a bomb in the president's office. You survived, but it took twenty-three surgeries just to restore your face, and God knows how many more to fix the rest of your body."

Nadia reached up with both hands. Her face felt strange and rubbery under her fingers. She closed her eyes, trying to remember what she felt like before. It wasn't coming to her.

Becca's smooth, comforting voice went on. "John Bowman, the owner of Bowman Communications, personally rounded up the best surgeons in the country to fix you. That was, as I said, over three years ago. Everyone missed you."

"What about those people, the ones who were here? Why were they here?"

"We called your station as soon as you started showing signs of coming back around. Mr. Hicks, Mr. Glass, and Mr. Olsen wanted to be here so you could have familiar faces around you when you woke up."

Becca stood and took Nadia's hand in both of hers. "We're all so glad you're back. You've had thousands of letters and cards from your fans. I'll bet your email is a sight to behold."

Nadia, tearful, pushed her away and tried again to sit up. Finally, with great difficulty, she reached out and grabbed the bedrails, pulling herself up to a sitting position. Pain yanked at her arms, her back, and her legs as she tried to move them. "Familiar faces? *Familiar, hell*! I don't know any of those men! I have to go," she muttered. "I have to get out of here!" She began to claw at the tubes in her arms.

The doctor reached out quickly and grasped her hands, pinning them to the bed. She leaned over and looked closely into Nadia's face. "Listen to me. You're not strong enough yet. You need some time to recover. It's been a long time since you even opened your eyes. Frankly, it's a miracle you can even talk." She released one of Nadia's wrists and gently pressed on her chest to help her lie back down.

Nadia tried to resist, but was too weak to do anything but comply.

She sobbed as Becca went on. "Please; work on getting better a little at a time, Okay?"

Becca settled Nadia in and poured a cup of water from a pitcher on the tray table. She elevated the bed's head and offered the drink to Nadia, who took it hesitantly and sipped. The water went down with some effort, and felt uncomfortable on her stomach, but stayed down. She sipped again, and it helped her calm down, giving her something on which to focus. As the tension faded, An overwhelming tiredness overcame her, as if this one visit had been a great effort. She handed the cup back to the doctor. "Thank you."

The door opened and a nurse came in with a syringe. Wordlessly she found a lock in one of Nadia's tubes and injected a clear liquid into it. Seconds later, A cold sensation crept up Nadia's arm, and, by the time the nurse put the empty syringe into the sharps container by the door and walked out, she began to feel sluggish. But the pain was beginning to subside.

"Becca? I'm sleepy. Can I sleep for a while?"

Dr. Mitchell rose and stepped toward the door. "Of course. The call button is at your left hand. Press it if you need anything." As she walked out, Nadia drifted off to sleep.

She dreamed of a man named Phillip.

Chapter Two

"At least it's warm today," said Nadia. The lift stopped at the bottom of the therapy pool and Nadia floated free from the chair, supported by Jenna Paine. She eased Nadia out into the middle of the water, chest-deep on the petite therapist.

"Okay, yeah, sorry 'bout that last time," said Jenna. "But remember, it was cold for me, too. Now remember, the water is here to support your weight and provide resistance for your workout. Let's get moving, now. Start with your arms."

It still hurt to move. Strength was coming, but too slowly for Nadia's liking. "Tell me something," she said as she worked, "Why is it that I can speak as well as you, but I can barely move my limbs?"

"Bigger movements; come on," coached Jenna. Nadia complied, and Jenna began to explain. "Your facial muscles operate from a different part of your brain than your limbs. They also use different neural pathways, different nerve trunks. Your long-term memory center took the worst of the damage. Besides, your brain spent three years disconnected from your body. Some of those neural pathways need to reconnect. Your body is perfectly fit. Your brain just needs to learn how to talk to it again."

Nadia continued stroking her arms through the water, rebuilding strength against the fluid's resistance. Finally, her shoulders began to loosen up. "How bad was it, really?" she asked. "When I came here... how bad was I...?"

Jenna's answer was brisk, almost impatient. "I wasn't here when you were first brought in. Okay, let's work on your legs. I'm going to stand you up, and I want you to try to bear weight.... Good, that's excellent!"

Jenna stepped up the workout, keeping the pace just brisk enough to keep Nadia at her physical limit. When Nadia finally returned to the chair, she was so exhausted she couldn't think of anything other than getting back to her room.

When the lift came out of the water, she felt the transition from the relative weightlessness of the pool to her true weight, and found she could barely raise an arm. Jenna rolled the chair off the lift and into a locker room where she helped her change into a dry set of scrubs that served well enough as pajamas. A large, cubical bin squatted in one corner of the locker room. Jenna opened the top and drew out a warm blanket, wrapping it around Nadia before rolling her back out into the hallway on the therapy floor. Nadia relished the warmth and comfort against her skin, and soon it spread into her weary body. "So how am I doing?" she asked as they approached the elevator.

"Amazing, hon. Believe me, you're coming along just great."

"It seems to me I should be able to do more than just wheel around in a damn chair. It's been a month already, and I'm tired of being so tired all the time."

The elevator doors opened and Jenna pushed the chair in. "Give it some time yet. Patience is your best friend right now."

"Oh, Lord, give me patience...now!" The doors slid closed and they rode back to the seventh floor.

* * * *

The next morning, Nadia was in the middle of her breakfast when Jenna came into her room carrying a file folder about six inches thick.

"What's up, Mistress Pain?" joked Nadia as she pushed some egg yolk around her plate with a biscuit.

Jenna ignored the play on her name; it had become a regular routine for Nadia to pipe up, "Where there's Paine, there's pain," whenever she saw the therapist coming.

"Here it is," said Jenna. "I found your file. You can either spend the day reading it, or we can work out again; your choice."

Nadia paused, looking at the sheer size of the folder. "What's in it?"

"Everything from Nigeria to now," said Jenna. "Right here."

Nadia put her tray aside and reached out to take it.

Jenna put her hand on top of the folder, pinning it to the table. "Before you open that, think about what you really want to know, Nadia. It's not pretty." A light shone in Jenna's eyes that Nadia had never seen before. A warning? "It's your past; it's over and done with. Do you really want to relive what put you *here* for three years?"

"But that's *me* in there, Jenna. I want to know who I am."

13

"This," said Jenna, patting the file, "is not *you*. This is what happened *to* you. Now, you can live with letting things keep happening *to* you, or you can turn your back on this, move on, and start making things happen *for* you. What'll it be?"

Nadia thought for a long moment. She could know. But what exactly *would* she know, and how could it help her get her life back? But if there *was* something in there.... "Maybe just some highlights," she finally said. "I probably wouldn't understand anything in it anyway."

"Okay, I'll just pull out one or two details then, and when you've had enough, we can be on our way."

Jenna opened the file and leafed through, picking out a sheet here and there. "Here's an MRI report from your first week: 'Shattered mandible left side, Vertebrae C3 through C6 shattered, spinal cord trauma, cervical; left scapula fractured, left lung perforated, six broken ribs, left temporal bone broken and displaced, temporal lobe trauma, frontal lobe trauma—' There's about three pages all told, but it's some list. Wanna read?" She offered the file to Nadia, who waved it away.

"No, I think I'll pass. Let me just finish up here and brush my teeth and I'll be ready to go."

"Very well, then; I'll get this back to the nurses' station and they can make sure it gets back to the file room. Be right back."

Jenna breezed out with the file and came back empty-handed just as Nadia finished freshening up. She didn't bring Nadia's wheelchair over to the bed; she parked it across the room and locked the rear wheels. After lowering the bed's side rail, she stood back with arms akimbo and a sly little grin on her face. "Ready?"

"I can't make it all the way over there," said Nadia.

"Keep saying that, and it'll never change. Come on, I want to see you try."

"Help me sit up, anyway," said Nadia. Jenna stood closer and offered a hand. Nadia grabbed it with both of hers and pulled herself upright, straining until she trembled from the effort. She sat at the edge of the bed for several seconds, glaring at the chair on the other side of the room. Jenna took her hand away and stepped back. Nadia dropped her hands to either side of her bottom to steady herself, and tried to scoot forward off the bed.

14

"Come on, Nadia, push with your hands. Now lean forward, that's it. Strength isn't your problem; it's coordination. Don't think about it so much. Just do it; come on."

Nadia pushed with her hands, and her bottom came off the bed. Her knees shook with the effort.

Jenna continued to encourage her. "Come on, just like in the pool. Get your balance and stand up."

Nadia stood trembling for some seconds, and then slowly took her hands off the bed. It was then that she realized she hadn't been breathing, and she gulped in a deep breath. She wobbled uneasily, her hands waving for balance, and then settled down. "I'm standing!" she shouted, "I'm standing up!" Suddenly she laughed, breathless, and nearly fell over.

"So you are," said Jenna approvingly. "Just stay there for a bit. Get yourself centered. Okay now; as soon as you're ready, I want you to try taking a step."

Nadia held her arms out for balance, willing herself forward, but as soon as her foot came off the floor, she fell forward. Jenna caught her quickly before she hit the floor and helped her stand back up. She helped Nadia sit back on the bed and fetched the chair. "More practice in the pool, I think. Come on, hon. Let's go...."

"I tried," said Nadia weakly, as she let Jenna help her into the chair one more time. "I'm sorry I couldn't—" A lump in her throat cut off her sentence. Her vision clouded with tears.

"Stop it." Jenna locked the wheels again and came around to look Nadia square in the face. "You just gave me more than I could have hoped for, this early in your therapy. Do you know how many coma patients I see that never get up on their feet again? Hon, you really have to be patient with yourself. Now, we're going to try this again tomorrow, so I want you to work extra hard in the pool today. I can see what we need to work on. Now, without further ado...." Jenna swung back around behind the wheelchair and pushed it through the door. It was going to be a good day.

Chapter Three

A few good days and several bad ones later, Nadia took her first, tentative steps. Before long, she graduated to a walker, and from the walker to a pair of forearm crutches, and then to only a cane. Every new day brought another breakthrough as Nadia applied herself stubbornlyto the task of making herself well, and Jenna never gave her a moment's break. The work was hard, but the results finally bore out.

They moved her to another room soon after she first woke, one with a window and a small balcony on which she would sit and take lunch or dinner, or just enjoy the fresh air. Afternoons, one would find her meandering along the nature trails of the spa's resort area.

* * * *

Nadia stood at the balcony rail and surveyed the remote mountain valley around the Twin Oaks Resort before her with a sense of wonder matched only by that of a child's first snowfall. The rugged beauty and remote grandeur spread out before her never failed to inspire awe; it was as if there was not another civilized place on earth. Great, jagged peaks rose all around the little valley, embracing and guarding it like a jealous lover, or a miser hoarding a precious treasure. The valley itself was filled with aspen and redwood trees and laced with well-manicured nature trails. One could find marked paths that ranged in difficulty from ones which a wheelchair could roll easily, to rugged tracks up and down mountains that would challenge any experienced hiker.

Physically, she was as sound as if she had never been wounded. Her memory, however, was another matter altogether. She knew her name, and she knew she was a television journalist. For some reason, nothing else seemed to come back. She had no idea where she lived, had no recollection of family or friends, or of anything from before. Every time she looked in the mirror, a stranger stared back at her. Obscure, furtive impressions crept around the dim edges of her mind, and every time she tried to focus on one, it faded into a black oblivion, leaving another question without an answer.

Her friends from work stopped in often to see her and lifted her spirits considerably. Steven Olsen, the huge cameraman, came by on a regular basis, as well as Rolf "Red" Hicks and Roger Glass. Rolf told her he wrote copy for her, and Roger was her personal assistant. They all brought Nadia flowers by the basketful, and the four of them sat and talked for hours, trying to catch her up on what she'd lost.

She was one of the west coast's top journalists, with a wall full of awards and a tally of interviews that included world leaders of industry, economy, and politics. She owned an apartment in San Francisco overlooking the Pacific Ocean where she spent her spare time reading classic literature and growing potted flowers in her greenhouse on the roof. Whenever she asked about anything from before she came to 'Frisco, however, they couldn't answer.

She no longer dreamt about Phillip, whoever he was. No one else spoke of a husband or boyfriend and it seemed to confirm that she was unattached, at least for the moment.

Six months had come and gone since she opened her eyes and now, as she looked over Twin Oaks, Nadia began to wonder when, if ever, she would regain the rest of her memory. Maybe, she concluded, the past was not as important as what she would do now, with a fresh start. She couldn't think of anything or anyone she had to return to.

She took a deep breath of mountain air and listened to the birds. A deer made a rustling sound in the brush below, and she watched it for several minutes as it grazed.

A soft sound behind her interrupted her reverie, and she turned to see Drs. Hamund and Spielberg coming through the sliding glass door of the balcony. Dr. Hamund wore slacks and a lab coat today. A pair of bifocals made him look older than when she had first seen him, almost comical. Dr. Anna Spielberg stood silently next to him similarly dressed, in a more feminine version of the slacks and lab coat. Her long, straight dirty-blonde hair was tied back in a ponytail. The sunlight betrayed her age, making her look more tired than she normally did. She was actually almost twenty years older than Nadia had at first thought.

"It's a beautiful day," Dr. Hamund observed as he crossed the deck to stand beside her at the rail.

"Yes. Yes, it is a beautiful day," said Nadia. Her long, curly blonde hair blew across her face as she turned her head, and she brushed it casually away from her eyes. They shared a smile as she looked at the man who had overseen the surgeries that had put her back together. It had been a long, rough row to hoe. Dr. Hamund had been there every step of the way as well as Drs. Mitchell and Spielberg, and Jenna Paine, her physical therapist.

"I have news," announced Doctor Hamund in his thick accent. "I believe we are at the point now where we can no longer do anything for you here. You're going back to San Francisco."

A thrill began in her abdomen, but then a wave of dread suddenly hit her. "What will I do? I don't have any skills anymore. I'll be alone, won't I?"

Dr. Hamund laughed. He had a good, honest laugh and she liked hearing it. He looked down at her and shook his head. "No, we won't leave you alone. Your producers have been watching your progress very closely, and they are eager to get you back on the news staff. We've been sending them regular updates. They have seen the way you handle yourself, and they all agree that you have not lost your journalistic instincts at all. You even have another international assignment in the works. Your staff will make sure you have a smooth transition, and Dr. Mitchell will always be here for you. If we can't help you remember your past, we can help you create a new future for yourself."

Nadia couldn't contain herself. She threw her arms around the doctor and kissed him on the cheek. When she drew back, her eyes were brimming with tears. "Thank you. You've all done so much for me; I can't believe it. When can I go home?" Suddenly she felt light-headed. "Oh, Jesus, where is home? I have no idea where I live!"

"Miss Paine has volunteered to move in with you until you become acclimated to your new life. She'll help in any way you need, as long as you need her."

"Oh, thank you, Dr. Hamund," she gushed, and hugged him again. "When can I leave?"

"You may pack right now. We just have some discharge forms for you to sign and you can be on your way. Your network has a Learjet waiting on the ramp at the airport." She began running to the door when he stopped her one last time. "I'll expect to see you in three months for a follow-up, Nadia." She smiled, winked, and passed through the door.

* * * *

She never saw the shadow that passed Dr. Hamund's face after she left.

"Perfect. Almost a shame," he muttered to Anna Spielberg. "Are you sure about the memory? It would be unfortunate...."

"Don't worry, Petr," said Anna flatly. "She doesn't remember a thing. She is perfect, just as you said."

"I hope you're right. There have been questions, and I have almost run out of answers."

"So what's one more little white lie?" asked Anna off-handedly. "In another year it won't make a difference anyway." She leaned on the balcony and stared off over the vista below as Petr Hamund sighed and went back inside.

Chapter Four

The director's finger knifed down and the theme music rang through the studio speakers. The red light on Camera 2 lit up and the studio lights dimmed on. The clean-shaven, ruggedly handsome man in the power suit tapped his token blank pages neatly on his desk and smiled into the Teleprompter. He waited for the music to fade before speaking.

"Good evening, San Francisco. I'm Peter Simms, and welcome to KBGX Action News. Our first story for tonight is one over three years in the making. It brings me great pleasure to announce the long-awaited return to the news desk of our very own, Nadia Velasquez. Welcome back, Nadia." He finished speaking and Roger Glass brought in a huge bouquet. He handed it to her and she received it tearfully.

"Thank you so much, guys." She wiped her eye with one hand, trying not to smear the makeup. "Oh, I love daisies!" She sniffed deeply to show her appreciation and set it down behind her desk before looking into the camera zooming in for a close-up. The happiness in her face was unmistakable. "It feels great to be back, and hopefully I haven't forgotten how to do my job." The studio personnel laughed at her joke and she plowed ahead.

"Next up, a new city ordinance could have downtown business owners paying more in property taxes. Could this mean higher prices for consumers on goods and services? Our own Phyllis Newton is at MacGruder's Restaurant with more. Phyllis?"

The camera cuts, video feeds, and director's cues flew by, and before she knew it, Nadia's first night back was over. Don Bailey, the director, came into the ring of studio lights and joined the throng around her, and they all shared a quick hug. "Damned fine job, Nadia! Now, go home and rest up. We'll keep you on short shifts this week, but next week I want you for the seven o'clock and eleven o'clock slots. Think you can be ready for it by then?"

"Don, I'll be ready to wrestle a grizzly bear by then," she beamed. Another laugh filled the studio.

"One step at a time. Hit your dressing room, and we'll see you here tomorrow at three. All right, people," he shouted to no one in particular and everyone in general. "Let's wrap this up and get ready for the teasers. Pete, you can handle the first two; Phyllis is coming back in to take Nadia's chair for the late edition...."

Don's voice faded behind Nadia as the studio doors closed behind her. She danced down the hall to her dressing room and when she opened the door, Roger was already there with a glass of champagne in one hand and an envelope in the other. "The champagne is a Dom Perignon of excellent vintage, from Mr. Bowman himself. The note, however...." His voice trailed off conspiratorially as he handed her the envelope. She took the glass and the envelope and carried them to her dressing table. She sipped from the glass and nodded. It was indeed an excellent wine. Then she read the envelope. It was hand-written, addressed to her personally in a now-familiar script.

He'd written her several times before, care of the studio. He'd never let her know as much as his name, let alone anything else about him. The first note came to the hospital a week after she first woke up from the coma, and there had been at least one a week since. She opened the envelope with a brisk sweep of a finger and took out the note. As all the others had, this one brought a wistful smile to her face. "How sweet." She turned the missive over, looking in vain for some clue to his identity. "Are you sure you don't know who it is?"

"Maybe the next letter," said Roger.

"Any other mail?"

"Nope. Anything else I can do for you before I leave?"

"Go ahead, Roger," she smiled. Suddenly she reached up on her toes and kissed his cheek. "Thanks. For everything. I'll see you tomorrow."

Roger stepped back, his face flushed. Without another word, he turned and left her alone to change clothes and makeup. As the door closed, she took another sip of the champagne, savoring it in her mouth. *It's good to be back.*

Chapter Five

There was a neat little grocery store a couple of blocks down the street from Nadia's apartment. It was a short walk she had begun to enjoy immensely in despite the apparent sense of drudgery grocery shopping inspired in everyone else she knew. She had enjoyed Jenna Paine's company for the last six months, but she also longed for the occasional trip on her own. She was given a clean bill of health at her last checkup, and Rebecca Mitchell had released her from psychiatric care, but Nadia still felt out of place, like a stranger.

Her return to journalism excited her the most. She had a career. She had begun to make a life for herself. It made her feel almost normal. It was exciting to sit at the desk and deliver news to people. It was even more fun to get out on the road with Steven, her cameraman. She loved interviews more than the anchor desk, she found. It made her job more personal and intimate. She also was privileged to meet some of the most powerful and influential people in the world. Visiting VIPs from many nations on sojourns to San Francisco never failed to book an interview with Nadia Velasquez. She handled the tough questions with dogged determination, and still made every guest glad they had spoken with her.

She only had one concern: her own privacy. It always seemed there were a dozen or more people asking for autographs at every turn. If that were all there was, she could have handled it. But at the studio and home she was never left by herself. Steven, Roger, Red, or somebody was always around at the studio, unless she was in her dressing room, and away from work Jenna was her constant companion. She began feeling closed in, and said so once to Dr. Mitchell. Soon after that, she noticed she could have little snatches of "me" time in the afternoons and evenings after work: sitting with a book at the library, a brisk walk around the block or, as tonight, a shopping trip to Bill Shelton's little corner market.

Nadia browsed every aisle, carefully choosing the exact ingredients for a new dish she wanted to try. She loved the smells of this market, especially the coffee aisle. After spending several minutes there, just taking in the rich aroma of roasted beans, she chose a blend she'd never tried before. Her hand froze as it touched the chute over the bag. The name of the roast seemed to penetrate something in her mind, and the aroma suddenly felt so strong she could almost hear it shouting at her.

A wave of dizziness slammed into her mind so hard she had to grab the shelf to keep her feet under her. Then it hit her like a cinder block… *Staley's! There's a Staley's coffee shop on East 42nd Street, just around the corner from…The Chrysler Building!* She spun around, spilling beans in the aisle. "Bill!" she called to the proprietor, "Bill, where's the Chrysler Building?"

Bill, a spindly old black man in weathered jeans, came around the corner of the aisle with a puzzled look on his face. "What Chrysler Building, Miss V? Hell, that's in New York City! What, you rememberin' stuff from befo' now?"

"Maybe," she answered breathlessly. "I don't know. But there's a Staley's just around the corner from there, on East 42nd Street."

"They's a Staley's just 'round the corner from every dam' where in New York, girl," Bill muttered and went for a broom, laughing under his breath as he shook his head.

Nadia threw her hands over her head and danced round in the coffee aisle at Bill Shelton's Grocery. It wasn't much, but she *knew* it was something. She'd have to tell Jenna when she got back. Drs. Hamund and Mitchell would want to know, too.

She hurried through the checkout and unfolded a small hand-dolly for the bagger to load the groceries. After giving him a generous tip, she pulled the dolly out the door and down the sidewalk, an excited grin pasted on her face. Maybe she could start remembering more, now.

The sidewalk traffic was light, the rush hour having run its course. Nadia tugged her dolly behind her as she made her happy way back home.

Passing an alley, a sudden movement caught her eye. A soft noise reached her ear: a moan…a low cry for help? Looking into the dim alleyway, she saw a leg sticking out from behind a dumpster. She glanced around. There was no one else on the block. She parked the dolly at the street and walked a few tentative steps into the mouth of the alley. "Hello? Are you all right...?" A rough hand shot out and dragged her back into the shadows before she had time to react.

Nadia never thought about what to do. Something automatic seemed to take over her body. She spun into her assailant and her right hand shot out on its own, driving its heel upward into his nose. She felt a crunch, and blood sprayed past her fingers as the hand let go of her arm. A startled cry of pain and shock echoed down the alley.

Another figure stepped up behind her and clapped a hand over her mouth. She bit down as hard as she could and at the same time snapped a heel up into her attacker's groin. He grunted and fell back against the opposite wall as the first man came at her again. Nadia dropped into a crouch and shot a fist out, catching him square between the legs. As he dropped down, she followed up with the other hand, catching him in the side of the head with a perfect left hook.

A sound behind her betrayed the second man's approach. Jumping straight up, she spun a foot into his head that sent him crashing to the ground. She landed lightly on her feet and stood, feet apart, hips forward, and fists clenched. Then the significance of the moment hit her. Shocked, she stood shaking. How did she know how to do...*that*? Her knees weakened and her head swam.

Nadia staggered back out to the sidewalk and reached out to grab the dolly, still standing where she'd parked it. There was blood on her right hand, the one that shattered the first man's nose. She glanced back over her shoulder. One man was still down; the other was gone. A crash down the alley confirmed he was on his way somewhere else.

Nadia was still shaking when she dragged her groceries into the elevator going up to her apartment. The blood on her hand was already drying into a red, coagulated mess. How was she going to explain this to Jenna? Why did she worry so much about what Jenna thought, anyway? The answer came, simply. They'd never let her have any solitary time if they knew. *So keep your mouth shut, girl. What they don't know won't hurt you.*

She hit the stop button halfway up and hastily dug through the top bag until she found a jar of pickled okra. With shaking hands, she unscrewed the top and set the jar on the floor. Then, kneeling, she dipped her fingers into the jar and splashed the juice over the blood-smeared hand, cleaning it off as best she could. She let the stained juice run back into the jar. A few drops landed on the elevator floor, but that couldn't be helped.

24

Then she pulled the stop button back out, pushed the button for the floor below hers and put the lid back on the jar. When the door opened, she exited the elevator and strode to the end of the hall. She opened the window and, making sure no one was in the alley below, threw the jar down into the darkness. A few seconds later, she heard the crash as it broke in the alley.

Nadia leaned against the sill for a while, thinking. What kind of five-foot reporter can take down two attackers with just a couple of punches? And where in the world did that *kick* come from? What else didn't she know about herself? Would it start coming back now, in some ugly rush? Her friends had never mentioned anything about martial arts from her past. Why?

After several more minutes, Nadia felt herself calming down, and she took one last, deep breath at the window before she took up the handle on her dolly and returned to the elevator. For now, this was all going to be a secret. Why, she wasn't sure. But something told her it was what she needed to do.

Who was she, really? Where did she come from? What else *didn't* she know about herself? She would have to find out, beginning with that Staley's coffee shop. With or without their help, she was going to find out.

Chapter Six

The flight to Tehran began smoothly enough, although Nadia had precious little recent experience from which to draw. She figured it was going well from the first leg out of San Francisco, mainly because Steven was in a good mood. One thing she'd picked up about her giant cameraman. He was a perfectionist, often to the point of belligerence if he couldn't get his shot, and especially if bystanders came too close to Nadia.

On the leg from 'Frisco to New York they worked on questions for their interview with the president of Iran. The gate at LaGuardia was packed. Steven grabbed his camera cases from the overhead and ran block for them both, forcing his way through the crowd, shouting and cursing as only he could. Nadia tucked herself behind his hulk and followed. As they cleared the gate area and reached the concourse, they read the screens for their next gate, three concourses away.

"Hey, Steve, you go on ahead. I have to visit the little girls' room."

"It's nothing, I'll just wait over there," he said, nodding to a bench situated near the restroom door.

Nadia looked nervously at her watch. "The plane to London leaves in ten minutes. You better get there and hold the flight or we'll miss it." Steven opened his mouth to object again, but she cut him off. "Steve, we're wasting time here. Just get there, and I'll catch up to you at the gate, okay? I'm a big girl; I don't need anyone to hold my hand."

Steven looked hesitant. Then he turned down the concourse and began walking. "All right, but you better get there quick," he grumbled.

Eight minutes later she still had not caught up and Steven was neatly being undone by a woman half his height and twice his age. "I'm sorry, sir, but we have first class overbooked on the flight to London. One of you will need to ride in coach." She was sincerely apologetic, but Steven was still pressing the issue.

"So why pick on the West Coast's premier anchor and her cameraman? Why can't someone else get bumped back?"

The gate attendant became more firm. "Sir, the plane is already boarded, except for you two. The captain has asked me to relay this message

26

to you, and I have." She stepped out from behind the counter and stood her full height with her arms akimbo, like a mouse standing down a lion. "Now, it's your choice. Someone rides in coach, or you can both stay here and catch the next flight."

Steven towered over the tiny woman, assuming a threatening pose that made most people cower. "Bump someone else back," he growled.

The phone at the gate counter rang, and the attendant picked it up without taking her eyes off the big man. "Yes, sir.... No, not yet. Yes, sir." She hung up and looked harder at Steven, unimpressed. Her gaze never wavered as a sly, condescending grin dawned in her expression. "That was the lead flight attendant. The captain says either you get on board right now, or he leaves you here. He has a schedule to keep. Now, what's it going to be, sir?"

In reply, Steven grunted and picked up his camera cases. Glaring at the gate attendant, he started down the skyway toward the waiting jet. "You make sure she gets on board, you hear me?" he snarled. He glanced one more time back down the concourse and saw a distinctive blonde mane running toward the gate. With a satisfied nod, he turned back and boarded the plane.

He had no sooner settled into his seat in coach than the plane began to back away from the terminal and the flight attendants started the pre-takeoff passenger briefing. He nervously rose up and entered the aisle, advancing toward the stairway to the first class section on the jumbo when a male attendant came toward him. "I'm sorry, sir, you need to be in your seat. We're getting ready to take off now."

"Stuff it, Punk," Steven said as he strode toward the stair. Another figure rose and came toward Steven and the attendant. Steven didn't need to be told this was a sky marshal. "Look," he hastily added, "I have to check on someone in first class—"

The marshal interrupted him. "Sir, first class is full. There are no seats available there. Now, sit down."

"Look, Stupid—" Steven started, but got no farther. The marshal was reaching inside his jacket. "Okay," he said, backing down. He held his hands out and backed away. "Okay, just take it easy. I'm going to sit down. Could you just make sure Nadia Velasquez made it on board?"

The marshal relaxed and took his hand away from his jacket lapel. "Oh, a fan? Well, I'll just see if I can get you an autograph."

"No, I'm her cameraman. This is like, the hottest interview of her career, we're heading for. If she didn't make the flight—"

"Okay, come with me," the sky marshal offered. "We can at least see if she made it on board." They mounted the staircase to the upper passenger deck while the 747 taxied to the runway. As they reached the top and looked forward, Steven took a step up the aisle but the marshal grabbed his arm. "Uh-uh, Sport. Not enough time. Can you see her from here, quickly?"

Steven glanced up the rows and spotted the blonde, curly mane spilling down the back of a woman's head. "Yeah, that's her, there," he admitted, pointing.

"Cool," the sky marshal said, guiding Steven back down the stairs. "She made it. Now get back downstairs. We're about to take off, and you don't want to be out of your seat when Smitty boots this thing in the rear, okay?"

"Yeah, okay," Steven said. He made his way back to his seat. He could always see if someone would be willing to trade places later, after they made their cruise altitude. There were still a lot of details to settle, and damned few of them had to do with an interview.

* * * *

Back in the concourse, Nadia checked her watch one more time. *Good, they had to have taken off by now.* She opened the stall door (*appropriate term*, she thought wryly) and came back out of the women's restroom, turning down the concourse in the opposite direction her cameraman had gone a few minutes before.

Her heart slammed in her chest like a thousand midget carpenters. She was throwing a wrench into her career for this. But there wasn't going to be another chance to find out, on her own, without being spoon-fed bits of information from someone else. No, this was something she had to do on her own, right now, if she was going to find out the truth.

In another five minutes, she was in the loading zone. A taxicab stopped in front of her, and, before she knew it, Nadia was in the back seat, heading toward the Chrysler Building as the plane with her cameraman took off for London. She would probably lose her job for ducking out like this, but she couldn't think of another way to find out for sure if she had indeed seen this place before. Maybe she could catch up to some more of her ever-elusive memory.

Oh, well. Maybe if I play my cards right, I won't get into too much trouble. It would be worth it, just to touch something that was hers alone, something she wouldn't have to share.

Nadia looked out the cab's windows at the skyline spread out before her as they crossed the Queensboro Bridge. There arose in her consciousness a disturbing kind of tingle, like another part of her was awakening from some deep and hidden slumber.

She wasn't sure exactly when she began suspecting Petr and the others were holding information from her. But now she was positive they knew something they weren't telling her, and that made her more determined to find out exactly what it was. If they wouldn't tell her, then she'd just find out on her own.

Right now.

The taxi ride was over before Nadia knew it. She did not remember paying the cabbie and getting out, or how long she stood on the curb staring up at the hulking profile of the Chrysler Building. Her mind buzzed and her knees shook as she walked down East 42nd Street until she saw Staley's.

She stepped through the door and waited in line until the counter attendant took her order. She ordered automatically, what she had always ordered, but somehow her voice seemed not to be her own. "Double-decaf-mochaccino latté with a cinnamon stick, please."

As she turned away from the counter with her cup, a strange pressure mounted in her head. *This place is important somehow. But how, exactly?* She was so distracted and lightheaded she bumped unsteadily into the man behind her. "Sorry, Jake," she started off-handedly, but then the man's face came into view. *Jon?* He had shaved his beard, but those eyes… *Jon!* A rush of recognition crashed into her mind and, as she started to fall toward the floor and her vision closed in, she heard him ask, "Do I know you…?"

Chapter Seven

"Ladies and gentlemen, welcome aboard and thank you again for choosing Trans-Atlantic Airways. Once again, this is Flight 6237 non-stop New York to London. We're currently cruising at an altitude of thirty-three thousand feet, and an airspeed of six hundred and forty miles per hour. The captain has turned off the seat belt sign, and you are now free to move about the cabin.

"We remind you, however, that we may experience turbulence at any time, so while you're in your seat we do ask that you keep your seat belt fastened and secure around your waist.

"Our flight attendants have begun circulating, and we have snacks available for one dollar a bag. Cocktails and beer are five dollars in coach and complementary in first class. Soft drinks, as always, are complementary in all classes. Dinner will be chicken-fried steak and mashed potatoes, and will be served in two hours. If you have any special dietary needs, please inform the nearest flight attendant, and we will do our best to accommodate you.

"The movie in first class will be *'Bladerunner'* starring Harrison Ford. If we can do anything else to make your trip more comfortable, press the call button located in your overhead console, and an attendant will be with you shortly. Once again, we thank you for choosing Trans-Atlantic Airways; enjoy the rest of your flight."

The attendant signed off and Steven unbuckled his seat belt. He wasted no time getting to the staircase, looking purposefully at the sky marshal as he climbed. The man shook his head slowly and returned his attention to his paperback. Reaching the top of the staircase, Steven scanned the heads again until he spotted the woman with the blonde mane. He stepped quickly up the aisle. As he approached, he noticed something very wrong. He distinctly remembered Nadia wearing black slacks and a cream-colored blouse, but this woman wore jeans and a blue blouse. Coming nearer, he could see that this was not Nadia at all, but someone entirely different.

He cursed under his breath and looked around desperately, trying to remember if he had seen another head like Nadia's earlier, but for his life he could not bring to mind if he did. Desperate, he scanned the toilet kiosks, but all were unoccupied. He entered the last one, closed the door with shaking hands, and took out his cellphone. They had been in the air for close to an hour. *This is bad. This is extremely bad.*

Chapter Eight

When Nadia came around, she was lying on the floor of the coffee shop with twenty people looking down at her. She heard the whispers in the crowd and a warm flush of embarrassment rose in her cheeks. She started to rise, but a hand on her shoulder stopped her.

"Why don't you lie back down, Miss? An ambulance is on the way."

She shook off the hand and rose shakily. "No, that's not necessary; I'll be fine. I'm sorry; I'll be on my way."

"Well, at least let me replace your drink." He quickly rattled off the order and helped her to her feet. "Are you sure you're okay, now?"

"Yes, yes; I'm fine," she repeated. The steaming cup was offered and, without thinking, she took it and sipped. "Oh, this is exactly what I ordered. How did you know…?"

"It's the same thing a close friend of mine used to get all the time." He paid for the drinks and they walked together toward the door. "How did you know my name, by the way?"

Nadia stopped on the sidewalk and looked at him again. Recognition was no longer there. "Do I know your name?"

"Yeah, you called me 'Jake' in there. That's my nickname, but only a few people ever used that since I was a kid. I know I've seen you, but I can't recall where."

"Oh," she said, hastily stepping aside to let other customers in and out of the coffee shop. She held out her hand. "I'm Nadia—" She suddenly stopped. That same something inside her that kept her secret in San Francisco told her to keep her profile low here. Jon took her hand and did not seem to notice the hitch in her voice as they shook. His grip was firm but trembling, his gaze penetrating. She could not help but feel as if she were under some kind of microscope. It made her quite uncomfortable in a way that being on camera never did.

"Jon Daniels. Are you sure we've never met somewhere else? You seemed to know me in there, and now you seem pretty confused. Are you sure you're okay?"

32

"Look, Jon, I can't be sure about anything right now. I came out…of somewhere else…a few months ago. Maybe we met each other before—" Just then, an ambulance pulled up to the curb and a couple of EMTs came out and headed for the door. Nadia turned her face away.

"Hey, boys; here she is."

Nadia turned on him then, eyes blazing. "Thanks, but no thanks! I said I was fine. I don't want an ambulance, okay?" She backed away as the EMTs took a couple of hesitant steps toward her. They looked questioningly at Jon. He held his hand palm-out to them while he continued to talk to Nadia.

"Okay, if you're positive, we won't force you," Jon said, "but what made you faint in there?"

"I don't know," she answered, curtly. "It doesn't matter, okay? Look, I won't bother you anymore, it's just…." Nadia's voice dropped, and Jon had to lean close to hear her above the noise of New York's rush hour streets. "I thought you were someone I knew." She turned and walked away, toward downtown. Why was she acting this way? She had no idea. What was she even doing here? *My producer is going to have a cow*….

Jon quickly dismissed the EMTs and caught up with her. "Hey. Hey, where are you going?"

"To see if I have a job left," she muttered. Her cellphone rang, and she took it out and opened it. "Yes? Okay, Steve, I'm sorry; I got caught in the crowd. I'll catch the next flight, okay? Yeah, I'm at the gate right now. Well, don't panic, I'll see you in Tehran tomorrow. Call the show, have Don get hold of the president and reschedule the interview for Wednesday, okay? I'll get there as soon as I can. 'Bye, now." She snapped it shut and put it away, then rested her forehead against the building and sighed heavily. When she looked up, Jon was still there. "Don't you think I've caused you enough inconvenience yet? It was nice to meet you, Jon, and I'm sorry—"

"Can I at least get you some dinner? I'd feel a lot better leaving you alone if I knew you were going to be all right."

Nadia sighed again and lifted her eyes to meet his. The shock was no longer there, but she knew she had felt it before. There was something nagging at her memory, even now. Maybe if she spent some time with him it would come back to her. He waited for her response, an expectant smile crossing his face.

It was a nice face, she noticed. Jon looked to be in his thirties, a tall, ruggedly handsome man with short brown hair and a clean-shaven chin. He was dressed neatly in a dark gray business suit, no Armani special, but well-fit just the same.

She searched her mind carefully, trying to find some kind of memory that could tell her more. Could she trust him? *Should* she trust him? She had known him once, by a nickname that only his mother used. That, at least, was a point in his favor. Oh, well, she had some time to kill anyway. All at once, she realized how hungry she was. "Okay; but I'll buy my own dinner, no offense."

Strangely, his look became more intense, more puzzled. The smile faded for just an instant. Just as suddenly, he recovered. The smile reappeared, and he held out his arm. She slid her hand through his elbow and they walked together down the busy sidewalk. "I know just the place to grab a good meal," he said. "You won't find a place like this outside of New York, and I know that for a fact...."

Chapter Nine

A continent away, a phone rang in a mahogany-paneled office. The hand that picked it up was neatly manicured; the ear to which it was held was framed by immaculate grey hair over an expensive jacket a couple of shades darker than the hair.

There was no greeting, just silence for several seconds while someone at the other end of the line spoke. Then he began to ask questions. After each question, he listened carefully and patiently to each response.

"Could you please repeat that, Mr. Olsen? How could she have missed her flight? Do you have any idea where she is? And you believed her? Why did you let her out of your sight? Where are you now? Are you sure she's still coming? When you get to London, check in at our hotel there. We'll reschedule the interview. This has to go through as planned. We must remain calm, Mr. Olsen. Don't fret so. I'll take care of things here personally. Thank you for calling."

The hand held the receiver to the ear after the other party disconnected, then the man's other hand came out and pressed the hook switch on the desk phone. A number was dialed, a pause and then, "Round up your team. We may have to clean something up. New York. Tonight. Don't go commercial, you'll need tools. You have the Gulfstream. Call Miss Preston right away. She will take care of the arrangements. Yes. Don't take any chances. Bring it back safe. Thank you."

The hand with the receiver hung up the phone, and met the other on top of the massive desk. His nervous fingers wandered to the left hand's ring finger, fidgeting softly with the band that dressed it: large and gold, adorned with a single, polished ruby. On the bottom side of the ruby, nearly concealed in the blood red of the stone, was an emblem, unnoticed by anyone who did not already know it was there: an upside-down V with three lines radiating from the tip, and a small dot in the middle. A mysterious slogan in Latin

35

was engraved in the gold around the setting: *Praestat facere rex ac esse rex*. He studied it for some time.

Finally, the figure stood, walked around the desk, turned off the lights and locked the office door before he left for the night.

Chapter Ten

By the time they reached D'Antini's, Nadia knew she was in the company of a friend. She and Jon made small talk while they waited for the maitre d' to find them a table in the middle of the sumptuous dining room, and she almost forgot about having to explain herself to her station staff.

The appetizers were amazing, if unidentifiable. Nadia asked what was in them and Jon just smiled and held up a hand. "You really don't want to know."

Nadia almost spit out the latest mouthful, but thought twice about it as she looked around. This was too nice a place to be so rude. Her eyes widened in mirth as she tried to laugh around it and almost choked trying to get it down. She grabbed her water glass and took a drink, waving a hand at her face.

"You jerk," she laughed softly, when her mouth became free. "All right, seriously now, do you take every woman who faints in your arms to a place this fancy?"

"No," he answered, "just those who remind me of a dear friend." The smile faded from his face and he became pensive for several seconds. Then he placed a couple more appetizers on her salad plate. "Here," he said, suddenly brightening, "have some more...brown, crusty...things."

She chuckled again, pushing the plate away. "No, thanks. A moment on the lips...." She let the rest of the cliché fade away while she rearranged her napkin in her lap, trying to buy some time before she had to plow ahead. "So why am I here with you? Because you're concerned for me or because I remind you of someone else?"

"That is an entirely unfair question, Miss Velasquez. I was wondering that very thing myself. Maybe a little bit of both. Is that okay?"

"How did you know my last name?" she asked. It was not as if she were a necessarily private person, it was mainly that she hoped he would not recognize her from television. She was already AWOL. She may as well put in her resignation as soon as she got back to 'Frisco.

"I heard you lie to 'Steve,' whoever that is. When you talked about an interview with a president, I pegged you right off the bat. I've been to the West Coast on business a few times."

"That's where you saw me before. Well, that answers that, then."

"No, it doesn't." Jon looked at Nadia again, the piercing gaze locked on her face. "There's something else, and I can't explain it yet. Just less than four years ago I lost my best friend and her family…."

"Oh, I must look like her, then—"

He cut her off. "How's Phillip?"

Nadia's hand stopped halfway to her water glass. She felt paralyzed. The blood drained from her face, leaving it ice cold. The memory reconnected like a switch in her mind. The question trickled weakly from her lips, her voice quavering. "Who's Phillip?"

Jon's voice took on a steely edge. He wasn't becoming hostile, just insistent, but insistent in a way that made her feel like she was being peeled away, layer by layer under a microscope. "You know full well who Phillip is."

The trembling in her hand increased to a violent shaking. She remembered someone telling her, "*It took twenty-three surgeries just to reconstruct your face.*" Her breath came in gasps; her voice weakened. *Phillip. Phillip was—* She found herself unable to get up, incapable of walking away, too terrified to run, like a bird in the gaze of a snake. "What are you talking about?"

"Why did you skip out on your flight, Nadia? Why did you come to the Staley's at 42nd and Lexington? Why at *that* particular time?"

The questions gushed from Jon's mouth, one right after another, and Nadia had no chance to answer any individual one. He became more agitated as he went, until Nadia thought he would reach over the table and strangle her right there in public. "Why did you order a double-decaf-mochaccino latté with a cinnamon stick? Why did you know my nickname and then faint as soon as you recognized me? Why are we sitting here right now, while the chef in the kitchen prepares Steak Hélène rare? Before the appetizers came, why were you doodling Betty Boop figures on your napkin and playing with your left ear?" *Twenty-three surgeries.* "Nobody has called me 'Jake' since I was ten, except for her and my mom. And you absolutely hate Merlot, don't you?"

Nadia's hand never made it to the water glass. She couldn't think. A sound roared in her head, like ten thousand voices screaming in terror. An icy spear of fear shot through her chest. Hot tears rolled down her face, and her chest heaved as she gasped for breath.

She hoped with everything inside her that no one else was watching these two terrified people having this horrible, strange confrontation. Her vision started to close in again, but she fought it off. As it was, she nearly fell out of her chair. Her voice was strange and weak. "Do...do you know who I am?"

Jon bored into her with his eyes for what felt like forever. Then he suddenly relaxed. His clenched fists went slack. He let out a breath. Nevertheless, Nadia could see that his hands were shaking, too, as he reached for his own water glass. "I guess the question really should be, 'Do *you* know who you are?'"

She buried her face in her hands. "I'm so sorry, Jon. I don't know why....Oh, God, I'm a wreck. And I'm going to get fired for missing my flight, all for this." She wiped her face with her napkin. "Look, I have to go. Maybe I can get to Tehran and at least salvage my career. I'm sorry for all this...."

"I'm sorry, too, Nadia, because I can't let you leave." Jon's voice took on its edge again as he continued. "You see, I'm a special agent for the FBI." He took a badge out of his jacket pocket and showed it to her, careful to be discrete as he did so, so as not to attract attention from anyone else around them. "I have reason to believe you know more about my friend than you're letting on."

So much for not making a scene. This was too much. Nadia's face exploded in disbelief as she shot to her feet. "You're crazy! Are you arresting me?" The people at the tables around them turned to look, and the restaurant fell silent. She leaned in close to Jon's face and her eyes narrowed. "With what exactly do you intend to charge me, Special Agent Daniels? Acting like someone you know? I'd like to see you make that one stick in court." She snatched her purse from the table and spun around, heading for the door.

She took ten steps before she heard Jon start after her. After they made the street, he reached out and caught her arm. Reflexively, she wheeled around and caught him with a wicked chop to the ear. He reeled from the blow, staggering back against the brick building. Nadia stood her ground, trembling, shocked at what had just happened. Jon held both hands up in surrender.

"No, please! Look, you're right, I can't arrest you. But listen for just a minute, will you? I don't understand this whole thing any more than you do. I don't know why, but I can't lose track of you. I just can't."

He stepped toward her carefully, both hands still out. "Let me at least see you to the airport. We can talk on the way. And when you return, you can pass back this way, and we can work this out, okay? Maybe get to the bottom of it all."

Nadia began to calm down. She was beginning to see that he was at least as frightened as she was. *Maybe he's not a psycho after all.* She had thought coming to New York might answer some nagging questions, but all it did was open a Pandora's Box for her and now for him, too. Maybe they owed each other some answers. "Okay," she said, "but just you pull that badge out on me again, and I don't have to tell you where I'm going to stick it."

Jon rubbed his ear and smiled nervously. "Deal. First, let me pay our check before we both get busted for skipping out."

Chapter Eleven

The Gulfstream V touched down at precisely ten-thirty-seven on Runway Zero-Six at Teterboro Airport. It taxied to a halt on the ramp in front of the business terminal and an air stair unfolded from its side. Three figures descended the steps, carrying shoulder bags and suitcases. After they threw their bags into the trunk of a waiting car, they climbed into the back. The driver started the engine and set off for the Lincoln Tunnel.

There was no conversation among the passengers in the limo. They exchanged no words with the driver; he already knew where, and had no need to know why. Being a company man, he knew better than to ask any questions. The only sounds were the faint hum of the engine and the traffic outside as they made their way across Manhattan.

As they approached the Queensboro Bridge, a taxicab swerved wildly around them, missing the front bumper by scant inches. The driver laid on his horn and cursed a blue streak about foreign drivers until he remembered who it was he had in the back. He quieted down and drove the rest of the way in nervous silence.

* * * *

Inside that taxicab, Nadia listened as Jon chided their driver from the backseat. "Hey, you don't need to kill us getting there, Buddy!"

Nadia looked at her watch, a hollow pit of unease growing in her stomach. She didn't see how they were going to get to the airport, much less to her gate, before the plane took off. She felt fortunate that the airline agent who took her call was efficient enough to get her a last-minute seat, though at some considerable expense. *Oh, well, that's what credit cards are for,* she mused. Part of her secretly hoped she would miss the flight so she could spend more time with this man who seemed to be connected with her past.

They had started the ride with some small talk about New York, and her first impressions of the grand metropolis. Soon, however, they knew they had to address the issue at hand, namely the reason they were here, now.

Nadia wondered if she could, or even should, trust Jon with her whole story. Could he handle the truth about her? She wasn't sure she could handle much more, herself. But if they were ever to get any answers to their questions, she had to trust someone. Could she really trust *anyone* right now? She looked at Jon. He watched her expectantly. He looked as confused as she felt. Before she knew it, Nadia was telling him about her injury, coming out of a coma a little less than a year ago, and all she had learned since then.

"Hell, that was more than an assassination attempt," he countered. "President Bello was killed instantly, along with twenty other people. Most of the presidential palace was reduced to rubble. Yet you managed to live through that? How?"

"I honestly couldn't tell you. I don't remember any of that. I do remember that when I came out of it, they were asking me about someone they thought I knew; I forget the name...."

"Phillip?" asked Jon.

Nadia's head swam at the mention of that name. "Who the hell is Phillip?"

"Alicia's husband."

"Who's Alicia?"

"I think you were," he said.

The rest of the taxi ride was very quiet.

Chapter Twelve

At La Guardia, Jon struck a brisk pace in front of Nadia, forcing her to run in order to keep up. Even this close to midnight, the main concourse was a solid mass of humanity, seething to get to a million points at once.

They had hardly said a word to each other since Jon dropped that bombshell on her in the taxicab, and now he seemed to be avoiding saying anything else. "Hey!" she panted. "Geez, Jon, my flight doesn't leave until 1:27 AM. What's the rush?" At her cry, he slowed down, and then stopped, turning in the massive corridor to face her. When he reached out and grasped her upper arms, she noticed his hands were still shaking.

"What does all this mean to you, Nadia? Me, I...just can't seem to find a handle on what I'm experiencing here. There are just too many coincidences here to be...well, coincidence. I...just...want to get you to your gate so we can talk. I'm trying to think of something to say. And there's a part of me that doesn't want you to go.

"There's a million questions exploding in my brain right now, I have no idea which one to ask first, and I'm afraid of each and every one of them...." His hands dropped to his sides and they stood, looking at each other.

"Yeah. I know what you mean," she said quietly. She strode past him and started for the gate again. "When I get back from Tehran, I'll stop by and look you up—"

A cry in the concourse interrupted her. "Nadia! Nadia Velasquez!"

She turned to see Red Hicks waving at her from the end of the concourse. He smiled and started running toward her.

"Red?" She started walking back toward him. She turned back to Jon to introduce her new friend to her old one, and someone blundered into her from her blind side, knocking her to the ground. They sprawled together in the corridor, tangled up in each other. When Nadia tried to get up, she kept getting tangled in the other person. Rising seemed to be impossible.

Jon reached to help her, but Red ran up and threw a block into him. She saw Jon go down hard and felt another set of hands around her, dragging her to her feet. Someone she could not see pressed some kind of object against the side of her head.

Until now, she had been dazed. Suddenly something else kicked her into action. Nadia threw her head forward, away from the object just as a sharp, electric *snap* reached her ears. She swung a leg forward, bending at the knee and snapped it back hard against someone's kneecap. A loud *pop* erupted in the concourse, followed by a woman's scream of pain. The hands that had held her were now gone, occupied with holding a broken leg.

Her left hand shot out, fingers extended, and found a throat without looking to see it first. Penetrating the rushed block with her other hand, she easily pivoted and threw a roundhouse kick that landed on the side of Red's head just as he stood up. Red went down, and Jon rolled away, scrambling to his feet and grabbing Nadia's hand.

"Come on," he gasped, "we have to get out of here."

She yanked her hand away from him. "Wait! I'm not going anywhere until I know what just happened."

"What just happened is that you took down three people who were trying to kill us. Now let's get going before they can finish the job."

"Wait, let's wait for the police—" she started, but a sound reached her ears. Red was getting up, and she saw him reaching inside his jacket for something. The look on his face was something she'd never seen before, a terrifying blend of fury and hate. Other figures in the crowd began closing in.

Jon grabbed her hand again. "Let's get out of here!"

Before she knew it, Nadia was running with Jon back the way they came, futilely trying to explain why some of her best friends attacked the two of them in an airport. "Maybe they thought you were trying to kidnap me," she panted as he dragged her out of the terminal and flagged a cab.

"Okay. Maybe so. But how did they know where to find you?" Jon waved his arms at an approaching driver. The taxi swung to the curb and he opened the door, pushing Nadia in first. He got in and slammed the door, then stabbed the lock down. He gave the driver a Manhattan address as the taxicab drove away.

Looking out the rear window, Nadia saw Red Hicks and Roger Glass stumble out the terminal door. They looked around desperately. Nadia saw Red point at their cab. Then she lost sight as the car swept around the curve of the terminal drive and out toward the freeway.

"I told Steven I was still at the gate for the Iran flight, remember?"

"Granted; but why didn't your producers just call you and schedule another flight? Who was the guy with the red hair?"

"That was Red Hicks, my script man…." Nadia felt her voice catch in her throat as her mind raced toward the same conclusion she knew Jon was reaching with his next question.

"All right, then. Why would your producers send your script man all the way across the country to get you? And what was that thing the woman held to your head?"

"Okay, I don't know. Look, this is all happening too quickly for me right now. Could you just tell me now if you're kidnapping me so I know if I have to, like…*karate* you, or something?" She tried to hold her hands up in a threatening way, but somehow couldn't manage to feel dangerous enough.

He smiled sardonically at her display. "You can't sandbag me that way. Where did you learn how to fight like that?"

Nadia pondered for a long moment. "I don't know. I never thought about it, I just…did it. I don't remember ever taking any lessons…." She faded away into silence again. She turned her face away from Jon so he would not see the tears of confusion and fear rise up in her again.

This day was just so wrong, on so many levels; she couldn't even begin to explain it to anyone. *Twenty-three surgeries….* "Jon?"

"Yeah?"

"Who am I?"

She felt his arm over her shoulder and found it strangely comforting. "I'm not sure," he said. "But I aim to find out."

Jon got them out at Central Park West and made sure the cabby saw them head into the hotel. They stood idly in the lobby for a few more minutes and then took another cab to New Jersey, where Jon checked them into a small motel in Hasbrouck Heights.

He opened the door with the keycard and went in first to clear the room. He motioned for her to come in, and she entered hesitantly.

Jon took a pillow from the bed and threw it onto the couch, and then found some extra blankets in the top of the closet. "I'll let you have the bed. Let's get some sleep. Tomorrow's going to be very busy for both of us."

He stretched out on the couch and closed his eyes.

After she turned the light off, Nadia lay quietly in the darkness for a few minutes, trying to sort out everything that had happened since she left Steven in the terminal at LaGuardia.

Before today, she had more than she could have hoped for: a great career, good friends, altogether a happy life. But now, everything she thought she knew about herself was in question. Could it be that she was really someone else? Why were her friends suddenly behaving so strangely? Did they know who she really was? Why were they hiding her from herself?

Jon was already snoring softly across the room. She found herself wondering: Was he really an FBI agent, or was she in some terrible danger from this man? How did he know so much about her? Was he, in reality, a stalker?

What in the world had she gotten herself into?

Sometime during her musings, fatigue overcame her and she fell into a fitful sleep.

Chapter Thirteen

Nadia woke up, not because she wanted to, but because the shower was running. She still wore the blouse and slacks she had on the night before. The couch was empty, save for the pillow and blankets Jon used, neatly folded and stacked on the left arm. Well, if she was being kidnapped, at least he was being decent about it. She had no idea how much sleep she had gotten, but it didn't feel like nearly enough.

She stumbled to the restroom and was relieved to find the shower had its own door separate from the toilet. Concluding her business and washing her hands, she found a small, four-cup coffee maker and started a pot while she waited for her turn in the shower. Usually the morning would find her watching the latest television news, but today she wanted to digest what had happened over the last twenty-four hours.

Yesterday had started out so well, preparing for the trip to Iran and the interview she had been trying to get for the last three months with President Javad. Yesterday she had been a top television journalist. Yesterday Red Hicks was her friend, and she didn't know Jon Daniels at all.

Then there were the stray memories of a life she thought she might have had before the hospital, before the incident that landed her in a three-year coma. All she had wanted was to find something familiar, something that could give her some clue about her past life. Now, she was in a small motel somewhere in New Jersey, with a man she didn't know from Adam, running from a supposed friend who acted for all the world like he was trying to kill her. She would probably never work on television again after this. In addition, the man in the shower was acting as strangely as she was.

Just as she finished her first cup, the shower stopped. A minute later Jon came through the door with a towel around his waist and his clothes in a wrinkled mass held against his chest. "Your turn."

"Okay," she said, passing him the other way. "But you'd better hope you didn't use up all the hot water. I can be downright nasty in the morning."

Jon smiled at the remark. "Hey, look at the clock. It's after noon. Pass me your clothes and I'll press them for you while you're in there. It won't be the same as washing, but at least we won't look like bag people. We can get some more clothes later."

When Nadia got out of the shower, she found her slacks and blouse neatly pressed and folded on the toilet seat, and the outer door closed. She could hear the TV through the door as she dressed, something about an incident at LaGuardia last night, a news crew being mugged on the main concourse. She was still toweling her hair as she came into the main part of the room. "They can't be serious about that, can they?"

Jon turned, a cup of coffee in his hand. Nadia couldn't read his expression. "You tell me. This is your business."

"For your information," she shot back, "I have never changed facts in a story—"

"That you know of. Who knows what drivel they plugged into your script?"

Before she could dig in any more, he changed the subject. "We'd better get some lunch. Then I'll rent us a car and we'll hit the road."

"Why?"

"This is going to sound weird, but after everything else I've been through the last twenty-four hours, it somehow doesn't surprise me." He began to chuckle. "News people are trying to kill us."

Hearing it said aloud, Nadia had to laugh. It sounded so ridiculous that before long the two refugees stood giggling at the situation, letting the stress and confusion melt away for a few minutes of simple foolishness.

Something on the television screen dragged them back to the moment: security footage from the terminal the previous night. Unfortunately, it showed a pretty good view of Jon grabbing Nadia's hand and dragging her away from the scene. The reporters went on about the "alleged kidnapping." Nadia could not believe the degree of embellishment applied to the story.

Jon grimaced. "Well, looks like a rental car is out. Someone sure is desperate to find you. If I try to rent a car, someone is bound to recognize one of us from that video, not to mention the paper trail that would leave."

"Well, duh," she blurted out. "I don't belong here, and neither do you. As far as they know, I *was* kidnapped. For all I know, you could be a stalker who set all this up just to get me alone in a motel room."

He looked at Nadia, and his eyes grew wide. "And I'll ask you one more time: what were you doing at that Staley's instead of making your scheduled flight to Tehran?"

That's it; this is too much to take. Nadia stood with an exasperated whuff and made it to the door before stopping, one hand on the knob. "Touché. So much for trying to put a normal spin on this thing."

"I thought you said you never spun a story." He barely managed to dodge the pillow she plucked from the couch and threw at him. "Let's go, then. We're not finding any answers here, and besides, I'm starving."

"Where to? No car, remember?"

"Ever see a TV in a taxicab?" Jon picked up a phone. "We have maybe a couple of hours before my picture gets out enough to interfere with us moving around. Restaurants are out for now. I could get us something at my place but I'm not going to count on not being recognized. The building's probably under surveillance by now." He continued as he dialed. "I'm getting us a plane. We're going to Washington DC for a little while."

"You have enough pull to get us a plane to DC, just like that?" asked Nadia, impressed.

"No, not ordinarily. But someone owes me a big favor." She could hear someone pick up on the other end, and he turned his attention back to the phone. "Hey, Pete? Jon. Look, I have a situation, here…yeah, another one….Yes, I remember, but I seem to remember something I did for you just last week….Yes, that counted! Why would you think that didn't count? I need the Citation. Teterboro to Dulles…. No, we need speed; better make it the Lear. With lunch for two…. Don't be a wise guy, all right? Just lunch. I'll call from the plane. Thanks, Pete. Now I owe you one." He hung up and stood. "All right, let's go. We have ninety minutes 'til lunch, but there's nothing to be helped."

"Why are we going to DC?" she asked.

Jon looked her straight in the eyes, the same intense look he had last night in the restaurant. "We're off to see the wizard."

Chapter Fourteen

The phone rang in the plush, mahogany-paneled office. "Excuse me, gentlemen," the grey haired man announced, looking at the caller ID on the display. "I must take this call privately."

The two junior aides nodded, stood, and gathered their things. As soon as they left, he set the remote control lock on the door, picked up the handset, and placed it to his ear

"Yes? Ah, Mr. Glass. Do you have an update for me?" He listened for several minutes, only asking questions for clarification: "Why didn't you call me right away? How is Miss Paine? Is Mr. Olsen still in London? How soon can he return?" He heaved a deep sigh. "No, whatever you do, don't use the codelite. There seems to be a programming error; it might go off prematurely, and I don't want you to place yourselves in harm's way. Just neutralize it with the stunner and bring it back to me. I don't want to have to start over; we've waited too long already.

"Have you found out who the gentleman is? As soon as you know, call me back. We'll have to bring in some of the other teams to help…no, no, don't feel badly, Mr. Glass. You've done very well so far, well beyond what you've been asked. No apologies are necessary or warranted at this point. I don't know what went wrong with its programming, but Dr. Hamund assures me it can be fixed. I'm sure you can find it, Mr. Glass. You're one of our best, and you have a crack team. Mr. Valdès should serve well as a substitute for Mr. Olsen until he can get back from London. Any further developments must be forwarded to me without delay, is that understood? Yes, thank you. Carry on, now, and may good fortune be yours."

He hung up and dialed another number, drumming his ring lightly on the desk while the line rang. With every ring, the hand that wore the ring trembled just a little more. When the party at the other end picked up, he said, "Please tell me you've found a way to reboot it, Doctor... how much more time do you need before you can tell me? That was not what I wanted to hear." As he listened, he shook his head, running his fingers through his hair. "Unfortunate... I'm sorry, Doctor, I can't understand the technical aspects of the project; that's your area of expertise. Please keep working on the solution. Mr. Glass has run into a problem. Miss Paine has been hurt, but not badly….No, a replacement isn't necessary or useful yet. This doesn't need to go any further for now. Thank you, Doctor. Goodbye."

He unlocked the door and called his personal assistant. "Please send my aides back in, we have much business to attend. Thank you, Denise. Oh, and take the rest of the day….You're welcome."

Chapter Fifteen

Roger Glass hung up his cell and heaved a sigh. The other team members gathered with him in Jenna's hotel room, where she had her broken leg propped up on pillows. The hot pink cast already sported a dozen signatures, mostly from the male staff in the ER, as well as Roger and Red.

Roger paced back and forth. "What I want to know is how in the hell she learned to fight like that? I thought she was a blank slate."

"Maybe Hamund left that intact in case she needed it for her job," said Rolf "Red" Hicks. He sported an angry, purple bruise on his face where Nadia had delivered a haymaker of a kick the previous night.

"Whatever," rasped Roger. He rubbed the welt on his throat, fully aware of what would have happened had Nadia's hand strike not missed his windpipe. He continued to wander around the room. *Did I let my edge slip? Did my feelings for Nadia get in the way? Maybe I need to get off this job before someone on my team gets killed.* "We need to find her, and this time, make sure she doesn't hand us any more surprises. Anybody got any suggestions?"

Red spoke up. "We could track her using her cellphone; it's got a GPS board for 9-1-1 calls, right? Just hack into the satellite network and give her a call."

"Okay," said Jenna Paine. "So what if we do find her?" She held up a small metal rod with a pushbutton on one side. "I couldn't even get the stunner in place long enough for a shot before she trashed my leg. Can you big, strapping men tell me exactly what we're going to do with her then? She kicked our—"

"Why do you people have to make this so hard?" A fourth man stood and shrugged. "All we have to do is sneak up behind her—" he drew a small pistol from a shoulder rig, pointed it at an imaginary target with one arm outstretched, "and unload one into her brain. Take the guy out, too. Look, if you all are squeamish—"

"Shut up, Valdès!" snapped Roger. "You just got here. You're only on this job until our regular gets back. You obviously don't have a clue what would happen if you did something that insanely stupid, so just shut the hell up, okay?" Roger Glass was getting fed up with this creep, and it was about time to let him know who the team leader was.

Valdès wasn't impressed. He turned toward Glass, his eyes blazing. "Okay, smart guy. So why don't you tell me what would happen if I did, huh?" He still held the pistol in his hand, now lowered at his side.

Red Hicks broke in between them. "Dave, you don't need to know that. Just suffice to say it would be a very bad thing to do, and let it go at that, okay? Now let's not get all 'Die-Hard' and all that crap just yet. We can come up with a plan to recover her and get rid of the guy, but the important part is to not lose track of Nadia. Is everyone okay with that? You two can blow each other's brains out on your own time, but right now, we need to find her again. Let's get back to the plane and use the office there so we don't leave a trail here."

Roger relaxed and backed off. "Okay, Red. But it still doesn't answer my other question, Jen. You lived with her. You were supposed to be watching for any change, any aberration in her programming. What happened?"

"Okay," she shot back. "What exactly was I supposed to notice, Sherlock? She's a *walking* aberration, thanks to Hamund and Spielberg. Becca probably would have been a better choice for a monitor. She would have spotted the problem a lot sooner than me."

Roger spoke as he rounded up his things. "Jen, you have a fourth degree black belt. The only degree Rebecca Mitchell has is hanging on her wall. She's a great psychiatrist, but she wouldn't have been able to take care of herself if something went wrong. And something obviously has gone wrong."

"Yeah, you sure took care of yourselves, Glass," grumbled David Valdès. He grabbed a small black duffel bag with one hand, and slung Jenna's bag over his other shoulder.

"Hey, Dave that wasn't exactly fair," said Jenna. "We were damned lucky. None of us were prepared for what we ran into. Every move she made was potentially incapacitating or deadly. Look where she caught Roger's neck: half an inch to the left and he'd be pushing daisies. She snapped my tibia like a matchstick, and that must have been a beautiful roundhouse kick she gave Red, judging from that bruise." She paused while she reached for her crutches. "I'd hate to see what she does to people she *doesn't* like. You weren't there, so I don't expect you to understand. Just hang back a little. Roger knows what he's doing."

Roger and Red helped her up, and the group headed for the door. "I think we'd better find out where that imprint came from," said Roger as he turned out the light.

Chapter Sixteen

"Learjet November 313 Fox-Bravo, you are clear to taxi Runway Oh-Six via Taxiway Hotel, hold short of the active runway for traffic. You are in line behind the Challenger."

"Teterboro Ground, Fox Bravo, copy Hotel, hold short at Oh-Six, I have the Challenger in sight," the Learjet's pilot called into the airwaves. Teterboro International looked for all the world like a giant beehive. Built to handle the corporate and private traffic for the New York/New Jersey area, the ramps and taxiways were filled with planes of all shapes and sizes, from light piston aircraft up to huge corporate-owned giants that carried busy executives and VIP's all around the world.

Jon and Nadia were oblivious to the bustle as a Global Express business jet took off, making a roar that reverberated throughout the little Lear 31. They were busy wolfing down packed lunches that were provided for their trip to Washington, DC.

The jet was small, but comfortable. Three single, leather-upholstered seats occupied the left side of the little cabin; a divan and one other single seat were set in along the right, positioned behind a small, wood-grained galley cabinet. There was a cramped baggage area with cargo straps in the aft section of the cabin, behind a tiny lavatory equipped with a commode and sink.

Jon and Nadia were the only passengers. The pilot and copilot were so occupied with getting ready for takeoff they wouldn't notice anything said behind the cockpit bulkhead. As Nadia ate, she listened to the crew going over checklists, flipping switches, and coordinating with Ground Control over the radio.

Jon and Nadia finished their lunches and packed the empty cartons and cans away just as the Lear made the turn onto the runway threshold. The pilot threw the throttle levers forward and the little jet leaped forward like a stallion out the gate, throwing everyone back in their seats. In no time at all they were in the air, climbing out under maximum power, making a wide turn to the south once they cleared the traffic control area around New York and Teterboro. The flight would not take very long.

Neither one spoke until the Lear leveled off at cruise altitude. The sound-insulated cabin only allowed the barest whispers from the engines to penetrate, and the wind rushing past the cabin at five hundred-plus miles per hour made a soft hiss on the windows. Nadia listened to the life-pulse of the little jet for a while, letting it soothe her nerves. She unfastened her lap belt and leaned her seat back. Glancing at Jon, she found him staring at her, eyes and face blank. She held his gaze and he looked away. Finally, she broke the silence. "So, what was your friend like?"

"She was like you. She *was* you, I'm sure of it. Okay, she didn't look like you, not a thing like you. But I don't think anyone who knew her could miss her in you." He looked up at the top of the passenger compartment, grasping for concepts he could put into words.

"So, what did she look like?"

"Five feet-ten and black."

"What, black hair?" She didn't know why she was asking. Maybe it was her own natural curiosity. She chuckled cynically to herself. Was anything "her own"?

His flat response surprised her. "No, black. Skin so dark it was black. I never knew anyone else that dark. Her hair was black, too."

"So what in the world would make you mistake me for her?"

"It was the way you moved. Alicia didn't strut or swagger, but she was confident—and it showed in every step she took, every word she spoke. She was one of a kind. That, and when you called me by my nickname in the coffee shop. No one but her and my mom ever called me 'Jake.'"

"So you think someone took a tall, African-American woman and crammed her into me. Don't you think that's a bit of a stretch?"

"But maybe there's some hypnosis involved here somewhere. You are just too much like Alicia for coincidence. Maybe you lost so much of yourself in the coma that they needed to put someone else in to make up for what was lost."

"And that's bad exactly how?"

"Well, for one thing, it may not be entirely legal. My friend is dead, after all. How did someone get hold of her mind? For another thing, it may not be safe. There may be conflicts between your mind and Alicia's, and that's why you started to get confused." He paused and took a deep breath, letting it out slowly. "And then there are your 'friends' who tried to kill you the minute you stepped out of line. Does that sound like a safe, *legal* situation, to you?"

Nadia paled, thinking about the sudden violence inflicted upon them by Red and the others.

Jon fixed her with his gaze. "How *did* they get hold of Alicia Burgess' mind? And further...." He leaned over as he continued, lowering his voice even more. "Why hasn't anyone tried to contact you since yesterday? I mean, besides that little reception at LaGuardia last night, no one else has even tried to call you. Have they?"

As if on cue, the phone in Nadia's purse rang. Hesitantly, she drew it out and opened it, placing it to her ear. "Hello?"

* * * *

Some distance behind them, on the ramp at Teterboro, a signal appeared on a small, handheld box with a display screen. Numbers flashed up on the screen, and a tiny beep issued forth from the box. Jenna Paine picked it up quickly and wrote the digits down. "We have a signal!" she announced to the rest of the team.

* * * *

The voice on the other end of Nadia's phone sounded fearful, almost desperate. "Nadia? Is that you? This is Dr. Mitchell. What is going on? I heard you were kidnapped. Where are you?"

"I'm...traveling." Nadia watched Jon, trying to get some indication of how to handle this. He made a motion with his hand, closing his fingers together with his thumb, and then laying his index finger to his lips. "No, Becca, I'm not being kidnapped. I think the New York studio has its facts mixed up."

"Nadia, we need you to come home right away. Come in and tell me what's going on, okay?"

"Maybe you need to tell me what's going on. Am I really someone else?"

"What are you talking about, Nadia?"

"I mean, is my head really my own, or did it belong to someone else?"

The pause on the line was too long, and Becca's response too artificially calm. "Whatever gave you that idea?"

"You're a lousy poker player, Doctor," said Nadia, and hung up.

* * * *

Back on board the Gulfstream on the ramp in Teterboro, the signal light went out on the small display. Curses went up from the crowd gathered around Jenna. Roger snatched the paper from her hand and handed it to the pilot. "Plot these numbers and tell me where they are," he barked.

* * * *

"I'm not me," Nadia moaned, curled up in her seat. She wrapped her arms around her knees. Her hands shook. "I'm somebody else, and I'm not me anymore. I never *was* me, was I?"

Jon leaned over to touch her on the shoulder, but a hand shot up and she writhed away. "Don't touch me. Don't even come close to me," she cried. He could see that her cheeks were already wet. She cried softly to herself, "If I hadn't known, I could have gone on. If I hadn't known—"

"If you hadn't known," Jon interjected, "You'd still be wondering who Phillip was. If you hadn't known, you'd still be in their hands."

She looked up, indignant. "Those people saved my life, Jon. They said it took more than twenty surgeries, just to save my face. They put that much into me so I could have a life again. They even had Jenna move in with me so I could adjust—"

"Or be monitored," said Jon.

"What are you talking about?" Her eyes flashed angrily.

"Have you ever, at any time, been left alone since you woke up?"

"Of course," she snorted. "I went to work—"

"To be with the people who just tried to kill you."

"I went shopping by myself. There was a little grocery store just around the corner." She stopped and went back to hugging her knees.

"What happened there? Alicia, what happened to you?"

"Don't call me that!" Her voice lowered threateningly and her eyes flashed. "Don't you call me by that name."

"Then who are you? What do we call you now?"

"I don't know." She sat curled up on the seat, her eyes locked on the lighting control panel by the cabin door. He watched her for a while, her chest wracked with silent sobs.

58

Jon got up and rummaged through the tiny galley behind the copilot's seat. He opened a drawer and took out a couple of small bottles. After he opened them both, he sat back down and held one out to Nadia.

"Peace?" he offered. She said nothing. "Nadia, I'm sorry. I should never have said that. I don't think I can ever understand what you're feeling right now. But maybe we can relax a little and figure some of this out."

Nadia didn't respond at first, but after a few seconds, she released her knees and dropped her feet to the floor. She took the bottle of Scotch and sipped it. Her face wrinkled in disgust and she almost spat it back out. Holding the bottle up, she tried to read its contents through watering eyes. She couldn't seem to make words come out of her mouth.

"It's Scotch," Jon offered. "Don't tell me you've never drank alcohol before."

Finally, she found her voice. "I can only answer for one year. And the answer is 'no.'"

"I can get you some water, if you want."

"What does this do?"

"It relaxes you."

"I think I need this more," she said, tossing back the bottle in one swallow. She squinted hard and gulped once, then lay back in her seat, feeling the warmth radiate from her stomach. "Let me know when we're there, please. I want to close my eyes for a little bit."

"Sure, Nadia."

Jon picked out a magazine from the rack in front of his seat and tried to read it, but couldn't concentrate. He kept stealing glances at the petite figure of the woman across the aisle. Her blonde hair poured in a golden, curly waterfall past her shoulders. Her squarish face complemented the slim build. From first appearances, it didn't seem as if she wore any makeup, but as Jon studied her full lips, he noticed a subtle shade of lipstick, and just a trace of makeup around her closed eyes. *Brown*, he remembered. *Captivating, almond-shaped, brown eyes. A guy could fall into those eyes and never want to come back....* He admired her figure for several seconds. *Give it up, Daniels; she's work, not play. And besides, she's way out of your league*, something inside him whispered. The flight continued, silent save for the drone of the engines and the muffled conversation in the cockpit.

Chapter Seventeen

"What do you mean, the Atlantic Ocean?" cried Red Hicks. "You mean, in a boat, or what?"

Jenna had her laptop open, plugging numbers into a spreadsheet. "No, the digits were changing too fast. She must be taking a flight somewhere."

"Okay, where?" asked Dave.

"Somewhere south of New York," said Roger. "We lost the signal from her phone when she hung up." He straightened up and rubbed his eyes. "We're losing a lot of time trying to track her this way. If we knew the man she was with, it might help. Where the hell did he come from, anyway?" The cabin phone rang. Roger picked up. "Glass."

"Roger, this is Anna Spielberg. I have some information for you on Nadia. It seems there has been an oversight on our part."

"What's up, Doc?" Roger loved that phrase and never let a chance to use it slip by. He smiled inwardly as he imagined Anna's eyes rolling in exasperation, even considering the seriousness of the situation.

"It seems that the download came from a woman named Alicia Burgess, wife and mother of three who was killed in an auto accident in the Cascades."

Roger held his breath for a moment. *There has to be another shoe to drop here.* "You mean we got our butts handed to us by a soccer mom? So, was she into Tae-Bo, or something?"

Dr. Spielberg paused. "She wasn't exactly a soccer mom, Roger. Try the FBI's number one hand-to-hand combat instructor. Eighth-degree black belt in three different styles and National Karate Women's Champion runner-up. She was a special agent out of the New York office."

Roger laughed and looked at the others, rolling his eyes and shrugging. *This is just too good.* He turned back around. "So, Doctor Spielberg, you're telling me that we downloaded a human weapon into a…." He stopped short and looked around. Dave was watching inquisitively, as were the others. Roger lowered his voice and spoke again. "What else can you tell me about her?"

"She had a partner for four years out of her last five, a man named Jonathan Daniels. I have an address—"

"Never mind the address, Doc, just fax a picture to this plane. If this is who we think it is, I know where they're going. Thanks." He hung up and turned to the rest of the team. "Let's get ready to take off. We're going to Washington. Let's just hope we get there before 'Show-and-Tell.'" After giving instructions to the flight crew, he came back and made his own preparations. A few minutes later, the luxurious jet's air stair retracted into its side, and the engines spooled up. After another fifteen minutes, it took off into the skies and swung south, destination: Dulles International Airport.

Roger filled in the rest of the team when the plane attained its cruise altitude. There was a space of minutes while the information sank in. "We need to get to FBI HQ. If they're in the air, that's where they're going."

"So what do we do once we get there?" asked Red.

"We can't let anything happen to Nadia," said Roger. "I think we need to have a talk with Agent Daniels, find out what he knows."

"And if he knows?"

"Let's hope he doesn't. Either way it goes, I wouldn't want to be him right now."

Chapter Eighteen

Jon led Nadia past the front desk without saying anything to the receptionist. "Just walk in like you own the place, and stick with me," he told her, "I have some friends inside who might help us." And so he led a brisk pace into the grand building, through three sets of double doors, and down endless halls and steps. In the basement, he led her into a small waiting room. "Just wait here, okay? I'll be right back." A few moments later, he returned with a heavy, middle-aged man in a lab coat.

The older man didn't look very pleased. "What did you do this time, boy? I saw your face on the news this morning."

"We have a Jane Doe here," Jon said vaguely. "She can't remember who she is."

"Well, the TV doesn't seem to have any trouble knowing who she is, Jonny." The doctor's voice was tense, and he looked sideways at Nadia, puzzled. She said nothing.

"Look, there's a lot more going on than meets the eye," said Jon hurriedly. "There's reason to believe she isn't who *anyone* thinks she is. We were attacked in that airport, both of us, and we barely made it out with our skins. I wasn't kidnapping her. I was protecting her—from them."

"From who?" asked the doctor, his arms folded across his chest.

Jon's face flushed crimson as he fought out his reply. "From…news people…."

The older man looked at Jon in disbelief, and then at Nadia, who nodded silently. His brow furrowed and he shook his head. "So what do you want from me?"

"Just give her a quick physical. Look for anything strange."

"Just how thorough do you expect me to be, boy?"

"You're the doctor; you tell me."

"What are we talking about here, amnesia?"

"To start with, yes."

"That could be caused by a head trauma, tumor, or nothing in particular. What makes you think she has amnesia?"

"I'm not who I thought I was," piped Nadia. "I've had some… episodes…recently, and I know I'm somebody else. I just don't know who."

"And you think this is why you got attacked?"

"The people who attacked us were my friends, before I met Jon," she said.

The doctor leaned his head toward Jon. "He has that effect on people. And you're sure *they* weren't protecting you from a perceived threat?"

"I guess you had to be there, Uncle Mike", said Jon. "Look, we don't have much time. What can you find out quickly?"

"I can see if there's been any trauma to her head. Run a couple of blood tests. Look for antigens for viral agents, stuff like that. Anything more is going to take time." He held out his hand to Nadia, who took it. "I'm Mike Alverson, Miss," he said warmly. She saw his eyes smiling behind thick, wire-framed eyeglasses. "Could you come this way?" He escorted her through a small door to his own office and had her sit on the edge of his desk while he fetched a small stool from the lab.

"We're not a medical facility, we're a crime lab, so we don't have full facilities," he apologized as he returned. "But I think we can make do. I was a country doctor for twenty-three years before I started working for the Bureau. Jon, I want to ask you some questions but I want you to stand over there." He pointed to the far corner of the room. "I want to preserve this young lady's modesty. Thank you. Now, turn around and face the corner."

Jon grinned as he turned. "Am I in trouble, Doc?"

"More than you know, boy," the doctor muttered. He took her pulse, nodded and reached for a tray of instruments, grabbing a small otoscope. "My dear, I want to check for evidence of any physical head trauma." He shone the light into her left eye as he scolded Jon. "Son, you know there's channels for these types of investigations."

"You know me, Uncle Mike. I like to take the bull by the horns."

"Uh-huh," grunted the doctor. "Well, your bull-grabbing sure started a spit storm upstairs. Scuttlebutt said Congressman Brady called the Director, and you were the main topic of conversation. Bad news travels quick 'round these parts," he muttered. "You better check in before someone swears out a warrant on you again."

"*Again?*" asked Nadia, shocked. She looked around the doctor's bulk at Jon. "What the hell kind of cop are you?"

"One who doesn't play by the rules when they don't suit him," said Mike. "You're just another case in point, Miss." He gently took her chin in his hand and brought her face back around to face him. The light shone in Nadia's right eye. "By all rights, you could swear out a warrant yourself—" Mike nearly dropped the light. "Well," he said, "What have we here? Hold still, dear. Yes, just like that. I'll be damned...."

Chapter Nineteen

The Gulfstream was still in the air when the cabin phone rang again. Roger picked up. "Glass. Yes, sir. Did Dr. Spielberg call you, then? No, sir, I don't think it'll be problem, we know what to expect now.... Yes, Jon Daniels. He used to be her partner....I guess that's something that just slipped through the cracks. Ah, sir...how do you want us to turn her off? So, you want her intact, then. Okay. And Daniels? Copy we have the green light, sir. Count on us. Thank you, sir. Goodbye." He hung up and turned to his team.

"Okay. Jenna, gentlemen, and you, too, Red...." He grinned at his own joke and dodged the pen thrown his way. "Here's the latest. They're at FBI headquarters right now. One of our assets there saw them come in. Nadia needs to stay in one piece, Daniels is toast. Dave, park outside on the opposite roof. As soon as you have the shot, take it. Red, you and I will have to take Nadia ourselves. As soon as Dave takes Daniels down, we move on her. She should be disoriented enough—"

"You're talking like she's a real person," said Red.

"She's programmed to be a real person, ain't she?" Roger shot back.

"'Programmed to be a real person?' This is getting real good," said Dave, sardonically. "How's about you morons tell me what's what before I walk out on this op and let you have it all to yourselves. That'd be a real gas, wouldn't it?" Roger looked at Dave as if he had three heads. Red flumped down in his seat.

Jenna broke the silence. "Better tell him, Rog. He'll need to know sooner or later, especially if Steven can't catch up with us before it's done." So Roger told him everything.

Dave nodded, slack-jawed, as the final truth hit. And when Roger finished, he sat, sipping a soda. He said nothing else for the duration of the trip.

Chapter Twenty

"Jon, I don't understand. What makes this a Jane Doe case? You yourself told me she knows her name."

"But she doesn't have any recollection from more than a year ago. She could be…a critical witness to a cold case." Jon hated to lie, but at this point, no one was going to believe what he thought: that someone had hijacked his former partner's personality via some strange hypnosis and placed it somehow into this woman. Doctor Alverson looked at Jon through squinted eyes.

"Don't shine me, boy. There's something else going on here; but I'm betting you don't know enough to figure out the *what*, let alone the *who*."

"Well, can you help, or not? I know she's not who she's been told she is, okay? I promise you, I'll find the right channels to make something stick, but right now I just need something positive."

"All right, boy, but I don't think you're going to like the answer this is heading for." The doctor prepared a phlebotomy tube and pushed up Nadia's sleeve. "My dear, I'm going to take a blood sample. Please forgive me ahead of time. I don't do this very often anymore, at least on a living person." With shaking hands, he held up a syringe. "This may hurt just a little." She tentatively held out her arm, and was semi-pleasantly surprised to see his hand settle down as he concentrated on the task.

"Just a poke, now," he said, and pushed the needle smoothly into her arm. As the syringe filled up, he gasped.

Jon turned around to see what was going on, but his uncle had already stuffed the tube into a pocket of his lab coat and twisted another tube onto the needle, filling it as well. He kept both tubes concealed from Jon's prying eyes. "I said, sit down there, boy," he growled, and Jon sat back down in the corner. The doctor withdrew the needle from Nadia's arm and pressed the site with a small gauze pad. "H-Hold this here," he said to her. He sat back on his stool with a grunt. Burying his head in his hands, he said, "I'm getting too old for this."

* * * *

David Valdès set up on the roof opposite FBI Headquarters with a casual air that betrayed his experience as an expert sniper. Having carefully cleared the area, he squatted down behind the façade and unzipped a modified structural-foam guitar case. Neatly packed inside, in four pieces, was the most formidable shoulder-fired weapon ever developed: The Barrett M107, .50-caliber rifle. He was proud of this weapon, and took care of it with all the loving care a virtuoso musician might bestow on a beloved instrument. Dave was a virtuoso, in the same sense that there were few on this planet that could surpass his skill with his chosen instrument. Death was his magnum opus.

He spread his jacket on the rooftop, lifted the barrel and flash suppressor/compensator assembly gently out, and inspected it. Finding everything satisfactory, he laid it on the jacket. Then he went through the same procedure with the scope, butt/action assembly, and bolt assembly. In another minute, he had the weapon assembled, inspected, and checked.

It was black and huge, and every line and corner betrayed its purpose. It looked like Death. A meter and a half long, there was no friendly curve, no grace about it. The flash suppressor was a flat, rectangular block with side ports, three on a side. Its barrel was straight and heavy, and met squarely against an octagonal receiver/action assembly. The buttstock was a massive right triangular shape. A pair of bipod legs lay unfolded from the front end of the barrel to support its 20-pound mass.

Reaching back into the case, he opened the storage bin and took out the magazine. He unloaded it and spread the rounds next to each other on the jacket. He'd loaded every one himself. He'd balanced each bullet, mixed the powder, chose the primers and pressed each round with tender-loving care. He hefted each one up and inspected it meticulously. More than three inches long and bottle-shaped, with the copper-jacketed bullet a full half inch in diameter, this cartridge could dispense instant death to anyone he chose within a half mile radius. This was the power of death, and David Valdès held sway over it. This small, metal-jacketed fiend was his familiar, a private little assassin all on its own, as trained and as ready as he himself. And, as in many instances before, it would do his bidding.

Tenderly, he loaded five rounds into the magazine, inserted the magazine into the action on the massive rifle, and drew back the charging

67

handle, watching the tip of the first cartridge ease forward into the chamber. Then he let the bolt snap forward the rest of the way on its own. *Locked, cocked and ready to rock.*

Cradling the death-giver in his lap, he placed his jacket over the edge of the façade. He laid the barrel over the jacket and settled the scope on the door across the street. He twisted the focus, estimated and set the range, and checked the wind. The day was still, and a light overcast obscured the sun.

This was going to be an easy shot, but timing would be critical. He mentally went over his planned escape route, analyzing his options. He should have about ten seconds after the first shot before agents started coming out of the HQ like fire ants. He could probably get one more off if he had to, but a third would surely give his position away and he wouldn't have time to make good his escape.

Let's hope it only takes one, then.

* * * *

"Son," said Dr. Alverson to Jon, "You have no idea what you stepped into, here. You may not have the shoes for it." He turned to Nadia. "Are you sure you don't remember anything beyond a year ago?"

"Only bits and pieces," said Nadia. "I have dreams every now and then about people I feel I should know, and there was something strange when I met Jon yesterday—"

The doctor held out a hand to stop her, and stood. "Don't say any more here. I have to round up a few things. You two stay here until I get back. They'll be looking for you down here soon; we don't want to be here when they do." He took the tubes and disappeared through the office door into the outer room; they heard another door slam.

Jon sat in the corner after his uncle left, trying to get the look of shock out of his face. He'd never seen his uncle that shaken. The doctor came back in, breathless, and rounded up a few things that he tossed into a metal briefcase he had already begun to pack: extra syringes, a paper package of sterile swabs, a hand-held tape recorder, some pipettes, and a small bottle of hand sanitizer. Mike slammed the lid and locked it.

"Grab my laptop, Jon. We're getting out of here. We'll go to the cabin and look into this." Mike took Nadia's arm, guiding her to the door. They turned the opposite way they had come in; instead of returning to the main floor, they continued on, corridor after corridor, coming out into an underground parking garage. Mike led them to a grey Mercury luxury sedan at the far end of the aisle.

He tossed the keys to Jon. "You drive. I'll get in the back." The engine started easily. "We have plenty of gas to get to the Shenandoah," said Mike from the back seat. "If I have to, I can work from my office in Front Royal. But this computer will be our sole means of communication from the cabin. Drive. I have some work to do."

Jon backed out of the slot and goosed the accelerator hard. Tires squealing, the car sped from the garage.

* * * *

Dave was watching the front door when the call came in his earpiece. "The garage! They're in a grey or silver Merc, coming out right now! Three, do you copy?"

"Three copies," said Dave quietly. "I do not have a visual....wait, I can see them now."

"Three, you have the green light. Stop the vehicle."

"Three copies," Dave said again, fixing on the vehicle as it sped down the street in front of him. This wouldn't do. They were traveling too fast for a shot from this angle. He got up and trotted to the right end of the building, where he could get a following shot. He set the bipod quickly in place, sighting in on the rear window of the car. "Who's driving?" he spoke into his microphone.

"Target male is driving, target female is passenger. There's someone else in the back seat."

"Three copies," said Dave. "I have the shot...now!" The car sped down the street as David brought the weapon to bear and squeezed the trigger. The death-giver roared and belched flame like a legendary beast as the bullet ripped through the air. It found the rear end of the Mercury and exploded through the rear window. Glass flew everywhere as the round carried through flesh, bone and seat, finally passing through the floorboard. It ricocheted back up off the street to lodge in the engine's drive train, tearing chunks of steel loose with adamantine claws.

In the back seat, Jon's uncle grunted and grabbed his lower body as the car ground to a stop. Jon looked back over his shoulder and yelled, "Uncle

Mike!" He got out and tore open the rear door, dragging the doctor into the street between the car and the curb. Huddling down in the shelter of the auto's hulk, Jon checked his uncle over.

Blood poured from Mike's lower abdomen and right leg where the huge bullet had ripped through. The shattered leg was hanging on by shreds of flesh. His face was pale, a horrid shade of white.

"Dammit, Uncle Mike!"

Mike Alverson's face turned up as his nephew looked around for something to stop the flow. People who saw the incident began to gather around.

"Jon," the doctor moaned, "Get out of here, now. Get to the cabin."

"Uncle Mike, I'm so sorry—"

An angry buzz cut the air, cut short by a metallic *pong* and a loud, wet slap as the man standing next to Jon crumpled to the sidewalk, grasping his abdomen. An explosion ripped the air immediately afterward. The crowd scattered, screaming, as Jon looked frantically around for the source of the shot. "Nadia, get out of the car. Grab that laptop and get out!"

Mike grabbed his arm. "Jon, her blood…Donna Hermsen. You can trust her…email. She's not—" He groaned and Jon could see a sickly pallor coming over his face. "Get," he said. "I'll be all right, it's not too serious. Just go. Take the case."

Jon looked for the flight case his uncle had packed; he found it on the floor in the back seat of the car. A sound down the street stopped him short: a car's engine revving hard, coming fast. *Damn, no time.*

* * * *

Nadia scooted out of the front seat with the computer. Jon took her hand and they ran around the next corner, ducking into an alley as they heard tires screeching around the corner behind them. The vehicle, a brown mid-sized Ford sedan, sped by and then skidded to a halt in the street. It slammed into reverse and tires screamed in rage as it came back.

She heard the protest of horns, the crash of a fender-bender, and felt Jon dragging her down the alley. She held the laptop in a death grip as he swung her ahead and pushed her bodily along. "Run, dammit!"

The roar of an engine pushed to its limit echoed up the narrow alley behind them, coming like a great metal beast of prey. The growl increased in volume until Nadia felt its hot, steaming breath on her back, almost felt the tires reaching out like claws to rend, tear, and grind her body beneath them. She tasted bile in her throat as she ran, looking desperately for anything to hide behind, to get away from the death that pursued her.

Jon gave her a rough shove, and she fell behind a dumpster. He sprawled over her, protecting her with his own body as the car careened by, throwing debris and exhaust fumes contemptuously at them as it passed.

Jon leaped to his feet and picked up Nadia. They ran back up the alley. Behind them, the car skidded to a halt and began to back up. Once again, the beast launched itself at them, hungry for the kill. Jon spun around, drawing his weapon as he did. He fired three quick shots into the rear window as the vehicle bore down on them. The window shattered. Spiderweb cracks spread out from the holes, obscuring the driver's vision. The car swerved into the opposite wall of the alley, and metal screeched in pain. Quickly Jon dragged Nadia back out to the street.

They ducked into a small restaurant just as the car blasted out of the alley, skidding into a turn. With a sickening crunch, it slammed into the side of a car coming up the street, sending glass exploding everywhere. Jon watched from inside as people surrounded both vehicles to see if anyone was hurt.

"They'll be occupied for a while. Come on," Jon muttered as he led Nadia through the kitchen and out the back door. They snuck away while their pursuers were making their own escapes from the scene.

Chapter Twenty-One

Bunny Kalinsky had spent most of his life running: As a kid in Brooklyn, running from the bigger kids; as a teen, running from the bullies; and as a man, running from the police. It wasn't as if Bunny actually looked for trouble; it was just that Trouble spent a good share of *its* time looking for Bunny. The harder he tried to do good things, the more Trouble came into his life. He wasn't sure exactly when he'd crossed the point of no return, but he had no doubt it lay somewhere far in his past.

Younger than his care-worn appearance suggested, Bunny was quick-witted and intelligent. He had a round face, large, expressive eyes, and a wide mouth that turned down at the corners. A skinny little man with a bowed back, he had long, quick fingers that loved to fiddle and tinker, mostly with computers. But not anymore. He could have had a well-paying job for just about anyone as an information systems or network specialist. But Trouble had once again intervened, and now he had to settle for lying on his beaten-up old couch in pajamas and a T-shirt, thumbing sadly through the channels with his remote.

He started at the sudden knock on his door. It could only mean one thing, as he had no friends left who would call on him. But why now? He'd paid back Lenny the Face, so there was no reason for another beating from his thugs. Maybe they'd gotten so used to making the stop that it was just a habit now. Bunny resigned himself to his fate and rose. Maybe it would be over quickly, and he wouldn't get anything broken this time. *Oh, well, at least it wouldn't be the cops again.*

He could almost hear Trouble snickering wickedly when he opened the door to Jon Daniels. "J-Jon. Hey, buddy, how are you…?"

Jon barged in, forcing the door the rest of the way open. A beautiful blonde woman came in with him, carrying a laptop in its case. "Hello, Nurse!" he exclaimed, openly ogling her. She gave him a dour look. "Boy, Jon you keep gettin' the best partners. Put me in for the FBI, baby." He chuckled feebly at his own joke, but no one else seemed to find it funny, so he let it die mercifully.

"How's it going, Bunny? Been keeping it straight?"

A cold pit opened in Bunny's stomach. *What did I do* this *time?* "Jon, ah…look, guy, I been straight, okay? I don't even have a machine anymore. I threw away all my software, I got nothin' left—"

"Shut up, Bunny," Jon interjected. "This isn't business, at least not *that* kind of business. We need help, and I can't think of a nicer guy than my old pal." He punctuated it with a good-natured slap on Bunny's arm that staggered the smaller man. "Now," Jon said. "Can you help us with a problem, or can't you?"

"Geez, Jon, I don't want to go back up. If I so much as darken the door to Best Buy, they'll put me away for good. Hell, I drove through the parking lot last week and your buddy Markie had me followed for two days! No, man, I can't do no more like that, okay?"

"Okay, Bunny, let's just have a look around, shall we? Nadia…" Jon nodded to the woman, who promptly set the laptop down on Bunny's table. "Oh, what have we here? Why, it's a computer, Bunny! Weren't you under a federal court order? Oh, my, what shall we do?"

Bunny could only sputter. "Get that crap outta here, Jon. I mean it! I can't get caught with that here, and you know it. What the hell are you up to, anyway?"

Jon put his arm around Bunny hard, and patted him on the chest with his other hand as he kept talking. "Bunny, this is a recruitment drive. You're the best hacker the FBI has ever had the immense pleasure of sending up the river. And, now that you're back in circulation, I have an offer that requires your unique talent."

"Oh, I get it, Jon. You hate me and you want me to go back up, so this is a setup, right? Where's Markie?" he demanded, looking around. "Do I get a better lawyer this time?"

"Bunny, what would you say if I told you that I can help you disappear and get a fresh start on everything? No one watching you over your shoulder, no one telling you what you can and can't do with your life. How would you like to work for the good guys for once?"

Bunny thought for a long moment, letting the situation sink in. What did he owe this man? Jon took everything that could be taken from a man, and now he wanted…what, exactly? "What's in it for me?"

"Bunny, why would you ask a question like that? You can name your price, buddy. I know that whatever you desire can magically appear at your doorstep in six to eight weeks, sooner if you can hack eBay again."

"You know you're ruinin' my life here, Jon, you know that? I promised the judge I wouldn't get in no more trouble and here you come and right away *ph-h-h-h-ht*! Out the window. You know that, don't you? What do you want now?"

"I wish I knew, Bunny. That's what I need you for. Where're your car keys?"

Chapter Twenty-Two

The team set up house in a small apartment the Company owned in the DC area. Steven Olsen joined David, Jenna, Roger, and Red on his return from London. They gathered around the table in the kitchen area and discussed their progress. Jenna took notes and operated the laptop. Roger Glass passed out cans of beverage and sat down.

"Okay, Jenna, gentlemen. You, too, Red," he nodded with a smile. "We now have our work cut out for us. According to Dr. Spielberg, Nadia knows she's a download. At least she has an idea she is. She's probably ruled out contact with us, and she still has Jon Daniels with her. They picked up a doctor from the FBI's forensics lab, but Dave put the kibosh on that. Thanks, Dave." Valdès nodded in acknowledgement, and Roger carried on. "That wasn't a compliment, Valdès. Why is Daniels still alive? You had a clean shot at a stationary target."

David's voice was calm, but his face betrayed his anger. "You wanted the vehicle stopped. I stopped the vehicle. Second round ricocheted off the fender, or it would have been a perfect head shot. I don't recall, Glass— how long did it take for you to get your act together in the chase car?"

Roger held David's gaze. The room went silent as the tension mounted between the two. Jenna shifted uncomfortably. Steven began to get up. Red stopped him and shook his head. He sat back down and looked at each man. David's elbows rested casually on his knees. His brow knotted in anger, his eyes were lasers, boring holes through the air. Roger was perfectly still, his face almost angelic in peace. Steven knew Roger, he knew better. *Dave, don't try it, buddy. You'll just make a mess.*

Roger broke the silence. He still watched Dave as he started, but his gaze shifted to the others as he continued. His voice was perfectly even, unfazed by the confrontation. "Unfortunately, we trashed out a rental car trying to make the pickup. The good news is, I don't think the police will find anything useful in the rental. What can you tell us about the doc, Jenna?"

75

(☞ ⌣ ☞)

She opened a file on the laptop and read selected portions to the team. "He's been with the Bureau twenty-five years as a forensic coroner. Served in Korea. Graduated with honors from Stanford, served his residency at Hopkins. He was in private practice on the side for a while, and then his wife left him. He's Daniels' uncle on his mom's side, and the lab team leader. There's another team sent from up-line going through his house right now, getting any other information that could help."

Red said, "Their car got towed before we could get back to it. We could probably find out where it was taken to and get into it first thing in the morning."

"Problem," said Dave. "With gunshots involved, I think it's in a police impound. We have to find it tonight, or it'll be gone over by the cops before we have a chance to get anything useful."

Jenna spoke up. "Already on it." She pecked away at her computer for several seconds. "Okay, got the number for the nearest police precinct." She picked up the phone and dialed a number. "Oh, hello. Good evening, Sergeant. I'm special agent Paine from the FBI. There was a car involved in a shooting this afternoon, a grey or silver Mercury, just down from our headquarters…yes, that's the one. Where is it right now? Thank you. Yes, could you let them know a couple of agents will be there this evening? Agents Hicks and Valdès. Yes, this is a very high priority case. An agent was shot. Thank you very much." She hung up and looked at Roger. "There. Problem solved. It's at the precinct impound on 20th. See Lieutenant Pierce."

"Man, you're good," said Roger, smiling. She smiled back with a modest nod. "Okay, now next item. It looks like we need more information on our Mr. Daniels and what exactly went on downstairs. What assets do we have available in the bureau?"

Jenna took a note. "I'll have to run that through channels. It might make a better plan to just send an inquiry up-line and see what comes back so we don't compromise anyone inside. Being a priority case, it should come back pretty quick."

"Okay, do that. I'd like to have an action plan in place no later than tomorrow. I don't have to tell anyone what could happen if this goes any more wrong. Let's just hope she stays away from any metropolitan areas until we can round her up again.

"Dave and Red, see if there's anything in the doc's car that could lead us to them. Jenna can make up a couple of ID badges for you and you can be on your way. Jenna, make your call up-line and I'll send a report back out to Twin Oaks. Steven, follow up on Dr. Alverson. See if he's still alive, find out what he knows, and make sure he stays quiet. The last thing we need here is to have to go from clean-up mode to damage control. Tomorrow's going to get busy real quick. Okay, that's it."

Chapter Twenty-Three

Late summer in the Shenandoah River Valley received the trio of travelers in splendid, breathtaking style. The urban landscape of Washington DC gave way quickly to rolling hills lush with crops and dabbed liberally with patches of thick forest. Before long, they began to climb the Blue Ridge and dipped down into the valley between the Ridge and the Appalachians. Dairy farms and orchards spread across the valley floor. Fruit trees hung heavy with color, branches weighed low with abundance. The rolled-down windows of the beat-up little car let in the smells of the countryside.

Jon followed the highway into Front Royal where they picked up supplies: food, clothing, and sundries for a stay in a cabin. Several miles out of town, they slowed on a seemingly empty stretch of tree-flanked highway and turned down an overgrown dirt track. They wound along between the trees and up a ridge. At the top, Jon stopped the car for a moment. Nadia gasped. "It's so beautiful," she whispered.

"Yeah," said Jon. "It's been a while since I've seen it myself." He put the car back into gear and they headed down the trail toward the river.

They found the cabin in a small clearing surrounded by hardwoods and scrub undergrowth. Jon and Nadia got out and stretched the cramps out of weary bones while Bunny walked around, checking out the view. The cabin rested comfortably at the foot of a small ridge in the Appalachian foothills. The Shenandoah River itself was visible through the trees only a hundred yards or so away, winding away through the hills. The sunset of the early evening painted the hills and banks overlooking the river in hues no human artist could reproduce, an abundance of reds, violets, maroons, and blues brushed across the sky with masterful strokes and blended with tender loving care. A soft gust caressed the surrounding trees, who waved by proxy with their leaves. They could hear the warblers and wrens, blackbirds and thrush, smell the fresh breeze, and feel the solitude.

The cabin itself was a quaint, rough-hewn, log affair with a gabled, cedar-shake roof. Half of the front wall was occupied by a recessed porch about six feet deep and overhung by the roof. Double hung windows graced the walls in pairs, allowing sunlight and the spectacular view into every room of the place. A stone chimney jutted up through the roof, waiting for someone to send warm, comfortable smoke up through it. It invited the weary traveler with the promise of rest and refreshment.

"This is awesome!" cried Bunny. "Nobody'll ever find us out here!"

"One can hope," muttered Jon. No sooner had the words come from his lips than there was a shout behind them. A squat, old man advanced through the trees toward them, led by a basset hound on a leash. The old man shouted in a thick accent as he advanced, waving a stout walking stick in the air over his head like a cudgel. Nadia caught sight of coke-bottle glasses, a huge, bulbous nose and a worn-out Boston Red Sox baseball cap.

"Hey, you!" rang the voice, in a thick German-Jewish accent. "This is private property. Clear out!" Jon spun around, and then broke into a smile.

"Mr. Rats?" Jon called out. "Mr. Rats, it's me, Jon."

"Jonny-boy!" The expression changed suddenly and a huge grin split the ancient visage. "Yeesh, you got big!" he shouted. He toddled up to Jon and embraced him warmly. "When did you grow up? My Hilda, God rest her soul, she would have been surprised to see you all grown! My goodness, it's been years." He backed up and took in the small group. "Where's your uncle? And who's this?"

"Okay," smiled Jon. "In order: Uncle Mike…couldn't make it. We were going to spend a couple of weeks up here, but something came up. Let's get the introductions out of the way. Mr. Irving Ratzinger, this is…Mr. Kalinsky, a…good…friend, and this…this—"

Nadia offered her hand. "Alicia. Alicia Burgess."

Irving shifted his stick to his other hand and took her outstretched hand in a gracious, gentle squeeze. His smile was so infectious and genuine that she couldn't help but feel lighter just being around this man. "It's certainly a pleasure to meet you, young lady. Welcome to our little resort." He talked to Jon. "Jonny, I'll let you get settled in, but you all have to come and see me tomorrow night. Dinner's at seven. Don't bring anything but yourselves. It's good to see you," he repeated. He led the basset back around the corner of the cabin and disappeared the same way he came.

The screen door spring moaned in protest as Jon put the key into the lock on the inner door. It creaked open to reveal a dusty, silent living room scattered about with furniture rescued from garage sales or a curb, Nadia wasn't sure which. A worn sofa languished under the windows opposite the door. A scratched coffee table gathered dust in front of it. In the center of the floor crouched a threadbare easy chair playing peek-a-boo from under a sheet.

Looking to her right, Nadia saw a short, narrow hallway. On the left were two doors, and on the right side a single door hung open on its hinges. A narrow arch nearer and on the right wall opened into the small kitchen.

There was a slight, dank chill and musty odor in the air, a kind of respiratory atrophy from being closed up for extended periods.

Jon stepped around her and into the kitchen. There was a metallic creak and the decisive *pop* of a main circuit breaker, and the ancient, round-topped refrigerator in the kitchen began to hum. Jon made his rounds through the place, turning on a light in each room. "I'll get the water going. Who wants to unload the trunk?" Nadia looked expectantly at Bunny, who looked back at her.

"What, like your arms are broke?"

"Would you rather grab a broom and get busy?" she asked curtly. "There's no way I'm staying here until this place gets cleaned."

Bunny went outside and began emptying the trunk as he muttered indignantly to himself.

Nadia grabbed a scraggly-looking straw broom from the closet in the kitchen. She stifled a surprised squeal and swung the broom at a mouse that scurried from where it lay, through the living room and out across the porch, disappearing into the woods. Her heart thudded in her chest as she began to sweep the dust from the floor. *Sorry, little Mouse. I hope you weren't hurt.*

* * * *

An hour later, the sun had set and darkness was creeping furtively through the forest like a wolf stalking the fleeing daylight. Jon and Bunny were still setting things in order in the kitchen when a crash and a scream from the bathroom slashed through the cabin. Jon ran in and found Nadia on the floor, curled up in a fetal ball, lying on her side. "No, no," she cried, again and again. "No, no—"

"What's wrong? What's the matter?" Jon looked her over. The mirror that had hung on the wall over the sink for so many years lay in pieces on the floor. She lay in the middle of the shards, somehow without a single cut on her. Her hands clung frantically to her face, covering her eyes. Jon picked Nadia's trembling, hysterical form up carefully and carried her into the bedroom.

He sat with her in his arms, talking gently to her until she began to get control once again. The smell of her hair reached his nostrils, her warmth radiated into his body. He forced his mind to stay on task. "What happened?" he asked softly.

Bunny appeared in the doorway, a puzzled expression on his face. "Just go," Jon whispered. "I'll be right there, okay?" Bunny nodded numbly and retreated to the kitchen to keep busy.

Jon laid Nadia down on the bed and sat on the floor, reclining against the wood-paneled wall of the cabin's master bedroom. He listened to her unsteady breath as she continued to cry softly. The utter helplessness of her situation stung his heart and broke it. "Nadia," he said, "I can't begin to understand—"

"I'm not me, Jon," she rasped between sobs, "I'm not anyone, but I'm still me. But who am I?"

"I think that somehow—"

"But I'm not her. I look in the mirror, and I don't know that person anymore. I can see *her* eyes, and she's looking back, but I don't know her anymore. Jon, I'm afraid, I'm so afraid…."

He reached over and took her hand in a gentle grip, and her fingers wrapped around his. She was so soft, so…. That voice whispered in his head again. *She's work, Jon. Keep your head in the game.* His head was telling him one thing, but his hormones….

Nadia cried silently for some time, lying on her side. Then she sniffed and was quiet. Suddenly she spoke again, hesitantly. "Did you love her?"

Jon was taken aback. He didn't expect the conversation to go here. He let go of her hand. "That's ridiculous. She was married."

She sniffed and pressed on. "But you knew every little detail about her, didn't you? You knew how she liked her coffee. You knew about her favorite foods, the way she walked…the way...I—"

"She was married," he repeated, beginning to get irritated. He wanted to change the subject.

But the interrogator in Nadia stepped in, pursuing it. "You still didn't answer the question."

Jon lifted his gaze to look at her, and found her staring directly into his face.

Her eyes wet and swollen, she continued to push. "You were in love with Alicia, weren't you?"

Jon listened as the crickets outside called to each other in the warm night air and said nothing.

"And now you see her in me, and it's like having her back, only without him, isn't it? Without Phillip? Is that why we're here, Jon?"

"We're here because someone's trying to kill us, Nadia," Jon shot back. "We're here because we've been attacked with deadly intent, which is a felony, and pursued across state lines, which makes it a federal case. Right now, we're here in this cabin because I'm trying to keep you alive."

"For what?" she asked. "Am I just a witness, or something more?"

Jon heaved himself to his feet and started for the door. "I'd better get a broom and pick up that glass before someone gets hurt." He stopped at the door. "Get some sleep," he said flatly. "You look beat."

Chapter Twenty-Four

The next morning found the little cabin alive with activity. Bunny had the laptop open on the kitchen table and was pecking away at a furious rate. He and Jon had finished breakfast: pancakes, eggs, and bacon. Now Jon was busy cleaning up. Nadia's plate sat untouched. She had yet to appear this morning. Jon had checked in on her and found her still lying in bed on top of the covers. He had no idea whether she was asleep, but he decided not to disturb her.

"So when's the girl gonna come and eat breakfast?" asked Bunny.

Jon rinsed a plate and put it in the wire drainer on the counter. "When she's good and ready."

"So if she don't show, I get the leftovers, right?"

"You touch that plate, I'll break your arm," said Jon.

"Geez. Some people got no sense of humor." Bunny typed so quickly the keys sounded like pea gravel in a rock tumbler as his fingers danced their *paso doble* across the keyboard.

"What are you doing, anyway?" asked Jon. He dried his hands and refilled his coffee cup from the percolator on the stove.

"Hacking the Fed. We need cash." Bunny quickly added, "I was jokin', there, okay? If I really wanted to hack the Fed again, I'd never tell you. Actually, I'm trying to fish out the doc's password to the FBI server. Nice laptop he's got here—wireless modem with satellite capability. A guy could have a lot of fun with a piece of gear like this."

"Let's play carefully, Bunny. Right now I just want to get into his email account and contact a Brenda…somebody."

Bunny shook his head and grinned. "Oh, yeah, that really narrows it down, that does. You oughta be on TV with that photographic memory you got there."

"Donna," said Nadia, coming into the kitchen. "Donna Hermsen." She gave a wide yawn and grabbed an old, chipped coffee cup from the wall cupboard next to the fridge. After taking a sip, she sighed. "I could really use a mochaccino right now."

"Breakfast is cold," said Jon. "Want me to heat it up for you?"

"I don't know," she said. "Do I care?"

"Okay, hold on," said Bunny, changing the subject before Jon could respond, "I got his password for the email system. Donna, Donna, where are you…? Oh, here it is. He got a message from her about four o'clock this morning. It's marked 'urgent.'" He double-clicked on the message line to open it up as Jon continued to wash dishes and Nadia started in on her plate. "Well, Geez, guys, don't everyone try to read over my shoulder," he said irritably. "Don't anybody want to read this besides me?" Steel silence greeted him back. "Okay, here goes nothin'…. 'Michael, I have the sample processed and have the file. You didn't tell me where you got it from, but we have to talk about this in person. Stay where you are, I'll meet you on Wednesday. DH.' Boy, sounds pretty important to me, it's even got that 'urgent' flag an' everything…." His voice trailed off as he realized he wasn't getting any reaction from either side of the kitchen. "Geez, what crawled up your butt an' died," he muttered, and went back to work.

He copied the email and saved it, then deleted the incoming file from the email folder. For good measure, he backdoored the main server so that the message could never be traced. Then he went into Donna Hermsen's own computer through the server and erased it from memory there. *That should keep her safe*, he thought. *Whatever the FBI doesn't want to talk about has to be hot.*

He thought again about what he might be getting himself into, whether he was setting himself up to get arrested again, or worse. He could almost feel Trouble walking up behind him with that sly, malevolent grin that it always wore when it found him. He didn't like the idea of having the agent who'd brought him in five years ago to be the one encouraging him to do what got him into trouble to begin with. It didn't seem to make any sense.

And now these two were acting totally weird. He thought about getting up, taking the laptop, and walking out, but he wasn't sure what Jon would do. *As it is*, he thought to himself, *the guy's crazy enough to shoot me.*

So Bunny choked down another cup of coffee while he pecked away inside the FBI's most secret electronic corridors for anything he might find useful in the future.

* * * *

Back in DC, Roger called an impromptu meeting to order around the breakfast table. "Okay, Jen, gentlemen…."

"Red," the rest of the team interjected as one, bringing a chuckle from all, even Red Hicks. He shook his head and grinned.

"Let's take a look at what we have here. Dave and Red, let's see what you brought back from the good doctor's car."

Red brought out a piece of paper and read, "One metal airline case, containing one portable medical centrifuge, various small tubes of chemicals, one optical microscope, Bausch and Lomb sixteen-hundred-power, one heater plate, and three glass flasks. Phlebotomy kits, swabs, syringes, miscellaneous type stuff." He handed the list to Roger. "The cops at the impound yard wouldn't let us take the case, but we also found a specimen tube and managed to scam it out without anyone seeing it. I wrote down the names on all the chemical tubes, but I can't begin to pronounce any of them. I'll write it out a little neater so you can send it back with the sample. We also found Nadia's cellphone on the front passenger's floor."

"What was in the specimen tube?"

"I'll let Hamund make that call, I have no idea. Whatever it was, it was getting old when we caught up to it."

"Thanks, guys. Jen?"

"Up-line promised me complete files on Jon Daniels and the doctor by eleven this morning."

"Awesome. Steven?"

"I had to access the hospital unconventionally. The place is crawling with DC police and FBI. The doc was still in surgery when I got in, and the surgeon told me he wouldn't be conscious until tonight at least with all the blood he lost, and the tissue damage."

"He just told you?"

"Well, yeah," Steven responded simply, "After I convinced him I was the doc's nearest relative, he was real easy to get to talk."

"Great. Stay on top of that, will you? Jen, make sure and get with Steven when you get those files. He may have to cough up some family type information to keep his cover. As for me, the report went out to Twin Oaks, and they're beginning to get nervous. This has to stay quiet or the whole project will have been wasted, and other questions might be asked that can't be covered up. Let's keep our ears to the ground and see where the trail leads from here. That's all."

Chapter Twenty-Five

"Okay, may I ask what *that* was for?" Jon whispered to Nadia. The morning sun scattered a million playful beams through the leaves and a cool, gentle breeze blew down the valley. Nature flirted with their senses, but was ignored by both as they stood face to face on the front porch of the cabin.

Bunny was still at work in the kitchen. He had finished going through the FBI's system and was working on a couple of "side projects" on his own, and so Jon had dragged her outside to discuss what had happened at breakfast.

"Why couldn't you answer a simple question?" she shot back.

"*What* simple question?"

"You know what question, Mr. Daniels," she hissed coldly. "Last night I asked you—"

"What? You're still stuck on *that*?"

"Why didn't you answer the question? There are two choices: 'yes' or 'no,' and you couldn't even give a straight answer!"

"Because it's wasn't a simple question, and it wasn't fair!"

Nadia's voice rose. "Tell me what *is* fair! You have memories going back to your childhood. You know your family, you know who your friends are, you know who *you* are, and you know what to believe. Everything I ever had as an anchor in my life has been ripped out from under my feet in two days. I find out that the person I once was is hidden behind someone I'm not. You know how I know that? Because a soon as I meet you my whole life explodes into a million pieces, and somewhere inside I know I know you, but I don't know me anymore, because when I looked…." Her voice broke and tears welled in her eyes as she continued. "When I looked into the mirror last night, suddenly I was *her*, looking out. And I saw *me*, and I think I'm going schizoid or something, and I'm so afraid. I want this to be a horrible dream, I want to wake up, and I can't. I can't get away from it because it's here, inside me, and I don't know if I'm me or her, or if there even *is* a 'me'…." She started to cry again.

Jon took her in his arms, and she buried her face in his chest, pouring out her fear. He held her through the shuddering, the sobs, and tears. Suddenly, he bent down and kissed her. Holding her face in his hands, he said softly, "I will promise you this, Nadia Velasquez. When this is through you will be your own person. You will get to be who you want to be, and no one else will change that again. And I'll be with you through it all."

Nadia pulled away, and wondered if Jon could see the smile peeking around the serious look she painted on. "Mr. Daniels, that was probably the hokiest thing anyone has ever said to me. And, strangely enough, I feel better for it." She smiled and held him close, drawing strength from him.

Something washed ashore in her brain, a memory. Not just a displaced fragment, but an actual memory. The feeling was so intense she thought she was going to fall over, and she held on tighter for a moment until her senses cleared.

In that brief flash, she *knew*. She knew the answer to her question of the previous night. "Jon, I…" she started to say, but stopped. *You will be your own person*, he'd told her. *So that was something between him and someone else.* It was best if it stayed that way. All the same, a warm, soft glow rose in her abdomen at the thought.

She looked up. He was watching her, an expectant smile on his face. "Jon, I'm sorry," she said. "About this morning, and last night. You were right. It wasn't a fair question, and I'll never ask it again."

"I think," he said slowly, "we need to go fishing."

Nadia managed a smile. "Okay."

* * * *

At ten minutes before seven that evening, the three of them strolled through the woods to the porch of Irving Ratzinger's cabin. The smell of good cooking filled the air, calling through the woods like a silent siren's song. The trio couldn't guess from the aroma what was going to be served, but whatever it was, it was going to be good, and the anticipation served to lighten their spirits considerably.

Irving opened the door and escorted them all into his home. Since his retirement, he explained, he stayed on the river year-round, watching the other cabins for their owners. Four years ago, his wife Hilda, God rest her soul, passed on, and now he shared the place with Ralph the basset hound.

An old, beat-up TV sat silent in the corner, and a radio that looked like its life's purpose was to hold up the dust that had collected on its top. He only turned either one on when the Red Sox were playing, and the three visitors shared a guarded sigh of relief at the news.

As they visited, Nadia looked around at all the bric-a-brac Irving had gathered. There were photos on the wall of Irving and a woman who must have been Hilda, from black and white wedding portraits of a handsome young man in a tuxedo and yarmulke and a beautiful, dark-haired young woman in a white dress, to colorized photos of Irving in a green dress uniform and Hilda in a blue dress, to recent photos of a smiling Hilda standing in front of the cabin holding up a large, bronze-striped fish. The fish itself was mounted over the fireplace; she could tell by that small, oddly-shaped spot by its eye.

Shelves loaded with knick-knack souvenirs adorned all four walls in the small, comfortable living room: snow globes from the Grand Canyon and the Grand Tetons, statuettes from California and Colorado, little ceramic racing cars from Indianapolis and Daytona. There were memories all over this place, and, in spite of Irving's being alone, Nadia could tell that this was still a happy home.

An angry flash of jealousy raced around in her brain, growing despite her best efforts to chase it away. Then she felt guilty for being jealous. This man couldn't help having all these wonderful memories any more than she could help having none of her own. *But, dammit, it's just not fair!*

A gentle hand touched her shoulder. Jon looked at her, an eyebrow raised in question. From the smile on his face, he understood exactly what she was thinking. His touch gave her a distraction, something else on which to focus. She smiled back in silent thanks, and he gave a short nod in response.

Irving kept up his banter non-stop, not seeming to notice the subtle gesture. Dinner would be ready presently. In the meantime, would they care for a *schnapps*? He got up and went into the kitchen, dug in his pantry and hauled out a bottle of brandy. Jon and Bunny received their glasses readily, but Nadia was tentative, remembering the whiskey that she'd sampled the day before. The aroma of the strong liqueur was heady and rich, though, and after she sampled hers, she found the flavor more fitting to her palate.

Following Jon's example, she nursed the drink as they shared conversation and the sun sank beyond the far ridge on the other side of the river. Or, more properly, they listened as Irving regaled them with his tales of the woods, fishing, and the Bo-Sox. Hilda, God rest her soul, never got to see them win the 'Series, and that was the biggest shame of them all. Wade Boggs was still the greatest player in the game, and the Curse of the Bambino was finally broken.

Then Irving looked around and fell silent for a moment. "Oy," he said, "I must be boring you young people with all this talking and not enough eating! Let's have some dinner, now." He slapped his knees and stood, hobbling into the kitchen, his legs stiff with age. Ralph heaved himself up and followed, with a casual wag of his tail.

After placing his guests, Irving took off the worn baseball cap and produced a yarmulke, solemnly arranging it in place on his head. He raised his arms as he stood, and sang a short song of blessing in Hebrew over the meal before he sat down and invited them to dig in. Lifting his wine glass, he cried, "L'chaim!" and laughed. "Thank you, my friends, for coming to visit an old man. You make my day less lonely."

The meal started with tossed lettuce topped with mushrooms, sliced Jerusalem artichokes, almonds, and raspberry vinaigrette, a combination that Nadia thought redefined the term "salad." The main course was roast venison marinated in mulled red wine, served with wonderfully caramelized potatoes, carrots, and beans. Homemade rolls abounded, and the dessert was a fruit tart, golden brown and topped with a delightful glaze.

Nadia drank and laughed along with everyone else as they all enjoyed the best meal any of them had had in a long time. She finally asked Irving where he learned to cook.

"Believe it or not, this is Army food." He chuckled at the men's shocked response, and then explained, "I was General Dean's personal chef in Japan. I won an award for this dinner, except it was beef then."

The evening raced by, and before they all knew it, heads were thick and eyelids heavy. Nadia was the first to politely excuse herself from the festivities. She felt light-headed from the wine and brandy, but made her way back to their cabin without undue difficulty in the darkness. A few minutes later, Jon and Bunny came in together. Nadia was barely aware of their entrance by then, as drowsy as she was. She drifted off, listening to the counter melodies of crickets and katydids in the trees, and slept through the night for the first time in her short memory. No dream disturbed her blissful repose.

Chapter Twenty-Six

The next day was Wednesday. A few minutes after ten o'clock, a small blue Toyota coupe pulled up the driveway to the cabin. A tall, striking woman in her late forties got out. She had dark brown hair tied back in a severe bun, and wore a smart brown skirt suit and flat, comfortable shoes. Under her arm was a file folder. Looking furtively about, she knocked on the door. There was no answer. She looked about at the trees. "Hello? Anyone? Who's here?"

Concealed in the bushes, three pairs of eyes watched carefully. Bunny whispered, "That's her. That's Donna. I recognize her from her badge picture." The others looked at him. They couldn't even see a badge from where they were. "What? I downloaded her picture from her HR file yesterday."

Jon stood and came forward at the reassurance of her identity. "Dr. Hermsen? I'm Jon Daniels. Mike Alverson is my uncle." Nadia and Bunny followed her and Jon into the cabin where they all sat at the kitchen table.

Donna tossed the folder onto the tabletop and sighed. "Okay, I'm officially stumped. Can anyone tell me what's going on here?"

"First things first," Jon countered. "How is my uncle? We're kind of without contact out here."

A shadow crossed Donna's face as she spoke. "He'll probably live. He's hanging on, but barely. Whoever shot him used a fifty-caliber rifle. It caused extensive tissue damage in his lower torso and right leg, and they're still pulling fragments of upholstery and sheet metal from his wounds.

"Okay, your turn," she said. "Where did this sample come from?" She tapped on the file folder.

"He took some blood from me yesterday," Nadia volunteered.

Donna snorted impatiently. "Be serious, this can't be yours."

"Why not?" asked Jon.

"For one thing, it's not human."

"Then you better make sure you got the right sample," Jon retorted, "because my uncle got shot for it."

Donna went out to her car. When she came back in, she was dragging a large, metal airline case. She opened it and began to unload its contents onto the table as she spoke. "I thought you'd say something like that, Agent Daniels, so I brought the equipment to rerun the tests here." She produced a pair of rubber gloves, an alcohol wipe, gauze and a phlebotomy kit. "Mike...." She stopped and corrected herself. "Dr. Alverson told me in his message to keep this strictly confidential until I confirmed the results. Your arm, please, Miss."

Fifteen seconds later, Dr. Hermsen's hand shook as she held up the tube for all to see. Inside was a thin, milk-colored fluid tinged with light purple.

Jon sat slack-jawed. Bunny fainted off his chair. Nadia and Dr. Hermsen stared at each other, Nadia in confusion, and the doctor in fear. Then Nadia remembered, back in San Francisco, the color of the blood that was on her hands after fighting off the two men who'd attacked her in an alleyway: red; it was deep, dark red. Not like hers at all. Nadia felt her face drain, and her vision closed in. Then all was blackness and she felt nothing.

* * * *

When Nadia opened her eyes, she was lying in bed, her head aching. She must have hit the floor awfully hard. She tried to raise her hands, but found she was unable. Something was holding her down by the wrists. Curtains. They'd torn the curtains into strips and were using them as restraints. "What the—?" she started. Jon and the doctor sat near the bed, looking at her. "Jon?"

"It's okay. You're restrained."

"Why? What have I done?"

"It's not that. It's—"

"It's what you are," cut in Dr. Hermsen.

"You mean 'who,' not 'what,'" said Nadia.

Doctor Hermsen shifted on her seat. "Nadia, this is important. Where did you come from?"

"San Francisco."

"No. Before then."

Nadia's brow knitted in confusion. *What are they asking?* "Look, just let me up, I'll be fine."

"I have to have some answers first," said Jon. "I'm sorry, Nadia, but you're staying right there until we get something straight."

"What do you want? I've told you everything—"

"Then what about your blood? What kind of blood do you have?" He began to get more insistent. "Where are you from?"

"California, you idiot! I was in the hospital, you know that, and I told you everything I know...before that I don't have any memories of my own." Nadia lowered her voice and her eyes narrowed at Jon. "You know who I am. You know whose memories I have."

Jon leaned closer. "How did you get them?"

"You're supposed to be the one telling me that," she shot back, as frightened as she was angry. "I don't know...." Tears began to sting her eyes. She strained at her bonds. "Let me up —"

"Nadia, look at me," said the doctor, "I think we're all more than a little frightened here. Please calm down. Help us to help you, okay?"

Nadia lay her head back down. "Why are you doing this?" she moaned.

Jon stood. "You have to start answering some questions here, Nadia. Then, if we can trust you—"

"Since when have I done anything to you? When have I ever betrayed your trust? If there's someone here who needs to be suspicious, Mr. Daniels, it's me. Every friend I ever thought I had is out there trying to hunt me down and kill me. Are you in on this whole thing, too?"

Jon walked around the room, rubbing his face. "Nadia, when I first met you a few days ago, I thought there was something I needed to trace out to the end. But the end just keeps getting weirder and stranger with every thing we uncover. Those people who are after us are chasing us because of you. I don't know who they are, but I have an idea why they're after you. What's worse, I don't know if there are more...people like you. I thought I knew *who* you are. Now I don't even know *what* you are."

"Nadia," cut in Donna. "Please understand. Your blood isn't human blood. I have some other tests running, but I know you're not a human being. Now, where did you come from?"

Nadia's response was weak, hoarse, and desperate. "I don't know. All I know is that I woke up in the hospital at Twin Oaks—"

"Twin Oaks? Is that in California?" asked Jon.

"I...I think so. It's in the mountains. They flew me to 'Frisco from there in a plane just like the one you took me to Washington in."

"Bunny," Jon called over his shoulder, "Find a hospital in a town called Twin Oaks, within a Learjet's range from San Francisco, will you?"

Bunny's tremulous response floated down the hall from the kitchen. "Is that where their flying saucer landed?"

"Just shut up and do that, all right?" Jon turned back to Nadia, approaching the bed carefully. "Listen, Nadia. Do you remember anything at all before the hospital?"

"No, nothing," she said.

Donna left the room for a few seconds. She came back holding the folder of papers she had brought with her. She sat and sorted through the stack until she found what she wanted. Lifting out several sheets stapled together, she cited points from the report. "Her blood very nearly matches a Type O. Rh

95

factor is positive. The plasma content is the same as ours, but she doesn't seem to have hemoglobin. There's something else, a white compound that seems to be doing the same job, only it carries one helluva lot more oxygen. It's a lot like Oxycyte, only it's organic in nature. It's protein-based. I think her body makes it naturally. Jon, you need to leave."

"Are you sure?" Jon sounded fearful.

Donna looked intently at him, raising an eyebrow and nodding toward the door. He got the message. Donna waited until the door closed and then turned back to Nadia.

"Nadia, I have to explain something to you. I'm a doctor, but I'm not a medical doctor. My PhD is in physiology. That's the type of work I do for the Bureau. I want to examine you, okay?"

"Then let me up first," said Nadia, "or it's no dice."

"I hardly think you can do anything to stop me."

"I'll scream—"

"We're in the middle of the woods here. Who's going to hear?"

"Dammit, Donna, please! I'm not going to run away or hurt anyone. I want to get to the bottom of this as badly as anyone here."

"I think," said the doctor after a pause, "we may have over-reacted. But, to tell you the truth, you have all of us frightened right now." She looked at Nadia, reading what was in her face. Donna sighed and reached for the straps that held Nadia down. "Woman to woman, I think you'll be all right. Here, let's take these off...."

Chapter Twenty-Seven

"Mr. Glass, I put a lot of trust in your work. I asked you to take care of a simple problem, and yet it still remains outstanding." The hand holding the phone trembled. The malevolent glare of the ruby ring thickened the air with menace.

"Do you know where they are right now? How many more are being drawn into this? Do you realize how many innocent lives will be lost if it isn't found and dealt with? You have two teams now at your disposal, sir, and I recommend you put them to good use.

"Yes, anyone who's had intimate contact with her. Then I suggest that you make sure it stays that way.

"Please be able to report some visible progress by this time tomorrow. And, Mr. Glass? Don't give me cause to doubt your trustworthiness. Goodbye."

He hung up and dialed again. "Denise? Please call a meeting of the Council. I'll be off for the remainder of the day. Just leave me a voice mail where and when. Thank you." The mahogany walls of the office felt close, strangling. He needed some air to think things through before addressing the others. There would be some uncomfortable questions to answer.

Chapter Twenty-Eight

The moon cast soft shadows through the forest canopy outside as Donna Hermsen, Jon Daniels, and Bunny Kalinsky sat around the kitchen table. The kitchen windows yawned open, letting late summer's cool breeze blow through the screens. The sounds of the forest at night came in with the fresh air. A stray moth flittered around the single bulb over the table as they shared coffee.

"She's terribly stressed out," said Donna. "I gave her something that should help her sleep. She's promised not to run off or do anything foolish, and I think we can believe her."

"You took off the restraints?" asked Jon, unsure. "But what if—"

Donna held a hand up. "She promised to stay right here."

"And you believed her?" hissed a shocked Bunny. "What if she comes out here with lasers and blows our faces off? What if she's back there making offspring—?"

"Shut up, Bunny!" Jon glowered at Bunny before turning to Donna. "What did you find out?"

Donna took a deep breath. "Here it is, boys. Nadia Velasquez, the real one, must have died in the assassination of the Nigerian President. What we have here is the most magnificent work of art I've ever seen, and someone is willing to kill to make sure it doesn't become public."

"Wait a minute, Doctor. What 'art'?"

"Her first memory is that hospital. I think that was where she was made."

"Made? What do you mean? Is she a clone?" asked Jon.

"Yes, partly, and more than that. She's an artificial person. Perfect in every way they could have made her. She's organic, with organs, tissues, blood and bones, but chemically different in so many ways. Her skin is tougher than ours is, her bones denser. I did an ultrasound— it was the best I could do out here. She has organs that we don't have and she doesn't have…." Donna's voice trailed off. There was a long pause.

The moth flew closer to the light. Jon could hear an occasional *tap, tap, tap* as it bounced off the bulb, wooing it fervently. With every little tap, Jon saw, the moth left a powdery substance from its wings. A little more, and a little more... *so which am I, the moth or the lamp?*

Donna's voice broke the silence. "She could never have children."

The moth flew away, damaged and frustrated, up into a corner.

"Then don't you think she would have noticed by now that she's... different?" he asked.

"Consider this," explained Donna. "She's been surrounded by these people from the time she woke up. They've obviously manipulated what memories they allowed her to have, and most likely controlled what information she had access to. As far as she was concerned, she was normal. And when she did start to remember things from her past, things began to happen so suddenly she simply didn't have the time to think about her anatomy. It's obvious if you know what to look for, but I assume she wasn't supposed to ever get in...that type of situation."

"You mean 'it' then, don't you, Doc? That, in there...." Jon pointed down the hall, "...Is an 'it.' It's not a real person. Someone made it in a lab, and stuck Alicia's...." He stopped, unable to continue. *Stupid, stupid, stupid Jon. What were you thinking?*

"Jon, I haven't run a DNA test on the blood yet, but I examined a piece of her hair under my microscope, and it seems to be human hair." Donna paused again, thinking. "So you think that Alicia Burgess' personality was somehow bonded onto this woman's brain?"

"That much I can answer, Doctor, and that's a solid 'yes.' You should have known Alicia, she was just like...." He stopped again. Some things were better unsaid. "That's not a woman in there."

"I knew Alicia," the doctor observed, "and you seemed to be okay with Nadia a few hours ago. I saw how you looked at each other, comforting, supporting—"

"When I thought she was a real person, not a—"

"Damn, Jon, you sure have a way with words. What makes you so sure she's *not* a real person?"

"You just told me, she's not human! You said it yourself! Some Frankenstein made her...made *it*," he corrected, "in a lab."

"Do you have to be a human to be a person? She's still got feelings, and emotions. Don't forget that."

99

"Her own? For all we know, the only feelings and emotions she has are recordings of another person's, downloaded onto her brain somehow."

Donna's eyes brightened. She stabbed the table with a finger while she formulated the words, "Neurostructural Personality Transfer."

"What?"

She rushed on as the epiphany surfaced. "I was at a seminar a few years ago, listening to Dr. William Bainbridge talk about the neurostructural approach to personality transfer.

"Every brain has billions of neurons in it, and our memories, our reactions, some say our personalities and our very souls, are shaped and coded in the brainwave patterns and the unique pathways by which these neurons connect with each other throughout our lives. A new memory, a new experience, hence, a new neurological connection— a new circuit.

"Bainbridge supposed that if we could map these pathways, we could in effect save a person's personality, their soul so to speak, and implant it on another mind. If someone figured out a way to make this happen, we could be witnesses to history here: an artificial person with Alicia Burgess' brainwave pattern imposed on it."

Jon paused, considering the implications as he understood them. "If we could verify that, would it be sufficient evidence that a crime has been committed? Cloning a person is illegal by federal law, but creating a person and giving them a personality? I don't know."

Donna ran a fingertip around the rim of her cup. "You do know, Jon. Bainbridge's presentation stated that, in reading each neural path, the original is destroyed." She paused to let Jon catch up before she finished her point. "Alicia had to have been alive when they recorded her personality. She couldn't have been when they were through with her. Besides, if there were no crime, the people who made her wouldn't be trying to kill her now. Are you sure that's what they're trying to do?"

Jon thought out loud. "In the airport the other night, they tried to grab her, but I thought I saw this other woman stick something to Nadia's head, just before she went Xena-Warrior-Princess all over the place. They took a pot shot at us two days ago, and hit Uncle Mike. Just who they were shooting at, I can't be positive. They used a fifty-cal, for God's sake, so they meant to kill someone. I just can't prove who yet, and before I can press

100

charges I have to know. What I can't understand is what's on the news. I'm being made out to be a stalker and a kidnapper."

Bunny spoke up at this moment. "Okay, now I'm the one that's confused, here. Jonny-boy, you didn't tell me you kidnapped this babe."

"Shut up, Bunny," said Jon.

Bunny cut him off, stabbing a finger at Jon's face. "Hey! You been tellin' me 'shut up' ever since you hired me to come out here for you. 'Hire?' What a joke! We found some stuff out, sure, and now we get this bombshell dropped on us. You didn't even tell me people would be trying to kill you, Jon. Are they gonna try and kill me, too? 'Cause if that's the case, then you can't tell me to shut up again.

"You already had me hack the FBI, man, and if anyone finds that out, I'm gonna get sent back up the river and be Big Marco's girlfriend for life. I'm doin' this 'cause I like you, Jonny, and don't you tell me to shut up no more, okay, 'cause I'm liable to just walk out of here."

"Bunny, you walk out that door and I'll shoot you myself," growled Jon. "We have to get to the bottom of this, and I need your computer skills to help us."

"What's with this 'we,' Jon? You got a mouse in your pocket? You think I ain't never been threatened before? Ollie the Mug shot me in the leg just 'cause I talked to his girlfriend. Gettin' shot's nothin'. I just don't know if I want to be around when whoever made *her*," Bunny jerked his thumb in the direction of the bedroom, "gets hold of *you*. If they can put someone together, they can take 'em apart, too, know what I mean?"

Jon softened. "All right, Bunny, I get it. I need you more than you need me. I'm sorry. But I have to find out what happened to Alicia, and what we have to do about...." He waved vaguely toward the back of the cabin.

Donna touched his arm reprovingly. "Nadia, Jon. Her name's Nadia. Bunny, what did you find out about that hospital?"

"Well, Doc, I got somethin'. There's a ritzy resort spa up in Oregon in the Cascades, outside of Klamath Falls. There ain't no town called Twin Oaks, but that's the name of the spa. Big money goes to that joint. Big, powerful people go there for spa treatments and the hospital is exclusive. Only big shots like presidents and movie stars and that go there. Helluva time I had gettin' info, 'cause they ain't got, like, a website or nothin'. Maybe I could work out a deal with them—"

Jon felt his jaw drop. "You found all that out in a few hours' worth of work? How?"

"Look, you got the best cyber-slacker on the planet right here in this room, Jon. There ain't a system I can't get into. I just checked a few confidential records and found some that matched, okay? I found some account records from clients who paid those guys money that dreams are made of, just for a weekend getaway there."

"What else did you find out?" asked Donna.

Bunny patted the laptop in front of him. "Not a whole lot more with this equipment. It's not bad, but I need something with a little more guts if I'm gonna get any further. Where there's big bucks, there's some mighty big watchdog programs, and I ain't bustin' into no place blind. I need speed and memory this thing ain't got."

Jon heaved a sigh and buried his face in his hands for a moment. He shook his head at the ceiling. "I can't believe I'm saying this, Bunny, but whatever you want, it's yours. Just let me know what it'll cost, and I'll get it somehow."

"Cost?" Bunny laughed derisively. "Cost don't mean nothin'. Money's just bits in someone's hard drive, baby, and I can make it come out of nowhere. Just watch me."

Donna pushed herself away from the table. "I did not just hear that. I did not just hear you give a known cyber criminal the green light to rob someone else's money."

"You don't understand, lady," Bunny replied assuringly, "I don't need to take it from anyone. I can make it perfectly legal."

She tapped her finger on the table in front of Jon. "You have got yourself one terrible mess here. You know, it's not too late to get an official investigation going—"

Jon looked up at her. "No, Doctor Hermsen, I don't want it to go there just yet. All we have are some disjointed incidents that don't add up. How can I prove what happened to Alicia? I can't even get these guys on attempted murder because I can't prove *who* in Mike's car they were shooting at! I have to figure out what happened—"

"You mean how they got hold of Alicia's brain?" asked the doctor.

"Yes. Alicia was...a good friend to me. I owe it to her to find out what criminal activity was involved here. If someone killed her to get her brain...." Jon's voice dropped, but the passion still burned in his tone. "They're going to pay."

Chapter Twenty-Nine

The early morning sun had not yet cleared the ridge behind the cabin, but light was beginning to shine down into the valley, gently waking the Shenandoah River. The water sighed as it flowed over deadfalls and rocks along the shore, and an occasional ripple betrayed the fish beneath the surface.

Nadia sat on the edge of the wooden dock watching the sun come up. Her toes came just short of reaching the murky river. She could see the light growing brighter with each passing minute, and watched the mist float above the water, like a curtain waiting to be drawn, caressing her lightly as it passed with the river. Birds struck up their songs in the trees, awakening the morning. Behind her, a faint rustle in the undergrowth told her that a rabbit or some other small animal was beginning its busy day. She sat and thought of nothing. Or, at least, she tried to think of nothing.

In reality her mind raced, trying to understand what was going on around her. She felt caught up in something malevolent, something that threatened not only her, but anyone around her. She had no sooner met Jon Daniels than the two were running for their very lives. To find that her mind was not her own was a confirmation that something was seriously wrong with her. Finding out that she wasn't even human was a shock she wasn't sure she could handle.

She didn't feel different. She was still the same person she remembered being. She didn't have any memories of her own, because there weren't any. When she woke up in that bed at Twin Oaks, it was her first day alive. The only experience that she could even deem as close to normal was the dinner at Irving's cabin. She smiled, remembering the little man's hospitality and warmth, and the comfort she found in his house, in his presence. She wondered if she would ever find a place where she could feel that way again, where she felt almost like she *belonged*. But what would he say if he found out about her? What would he do?

She already found out what Jon would do. The man who had called himself her friend three days previously had all but thrown her out the second he found out about her anatomy. He stopped talking to her altogether, and only acknowledged her presence when he had no other choice. When she walked out the door in tears, he made no move to stop her.

She spent her days wandering the woods around the cabin, and ate by herself after the others turned in for the evening. Even Bunny got quiet, mainly when Jon was treating her like a piece of garbage someone left in the middle of the floor. As for Donna, she seemed to hold Nadia in some kind of awe. She brought more gear out from DC, ran more tests, and became both more confused and more amazed.

Nadia sighed and threw a twig into the water, watching it settle into the current and drift slowly downstream, carried away to who knew where. She felt like that twig, carried on by forces outside her will, not knowing where she would eventually end up.

She heard a noise behind her and turned. Irving was making his way down to the dock, grasping a white plastic, five-gallon bucket and a pair of fishing poles in one hand, and a tackle box in the other. He greeted her merrily and tottered out to the end of the pier.

"Would you care for a little company, young lady?"

She smiled and beckoned. "I like to come out here in the morning," he announced with a grin, sitting down next to her. "It's a great time to fish."

He opened the tackle box and began to rig a spinning rod with a small Rooster Tail. She watched his meticulous, steady fingers tie the lure on the line. Then he flipped it out into the water and wound it back against the current, making little jerking motions with the rod tip. The lure leaped out of the river as it neared the end of its travel, trailing tiny, diamond droplets of water from its skirt as it swung in the sunlight.

Irving set the bail and flipped it out again, drawing it back along some rocks. She could barely see it in the murky water, the little silver blade spinning happily as it came back to the pier, like a tiny puppy wagging its tail.

A dragonfly zoomed down and hovered inquisitively over it, and then sped off for parts unknown. Nadia said nothing. She just watched as Irving made cast after cast.

She didn't want to break the silence of this golden morning, but her curiosity finally got the best of her. "Don't you ever get bored, doing that same thing over and over again?"

"Nah, I've got nothing better to do. Do you?"

Nadia smiled. "No, I guess not. But what if you don't catch any fish?"

Irving winked and grinned. "Sometimes, fishing has nothing to do with catching fish."

She sat watching, quiet, and he went on. "It helps me keep my perspective out here." He spoke slowly, dividing his attention between the young lady next to him and his lure in the water. "I lost my Hilda, God rest her soul, four years ago. She was everything to me. We came out here all the time on weekends, and then after I retired we moved out here full-time, partly to watch the other cabins for their owners."

"What was the other 'partly'?"

"Well, if you had a choice of living out here or in Boston, which would you choose?"

Nadia looked out over the river, taking in the glorious morning scenery. The mist was departing, leaving thready traces here and there on the water, being dragged along by the current. A water bird swooped low over the river, and its feet drew a silent, silver trace across its surface. Somewhere in the distance, a bullfrog roared. Birds sang all around them.

The sky was an intense blue, that shade they call cyan, with nary a cloud to mar the skyscape. The quiet reminded her of the balcony back at Twin Oaks, that time after she woke up. Here was peace. She remembered living in San Francisco, with its business and noise, the traffic outside her apartment, the hustle of pedestrians. She'd enjoyed bits and pieces of both, but if she had to choose…. "I suppose I'd live out here," she said at last. "It gives a person time to think."

"But you have to be careful you don't think too much," said Irving as the spinner hit the water one more time. "Your brain has a way of getting you into trouble. That's why God put the fish out here, to keep your mind busy." He grinned at her again, and she couldn't help but smile back.

"Gotcha!" he exclaimed, and lifted the pole upward as the line snapped taut. The water's surface swirled and splashed as the struggling fish broke and twisted. He played it with confidence borne of experience, bringing it in a little bit at a time and then letting it run. Each time he let it work itself more tired, more fatigued. Then he would turn it around with a tug on the line, keeping the rod tip high. With a final splash and flash of scales, Irving hefted the big fish up to the pier.

He handed the rod to Nadia. "Here. Take it, and don't let go." She held it tightly as the fish strained and thrashed in the water below. She watched as Irving rolled up his sleeves and grabbed his bucket. He dipped it into the river and drew it back up onto the pier with a grunt. Then he took the rod back from Nadia and lifted it up, unhooking the fish over the bucket.

Irving placed the fish inside, where it swam around chaotically, banging into the sides for several seconds. Then it settled down and centered itself in the vessel, and Nadia watched its gills working, quickly at first, and then slowing as the fish calmed down. Irving had the rod back in his hand and was already casting back out into the stream when she looked up again. "When I'm out here, I think about my Hilda, God rest her soul, and how much she loved it here. But I don't take the time to think about how lonely I get without her here with me. Sometimes I think about that, but not too much. My Hilda, God rest her soul, she would say, 'Irving you have too much to worry about already. You can only do one thing at a time.'"

"She sounds like a very sensible person," Nadia said, watching the rhythm of his hands: flip the bail, cast, retrieve.

Irving paused before he answered. "Yes, I suppose she was."

They sat together in silence for some time. Irving fished and Nadia watched. "What's that on your arm?" she asked presently, pointing at where he had rolled up his sleeve, exposing his forearm.

"A memory," he said, "from a long time ago." He let the lure sink to the bottom and it stayed there as he explained about the Nazis.

"I was a German Jew, twelve years old when they rounded us all up and put us on a train. On a *cattle car*, we were loaded. It dropped us off at a place called Buchenwald."

He had to explain to her about the death camps, the starvation, the rape of the women and girls. He told her about the serial number that every prisoner wore, tattooed on the inside of their left forearm, and about the experiments. Then he told her about the ovens. She had to hear everything he could remember, every detail. To her it seemed more than a nightmare, something beyond comprehension, beyond Hell. His eyes were moist when he looked up. "I never got to tell my mother goodbye. She just…disappeared. My father threw himself on the electric fence one night, not long after. They just dragged him away and threw him in a pit. People," he concluded, "don't have any idea what it's like to be treated as less than human." He stared out over the river and said nothing more for a long time.

"Some people do," she whispered to herself. "I think some people do." A cold chill ran up her spine as she thought about what she had overheard two nights previous, and what had already changed in her short life, and how the last two days had changed even more. Moreover, she wondered what might lie ahead. Presently, she stood. "I need to get back to the cabin. Jon probably wonders where I am." *Yeah, right. He could probably not care less. Would you treat me any differently, Irving, if you knew?*

"Okay, then," said the old man. "Thank you, my dear, for your company. Come on by the cabin any time you want a good meal. You look starved."

Nadia made her way through the woods, taking her time as she wandered along the path toward the cabin.

Jon was rounding up firewood for the stove when she came out of the trees. He didn't seem to notice she was there, and she stood for a while, watching. She saw his face as he turned around. He seemed exceptionally distracted, uneasy. She strolled up closer. "Hi." He grunted in reply. "Can I help?"

He gave a curt "No," and went to the far side of their little clearing.

Nadia went up the steps and into the cabin. There was no sense in pursuing the issue; it would only compound the pain. *Why am I still trying?*

Bunny was pecking away at the laptop on the table. He lifted his head briefly, and then went right back to work. Still shaken, she watched him for a few seconds, almost afraid to open her mouth. What could be going through his head? He seemed to ignore her, as engrossed as he was in his work. However, there was no forced look of concentration on his face. He didn't seem to be deliberately ignoring her; it was just that he was so intent on his current project that she simply didn't exist in his consciousness. Finally, she had to break the silence. "Where's Donna?"

"Oh, she went into town to pick up a FEDEX for me."

"What's wrong with Jon?" she asked. "Did he tell you anything?"

"Oh, you saw him, did you?"

"Yes. He's outside trying to find the right club or something," she said off-handedly, trying to make light. "What did I do, Bunny? Did he tell you what the matter is?"

"It ain't hard to figure out from where I'm sittin', but no one 'round here asks me for anything except hackin', so I sit still an' keep my piehole shut an' my nose to the grindstone."

"Why does everyone call you Bunny?" Nadia asked as she looked for a coffee cup. She found one in the cupboard over the sink and filled it from the percolator.

"'Cause I was always too fast for the cops. They said tryin' to catch me was like tryin' to chase a rabbit through a briar patch."

"Someone caught you."

"Yeah, it was Jonny and Alicia finally caught up to me in Richmond. I made one too many mistakes, an' when I opened up my apartment door, right there they were with the cuffs."

"So, what's your real name?"

There was a pause. "Don't laugh, okay?"

"I promise," said Nadia, raising her right hand.

"It's Oswald." Bunny looked at her, watching for the response. She wasn't going to give him one.

Nadia sat down at the table. "I don't see anything funny about 'Oswald.' Okay, Oswald, what did you do that was so bad?"

"Wrote viruses. Just got bored, you know? So, I punched up a couple of codes. Boy, did they take off. Megasoft bought one."

"Megasoft? The software company bought a virus from you?"

"Yeah, it seems that they wanted to see if they could write a code to bust it."

"And?"

He chuckled and tilted his head to one side. "I put a couple of extra twists in it, just to make things interesting. Well, it blew up in their faces, pretty big. It's been five years, and I think they're still tryin' to get it out of their system."

"Sounds like somebody got scared. Did Megasoft press charges?"

"Not right away. Everyone thought that one was funny. But then I had to hack the Fed, and that got a whole lot of folks' attention."

"Oh, my…." Nadia's mouth hung open in surprise. "I've heard about that. That was you?"

"Yours truly," Bunny acknowledged, and took a short bow. "You may now give me accolades. I also accept cash, checks, and American Express."

Nadia set her cup down to laugh. "So, then Jon caught you."

"Yep. It was five to ten, courtesy of the federal government from there. I got out on good behavior with a promise never to set foot in a Best Buy again." They sat quietly for a few more minutes as Nadia finished her coffee, and Bunny's fingers buzzed away at the keyboard. Bunny spoke up again. "I think he's just freaked out, you know? Kind of in a 'my girlfriend's an alien' sort of way. No offense intended. That's what's got him bugged. He'll probably get over it."

"If you think *he's* freaked out, what about *me*? I was just as in the dark about this whole thing as he was. And I'm the one who's the 'alien.' So, no offense taken. Tell me something, Bunny. Why would you treat me like a real person, and not him?" She nodded toward the door.

"You shoulda seen me a couple nights ago. I thought you were gonna mate with us and then eat our faces off or somethin'."

Nadia smiled. "You seem to be okay now."

"Let's face it, I got what they call a 'birth control face.' It's not like some beautiful alien lady is gonna *wanna* mate with me, let alone get to the part where I get my face ate off. Besides, human or not, you seem like a pretty nice person."

"When this is over, Bunny, you have to come back to 'Frisco with me. There are beautiful alien ladies on every street corner who would love to eat your face off."

"You're okay," Bunny laughed. "You're one of a kind."

"God, let's hope so. So, what are you working on now?"

"I'm trying to find out more about Nadia Velasquez. You're pretty popular, out West. You started at KBGX in San Francisco about five years ago. How long you been out of the hospital?"

"About a year, now."

"What'd they tell you when you woke up?"

"That there was an assassination in Nigeria, when I was interviewing the president. I was caught in the explosion and spent three years in a coma."

Bunny's fingers danced a quick two-step, and then a *bossa nova* as the information appeared on his screen. "Okay, here's an article about you coming back to TV. That was about six months ago. Let's see…there's one about the assassination." He ran another quick search. "Wait, here it is on YouTube." He clicked and a page came up. Nadia came around the table to read over his shoulder.

The file opened, and Nadia saw herself from the camera's eye view, in a shot with a handsome, middle-aged black man in an Armani suit. She had just asked a question, and turned to the camera. There was a flash, then only static. The video ended. Nadia and Bunny stared dumbly together at the computer display for several seconds. "Wow…that's a start, anyway. You okay, Nadia?"

"Yeah…" she said quietly. "How did they get that video? Didn't everything get destroyed in the explosion?"

"Looks like they satellite-fed it, live, back to the USA. It must have been recorded and stored in the KBGX archives. This looks like it was recorded from something else, and then uploaded onto the web. Let's see…" He went to work furiously, and several silent minutes later nodded in satisfaction. "Here. This is the actual video file from the archive."

"How did you get that?" asked Nadia.

"You don't wanna know. Here we go." The video was clearer, and the status bar said the file was about an hour long. "This must be the whole interview. Let's just copy it real quick, shall we?" After a few deft strokes, the video was captured on Michael Alverson's laptop. Bunny backed out quickly and shut down the web program. "I gotta be done with that for a while. I need a break, and then we'll look at this again, all the way through. I took some notes on what else I got. Wanna see 'em?"

"What'll they tell me?" asked Nadia.

"Not much. Only that our Miss Velasquez is twenty-eight years old, and her birthday is October 13. She hails from Temple, Texas, and she moved out West to attend UCLA. She graduated with a degree in journalism. Her name shows up on a report for an auto accident shortly after she graduated. Then there's no public record for a while, and then she starts at the studio as an intern five years ago."

"Wait a minute," cut in Nadia. "You said there was a record of an auto accident after she graduated. How bad was it?"

"We'll have to see after I get my shipment. I'll be able to crawl around the briar patch a little easier with that."

"Can you find out how Jon's uncle is doing?"

"Only if they put his chart in the computer or if something bad…." His voice trailed off.

"Could you find out what you can, Bunny? It might help things if Jon knew how his uncle was doing."

"Tell you what," he said. "Give me a few minutes to shake the cobwebs outta my head an' we'll take a stab, okay?"

"It's a deal," she smiled, and stood with her cup. "I'm ready for a refill. Want some?"

Chapter Thirty

"Okay, team, let's get it together. Jen, you're first." Roger opened the fridge and grabbed a six-pack of Pfalzlagers, passing one out to each team member. He took one himself before putting the stray can back on the refrigerator shelf. Jenna opened her laptop on the table. While it booted up, she cracked her beer and took a drink.

"Good stuff, Rog," she stated, opening the relevant files. "Team B went through his house with a fine-toothed comb, and we checked out his records at County. He has a deed for some land in Colorado, and a cabin over by Front Royal somewhere. Exact location isn't specified, but it's a share in a resort community. They might have been heading out that way when we intercepted them. I had a family file printed off back at home and sent here via FEDEX for Steven to go through, so he can fake his way through any questions and stay in contact with the doctor.

"Jon Daniels is thirty-three years old, and he's been with the Bureau for eight years. He has several citations in his file for excellence, and three incidents of reprimand: one for conduct unbecoming a federal agent, and two for violations of policy that led to dismissals of charges against major crime figures."

"Awesome," said Roger. "Great job, Jen. Steven, what about the doc? How's he doing?"

"Not good. He's still unconscious. The staff is thinking there's an infection brewing."

"He's your hot project," ordered Roger. "Do whatever it takes to make sure nothing about Nadia gets out where it can cause more trouble. That includes extreme measures, but only as a last resort. Understand?"

"Got it, Chief."

Roger's cellphone rang, and he looked at it. "I have to take this. Stand by." He opened it and put it to his ear. "Glass... Are you sure? What file? Why wasn't it deleted before? Okay, thanks. Any idea who? Uh, huh. Thank you. That helps. Goodbye." He slapped it closed. "That was the studio. They've been hacked. Someone accessed the Nigerian interview files. I'm thinking it was Nadia and her pal Daniels."

He ran his hand over his shaven pate, and stood silent for a span of several seconds. The situation now balanced on a razor edge. If it fell the wrong way, God only knew what kind of hell would break loose. "All right, then. Steven, stay on the doc. Do what you have to do. Jen, Red; head back to Twin Oaks. Dr. Hamund may need an extra measure of security out there. Dave, you and I need to find this cabin. Jen, who's in charge of Team B?"

"Up-line made the assignment, Roger. We won't know who's on that team."

"Okay, then. Call up-line and have them thank Team B for their time. They stand relieved as of now. Oh, and Jen? Get into Daniels' file. Find out any associations he has with computer experts. I want to know all his friends and family, and anyone he's busted who could hack the studio's secure net like that. All right, folks, let's get to it. I'll file the report to up-line, and we can be on our ways."

Chapter Thirty-One

Jon swung the maul down hard, splitting another hunk of oak straight through. The pieces fell away to either side of the stump, and he grabbed another hunk off the pile. He'd been gathering and splitting wood all day, just to keep his hands busy and his mind occupied. That, and to stay as far away as possible from...*it*.

This was more than his mind could wrap around. Here she was, his best friend, and yet not even close. Alli was dead; there was no way around it, and then she walked back into his life without so much as a how-do-you-do, and turned his world upside down all over again. It was bad enough when she was alive. On top of it all, there was so much that she didn't remember. Maybe that was a good thing. Maybe she wouldn't remember how he'd screwed everything up. But then again, she wasn't even a *she*; she was an *it*, something not even human, not a *person*, and it angered him to think about Alicia as less than who she was.

Donna came back with a package for Bunny, had lunch, and left, taking her paperwork and fresh samples of Nadia's blood with her.

As the afternoon wore on, Jon's muscles announced that, whether he liked it or not, they were through splitting wood for the day. He thought about Uncle Mike's lounger, a cold cola, and a sandwich. And then he thought: *It's in there. Do I really want to be in there?* He wandered in circles in the yard for a full minute. *This is ridiculous. It's my uncle's cabin. I belong here, she...it...doesn't. Just walk in there and own the place, already.* He was getting one hellacious headache. He put a hand to his head and crossed the yard, leaning the maul against the woodpile as he passed.

Entering the cabin, Jon flumped into the lounger. He reclined it, sat silently, and closed his eyes.

A few minutes later, Nadia came in with a cola and sandwich, and set them on the end table next to the chair. She disappeared into the kitchen without saying a word, leaving only the lingering bouquet of her perfume. She still smelled like Alli. Jon listened to her and Bunny whispering in the kitchen, unable to hear what was being said. He picked up the sandwich and lifted the top slice: roast beef on rye, sliced thin and heated, stacked with

115

pickle slices and Muenster cheese, the top slice spread with salad dressing. Jon's favorite. He cursed himself inwardly, and then set to on the sandwich.

As soon as he finished, Nadia came back with a chair from the kitchen. She set it on the floor in front of the lounger, facing Jon. He tried to look away, but felt stupid for even trying, so he met her gaze.

Finally, she spoke. "We're both in this, Jon, whether we like it or not. I need to know what's going through your mind right now, because I can't handle this change in you." Jon stayed silent, letting the ice melt in the half-empty glass of cola.

Nadia continued. "I'm trying to get a handle on this whole thing, too. The difference between you and me, though, is that you can walk away from it. I can't. I have to just suck it up and deal with not being human. I know what I am to me, and I can't help it. But what am I to you?"

Jon sighed and brought his glass to his lips. He looked into it as he spoke. "I don't know. You're certainly not what I thought you were."

"I'm not what you were hoping for, in other words? And what was that?"

"I don't know that, either."

"I don't buy that, Jon. Look at me." Jon looked up, his mind and face blank. "Who do you see?"

"I don't see anyone."

Nadia's face flushed, and she looked away. When she looked back into Jon's eyes, her lip was quivering. "Then why are we still here? Why are you here? Why am I here?"

"You're evidence," said Jon. "Donna said in order to capture Alicia's mind, it had to be destroyed while they recorded her personality. That means she must have been alive when they got to her. Someone committed murder, and right now you're the only evidence I've got. You're the only marker on the trail."

"So I'm no one, just 'evidence'?" Nadia's voice hardened. Her hands clenched in her lap. "Exactly how are you going to fit me in your little Ziploc 'Exhibit A' bag, Agent Daniels? When this is over, are you going to lock me away in your little evidence closet back in DC? Am I that dead to you?"

"Well, you're not human, are you?" Jon said.

116

She said nothing in return. She looked down at the floor, her lips pursed tightly.

Jon pressed on. "Well, are you? What exactly are you, Nadia? Someone's twisted science fair project? Some show-and-tell from hell? Is Dr. Frankenstein even now throwing together a Nadia Mark II, using a dead woman's DNA, and another dead woman's brain patterns? What do you want to bet there's a serial number tattooed on your left—"

Jon should have expected the slap, but even had he seen it coming, it was lightning-quick, and hard enough to sprout stars in his vision. When he recovered enough to see, Nadia's eyes still burned and the low growl was just fading from her throat. He sat back, shocked.

"Was *that* dead, Jon? For your information, sir, I am alive. I'm sitting here right now, in front of you, alive. Okay, I was made by someone else. Am I worth less because of it? As I recall, you didn't see the difference when you kissed me out there on the porch. You promised me then that this would be over, and I could be my own person, do you remember that?"

"That's before I knew—"

She cut him off, her voice rising in anger. "I'm not letting you off that easy, Jon Daniels! You think that a promise made to a non-human isn't binding? What if I was a dog? Do people make promises to their dogs? Or do I not even deserve that?"

"Quit! That's not—"

"Not what, Jon? Not the same? Let me ask you something else. Did it mean anything to you when you kissed me?"

"What?" he sputtered. "That's not fair!"

"You know what's not fair, Jon? Waking up in a hospital with no history, no memory. Getting lied to for over a year just to find you'd have been better off being someone's stupid little pet! Finding out what you are, but not why! Trying to be you, when everyone else around you is trying to make you be *their* someone else! Well, Jon, say goodbye to Alicia, because I'm going to be me, and to hell with her!"

"Don't you say that!" Jon shot to his feet, his hands balled into fists. "You have no right—"

"I have *every* right!" Nadia stood toe to toe with Jon, glaring back up at him. "You've been comparing me to her ever since we met. What really makes me mad is there's a part of me that *is* her. So right now am I me, or am I her? I could go *nuts* trying to sort it out. I don't care anymore."

Nadia's voice dropped, but she stood her ground, looking up into Jon's eyes. "And I can be okay with that, because now I understand why I don't remember before. I'm getting answers. They're not the answers I wanted, but they're answers."

Jon's hands relaxed. He looked away from Nadia for a few seconds before speaking. "You asked me something the other night. You asked me if—"

Nadia held her hand up, shushing him. "No. Don't tell me. I know." She took a deep breath before going on. "Did you know she cried, Jon? That night in Chicago, she cried in your arms, and you never asked why. It was because she was wishing she was someone else. You never knew how she felt, because she couldn't afford the consequences, and neither could you."

"Why—" began Jon, his voice breaking.

"Because she has to be gone, and you have to go on. Because if you can't treat me like a woman, maybe you could treat me like a person. Maybe even a friend." A tentative smile appeared on her lips. "God knows I could sure use a friend right now, because I'm scared absolutely witless of myself."

Bunny called from the kitchen. "Hey, guys, you might wanna get in here, like right now!"

Jon and Nadia looked at each other for another moment before Jon answered. "All right, Bunny. We're coming."

As they entered the kitchen, Bunny was working on his new desktop system and printer. His hands shook as he prepared the program. "Watch this." He explained as he cued up the file at the beginning of the clip. "Here's the file I copied from the computer at KBGX. It's the whole interview from Nigeria, four years ago."

Jon and Nadia pulled up chairs as the file began to play. Jon kept one eye on the video, and one on Nadia, watching her reactions. She muttered nervously as the video played: "Strange, I don't feel anything...I don't remember this at all. It doesn't trigger a rush or any memory at all... Is that really *me*?"

They watched the Nadia on the file conduct her interview with President Bello, exchanging laughs here and there, getting more serious in other spots. The video segment was unedited, and so contained parts where she looked into the camera and asked Steven to change angles, and parts when the president's aide served drinks. The entire file was about an hour long.

"This is where the YouTube file ends," announced Bunny, "any second now." But it continued for several more minutes. Now they were all in unmarked territory.

Jon saw the lighting shift as one of the set lights burned out in a flicker of flashes. Steven's voice behind the camera told her he needed to get another light from the truck. President Bello and Nadia continued to make small talk for a couple more minutes, and then something happened. Nadia froze in place. She seemed to grow pale, or was it some variant in the video file? President Bello touched her shoulder tentatively. Then the screen exploded in a white flash, and the video file ended.

Jon, Nadia, and Bunny sat silently for some time. Jon finally spoke, in a weak voice, "What the hell did we just see?"

Bunny backed up the video about thirty seconds and let the video play until just before the end. He paused it, and advanced one frame at a time. They watched Nadia slow down and grow still. All three were watching the screen for every detail. Jon picked out the first change. "There! See what's happening? That's not an aberration of the video file. Her face is getting pale, like she's fainting." They watched closer as the transformation washed over her skin, leaving her clothes the same shades of pastel blue and black as before. She was frozen in place.

Nadia saw the next event. "Wait, Bunny! Back it up again and go more slowly…there! Stop. What's that light reflecting off my eye? It's only in the right, that little flash. One more frame. No. That light's coming *out* of my eye; it's not reflected in it!" Five seconds later, they found out what killed the President of Nigeria, his aides, and his senior minister, and destroyed half of the presidential palace in Abuja. Jon, Nadia, and Bunny sat in stunned silence for the second time that evening.

This time it was Bunny who broke the shocked stillness. "Jonny-boy, you better quit gettin' her mad."

Chapter Thirty-Two

The rented SUV left the highway and wound its way down the tree-lined tracks as the sun began to set behind the Ridge. In spite of the growing gloom in the forest around it, the headlights remained off. Three hundred meters in, it turned off the track and into the woods, where it stopped. The engine shut down, and the front doors opened quietly. Two figures, dressed in dark camo BDU's, stepped out onto the ground and listened to all around them. The night was coming alive with the sounds of frogs, crickets, and the occasional owl.

One figure produced a small flashlight and they hunkered down behind the vehicle, concealing themselves from passersby. After applying dark grease to their faces and unloading their packs from the truck, they set out together, moving silent as death through the trees, as the final rays of the sun receded behind the ridge along the banks of the Shenandoah. They soon disappeared, leaving an abandoned SUV in the woods as the only proof that anyone had been there at all.

* * * *

Bunny pulled a thumb drive from the machine and handed it to Jon. "Here you go, Jonny, I copied the movie onto this for you. Put it in a safe place." Jon reached out with shock-numbed fingers and took it, placing it in his pants pocket.

"Oh, my God, did you see that?" Nadia kept whispering, horrified, at what she'd witnessed. "I just…Oh, my God, I can't believe—"

"Nadia, that wasn't you. That couldn't have been," said Jon. "There was no way you could have actually *been* a bomb like that."

"Jon, believe it," said Bunny. "Look, the last frames prove it. The shock wave, and all that energy, coming from her body." His hands still trembled. His face was a blank mask. He rubbed the meager stubble on his chin anxiously as he stared at the computer screen.

"Then how is she still alive, Bunny?" Jon said. "How is it that she's here?"

Nadia answered the question herself. She spoke quickly, as if worried that if she stopped she would never be able to speak again. "I'm starting to see it all, now. That wasn't me. It wasn't me. Watch how she behaves, how she acts. Watch the video again. Jon, I was supposed to interview the President of Iran when I left the airport and met you at the Staley's in New York. Steven was so hesitant to split up, even for just a moment. Then, when they did catch up with us, look how they all behaved. They attacked us. They shot your uncle."

"Yes, but who?" asked Jon. "We don't even know who we're running from."

"News people!" cried Nadia. "They were my news crew, remember?"

"News people don't go around killing people, Nadia. News people don't put bombs in artificial people as weapons of assassination. Someone else is behind all this, someone with a lot of money and a lot of power. NSA? CIA? Who would have a vested interest in assassinating President Bello?"

"Who owns the studio where you worked?" asked Bunny. "Maybe that's where we should start lookin'."

"Didn't you hear me? It's not news people we're after," said Jon.

"Yeah, I heard you. But how did they manage to plant all those people at the studio, all in one area, just to watch one reporter? I'm tellin' ya, Jon, someone in there has to be in on it."

"What makes you think that? Why couldn't it be someone on the lower echelons of the company?"

"Because of the watchdog program on their network." Bunny got up and opened the fridge, grabbing a soda. "When are you gonna start stockin' somethin' decent in here? I could go for a Dew right now." He sat back at the table and popped the can.

Bunny took a deep drink and continued. "Anyway, it's like this: Hackin' is an art form. You gotta be real careful with it. Companies and organizations of all kinds, they got watchdogs an' firewalls, and all sorts of stuff to keep us out. What ya gotta do is find out what watchdog you're dealin' with. Then you try an' pat him on the head and just ease on by. Sometimes the dog bites you, and sometimes you get lucky and he don't. My point is, the bigger the dog, the more secrets the company has to keep. The Fed, that was a mighty big watchdog, my friend. And for the record,

Jonny, I never took no money from them. In fact, I gave 'em some. But back to what I'm sayin'.

"The Fed had a mighty big watchdog, but I got around it. KBGX has a bigger watchdog than the Fed, one that takes lots of money to install and maintain. The FBI don't even have a dog this mean, Jonny. I got by it, and came back with this video. But I wasn't usin' top-grade equipment, just your uncle's laptop, before Doc Hermsen dropped this off." He patted the top of his new monitor. "I think I was detected."

Nadia gasped.

"Now, don't go off just yet. I don't think they can place us here. But I'm just sayin' that no IT department can hide the kind of cost it would take to install this watchdog. This ain't no dog. It's more like a big, green dragon. And this stuff here…" He patted the desktop again. "is gonna get me back in there, and I'm gonna find out who's in charge."

"Can I ask something?" The men looked at Nadia. Her voice was very small, and she looked shaken. "What set off the bomb?"

Jon took her hands and pulled her to her feet. "Look, Nadia, it might seem impossible, but I want you to try and get some sleep. Go lie down, and we'll find out what we can. Are you okay?" Her face pale, she nodded and excused herself. The men heard the bedroom door close. Jon pulled his chair closer behind Bunny. "Okay, my friend, let's back this up. I think I know where to look."

* * * *

In the woods outside, the crickets paid no mind to the two shadows creeping closer to the cabin below them. They came down the ridge, approaching from the rear. A light came on in a window, and went out again a minute later. They moved slowly, taking their time. Silence was their top priority. The noise would come later. But first things first: acquire the target. Down below, a wooden screen door opened and then slammed shut. A set of heavy footsteps advanced out onto the porch. A yellow bug light came on on the other side of the cabin, and a figure slumped into a creaky chair. The sniper felt a tap on his shoulder and turned to the other. A few hand signals were exchanged, and the other crept silently away into the darkness.

The sniper backed up the ridge several yards until he found a fallen tree, wedged sideways across the slope and resting against two upright trunks. He slunk over to the uphill side and settled in. Bringing out a chewy bar, he sliced the packet open with his knife and gnawed on it while waiting for his companion to return.

* * * *

"There! Stop the video, Bunny!" Jon's finger shook with excitement as he pointed again at the screen. "Now, can you run it real slow, and let's watch carefully." He was standing behind Bunny, watching over the hacker's shoulder.

"I think I'm on the same page, Jonny-boy." Bunny manipulated the file, slowing the playback down to two frames per second. They both saw it. "Right there. Right when the light goes dim. There's a funky little shimmer in the light, and right after that, the cameraman makes an excuse to go out to his truck. Like he don't carry no spare bulbs with him for an interview this important. I'll slow it down a little more—"

"Bunny, look! There's a series of flashes from somewhere off to the left, right after the light goes out on the right side. Then look at her right eye. There's a little flash! Did you see that?"

Bunny pushed back his chair with a grunt and stood up. "Jonny, we gotta have enough for your buddies to open somethin' official, don't we? I mean, she was bein' sent to murder Iran's president, an' we got proof right here!"

"Bunny, everything we have, we got by illegal means. It'll never stand up in court. We have to find out who's behind this and bring them down legally."

"Suivez-la Piste," muttered Bunny as he cracked open another cola. "You really oughta see about gettin' us some beer or somethin'—"

"Swivvay the what?" asked Jon, puzzled.

"Oh. 'Suivez la Piste' means, 'follow the path.' It's French."

"O-o-o-kay…." muttered Jon.

"Follow the money, Jonny." Bunny sat back down. "Whoever set her up like a nine-pin, spent a lot of cash to make a person-bomb…." His voice trailed off and his eyes grew wide in realization. "Out in the middle of the Cascades!"

Jon was right with it. "What was that hospital she woke up in, Bunny?"

"Twin Oaks." Bunny leafed through the stack of notes on the table.

123

"Whose names are on those billing notes that you collected?"

Bunny pulled out another sheet on which he had hand-written some notes earlier. "Okay, let's see who the cat dragged in: Walter Brady—"

"The congressman? He was on the FBI director's case about me when I snuck Nadia into the basement at FBI Headquarters. My uncle was telling me…." He grew quiet, and Bunny knew what he was wondering.

"Jon, I did a little research on that earlier today. I was kind of waitin' to tell you…."

Jon sat down. He looked down into his lap for a few seconds, steeling himself. Then he looked at Bunny. "He's dead, isn't he?"

"Last night. Infection and trauma. His heart just gave out. I'm real sorry, buddy."

Jon fell silent. He swallowed several times, hard. Then he rubbed his eyes and stared off somewhere else for several seconds. His eyes were moist, and his voice was shaky. "Who else is on that list, Bunny?"

"She wanted me to check for you, you know. She ain't so—"

Jon stabbed the table with a finger, his face thick with anger. "The list, Bunny. Who's on it?"

Bunny looked back down at his stack of printed sheets and they went over the list: Congressmen, billionaires from all over the world, industrialists, movie producers, and people of influence from all halls of power. Names filled the page, stupefying the two men.

* * * *

Two shadows met each other in the darkness over the river. Through hand signals, the lookout told the sniper they had to continue their search. Setting off down toward the bank, they worked their silent way along the water's edge. They came to another cabin, this time swinging through the trees around the front side where they could see the door. There was a light on, in spite of the late hour.

The one with the rifle once again took a position of waiting while the other crept forward. He came in close to the cabin and crouched, listening under the windows for several minutes. When he finally came back to the trees, he was shaking his head. *No, wrong again.* The two then set off once more, checking the next cabin down the line. A bleary false dawn glowed in the eastern sky when they gave up for the night and headed back up the ridge to make camp. They would continue after a few hours of sleep.

Chapter Thirty-Three

Nadia came into the kitchen early the next morning to be greeted by the mess from the previous night. Stacks of printouts and notes littered the table; cans and cups filled the sink. Jon and Bunny were nowhere to be seen. "Men," she muttered, and began to clean up and prepare for the morning meal. They were usually up by now; it must have been a late night.

As the sink filled, Nadia's mind wandered to what she had seen the night before. When Jon asked her to leave, she felt too numb to resist. It was impossible for her to believe. They had told her that she'd survived, and here she was. But the video: the video showed what had happened. There was no way she could have lived through that. She wasn't caught by the bomb, she *was* the bomb. *The bomb. I was supposed to go to Tehran!*

The horrid truth hit her like a brick in the face. They were sending her to die. How close she came…She began to tremble. Fear erupted from her throat in a sob that echoed from the walls. Her knees buckled, and she leaned forward to support herself against the sink. The dishwater began to overflow as she became lost in her nightmare.

"Please, God, let this be a dream. Let me wake up…." The remainder of her strength left her in a rush and she slid to the floor, her face buried in her hands as water cascaded onto the floor, pouring over her helpless form.

She heard someone screaming, a tormented howl that shook her soul. Something in her mind told her it was her own voice, but it all seemed so distant, so far away. She felt paralyzed, so out of control that even movement was beyond her. Terrified beyond measure, she lay curled on the floor, a bedraggled, soaked, helpless heap.

She never heard Jon come into the kitchen and pluck her limp form out of the quickly spreading puddle of soapy water.

Bunny staggered blearily around the corner, a puzzled look on his face.

Jon carried Nadia through the doorway into the living room. He spoke to Bunny in a low voice as they passed. "Get the sink, please." Jon lay her gently in the recliner.

"I don't want to die," she cried as he let go and kneeled in front of her.

126

Jon took her face in his hands, forcing her to look at him. "You listen to me. You're not going to die on me, you hear me? Not again. We're getting to the bottom of this whole mess and then—"

Her eyes bulged. "And then what? Then I blow up? Or someone decides they want to see how I work and takes me apart?" She grabbed his wrists in her fists. He winced, but did not pull away. "Tell me, what happens then?" She let go and pushed him away. "Will I be worth anything, or am I still just evidence?"

Jon sat on the small couch opposite the recliner and rubbed his wrists. "I think," he said slowly, "I've been treating you badly. I'm sorry. I just don't know how to take you right now. I thought…." He paused, and his mouth worked in vain to find words.

Nadia spoke, so low that Jon had to lean forward just to hear her voice. "I think I know what you thought. Maybe I kind of thought the same thing, at one time. But it just doesn't make sense anymore, does it? Nothing makes sense anymore."

"No. Nothing makes sense."

She wiped her eyes with shaking hands. "I guess I need to quit being such an emotional train wreck, huh?" She sniffed and looked at the ceiling. "I'm just having a hard time getting around the last week." She laughed sardonically. Another tear formed and ran down her cheek. "I must be pretty damned pathetic."

"Gee, I don't know," said Jon. "In less than a week to find out that you're really someone else, and not only that, but that you're someone's weapon and totally expendable? Hey, sounds like a reason to celebrate to me. Hang on." He walked into the kitchen, and returned with a paper towel, holding it out so she could take it.

Take it she did, and wiped her eyes and nose. "What did you find out last night?"

"Right when the light burned out in the video, there was another light source that flashed some kind of coded stream at you. Then the cameraman made an excuse to leave, and about two minutes later you went—"

"That wasn't me," she insisted. "That couldn't have been me. How could anyone have survived that? And if that was the trigger, why am I still here? Why didn't I get triggered last night, just watching the video?"

"I don't know, Nadia. Maybe the digital file couldn't capture the whole code or something. I guess there's more to find out."

She fixed him with a stare. "I'm going to hold you to your promise, you know."

"What promise?"

"You said you'd be with me through all this. I need you to keep that promise. If you do nothing more for me, Jon Daniels, I need you to keep that promise."

He lowered himself to look her straight in the eyes and took her hands in his. Nadia felt the soft comfort in his voice. "Okay," he said. "You got it."

* * * *

In the kitchen, Bunny turned off the water and grabbed a mop out of the broom closet. With a sigh, he went to work on the kitchen floor. After wringing the yarn mop head over the sink, he picked up the rag rug from in front of the sink, and took it outside to hang over the porch rail. When he came back into the kitchen, he noticed a perfectly round knothole in the floor under where the rug lay. It sat between two knots on the adjacent planks, such that it seemed to form a little, gaping mouth in a startled, lopsided face. He nearly laughed at the thought of such an expression on a human face. *A human face.* Bunny never in his wildest dreams thought there could be any other kind of face on a person.

Chapter Thirty-Four

"Dr. Hermsen," said the assistant's voice on the phone, "the director would like to see you right away."

Donna hung up and sat down in her chair. *Ducks in a row, girl. Someone took it upstairs, you better think fast.* She'd been analyzing blood and tissue samples from Nadia Velasquez, and even had some of her assistants take on different samples, not enough so that they could figure out where the samples came from or what case they were attached to, but enough to help her to get the job done faster. She did not know what was going on, but it was something that more than piqued her scientific interest. An artificial person? She could just about get around the concept. But why? She had to finish her analysis and get back out to the cabin. Maybe Jon and Bunny had some more information.

She left the clean room area of the lab and unzipped her "bunny-suit" in the vestibule. Then she straightened her business suit and primped her hair in the mirror. Why else in the world should she be called to the director's office? An official investigation on this would be a very bad thing right now. All she had were dots, with no connections yet. *Maybe I should have updated my resume.*

It took fifteen minutes to negotiate the elevators and hallways between the labs and the Office of the Director of the FBI. She tried not to act nervous, but her palms started to sweat before she was halfway there.

The director's secretary nodded as Donna entered the outer office. "Go right in. They're waiting for you," she said with a smile. *A smile: That's good, right?*

She opened the door and walked in. Director Standish stood as she entered. There was no mistaking the man in the chair next to Standish's. She had seen his face on TV often enough. If she was nervous before, now was a good time to panic.

Donna stepped through the door and the assistant came up behind her and closed it softly.

Chapter Thirty-Five

"Okay, boys and girls, we got thirty-seven names here," Bunny announced as he continued sorting pages coming off the printer. "I got quick biographies, business associations, and college fraternities, along with medical histories on most. Why are we doing this when we know where she was…where she came from?"

Jon grabbed the first twenty pages off the printer and started to sort them by name. "Because, Bunny, it's not enough to go after the hospital. We have to get the right dirt on the moneyman behind the research. And we have to know who would want two third-world leaders dead if we want to make sure that this never happens to another…person," Jon said, glancing at Nadia, who sipped her coffee and tried not to look uncomfortable. "It's no good putting a band-aid on a cut and ignoring the cancer underneath. We have to get to the bottom of this whole thing or it's going to keep happening. The next bomb may never wise up and we'll lose another president, or worse."

"Okay, then, we'll need a program to track what's connecting these fine folks," said Bunny. "I can have a code punched up in a couple of hours. Are we gonna assume that all these people are connected, or just some of 'em?"

Jon scooted his chair forward. "I'd say anything that connects at least five should be looked at closely. Nadia, could you take these and go through them?" He handed her a stack of impromptu dossiers and divided the rest between himself and Bunny.

"Looks like a fun day ahead," she muttered as she began to sort names and facts. Almost immediately, she held up a sheet. "Hey, I interviewed this guy. Jon, isn't this one your boss?"

Chapter Thirty-Six

"Dr. Hermsen, I believe you know Vice President Gutenberg, at least by sight. Mr. Vice President, this is Dr. Donna Hermsen, one of our top lab technicians." Director Standish picked up his phone and dialed his secretary. "Bring water, please, and make sure we're not disturbed."

The vice president stood and offered his hand. "Call me Charles, please. All these fancy titles are for someone else."

Donna took the hand. "You can call me Donna, Mr...sir," she stammered, and too late realized she forgot to wipe the nervous sweat from her hand. She pulled her hand back and wiped it on her blouse.

"Donna, Charles, please have a seat," said Howard Standish. He leaned back in his chair, pulling out a small file. He was a husky black man with short, salt-and-pepper hair and a *basso profundo* voice. Donna couldn't read Howard's face; no one could. His chiseled features seemed always to be frozen in a half-smile, whether he was talking about the weather or chewing out a subordinate. She knew he wouldn't have called her up here to talk with the Vice President of the United States about the weather.

"Donna, I asked you to come in here so we could talk about some of the things going on with Agent Daniels and the woman he's with right now. But first, I want to congratulate you."

"S-sir?" she stammered. She thought she was prepared to cover her story, but it looked like it was too late for that now. *Okay, now what?*

"Donna, Mike Alverson left the lab chief's position open. I want you in that position starting tomorrow." He leaned forward, pushing a piece of paper toward her. "Just sign the line to acknowledge the promotion, and I'll make sure the office has your name on the door by the end of today. Your first order of business is to get rid of that squealing little pig, Albert McCormick, even though he's the reason Charles is here with us today."

"Sir?" Donna was aware that she was beginning to sound redundant, but she was still trying to get around the situation.

"He's a security risk. Thank God he came directly to me, or the wrong people may have heard about your research. You can't afford that with the program you're going to be taking on for us, Donna. Fire him, move him, I don't care. Just get him out of that lab. Okay, that's done. Mr. Vice President, you're on."

Charles Gutenberg was smaller than Donna imagined, a slight man with a ring of silver hair around a clean-shaven face and honest, blue eyes. He lifted a briefcase off the floor and opened it in his lap. "My first order of business here, Doctor," he began as he rifled through the papers in his case, "is to say that everything in this room is considered classified 'Eyes Only.'" He paused, fixing Donna with his gaze. "That means, anything that gets revealed about the proceedings in this room could get someone killed, and definitely will land you in prison for a very, very long time. Do you understand?"

A lump rose in her throat, and she swallowed hard before answering. "Yes, sir."

Charles drew out a short stack of papers and set them on Director Standish's desk. "Dr. Hermsen, please tell me what you know about the woman staying with Agent Daniels."

"Sir, I…" she began. What kind of danger was she in right now? Donna found herself unable to continue.

"Donna," said Standish, "I realize it's difficult to know who to trust right now, and I appreciate your care. You must be concerned for Ms. Velasquez's welfare, and I admire that. But if you want to save her life, you must trust us. You may end up saving the lives of millions in the process."

"Jon didn't kidnap her," Donna found herself blurting. "The news has the story all screwed up—"

"We know. That's being taken care of," said Charles. "We know the name of the group that made her, and we know what she's capable of. What we don't have are individual names or motive. We don't know what makes her work."

"So you want me to bring her in and take her apart?" asked Donna. "You want me to kill her?"

Howard was firm. "No, no. We want you to keep doing exactly what you're doing. We know she's a variable-yield weapon—"

"What?" exclaimed Donna. "Okay, now, I'm confused. What exactly are you talking about?"

A light rap sounded on the door. After a five-second wait, Howard's assistant entered carrying a tray with a pitcher of water and some glasses.

All conversation stopped until she set the water and glasses down and left again.

Charles handed Donna a tan envelope marked "Eyes Only" and explained. "When President Bello was assassinated, it was assumed that everyone in the room died in the blast. We sent an Air Force OSI team to help with the investigation, and found a level and type of destruction inconsistent with anything but an antimatter weapon—"

"Wait a minute, did you say, 'antimatter'?" blurted Donna. She immediately regretted the outburst. After all, she had just interrupted the Vice President of the United States, for crying out loud! But it was too late to do anything about it now.

"Yes, Doctor Hermsen, an antimatter weapon," said Charles, patiently. "How much do you know about physics?"

Her voice wavered. "Not much, I'm afraid. My degree is in physiology."

The vice president smiled. "That's okay. Mine happens to be in physics." Reaching into his briefcase, he pulled out another folder. Opening it on the desk, he consulted it often while filling her in. "You've heard of PET scans, right?" She nodded. "'PET' stands for 'Positron Emission Tomography.' It uses positrons generated in fission-type reactions in atomic colliders.

"Positrons are antimatter. They are the exact material opposite of the electrons that are part of our atomic model.

"Anyway, Doctor, when electrons of normal matter meet up with positrons of antimatter, they fall toward each other and destroy each other. The reaction releases massive amounts of energy."

"How massive?" she asked.

Charles consulted his notes again. "Bear with me. I just learned some of this recently myself, and I don't want to mislead you...oh, here we are.

"Are you familiar with Einstein's Theory of General Relativity?" He pulled out a piece of blank paper and a pen, and wrote, "$E=mC^2$" on it, and turned it around so Donna could see it right side up. "According to Professor Einstein, the amount of energy stored in matter," he pointed to the 'E' with the pen tip," is equal to the mass of that matter times the speed of light, squared. It gets much deeper, but you don't need to know any more than that."

133

He put his pen back in his pocket and went on. "Now, an antimatter reaction is very much like a nuclear reaction, in that matter is converted into energy in line with that equation."

"So, by 'nuclear reaction,' you mean an atom bomb?" asked Howard.

"Not exactly," said Charles. "Now, most chemical reactions involve a little bit of this conversion process. Gasoline converts about 8 to 10 percent of its mass into energy. The Hiroshima bomb converted less than one percent of its total atomic mass into energy." He paused for effect. "Antimatter reactions convert one hundred percent of mass into energy."

"Oh, my God," whispered Donna.

"The main difference between a nuclear explosion and an antimatter reaction is in the amount of residual radiation. Antimatter reactions release an incredible amount of gamma radiation, but it dissipates almost instantly, leaving nothing behind. Massive destruction, minimal fallout."

"So why aren't more countries making antimatter weapons?" asked Donna.

"Mainly because it's so hard to get enough together to make a weapon with enough power to make it worth the effort. Another problem is the way to transport the stuff when you do get enough together. It's horribly unstable, to say the least."

"So what do you hold the antimatter in to keep it from contacting any regular matter?"

"In a container called a Penning trap. It holds the antimatter in a perfect vacuum, contained in a magnetic field. It's a pretty good way to move the amounts needed for medical purposes. But even that method is only good for the short term." He sat back and heaved a sigh. "And for the amount needed to make a weapon, and keep it stable long enough to make it practical, would take incredible amounts of power. I just don't see how it can be done."

"But somebody did it," said Donna. "It's been done once. Maybe more than once."

Charles nodded. "But the Nuclear Regulatory Commission monitors how much antimatter is produced, and there hasn't been nearly enough made to make a weapon that effective."

"I think someone's been sandbagging about how much antimatter is being produced, first off," said Howard.

"And the evidence at the scene in Abuja, Nigeria definitely pointed to an antimatter reaction being the cause of the explosion," said Charles. "There was no way anyone could have survived, let alone a small woman who was right at ground zero. We kept our findings quiet because we didn't need an international panic, and at the time, we didn't know who could have been responsible, or how they smuggled the weapon into the palace.

"Last year, when Miss Velasquez made her return to television, we knew something was amiss, but we couldn't place it. There was no way she could have lived through what we saw. So we watched. Then we received an anonymous call from someone inside Twin Oaks about something called the NADIA project, but before we could find out any more, our asset disappeared."

"Killed?" Donna asked.

"We don't know," continued Charles. "They just disappeared. We can assume they're dead, but without a body, we can't prove anything. Now, Dr. Alverson is dead. We have two known murders and twenty-three dead in collateral damage on our hands, and someone playing God with people and politics. It has to stop, and you can help us."

"What can I do?" Donna asked.

Howard leaned forward, his elbows on his desk. "First of all, Dr. Hermsen, you can let absolutely nothing be said outside of this office on this issue. We three are the only ones in the know as far as the FBI is concerned. The vice president is organizing small teams from other federal agencies, but we won't know who they are."

"Sir, if I may ask, why not?" asked Donna, puzzled. "We have a hard enough time getting cooperation from NSA, CIA, and OSI without—"

Charles cut her off. "Because, Doctor, the Pinnacle may have several moles in each agency who could be feeding information on our doings back to them. If they know what we're up to, they can stay one step ahead of us and we'll never catch them. As with the other team members, you two will report directly to me."

"The Pinnacle?" queried Donna. "What is that?"

"That's the group behind NADIA. Like I said, we know the name of the group, but not who's involved, let alone who's in charge. We have people working that angle right now."

Charles fixed her with his stare. "What I want you to do is to keep in contact with Nadia and Agent Daniels. Become her physician."

"But I'm not a—"

"As of right now, you are. You know more about her physiology than anyone except whoever built her, and I don't want anyone else to know about her. If the NSA got wind that she's an artificial person, they'd want to dissect her like an animal and try to apply this technology to weapons systems of their own. Can you imagine what arms race will come from that?"

There was a long pause while Donna let that sink in. She felt a distant fear, the shadow of a horror unleashed on humanity that could destroy whole civilizations.

"No," Charles said finally. "There is to be no one else like her. She's too dangerous by herself, and we can't let anyone else get hold of her."

Donna wiped her palms on her slacks. "You said something about her *being* a weapon."

"Yes," answered Charles. "Our source at Twin Oaks told us what she really is. I assume you don't know why they named her Nadia." Donna shook her head. "It's an acronym. It stands for 'Nano-triggered, Antimatter, Demolition/Interdiction Apparatus.'"

Donna's jaw hung open. "What the hell are we dealing with?"

"To be honest, Doctor, we were kind of hoping you could tell us that."

Donna gathered her thoughts and tried to explain what she was able to put together from the tests she ran at the cabin. "The purplish tinge," she concluded, "seems to be caused by a concentration of tiny, sub-microscopic machines—"

"Nanobots," said the vice president. "They're called nanobots. What they're for is the question. I can help you find out. Do you have a fair-sized sample?"

"Yes. The blood sample we have downstairs has several hundred. I need someone to look at them and see if they can figure out what they do. I can let you have a hundred or so for now."

"Excellent," said Charles. "Bring them to Howard, and he'll make sure I get them. I can have some engineers on the problem in a couple of days." He paused, and Donna heard the tension in his voice. For an instant, she thought she detected fear. "Don't let anyone else see them, or where you keep the rest. Am I clear?"

"Yes, sir." Donna took a pen from her blouse pocket and signed the employee action form, stood and thanked the two men, and left. Her head swam as she made her way downstairs to the break room in the lab area. The vice president! She just had a meeting with the Vice President of the United States! *This better be a helluva raise.*

Chapter Thirty-Seven

Oswald Kalinsky never went looking for Trouble. Trouble just seemed to go out of its own way to find Oswald Kalinsky. As a young boy, he was smaller than 90 per cent of the other boys in his class, and they took great pleasure in the knowledge of that one fact. He'd been shut in his own locker, shut in girls' lockers, and had worn atomic wedgies and black eyes with the stoic dignity of the powerless. The one time he had tried to fight back, he was left in a bloodied heap in a back corner of the playground.

No adult at the school seemed to have the time for young Oswald, and even his parents were too busy making ends meet to worry about the letters from school, first about his falling grades, and then about chronic truancy.

More and more, instead of going to school, he hung out at the New York Public Library and hid among the aisles of books. Reading became a passion, especially about computers and electronics.

When Trouble decided that enough was enough, it found him again. Someone who knew his parents saw him playing hooky in the library, and that night, his dad laid into him like a rug. The next morning, Oswald Kalinsky was again enrolled at Brooklyn's PS238 and given back over to his tormentors, who had so dearly missed the lad and the many amusing diversions he had given them in the past. There was lost time to make up, and this they did with joy and aplomb.

Oswald never learned to fight, but he did learn one thing that was more valuable than he had ever hoped. To get around a failing grade in English class, he hacked the school's computer and changed his grade. His teacher never took the time to notice, but someone else did. Before long, Oswald came to realize that he was getting picked on less.

He began to believe his luck was changing, but Trouble was only taking time off to pal around with someone else for a while. When it once again turned its attention back to young Master Kalinsky, Trouble tried a different approach: the classic "set-up."

Sammy Calliuto approached Oswald, and suggested that it would be in his best interest to pursue changing grades and attendance records for fun and profit, the fun being that Sammy could afford to take a few extra days' vacation, and the profit being that Oswald could keep his skin intact, as long as he kept his yap shut and did what he was told. Oswald quickly saw the logic behind such an arrangement, and Trouble laughed out loud, knowing that that verbal contract was the beginning of a beautiful friendship with Oswald "Bunny" Kalinsky. Over the years, that relationship grew from changing grades to breaking security systems, creating false identities and erasing real ones, and then the deals with Megasoft and the Fed.

Right now, Trouble stalked the ridge overlooking a small collection of cabins in the woods of the Shenandoah Valley, looking for its old friend. Trouble missed Bunny, and there was so much lost time to make up.

Jon and Nadia were off fishing the river for some dinner and a small divertissement. Their day had begun with a good breakfast and several hours of inane sifting through papers and statistics, accounts and names, numbers and payments. Throughout the day, Bunny could see Nadia becoming more agitated as they went through name after name, trying to find common ground among the clients of the Twin Oaks Resort. She was talking more rapidly, muttering aimlessly, and her eyes were glazing over. Every name, every connection punctuated the reason she was here, hiding from the killers that created her.

Bunny twice more braved the "Big Green Dragon" guarding Twin Oaks' billing computers, and found several more names to add to the growing list. And yet, all they could do was guess, and guess some more.

So after lunch, when Jon invited Nadia to go fishing, she was happy for the break. They were gone for the rest of the afternoon.

Now, as the golden sunset began to paint the Blue Ridge, Bunny sat alone in the cabin working out how best to say goodbye. He knew Trouble was just around the corner, and it was only a matter of time before it found him again. In fact, Bunny wasn't so sure that Trouble wasn't outside licking its chops already.

Exploding, artificial persons topped the list of strange things that surrounded Bunny right now. News people with guns, and FBI agents who kidnapped people, were just icing on the cake. It all added up to more than Bunny could deal with. He'd packed his things in his car, just the basics. This computer was going to be left behind. He hated to say goodbye to such a fine machine, but he knew he had to cut and run, if he was going to make it out of this alive. Jon and Nadia could use this one. He could start over with the doctor's laptop. If he could just stay one step ahead of Trouble.

He'd just put the finishing touches to his farewell note and leaned over to reach for his coffee cup, when Trouble exploded through the window behind him and put Bunny Kalinsky down hard.

He felt a kick on top of his right shoulder and saw red chunks streaming in front of his vision. His face slammed onto the table and he bounced back onto the floor. The computer exploded into sparks and fragments, and papers went flying. He lay on the kitchen floor trying to get his breath, unable to comprehend why he couldn't move his right arm. *What the hell was that?*

Sparks from the damaged computer threw strange, blue flashes from the walls. The floor under him was growing slick with wet warmth as he struggled to grasp something to pull himself back up. His vision began to fog over. He had to do something fast.

* * * *

Up on the ridge, two figures separated themselves from the forest's early evening gloom. "He moved at the last minute, but he's down," said the one holding the long rifle, its barrel still smoking from the round that had torn and devoured flesh and machine. "That's our bait."

"Cover me," said the spotter. "The others'll be along. I'm going to see if I need to recover any information before they get back. If you see Daniels, take him down, but make sure you have a clear shot." He picked up quickly and headed down the ridge toward the cabin.

* * * *

Down at the pier, Jon and Nadia were putting their fourth rock bass on the stringer when a long, rolling boom echoed through the valley. They looked at each other for a full second, each hoping it was what they both knew it wasn't. Jon shook his head. "That wasn't thunder." He dropped his rod on the bank. Nadia was right on his heels, letting him crash their way through the bushes and trees back to the cabin.

* * * *

Bunny swam back to the surface of his consciousness and saw a yellow glow spread and grow as the sparks from the wrecked computer ignited more paper on the table.

He knew he was hurt bad this time. He couldn't feel anything from the right side of his neck outward. He struggled to move, tried to get to the door. Purely by accident, his left finger caught on the knothole in the floor by the sink and he pulled, trying to get to the back door. The section of floor came loose in his hand, leaving a meter-by-meter hole to the crawlspace under the cabin.

The table, weakened by the shot and flames, collapsed under its fiery load, blocking the doorway. The wall had already caught. He could hear the crackle and roar as the fire took off.

From out in the clearing, he heard approaching footsteps, heavy boots and a strange voice. Consciousness was leaving. Bunny was out of time. He pulled himself over to the hole and only dimly felt himself fall over an edge. Down and down…

* * * *

Jon and Nadia covered the distance as best they could, but nothing was fast enough. Coming through the forest, they could smell the smoke before they saw the cabin. "Oh no, Bunny!" Jon groaned, putting on an extra burst of speed.

He came out in the clearing to see a camo-suited figure with a green-and-black painted face standing on the other side.

On instinct, Jon reached for his holster, and his hand passed fruitlessly through his armpit. He had left his weapon in the cabin! The other man raised an automatic pistol and leveled it at Jon's chest, aiming for center-of-mass.

A foot-length section of rotted tree limb hummed past Jon's head from behind as he pulled up short. The assailant was taken off-guard, screened by Jon's body, and the whirling, wooden projectile caught him square in the face. With a grunt, he dropped the pistol and grabbed his nose, staggered from the blow. Jon dug in with his rear foot and dove for the man's midsection. The two men toppled over together, scattering dirt, twigs, and leaves as the struggle became a desperate brawl.

141

Nadia charged into the clearing. Something told her it was more than just a lucky shot that she'd landed with the limb, but she was glad it did. She couldn't tell who was winning the scuffle on the ground, but the cabin was engulfed in flames. She had to see if Bunny was okay. She made a beeline for the door, ducking down below the smoke pouring from the wooden structure.

"Bunny!" she shouted coming in through the living room. But as soon as she tried to take another breath, her lungs filled with fumes and she choked, her eyes watering. She caught a glimpse around the corner of the kitchen. Beyond the burning, collapsed table, she saw a dark pool on the floor, and the sole of a shoe. "Bunny!" she screamed again. There was no sign of movement from the shoe. The kitchen ceiling collapsed, sending sparks and embers flying into the living room. The heat wave hit her square in the face. Her lungs felt like they were going to explode.

Then a wave of panic hit her. She was in a burning cabin! She had to get out before something happened that she couldn't control.

She staggered back out through the door and saw Jon on the ground. The man in camo was on top of him with a knife in his hand, bearing down on Jon's chest.

"No!" she screamed, and threw herself at him. The man tried to break loose from Jon to defend himself from her attack, but Jon had a hold on his knife arm, and so there was no defense against the hundred and five pounds of flying clothesline that hit him from the side. He rolled over and came up barehanded, throwing a series of jabs that were deflected neatly by Nadia as she receded, giving him ground. She feinted, leaving him an opening. When he threw a full lunge-punch at her throat, she sidestepped and caught him with a roundhouse kick to the back as he passed. She heard the *whoof* of air leaving him.

The attacker ran a few steps to the edge of the clearing to buy some time and a couple of hurried breaths. He turned around and looked down the barrel of his own pistol in the hand of Jon Daniels.

* * * *

On the side of the ridge, the M-107 was sighted back downrange. The man at the trigger sighted in on Jon's head. It was a difficult shot, more because of the interposed trees than anything else. He reached up and adjusted the scope for elevation. One click, two. The hand returned easily to the grip and trigger. The thumb eased the safety off. Just a second more, and this would all be over.

A whisper of a sound distracted him, and he brought his head away from the scope just in time to catch a glimpse of two words speeding toward his eyes, branded onto a wooden—

He had no time to dodge, and the words crashed into his skull at the corner of his right temple, shattering the side of his skull and destroying his eye. Fragments of bone splintered off and penetrated deep into his temporal lobe. He couldn't get up. Warm numbness spread down his left arm.

The last thought that David Valdès had was a memory, one that was attached to those two words. He was five years old then, sitting rapt before the television. His daddy cheered when the big man swung the bat. It hit something really hard. He heard the *crunch. Louisville*, he thought. *Boggs*. The little boy before the television faded away. His father's face appeared in his vision "What's the matter, Davie? What happened? What happened?" *Daddy...Daddy, it hurts...* the words echoed as Daddy faded into blackness.

* * * *

"Roger? Roger, what the hell...?" Nadia stepped over next to Jon, staring incredulous at the man backed up against a tree on the edge of the clearing around the cabin.

Roger held his hands in the air while Jon held the gun on him. "I said, get down on your knees!" shouted Jon, and Roger sank down. "Put your hands on your head. Do it, now!" Again, Roger complied.

Jon stepped forward to finish taking him down, but as he approached, Roger's hands stabbed out. One hand knocked the pistol off line and the other swept Jon's arm wide. He came off his knees like a shot and rocked onto one foot to throw a lightning kick into Nadia's midsection. She grunted and backed up as Roger spun again and began to run into the forest. He made five steps when a ripping sound split the air and ended with a sickening, wet slap. Then the roar of the weapon rolled over them, fading off like thunder through the trees.

The bullet shattered Roger's spine and tore out through his stomach. It spent the remainder of its energy in the forest. The impact sent him tumbling end over end, and he landed awkwardly, splayed out like a torn rag doll.

Jon dropped to the ground, dragging Nadia with him. They scrambled for cover while looking desperately around, trying to see where it came from. The echoes died away, subdued by the crackling roar of the burning cabin.

They could feel the heat building as flames belched through the windows and out the open door. With a crash, the roof fell in. Jon heard Nadia's agonized cry. "Bunny was in there!"

"Stay here," Jon growled, and rose to a crouch. Looking around, he saw the pistol lying on the ground not ten feet from where they were, and he dove for it. There was no further shooting from the hill. He eased to his feet and looked around.

Jon stalked over to where Roger Glass lay, holding the pistol at the ready. There was no chance of any further tricks, he could see. Roger was lying on his back, his midsection a mass of torn and bloody tissue. His legs splayed out at awkward angles. His right arm moved; the fingers worked feverishly at the ground. Roger looked up at Jon, and his lips quivered as he tried to speak.

There was not much time. "Why, man?" Jon asked.

Roger's lips worked harder. His right fingers dug spastically into the earth. Foamy blood came from his lips as he coughed. "S-save the…world," he whispered, "s-save us."

Jon lowered the pistol, stunned. "What?"

"S-she likes…d-daisies," said Roger, and coughed once more. "Tell her…the notes…it was…me…."His hand slowed, and the fingers quit clutching at the earth. His eyes faded, and he was gone. A single tear ran down his cheek and dropped into the loam of the forest floor.

"Yeah, okay." Jon turned from the scene and shook his head, trying to snap the image from his mind. He didn't remember the pistol dropping from his hand, nor did he feel his knees hitting the ground. His brain felt suddenly swollen, and his stomach revolted. When he finished throwing up, he heard footsteps and looked up.

Nadia was coming to him through the trees, accompanied by Irving Ratzinger. He had a huge rifle slung over his back, and a bloody baseball bat in his hands. There was a small first aid pack hanging in a bindle pack from his shoulder, and a strange, faraway look was in his eyes.

Nadia reached down and helped Jon to his feet. She wrapped her arms around him, burying her face in his chest. He leaned against her, letting her support them both for a while, and then gently pushed her away. She was pale, stricken with shock.

The three walked through the woods toward Irving's cabin. Behind them, the fire roared its fury. Unable to spread far enough to get into the trees, it satisfied itself on the remnants of Michael Alverson's cabin.

Chapter Thirty-Eight

Jon accepted a small glass of brandy from Irving. "I thought you were a cook." Nadia already sat sipping hers next to Jon on the old, comfortable couch in Irving's living room.

"I was," said the old man, "for two years. When the North Koreans invaded the South, we were in Japan. There was no one else who could get there faster, so General Dean's division got the call.

"We set up in Taejon, and the Communists hit us with everything they had. We were outnumbered, outgunned...." Irving flumped into his chair. "In four days, they chewed us to bits. General Dean didn't need a cook anymore, not as bad as he needed someone to watch his back. So, I grabbed an M-1 carbine and a couple of bandoliers, and we tried to keep the Communists from crossing the river. I saw him destroy one tank with only a hand grenade and a pistol.

"They drove us out of the city and into the woods. He ordered everyone else to retreat, but he stayed behind. I stayed with him, and so did Dusty Ferguson, Jimmy DeBartolo, Manny Ramirez, and Mike Alverson. We got hold of a couple of bazookas and about sixty rounds, and went through the woods hunting tanks on foot for three more weeks.

"Dusty and Manny got shot and died there in the woods, and Mike and Jimmy got lost. Then it was just General Dean and me."

Irving's eyes grew moist as he continued. "We got found by a platoon of North Koreans one day, and we were fighting them all hand-to-hand. I took a bayonet to my chest, and they took the general and left me for dead. I didn't want them to get General Dean. We all would have died for him. He loved us all so. We were his boys.

"I never saw him again, but I heard he was a prisoner until after the war was over.

"When I woke up in the woods, I was hurt bad, and bleeding, and alone. I stopped my bleeding the best I could, and made my way south. Three days later, a South Korean patrol found me and evacuated me to a hospital in Seoul.

"I became a cook again, and served the rest of the war in Seoul.

"I saw your uncle again, and some of the others when we came home to the same out-processing center, and we stayed in touch, always. Mike and I bought cabins out here, along with some other families."

"I'm so sorry," he added, "I couldn't save your uncle's cabin." He took their empty glasses into the kitchen, then sat down again in his chair.

"Now, children, we must talk. My Hilda, God rest her soul, would say, 'There's a rat in the woodpile, Irving.' So why should World War III be breaking out in my back yard?"

Nadia looked at Jon. He shook his head at her and spoke for them both. "Mr. Rats, I wish I could tell you everything, but you'd never believe it if I did. And if I did, you'd only become a target yourself. Alicia is under my protection pending an investigation," he said, remembering the alias she'd given Irving when they were introduced.

"It would seem that someone figured out where you were hiding," said Irving. "Where is our young Mr. Kalinsky?"

"He was in the cabin," said Nadia. "He's gone."

"You know this?" asked Irving.`

"I saw blood on the kitchen floor, and I saw his foot...." She choked up. "It was too hot, the smoke...I couldn't save him..."

Jon's head snapped to face her. "Wait a minute—you went into a burning house?"

"I had to try and save Bunny! I had to try...." Her eyes welled up as she thought of Bunny.

"Irving, we need to leave," said Jon. "I've put you in more than enough danger, and I'm sorry."

"I'm not afraid for myself. I may be old, but I still swing a mean Louisville Slugger. It's a shame, though," he said, "Wade Boggs signed that for my Hilda, God rest her soul. He hit a home run with it in the 1986 'Series." He shook his head regretfully and stood again. "I have to get something. I'll be right back." Irving disappeared, and returned a few seconds later with a bank pouch. "Jonny, you come with me. Excuse us, please, my dear." He walked out onto his porch with Jon in tow.

"Jonny," he said in his thick accent as he nodded back toward the living room, "My Hilda, God rest her soul, would look on that one and say, 'Now, Irving, there's a real person.' You take good care of her."

Boy, if you only knew, thought Jon. But he kept that to himself.

147

Irving held out the bank pouch. "You need something to get to a safe place." Jon tried to open his mouth to refuse, but Irving waved him down. "No, don't worry about it. If the government wants to pay me back, it's their business, but I don't want a dime from you. Here." He grabbed Jon's hand and placed the bag in it. "Go with God." He turned and opened the door, motioning Nadia to come out. "My dear young lady, it has been a pleasure to meet you. Please come and visit me again in better times."

She gave Irving a tight hug. "You can count on it, Mr. Rats." She reached up and kissed the old man's cheek. "Please do me one favor? Take care of Bunny?"

"My dear, count on it," said Irving.

Jon and Nadia walked back through the woods to Bunny's old rust-beater. Jon was relieved to find the keys in the ignition. He started it up and they drove away. Once away from Front Royal, they stopped only long enough to pick up some basic necessities. They made Roanoke before fatigue forced them off the road. A small motel off I-81 offered a few hours' rest and a hot breakfast. With whispered thanks to Irving's generosity, they checked in and collapsed wearily onto lumpy, twin beds.

Chapter Thirty-Nine

Donna Hermsen drove through the hardwoods in the morning mist and came around the last curve in the wooded road to find a smoldering wreck in the clearing where Mike Alverson's cabin used to be. She felt the rush of blood leaving her face as her foot slammed on the brakes and the car skidded to a stop on the dirt. A small cloud of dust rose up from beneath the tires in pitiful imitation of the rising plume from the charred wood. The ridge, the winding path of the Shenandoah, the bent old red oak standing right there— all told her she was in the right place. She drove the last eighth of a mile to the cabin before turning the engine off and getting out. It was then that she saw the long, low mounds of fresh dirt at the clearing's edge. It didn't take Sherlock Holmes to tell what lay under those mounds. Fear slithered through her chest, and her heart pounded as she took in the scene.

"Oh, God," she moaned, "What the hell happened here?"

A cracked, dry voice caught Donna's attention. "Stop right there! Hands up!"

Coming around the backside of the wreckage stalked an old man. He advanced toward her holding a wicked-looking, sawed-off shotgun. Her hands trembled as he came closer.

"Who are you?" There was tightness in his voice, an edge that betrayed his fear.

She found her voice, though with difficulty. "Did you do this?"

"You first!" The shotgun came level. "What do you want?"

"I'm looking for Jon and Nadia. Look, that's a lot of gun—"

"Rabbits around here grow to the mean side. What do you want with Jon?"

Donna hoped she sounded calmer than she felt. "Look, I'm going to reach into my pocket, very slowly. I'm with the FBI. I'm a friend of Jon's."

He stopped a few paces in front of her, studying her face hard through the thick glasses. "Didn't I see you out here before?"

"I was out here with Mike Alverson and some other friends last summer. Can I put my hands down now?"

He said nothing, just squinted at her through those coke-bottle lenses. He didn't shoot her when she inched her hand to the breast pocket of her suit, so she reached in and pulled out her identification badge. Without taking her eyes from the muzzle of the shotgun, she proffered it to him. He didn't move to take it.

His voice was tight, tense. "I heard Mike died."

"Yes. Three days ago."

"He was a good friend."

"Yes," she said, a lump rising in her throat. She tried to look calm, but inwardly she knew what a miserable failure that was. She was terrified enough as it was, but when he mentioned Mike, the grief nearly overwhelmed her. "He was…a very good friend." A tear slid down her cheek. "We're trying to find out who shot him. Do you know?"

"Probably one of them," said Irving, nodding toward the mounds.

"Who—" was all she could manage to squeeze out.

"A couple of guys that Jonny and I took care of. He and Alicia got away last night." His eyes narrowed even more. "What kind of gun shot Mike?"

Was this some kind of test? If she gave the wrong answer, would he shoot her, just like that? Donna could almost picture a third mound, laid out next to the others. She closed her eyes and took a breath before answering. "It was a fifty-caliber rifle. A Barrett M-107."

"How would you know this?" His hands tightened on the stock of the shotgun.

She rushed to explain. "I work in the crime lab with Mike…." She stopped. *Not any more.* "We found the bullet. There was enough left to get an ID from the rifling. Please, I'm not armed."

The muzzle lowered and he stepped forward, offering his hand. "My Hilda, God rest her soul, she'd say, 'Irving, you gotta trust somebody sooner or later.' I'm Irving Ratzinger."

Donna relaxed and took the hand. "Donna Hermsen. Thanks for not shooting me."

"I can't shoot one of Mike's friends. He wouldn't like it."

"Can you tell me what happened here?"

150

"Sure. But you'd better follow me," said Irving as he turned around and cradled the shotgun in his arm. He plucked up a shovel that had been jammed tip-down in the earth as he passed, and led her through the trees to his own cabin.

Chapter Forty

Breakfast at the little motel was southern-style hash browns, eggs, bacon, and toast, accompanied by a steaming bowl of grits. The motel owner's wife made rounds with a coffeepot, warming everyone's cups in the sparsely populated dining room. Jon nodded thanks as she poured his cup full of the rich brown elixir, and waited until she wandered out of earshot before he spoke again. "We probably need to head back to California."

"Won't they be waiting for us out there?"

"Probably. But we have to start all over, gathering information on the ones who made you. The best place to look is right there. Maybe we can get some better information up close and personal."

"What about Doctor Hermsen? Don't you think you have enough to open an investigation so someone else can go?"

"Nadia, the only starting place I have is you, and I don't think that's the right place to open a case. How do you think you'll be treated when the world finds out about you?" He looked her straight in the eye, and the intensity of his face was disturbing. "They'll kill you, for sure. You're not a person to them, anymore that you were to me two days ago."

He reached across the table and laid his hand out, palm up. She hesitated, and then laid her own hand on his. His fingers wrapped around hers gently. "We have to keep you safe, at all costs. That comes before the case, before everything." He released her hand and took a last sip of coffee.

"Is that smart, Jon? Is it the right thing to do?"

He threw a pair of twenties on the table and stood. "It's what I'm doing now. Whether it's the right thing remains to be seen. But it's better than hiding out somewhere else and waiting for them to find us again."

They freshened up and checked out. Jon opened the trunk to put in their bags, and Nadia was getting into the passenger's seat when she heard a sharp stream of obscenities from the rear. Jon gazed into the trunk. "The little rat was going to take off on us," he said. "I didn't see this last night when it was dark."

Nadia went back to look. Bunny's clothes lay packed in a small brown gym bag on the bottom of the small trunk. Packed next to it, in its satchel,

152

was the laptop. Jon reached in and grabbed the gym bag, throwing it angrily into the motel's dumpster. The laptop, he placed in the front seat. "I can't believe this," he muttered. "After all I did for him!"

Nadia listened to the tirade until Jon's temper settled down and he stood over their bags, arms akimbo and chest heaving. She stood apart from him, feeling the sting of his words for the funny little man with whom she'd shared such a brief friendship. *Who would speak for the dead?*

When Jon took a breath, she did. "Precisely what *did* you do for him? Practically kidnap him? Put his life in danger? Set him up for more prison time? Steal his car? I'm lost here, Jon. I seem to recall you doing things *to* him, not *for* him. It seems to be the way you live your life, just ramrodding through, getting your way no matter who you hurt in the process."

"Shut up and get in the car," he growled. He threw their bags in the trunk and slammed it shut before getting into the driver's seat. With a protest of false starts, the engine in the rusty old beater hiccupped to life, and he revved it a couple of times to keep it going until it warmed up.

Nadia stood by the car. She stared at him with a steely expression, her arms crossed.

"Are you coming or what?" he demanded through the still-open passenger door.

She walked slowly around the front of the car and sidled up to the driver's window. Leaning down, she glared right into his eyes. "Why would I want to spend another minute with you? You treat other people like they exist only to serve you. Bunny did a lot more for you than you ever did for him, did you ever think of that? Did you even give him a chance to say 'no'? Face it, Jon. You needed him a lot more than he needed you. And now, for his trouble, he's dead. Am I going end up that way, too?"

"Give me a break, Nadia! If I had waited for the paperwork to catch up with us, you'd be dead now. If I ran around procedures, it was to save your life."

She cocked her head and stood up. "Okay, fine. I'm still here. However, what case do you have? Can you point to anything you have that is admissible in court, or can point to why I was made like this? Give me one good reason to get in this car, and I'll come with you. Or we can part ways right here. I already got more answers than I bargained for. I don't think I can handle any more."

153

Jon let the engine idle and stared silently for several seconds. "You're right. I need you more than you need me. Please get in the car so we can go."

"I'm still waiting for a reason, Jon."

"Why do you have to be so damned stubborn?" he sighed. "Okay, look; without you, we have no case against these people. Without you…" He hesitated, choosing his words carefully. "Without you, I can't do this. You know the area, you know the people, and…."

"And what?"

Jon sat at the wheel, his lips clenched in a tight line. His head hung for a moment before he spoke. "Irving was the closest thing to a grandpa to me. He told me to take care of you," he said, "And I'd hate to disappoint Hilda-God-rest-her-soul."

She strolled around, slid into the passenger's seat and closed the door. She looked at him intently, a slight smile on her face. "No, I suppose not."

Jon put the car in drive. "You would have loved Hilda. She made this coffeecake that was out of this world…."

They pulled out onto I-81 South, and made St. Louis before stopping for the night.

Chapter Forty-One

"When I heard the shot, I didn't have the time to get out my own weapon, so I grabbed the first thing that came to hand," said Irving over a flaky apple pastry. "Did I hear you call Alicia by a different name?"

Donna took a sip of her tea. "Her name is Nadia Velasquez, and she needs help."

"Jonny said she was under his protection."

Donna took another sip of tea. "Did they say where they were going?"

"No, but we should be able to get in touch with them."

"And how exactly could we do that?" asked Donna, puzzled.

"Would you care to take another short walk with me, young lady?" Irving pushed his chair away from the table and picked up the plate of pastries. "Grab that thermos with you, please." He led Donna out to his shed.

"There are several of us out here who carry no pretenses that our government is out for anyone's interests but their own," he explained. "We love our country and its constitution, but I would like you to think that this is our own way of taking care of our own. Come inside, please. Mind your step."

Irving stepped through the door into the gloom of the small shed and turned to the left. Donna heard him fussing with something, and a scraping sound came from that side of the door. When she entered, she saw an open door leading to a hidden staircase.

Irving turned on a light, and began to descend. "These cabins are on land which was once used by the Underground Railroad. Mike and I spent a lot of time upgrading the facilities and making them more comfortable for if there was ever an emergency."

He led the way down the concrete-lined staircase. At the bottom, he opened another door into a spacious basement. Donna could see that it was well stocked with enough canned food, dried goods, and drinking water to last for several months, if not a year or more.

There was more. A hall led off into the gloom, and Irving flipped a switch as he passed through the opening. A series of bare bulbs suspended

155

from the ceiling cast dim illumination before them. Donna noticed several doors on either side of the hall, all closed and bolted.

The concrete walls were covered with pine paneling, and rag rugs sprawled on the floor. At one door, Irving stopped. Donna heard a television playing low in the room beyond. Irving opened it and went in. A tired greeting in a familiar voice reached her ears. When she came around the edge of the doorway, her jaw dropped.

"Hey, Doc. What a sight for sore eyes, and boy are my eyes sore."

Bunny lay stretched out in a sleeping bag on a cot, his head propped up on pillows. His eyes were red and swollen, much of his hair was burned off, and his scalp was scalded. Bandages and dressings covered half of what was not covered by military surplus blankets. His hands and arms had been burned as well, and he had bruises on his face. A huge dressing covered the top half of his right shoulder, and the arm rested in a sling.

"Bunny! What in the world—"

"Seems Uncle Mike had a tunnel under the kitchen. I saw the thumbhole under the rug in the kitchen one day, and never had the time to check it out. Until I had to use it, that is. I fell down the stairs with a burning cabin comin' down on top of me. I don't know how long I was down there. But Irving found me and helped me get here."

"Alicia…the young lady," Irving corrected, "told me he was caught in the fire. I expected to find a body, but there was none. I came down here on a hunch and there he was, at the bottom of the tunnel at Michael's end. He's lost a lot of blood. He was shot, but at least that part's not too bad. I had some painkillers that Mike stocked in the emergency kit, and I gave him some of these." He held up the small bottle of antibiotics so she could read the label. "I was hoping you could maybe do something for him."

"Well, let's take a look," said Donna. "Do you have a place down here to wash up?"

Half an hour later, she had changed Bunny's dressings and looked at the bullet wound on his shoulder. The round had ripped loose a sizeable portion of flesh from the meaty part between his neck and rotator cuff, but it had missed the bone. No stitches would close that wound; it would have to heal on its own. She would need to get some burn salve and pain meds, plus more basic supplies. Leaning back in her chair, Donna took another apple

156

pastry and said, "Bunny Kalinsky, you are probably the luckiest man alive right now."

"Lady, I don't know what you been smokin' to think that."

"I'm thinking this, Mr. Kalinsky," said Donna, leaning closer. "You're dead. At least as far as the world is concerned. I can make that official for you. And you can make some things happen for me."

"Oh, Lord, here it comes," said Bunny. He turned his sad-sack expression on the older man. "Irving, you shoulda shot me again, just to make sure."

"Wait a minute, Bunny. Hear me out," Donna pressed. "I need a computer expert, someone who can get in where no one else can, and who can help me stay in touch with Jon and Nadia."

"Who gives a flyin' rat about Jon Daniels, anyway? All he's ever been to me is trouble, you know that? He steps back in my life after bustin' me to begin with, and thanks to him I'm layin' here all busted up, barely gettin' by…." He reached out and picked up a couple more of Irving's apple treats and popped one into his mouth, speaking as he chewed, "All this inhumane sufferin' and now you want me to make nice?"

Donna gave him her best cynical look and said, "How's the job search been going since you got out, Bunny? I hardly think a convicted felon has the world beating down his door, especially for a salary anywhere close to what I'm prepared to offer you."

"Salary or not, I'm still under a judge's order to never own a computer."

"Not if I can certify you're dead, killed in a tragic fire. You simply won't exist. You can come and go as you please with a fresh start on life. Work for me, and I'll take care of you. It's that simple."

"What if I say no?"

"Then the people who are after Jon and Nadia will probably kill them, but not before one or the other talks. Then they'll come out here and kill Irving, and find out you're still here. If you're lucky, they won't fry your brain and use you as a bomb, too."

"Some choice you're givin' me here, Lady," growled Bunny. "What kind of salary we talkin' about, here?"

"Well, let's start with a standard lab technician's wage and go from there." She gave him a figure. He seemed a little less reticent.

"And equipment? What do I get?"

Donna looked around thoughtfully. "Whatever you can fit down here. I can make the budget work. But I have to get in touch with them right away. What can you get by with to start?"

"Two hundred cases of Twinkies and a truckload of Mountain Dew," he answered promptly.

Donna started. "What?"

Bunny chuckled. "Hacker joke. Got somethin' to write with?"

She reached into her purse and brought out a small notebook and pen. He outlined a simple starter system and she nodded as she wrote. "Give me a couple of days to round this up. I'll be back then." Thanking Irving for his time, she allowed herself to be escorted back up to the shed's gloomy interior. She turned before leaving as he locked his shed door. "Are you sure no one else knows about these tunnels?"

"Only those you can trust with your life."

"Good. I need one more thing before I go. Can you get into Mike's office in Front Royal?" He nodded. She wrote while she explained, "I want Mike's lab equipment, and an exam table put in the room across from Bunny's little den. See if you can get some help. That table's going to be damned heavy. We'll also need his stock of medicine. Just bag it all and bring it along, we'll sort it out by type later."

"That's more than one thing." Donna looked up, and his eyes were twinkling. "But I can do it."

She pulled the page out and handed it to Irving, then got into her car and drove back to DC.

It was a beautiful day. The sun shone down, warming the valley. But she could sense the presence of a shadow, an unknown menace that hung behind the backdrop of this pastoral beauty.

Today, everything had changed. She'd always prided herself on being "by the book," guided by the structure of the laws and regulations that dictated how she did her job.

Sure, she bent the rules on occasion, to get red tape out of the way of true justice. But she'd always followed the spirit of the law, in everything she did. Now, with lives at stake, the rules had to bend even farther than she had ever tried before. She wasn't even sure right now if she hadn't broken some, in her deal with Bunny.

She thought about her situation as she drove along. She never asked for this; it was foisted upon her by circumstance. She now had leadership of a team consisting of a living weapon of mass destruction, a loose-cannon agent, a convicted cyber-terrorist, and an aged survivalist who she knew had killed at least two men. How in God's name could she keep this "by the book"?

"Desperate times call for desperate measures." *Who was it who said that? And could they have conceived how desperate this could get before it was over?* She probed her mind for some kind of an answer, and came up empty. *God, help me tread this water.*

Chapter Forty-Two

Nadia shot upright, her eyes wide in terror. Her arms flailed through the air. For several seconds her voice failed her, and all she could produce was a hoarse whisper in the air where a scream should have been.

The light snapped on, and Jon was out of bed, a large automatic pistol in a modified cup-and-saucer grip sweeping the room frantically. "Nadia? What's wrong?"

She felt paralyzed, unable to do anything but breathe in sharp gasps and pants. Her throat was as tight as a banjo string. She couldn't make any sound but a ragged wheeze.

Jon's face softened, and he put the pistol down. Stepping over to her bed, he sat down next to her and took her in his arms, holding her close to him. She clung to him, trembling as reason slowly returned to her mind, and she sobbed against his chest. He said no words, just holding and rocking her while she let it all out.

Her head cleared and she looked at the clock on the nightstand: it was four-thirty in the morning. What was she doing here? What was she thinking? Were they in over their heads on this? The answer whispered to her from somewhere inside: *most assuredly*.

Jon's arms felt strong around her, holding her safe and warm against the fear. She felt his chest against her cheek through his T-shirt, and when she inhaled, his musky scent reached her nose, stirring the shadows of another memory that refused to come forth and make itself known. What did come was the memory of a feeling so strong she was nearly overwhelmed.

She felt his hand stroke her cheek, wiping an errant tear, and she looked up, meeting his gaze. He bent down, and her lips met his. It was wrong; this was entirely inappropriate. She tried to break away, but found herself unable to, unable even to want to. After their lips parted, he continued to hold her close.

After some time, they released. Nadia got up and crossed the room to the light switch. The room went dark and she heard him lie back in bed. She padded back across the carpet, her heart pounding in her chest, and her hand found his in the darkness. She lifted it to her mouth and kissed his fingers, then slid beneath the covers.

"Please," she said. "Just hold me for a while?" She nestled next to him. He wrapped an arm around her shoulders and pulled her closer. She laid her head against his chest, her arm over his abdomen.

She could feel the fear still stalking her, just outside the door of their little motel room, but it dared not intrude now. He was with her. Here she felt warm, safe, and protected.

Nadia listened to Jon's heartbeat. Its steady, strong rhythm penetrated her, beating back the terror one beat at a time. A *human* heart. Did her own heart sound that way, too, or was there some difference, some nuance in the rhythm that made her...something else? She put her hand to her chest, feeling for her own heartbeat. It still felt the same as it always had, but everything was different now. *So different.*

The tears came again and her body shook in spite of her best efforts to remain still. She felt Jon caress her back, his gentle lips pressing against her head.

She closed her eyes and tried to sort out the dream, dreading the prospect of facing what had so terrified her, but sensing that she had to know. *I can do this.* She went back.

Children. There were children playing around her and she was happy. The sun shone and laughter colored the air. She was tickling a little girl, and her heart was full. The baby's full-hearted giggles rang in her ears.

Two small boys, one four years old and the other six, wrestled each other joyfully in the grass. The field was full of short bushes and brightly painted playground equipment. The boys chased each other around and over, under and through. Off to the side, a tall, handsome, dark-skinned man was watching and laughing. She stood and strolled over to where he stood, and her bare arms shone dark and beautiful in the sunlight as she reached out to embrace him.

But before they met, someone else appeared. She turned to see Steven, holding something out to her. He pressed a button on something, and an eerie flash came from the object. Her strength rushed from her, and she felt heavy, so heavy. She fell to her knees. A powerful shock slammed through her body. Her family ran to her. She tried to tell them to run, but nothing came out. She toppled into the grass and looked up into the astonished eyes

161

of her little girl. Nadia/Alicia found herself paralyzed. She felt the burning begin, felt the pressure increase, felt the explosion begin, saw the flash....

She remembered no more of the dream, but the ache of another memory tore through her soul, and she held Jon closer as the tears came again, finding comfort in his company. Would there be no end to this pain? "My heart hurts," she said as she wept. "You never told me I had children."

"You didn't." He ran his fingers through her hair. "Alicia did."

"Where are they?"

His fingers stopped combing her hair. She heard him take a deep, hesitant breath. "They're all right."

"I should find them—"

"You can't," he rushed. "They…wouldn't understand, okay? It would not be a good thing. Just let them…be, please just let them be."

She felt Jon tense up. He seemed…frightened. She opened her mouth to say something more, but thought twice about it. Maybe he was right. They wouldn't know her. By this time, they would have accepted that their mother was dead. If she suddenly showed up again, it just couldn't be the same.

"I miss them," she sighed. "I don't even remember their names. But they were mine, weren't they?" Her voice broke in a sob, and then she was quiet for a long time. She listened again to his heart beating against her ear.

"If I were real, could you love me like you loved her?"

A thoughtful pause followed. "No. No, I could only love you like I love you."

"Fair enough," she said finally, and kissed his cheek. He hugged her close against his side. She felt warm and safe and protected. She felt him relax and she snuggled closer.

She never remembered falling back asleep. When the alarm woke them in the morning, they were still lying together. Nadia turned off the clock and Jon went into the shower. She drew his pillow to her and closed her eyes again until he came back out, savoring his scent and the lingering sensation of his body next to her.

* * * *

162

Breakfast was quiet. Conversation was brief and uncomfortable. Jon tanked up the little car in St. Louis and they set out for Denver. The lonesome drone of the highway was the only sound in the car as Missouri rolled by outside. Nadia looked out the window as Jon drove. *What am I doing? Do I love him, or did she? Is it wrong?* She felt like she was impinging on something that wasn't hers. "I'm sorry," she said, still looking out the window. "About last night...."

His eyes never left the road. "Don't worry about it."

She turned to face him. "Jon, let's face it, I just look like a woman. I can't give you what you need from...." She fell silent for a few seconds. "I can't be with you...in that way. It wasn't fair to you, to put you in that kind of position, or to...I'm sorry, okay? It's important that I'm sorry, so please take it."

"What if I don't want you to be sorry? What if I don't care—?"

"Don't give me that, Jon Daniels! Back in Virginia, it sure made a big difference."

"Back in Virginia I was still freaking out. I'm getting to know you better, Miss Velasquez, and I see you in a different light now than I did then."

"Knock it off. It can't work and you know it. What are we going to do, settle down in a little white house with a picket fence?"

Jon sputtered for a few seconds, seeming to struggle to formulate his thoughts. "Excuse me for breathing, but are we remembering the same 'last night'? I mean, what was with that whole 'just hold me' thing? Are you going to tell me you weren't wishing for just a minute that things were different?"

"Two weeks ago, I thought things *were* different. But now I know better, and so do you. Wishing doesn't make it different." She looked away. "Wishing doesn't make me a person again. Wishing doesn't give me my children back."

"Those were never your children, Nadia. They were hers—"

"But *I* remember holding them!" she cried. "*I* remember carrying them, *I* remember loving them! And now I can't, and I never will again! And you can't give them back to me, either. It can't work, Jon."

He scowled and shook his head. "God, I'm never going to understand you."

163

"Don't feel alone," she muttered, watching the fenceposts along the roadside. An empty place inside her made its presence known. It had probably been there ever since she first woke up, but had waited to define itself until now. She knew that it would only get bigger as time went by. She could never love again. She could never let herself feel that way. She closed her eyes and hoped he didn't see her crying herself to sleep.

Chapter Forty-Three

Donna grunted as she bumped the door open with her hip and brought the bulky box into Bunny's underground bedroom. Irving came in behind her, carrying two more boxes stacked one on top of the other. "I called in a few favors and stole some crap. Now if you can walk us through the process, we'll get you set up, and you can get us back in touch with Jon and Nadia."

"Hate to break it to you, Doc, but we won't be able to get the 'Net down here. Satellite reception is blocked by the ground, and there's no cable—"

She set the box down and opened the top flaps. "I got a phone line coming down in a couple minutes. The satellite company is coming to the cabin tomorrow between ten and four. I'll run the extension down here myself. The permanent installation is coming a little bit later."

"It might save you some time if you could set me up with a wireless modem and a couple of line-of-sight repeaters. It'll also make it harder to find this place," suggested Bunny. Donna and Irving listened and nodded.

"We can make that happen," said Donna. "Now, let's get these boxes opened and start making some magic."

Chapter Forty-Four

The next day, Donna sat in Howard Standish's office going over the latest report on the nanobots found in Nadia's blood sample. "They're made of complex proteins," she said, "so it's likely they're produced naturally in her body. Three types are evident. Two are unidentifiable in function so far. The third type breaks down sugar faster than anything I've ever seen and seems to give off an electrical charge. But it needs oxygen to catalyze the sugar, a whole lot of oxygen."

"Electrical voltage?" asked Howard, "You mean like a power supply?"

"Yes, but what could that be used for?"

"Maybe they run a Penning trap," said Howard, reading from another page of the report. "Antimatter is so unstable that if it comes into contact with any type of regular matter, even air, it reacts violently, annihilating itself and an equal amount of matter. The destructive power unleashed at Hiroshima could be matched by less than one gram of antimatter. If she's actually an antimatter weapon, she must be powering a Penning Trap somewhere in her body."

"Charles said something about 'variable-yield'—"

"Yes," said Howard. "From what the informant said before they disappeared, she could release the equivalent power of anything from a couple of tons to two megatons of TNT."

Donna's jaw dropped and her mouth worked for several seconds before she could find words. "I have to get hold of her, see if I can get her to come back in so we can confirm that. There must be a way to make her inert."

Howard sat back and sipped his coffee. "You realize if we can't neutralize her, we have a major problem on our hands? There's no way the agency or the military would let her stay alive. As long as she exists, she's a threat to anyone in a ten mile radius."

"I'll find a way to make her safe," vowed Donna. "I can't let her get killed."

"Why is she so important to you?"

"She may not be a human, but she is a being. She's alive, Howard. Our own constitution guarantees every citizen the right to life, and she should be protected under that right."

"And who said Nadia was a citizen? What makes you think she's anything more than the literal embodiment of the term 'loose cannon'?"

He sighed. "Okay, Donna, this isn't the Supreme Court. I get it. This is a cause for you. Go ahead and take it on, but don't forget our primary objective is to keep our *real* citizens safe to the best of our ability. It may very well mean that we have to compromise one person's rights, in order to guarantee the safety of everyone else."

"Howard, you have to give me a chance. Let me find her. I know I can help her."

"I can't guarantee anything, but I'll do what I can."

"We may have to keep some things from Charles," she suggested.

Howard looked at her askance. "Do you know something we don't?"

She sat back, her hands clasped in her lap. "Nothing I understand enough to relate."

"You listen to me, Doctor." Howard stabbed a finger at her. "If I find out you're deliberately withholding information for your own purposes, I will have your resignation before the end of that day." His eyes narrowed and he leaned forward. "Is that clear?"

"Yes, sir, I believe it is," said Donna primly.

Howard nodded and changed the subject. "What did you find out about the two subjects that Agent Daniels killed?"

"We found their wallets in an abandoned truck a couple of miles from the scene." Donna opened a folder on Howard's desktop and read. "Subject Number One was Roger Glass, a studio hand at KBGX in San Francisco, the same station that Nadia was the evening news anchor for. One prior arrest for assault in 1999. Subject Number Two was David Valdès, a Marine sniper. He's supposed to be in the Gulf, according to his unit's PR officer."

"Now he's in a shallow grave in Virginia."

"He was awarded the Bronze Star for Valor last year, no arrests on record. The Marines are pretty tight-lipped about much else. We may need to come up with a warrant to get any more information."

Howard turned his coffee cup around on his desk with an idle hand. "I'd say AWOL is a good enough reason to get a warrant. And there has to be more on the other man, Glass. I will get someone to look discreetly into his other associations. We still need to keep this under wraps until I get clearance from the vice-president, but I might be able to get a couple of special agents assigned to look into the AWOL case. We may find something more there than meets the eye. Come back up here if you get any more information on Nadia, please. I don't have anything else to add right now. Why don't you leave those files with me, and you can be about your other cases?"

"Because I'm not supposed to trust you, sir." Donna rose and swept the files into her briefcase. Howard said nothing as she walked out of his office.

Donna Hermsen's mind worked frenetically all the way down to the lab in the basement. Something stank about this whole mess. What reason could Howard possibly have for threatening her job the day after he promoted her into it? Could there be another motive somewhere? *Really, Donna, who in Washington* doesn't *have an ulterior motive?*

If nothing else, Donna Hermsen had good instincts. In this instance, her instincts were screaming at her to hedge her bets. *Oh, well. What Howard doesn't know won't kill me.* The elevator doors opened in the basement area, and she stepped out into the hallway, heading back toward the lab. There was still much to do.

Chapter Forty-Five

They had almost reached Burlington, Colorado when the car gave out with a steaming, smoking gasp. Jon let it coast to the edge of the road, and they sat in the silence of the Colorado flatlands, watching the steam fluff out from under the hood in a dense, white cloud.

"Okay, what now?" asked Nadia.

"A.T." Jon opened up the driver's door.

Nadia got out and blinked in the hot afternoon sun. "What did you say?"

"Alternate Transportation. We walk." Jon got their things out of the trunk and set them on the ground. He took his bag and the laptop, Nadia shouldered her duffel, and they set off on foot the rest of the way to Burlington.

Two hours later, they arrived at a small motel on the outskirts of town, dusty, tired, and dehydrated. They were too exhausted to go anywhere to find dinner, and so they simply collapsed into bed, hungry as they were.

Nadia woke up again that night, and the hollow echoes of children ripped at her heart once more. In her mind, she could still hear them, still feel them, still smell them. It was as if someone was taunting her with those memories, cruelly dragging her brain through them to remind her of what she was no more.

Light from the security lamp in the parking lot snuck around an edge of the drape and filtered into the room, bathing it in dim illumination. Trucks on the highway rushed by, making time in the early hours. She could see Jon sleeping in the other bed, and choked back her tears as she rolled over.

Damn them. They gave her life, but it wasn't even her own. They gave her a mind stolen from someone else, and left her with the lingering echoes of a love she could never have again. She would never again feel her arms wrap, warm and soft, around her children. She could never share the kind of love that filled her heart.

Last night was impossibly sweet. Lying in his arms, just being together, filled something in her, a hollow space that she could never define until now. But it wasn't the same, it wasn't right. There was more, but she could never attain it. She could never be what she knew she needed to be for him. Everything she'd always wanted was just out of touch, impossible to reach.

Donna said they'd made her perfect. How wrong can one person be? If she was so damned perfect, why couldn't she love someone in a human way? Why could she never again feel life growing in her body? If she was so perfect, why could she never hold another baby, feel its breath on her cheek, feel it sleeping against her breast? The feeling of loss, the ache in her heart, overwhelmed her.

She was alone in the world, and there could never be someone for her. She was a danger to anyone around her, and on top of that, here they were, running headlong into the dragon's mouth. What if they got hold of Jon? What would they do? She couldn't bear the thought of dragging him into that kind of peril.

She reached out and drew a pillow close, wrapping her arm around it. It felt like trying to put a Band-Aid on a broken arm. She pushed it away and rolled back over. Jon stirred in the other bed, and she listened to his soft snoring for a minute. She put out a tentative hand toward him. There was nothing that she needed more right now than a human touch. Her fingertips fell just short. He was out of reach. She swallowed back the sob that rose in her throat at the thought: *out of reach*. She let her hand drop. Then a thought resolved itself in her mind. She couldn't go on *needing*, without hope of achieving. She'd been broken enough. *No. No more. Enough is enough.*

Nadia slipped out of bed, careful to make no noise. Tiptoeing to the window, she cracked the drape just enough to let the outside security lamps throw a few more lumens into the room. She packed her few stray belongings into her duffel bag, leaving it unzipped for silence's sake, and turned for the door. Jon started once in his sleep and she stopped, frozen, halfway between the bed and the door until she heard him begin to snore again.

When Jon awoke later that morning, the sun was already high in the sky. Nadia was gone, and so was the remaining money from the cash bag.

Chapter Forty-Six

Donna arrived at her office a few minutes early and sipped from a cup of coffee while she waited for her computer to boot up. She wanted to rifle through the day's assignments and get down to business: finishing her analysis of Nadia's blood. The karyotype report was due this morning, according to the lab tech to whom she had assigned it. That was something in which she was interested indeed.

She opened her email and scanned for new messages while she sorted out work orders for new cases. Her backlog was getting out of hand. It would probably behoove her to hire some extra help. The budget figures should allow... She almost missed it. It appeared as another spam email, and she was ready to delete it, but something in the subject line caught her attention: "Nadine Johnson's Missing San Francisco Boom."

There were too many coincidences to ignore it as spam. "Nadine Johnson" had to mean "Nadia and Jon". "San Francisco" was where she told them she was from, and "Boom" was self-explanatory. But what did he mean by "Missing"? She clicked on the message. It was only slightly less cryptic, but no less disturbing: "N gone. Yondering. Stranded at the coat factory. J."

Donna almost dropped her coffee cup. Nadia missing? What could have happened? Could the Pinnacle have gotten hold of her somehow?

Now is not the time to panic. There's only a two-megaton bomb wandering around loose somewhere, nothing to worry about. God, what am I saying? She knew one thing: Howard was not going to learn of this. No one was going to know, just yet. What could she do right now to help Jon? She didn't even know where he was. She looked at the message on her screen again: "Yondering. Stranded at the coat factory." She'd have to look that up. It must have some kind of significance that could help her narrow down his location without giving it away to the wrong people. She logged out and opened a web session. A search of "yondering" had as its most common usage a book by Louis L'Amour, an author of Western novels. So, he was out West somewhere. How could she narrow that down any further?

The part about the "coat factory" was particularly strange. The only coat factory that came to mind was...Oh, wait a minute. It had to be the name of a town somewhere out West. A quick Google search on "Burlington" returned too many results to search through. *Think, girl. You should have listened better in geography class*. She heaved a desperate sigh and rubbed her eyes. *Oh, crap, geography!* She opened a map and travel site, and clicked on the "maps" tab. She entered "Burlington" and left the state blank, then hit the return key. Ten towns came up. *Okay, now, let's look out west: Washington State, Colorado, and Arkansas. Western novels would be written in Colorado. Okay, so he's stranded in Burlington, Colorado. What in heaven's name would he be doing out there?*

She shut down the laptop and closed her office. After scribbling a note of instructions for her assistant, she grabbed her jacket and headed to the parking garage.

Chapter Forty-Seven

Steven's cell rang three times before he picked up. "Olsen here." He hoped it was Roger. Three days had passed since he'd heard from him, and that wasn't like Roger Glass at all. An unfamiliar voice was on the other end, an older man by the sound of it.

"Mr. Olsen, you are in charge of the team now. We haven't heard from Mr. Glass and can only assume the worst. I've spoken to Miss Paine and sent her home to recuperate. Mr. Hicks remains at your disposal."

"Th-thank you, sir," said Steven, trying to catch up with the situation. "Ah, who is this?"

"You should know better than to ask that, Mr. Olsen," scolded the older man. "A good soldier knows when not to ask questions."

"With all due respect, sir, how do I know you're my authority?"

"Mr. Olsen, the Pinnacle knows its members, and who belongs to them. You performed a service above and beyond the call of duty by your actions in Nigeria. You've been loyal to us for many years, and we reward our own richly. Look behind the picture above the couch in the safe house. You'll find a credit card and a telephone number you may call for logistical support."

"Very well, sir—"

"Our source at the Bureau has passed on some information. We want you to go to Burlington, Colorado, and find Agent Daniels. You will carry out the orders given to Mr. Glass. We will appoint replacements for Mr. Glass and Miss Paine, to round out your team. Do you have any questions?"

"Could you have the replacements meet me in Burlington?"

"Very well. They'll meet you at your hotel. We appreciate your loyalty, Mr. Olsen, and I have faith you will succeed in your mission. Good luck." The line disconnected.

Steven went into the living room and found a packet taped to the back of the picture above the couch. He tucked the credit card into his wallet and punched in the number on his cellphone before he tucked that piece of paper in as well.

After a couple of rings, a young woman picked up. "Support, Preston."

"Miss Preston? This is Mr. Olsen. Is the Gulfstream still on the ground at Dulles?"

"Yes, sir. When did you want to take off?"

"I'd like to be wheels-up in two hours, please."

"Of course, sir. I'll notify the flight crew and arrange for fueling as soon as you and I conclude. Do you need a car to the airport?"

Miss Preston seemed to know exactly which questions to ask, and in short order the trip out west was scheduled, the hotel reservations confirmed, and a rental car was secured.

Steven hung up the phone, shaking his head and smiling. *I could get used to this.*

Chapter Forty-Eight

The morning sun was high and the temperature climbing rapidly when the battered Dodge pickup pulled over in response to Nadia's outstretched thumb. She ran to where it idled on the shoulder and stopped at the rolled-down passenger window. "Denver?" she asked, hopeful.

"Get in, babe," said the young man in the cowboy hat.

She threw her bag in the back and climbed into the cab, slamming the door hard to get it closed. "Thanks. It's getting awfully hot out here."

"And you without a hat?" he said. "I'll bet you're not from around here."

"Frisco." She ran a hand over her head, laying her sweat-soaked hair back. "Trying to get back home."

"Thirsty?" He motioned to a cooler on the floorboard. She lifted the lid and found several bottles of Coke buried among the chunks of ice. Pulling one out, she opened it and the hiss of escaping carbon dioxide triggered a Pavlovian response in her mouth. She put it to her lips and let the cool drink pour down her parched throat.

"Wow, that's good," she said after taking the bottle down from her chapped lips. "Thanks," she smiled. When she turned to speak to him, her next words froze in her throat.

He was openly ogling her. His eyes shone with lust, and a strange, twisted smile slashed across his face. She considered asking him to pull over and just let her out, but this was the only vehicle that had stopped all morning, and she needed the ride into Denver. She'd just have to head this off before it went the wrong way.

"Okay, look, I appreciate the ride and all, but I just got out of a bad relationship and I'm not looking to rebound just yet. So, if you can get me to Denver, I'll at least pay for your gas, and we can call it a day. Sound good?"

A shadow flashed over the man's face. Was it anger? Disappointment? Or something else entirely? "Ah, yeah, okay, lady," he said hurriedly. "No harm, no foul, huh?" He then proceeded to fill the silence with a series of bawdy jokes that only made her feel even more uncomfortable.

Just south of Deer Trail, they pulled into a rest stop to stretch their legs and shake out the cobwebs from their minds. Their truck was the only vehicle in the parking lot. Nadia bought another Coke from the vending machine in the lobby and carried it with her into the ladies' restroom.

Nadia never heard him sneak into the women's room after her. She'd just finished using the stall and reached for the door when it exploded into her face. She flew back against the wall, striking her head, and slumped senseless to the floor next to the commode. In an instant, he was grabbing her ankles and dragging her out onto the floor, where he began to fumble with her jeans.

Nadia felt him sitting on her knees as his hands worked at her zipper, and she shook her head, clearing the fog. She felt the flurry of activity stop. A finger brushed her sore cheek; a surprised curse echoed off the wall tiles. When she opened her eyes, his confused gaze was fixed on his hand. It was wet with blood from her face: pure, pale white blood.

His shock bought Nadia a second or two, just long enough for her to get her bearings. She popped a quick sit-up and clapped her cupped hands hard over his ears. He hollered and rolled off her, grabbing his head in pain.

She scooted away from him and into a corner, grabbed the edge of the sink, and pulled herself up. He circled around, putting himself between her and the door, and came at her again from behind, cursing as he advanced.

She lashed out with a sideblade kick, but missed. He caught her leg and tried a throw, but she jerked back and threw a backfist at his throat. He drew back, but not quickly enough to avoid her follow-up, a right hook that landed squarely on the side of his head. She backed away again, quickly fastening her jeans.

"What the hell are you?" he growled, and whether it was anger or fear in his voice, Nadia couldn't tell. He cursed again and reached down to his boot, bringing up a large hunting knife. Hate and lust mixed in his eyes as he came at her again.

She watched his eyes for the giveaway: There! As he lunged forward, she swiped his knife hand aside and stepped in, punching straight through with her other hand in a lightning series of jabs to his face that rocked him back on his heels. As she gained a little more room, she leaped into the air and threw a scissor-kick into his chin. He landed with a grunt on his back.

The knife flew from his hand and clattered across the tile floor. He lay still, groaning unintelligibly.

Her sore cheek throbbed with every beat of her heart. She brought her hand up to her face and it came away wet with her alabaster blood.

The cowboy scrambled for his knife but she kicked it away and pushed him back down with her other foot. "Stay down!" His hate melted into fear as he saw the cut on her head bleeding. His battered lips sprayed blood and saliva onto the floor as he blubbered.

"P-Please," he begged, his hands held out in surrender. "Please don't eat my face off!"

She stooped to pick up his hunting knife, keeping her eyes on her adversary. He struggled to his feet, keeping his hands in her view. When she worked the lever on the paper towel dispenser to get something for the cut on her face, he whipped around and ran out.

Almost too late, she followed him out to the parking lot and managed to snag the strap of her bag, yanking it from the back of his truck as he peeled out of the lot and back onto I-70. "What is it with you people eating each others' faces off?" she muttered as she headed back into the rest area's main building.

Chapter Forty-Nine

Calm, Jon. Just stay calm. He fought the urge to throw the first thing he got his hands on as he paced the room. *She's gone, just like that. What in hell was she thinking? She could be walking right into their hands!*

He sat on the bed and hung his head. Freaking out was not what this situation called for. He'd kept his cool in worse circumstances; why was this different? Alicia would *never* have done anything this stupid! *Alicia. Damn. This was like losing her, all over again.* He shook his head. *Dammit, think! Stay clear! She's not Alicia, not anymore. She's a bomb, and she's out of control.*

He got up and started pacing again. *Priorities. First, decide what you can help and what you can't. You know where the lab is. You don't know where Nadia is. She may be headed for the lab, or just going back to San Francisco. Or, she may just go off somewhere God alone knows. As irrational as she is right now, you have a better chance of finding one particular grain of sand in the Sahara.*

He was trying to find the people who made Nadia. The last thing he wanted to do right now was to look for her as well. As Uncle Mike used to say, "When you're up to your elbows in alligators, it's hard to remember your initial objective was to drain the swamp." Nadia would turn up again, he was sure of it. At least, he hoped she would.

What he needed right now was a little help, and the only person he could think of was Donna Hermsen. He hadn't seen the news networks replaying video of him walking out of LaGuardia with Nadia in tow recently. There was no clarification from the news outlets, no admission of improper reporting. Nor had he heard any news that his name was cleared. The story just faded off into the black hole designated for such journalistic blunders. But Jon harbored no illusion that these people had forgotten about him.

If he stuck his head up too high, it was a sure bet they would find him again. The best thing to do was to stay low and trust that somehow Donna could muster up some help for him. Jon ate lunch and paid for another night's stay at the hotel with the last of his cash. Then he went back to the room to rustle up what help he could find.

Bunny had left notes in the laptop's case on how to access his uncle's account, and he had used that address earlier to let Donna know what was happening. He only hoped that he didn't give someone else enough information to put Bunny's killers on his trail.

There were no new messages for him on his uncle's account, so he logged into his own email. He found a message from some law firm, informing him that his uncle's estate was being settled, leaving him the sole beneficiary. It didn't look like spam or a phishing email, but it could also be a trap. If they traced him to Washington, and then to the cabin, could they be using the laptop against him?

He read the email again. This was damned quick to be settling an estate, and he didn't think Uncle Mike had anything set aside:

Dear Mr. Daniels,

The Law Offices of Gunderson, Peebles, Banks and Lewis, LLC were retained on behalf of Michael Alverson. Your uncle's estate is being settled, and as sole surviving family member, you are the beneficiary of said estate.

At your uncle's request, an account has been set up. To access the information, review the three links following the text of this message. Click on the link that contains the name of your first pet gerbil.

Best regards,

Alvin Gunderson, Attorney-At-Law

After reading it a second time, Jon noticed that one of the three links said, "Peanut." He stared at the screen for a minute, thinking it over.

It could be a trap. If it were, how long would it be before they showed up to kill him? Or, if he went to the bank to access the account, would someone be waiting for him?

It may not be a trap. After his mom died, he moved in with Uncle Mike. The gerbil was a gift to keep him company, but an hour after he named it, it bit his finger and he dropped it. Mike's cat was waiting at the bottom of that fall, and in short order, Peanut was no more. Irving and Hilda helped him bury the remains down by the river. Jon was so upset that he didn't speak for almost a week. The little animal was never mentioned again.

If this was a trap, then someone made one helluva lucky guess. He clicked Peanut's link, a last nod to the pet he almost had. A document opened:

"Mr. Daniels, please go to the nearest branch of the First Bank Savings Corporation and ask for the branch manager. Give the following identification code...." Jon wrote the number down. "The manager will verify the balance in the account. You have full and sole access. Goodbye, and good luck." He took a phone book out of the side table's drawer and found a listing for a First Bank Savings Corporation in town. It was a fifteen minute walk away from the motel.

He nearly choked when the bank manger told him the balance in the account. He withdrew a portion and left, his head still spinning.

Five minutes later, he walked into a nearby Hummer dealership. He drove off the lot after another hour in a brand-new machine with a clear title and a full tank of gas. A few stops later, he had a full camping outfit, two carbines that used the same 9-millimeter ammo as the Glock autopistol he'd had since Virginia, and ten boxes of rounds. He stopped back by the motel long enough to check out and hit the road for Denver. Wait until Donna heard about this!

Chapter Fifty

Irving was sitting on the porch when Donna Hermsen pulled into his driveway. He recognized her car and came down the steps with a big, friendly wave. "Welcome, young lady." His warm smile brought a grin to her face. "I have tea and fresh croissants in the kitchen, and lunch is warming in the oven."

"Irving, you're murder on my waistline. How's our pet rabbit today? I need his help with a certain project."

"He's safe in his hole. I'll just let you in and bring the tea down in a bit."

Bunny was sitting up when she came in. Somehow, he'd gotten hold of a T-shirt that said, "I WAS FAT-FINGERED. WHAT'S YOUR EXCUSE?" in large, petulant letters across the front, above a graphic of a finger pressing two keyboard keys simultaneously. "Hey, Doc," he said. "Have a Twinkie?" He nodded to a small box full of plastic-wrapped yellowcake pastries sitting next to his coffee cup on a wooden crate. Beside the box, a tangle of empty cellophane wrappers frolicked in an errant air current.

"No, thanks, Bunny," she said. "Something happened. I have to get some support to Jon."

"No sweat. By the way, don't use your company email no more, okay?"

"Why not?"

"I think you got a mole problem. I took the liberty of settin' up different email accounts for all of us that'll take a few days anyway for the bad guys to find. I also ordered a server that I can make secure—"

"Bunny, we have a pretty tight budget for this project. Hold off on ordering anything more until I can get it cleared, okay?"

Bunny gave her a serious look that made her freeze. "Doc, don't worry about budget. I have that all handled."

"I hope you're not doing anything illegal, Bunny. We can't put ourselves above the law for this."

"Doctor Hermsen, I would never put your career in jeopardy by telling you anything that I would or would not do entirely against any illegal Internet activity for which I am totally disinclined to admit."

"For some reason, Bunny, I think I don't want to know what you just said."

"Let's leave it at that, okay, Doc? Jon brought me out here to help him and Nadia, and I wanna keep doin' that, especially if it means gettin' a little payback for myself, you know?" Bunny rubbed his shoulder to emphasize the point. "I still can't hardly move my arm. I been shot before, but that one," he shook his head, "That one was bad, even for just gettin' winged."

"Okay, well, what can we do for Jon?"

"You can look the other way an' lemme handle it."

Irving came in with an insulated carafe of tea and a basket of croissants. He also carried a small platter with several hot meats, mustards, and cheeses. "Lunch is served," he announced, cheerfully.

Bunny winked at Donna and whispered, "You should try his pesto. Magic. Sheer magic."

Donna smiled. "I can see you've been suffering terribly." She grew somber. "Let's get down to some business, Bunny. You said something about a mole problem at the bureau."

"Yeah, that's right," he said around a mouthful of sandwich. "Look, I ain't got no proof, but I know someone besides me's been snoopin' around your files on the Nadia case. And it looks like someone deliberately left a few holes in your security firewall."

"So, what do we do about that?"

"Lemme try and find'em. Meantime, do regular business on your regular account, and anything about Jon and Nadia you do on this account." He scribbled an Internet address on a piece of notepaper and handed it to her. "An' I wouldn't trust that boss of yours any further than I can throw 'im, lady. His name came up on a list of people associated with the hospital where…." He gave Irving a dubious look. "Where it happened." He nodded at Donna. She said nothing, but nodded back. "I gotta start over with my research on the list, 'cause it burned up in the fire. But don't you tell Standish nothin' just yet, okay?"

"Yeah, sure," murmured Donna. This was getting more and more dangerous all the time. Who in the bureau could she trust anymore? She used to think she knew, but now she wasn't so sure.

Chapter Fifty-One

Nadia looked around for a first aid kit of some kind. She needed to clean up the cut on her face and make sure that no trace of her blood remained. The last thing she needed was to have to answer any uncomfortable questions.

Fortunately, the place remained deserted for the fifteen minutes or so that it took to clean everything up. She checked her cheek in the mirror and saw that the bleeding had stopped on its own, so she only had to cover it with a Band-Aid she found in the janitor's closet. Finding the man's knife still lying in a corner of the bathroom, she jammed the blade in the doorjamb and snapped it off, then threw the pieces into the trash.

She rested through the heat of the day, dozing to the lullaby of the traffic on the interstate. Some time in the early afternoon, a small family pulled up in a minivan, and two small children bounded out the side door, followed by a collie.

Mom and Dad shut the engine off, then came inside to stretch and refresh themselves. They had no sooner entered the building when the collie bounded playfully up to Nadia and nuzzled her shoulder.

"Laddie, no!" The older of the boys, a lad of about seven, ran up and grabbed the dog's collar, dragging him away. "Bad dog!"

"No, it's okay, he was just playing." Nadia reached up to scratch Laddie's ears, and stood. "What's your name?"

His answer wasn't rude, but he was firm. "I'm Todd, and I'm not s'posed to talk to strangers. C'mon, Laddie."

A woman's voice carried from the door. "Todd Faulk, leave that lady be. Take Laddie down to the dog-walking area." Todd's mom came out toward Nadia. "I'm so sorry, Ma'am."

Nadia smiled. "Not to worry. He was just telling me about talking to strangers, weren't you, Todd?"

Todd tugged at Laddie's collar and said nothing, just nodded, looking down at the ground.

"He's a bit bashful, isn't he?" asked Nadia. She wanted so much to take his chin in her hand, lift that face to hers, and kiss him, right on the forehead. *Willy. That was his name.*

"We're trying to teach them to be careful. You never know what kind of people are around."

"I know what you mean. I'm Alicia." Nadia held out her hand.

"Suzanne. Suzanne Faulk. My husband is Paul." She took Nadia's hand in a firm, warm shake. She looked back toward the parking lot. "I don't see a car. Is someone coming for you?"

Nadia ran her fingers through her hair, and smiled. "I was hitching a ride into Denver, and my ride…left."

"I think we can help, we have plenty of room. Let me talk to Paul." Suzanne turned and went back into the building. When she came back out, she said, "It's all set. You're riding with us. That is, if you think you can handle Todd and Billy."

Nadia warmed to her instantly. She had such a winning smile, and the thought of spending time with children again brought a thrill to her. "I believe I can make do." She grabbed her duffel, slinging it over her shoulder as the women walked to the minivan. Ten minutes later, they were back on the road.

Todd and Billy were seven and five; they told her so numerous times on the way to Denver, along with sharing the exploits of G.I. Joe and the Transformers. Paul kept admonishing the boys not to pester the nice lady, but Nadia told him she didn't mind, she had two nephews and a niece about the same age.

The longer the trip went on, the more fun they had, the adults sharing idle conversation and teasing the boys until they all giggled so hard their bellies ached. Coming into Denver, the Faulks dropped Nadia off at an exit indicating food and lodging, and she bid them a reluctant farewell. Then, shouldering her bag in the early evening light, she walked up the exit ramp toward the motel row on the frontage road. As she strode away, the ghost of a memory tickled her mind again, of a sweet long-ago time with another family. A wistful tear formed in her eye and ran lazily down her cheek. She let it fall.

She missed them. She missed them, so badly. This was the pain she'd felt over her children's loss, mixed in a bittersweet cocktail with the joy of her only memory of them, gleaned from a dream about a playground. In Todd and Billy, she could hear echoes of her own children's laughter as she tickled her little girl and chased the boys around the slide and through the swing set, scattering pebbles in a rattling, giggling, happy little riot.

Halfway up the ramp, she stumbled. When she put out a hand for balance, she noticed her vision closing to a pinprick in front of her. A thickness ballooned inside her head. Her duffel fell from her shoulder, and she slumped in the grass. It was as if her *self* was being drawn back inside her skull. Her face burned and tingled, and she felt a wave of nausea well up in her stomach. She found herself inside someone else's head, looking out, disconnected from her body. Looking through the dim tunnel of her vision, she willed her right hand to move. A pale, small blur moved into the center of her field of view. *Not mine. This blur is not my hand.* For one thing, it was the wrong color. Or was it?

As suddenly as it hit, the spell lifted. Her vision cleared. The nausea faded, and all that was left was a lingering tingle in her face and hands. The memories of her family receded back into the void, leaving behind them a sweet melancholy. Nadia was herself once again.

She struggled to her feet and took up her duffel. After a few tentative steps, the last of the effects of the episode lifted. She cut across the grass and climbed the hill to the top of the exit ramp.

Turning left at the end, she followed the frontage road until she came to a small mom-and-pop restaurant that promised a degree of privacy. The restaurant occupied one of the smaller storefronts in a minor strip mall. The front wall consisted of a row of picture windows with the name of the restaurant hand-painted in neat, two-foot high letters on the inside of the glass.

A small bell tinkled as she opened the door and walked in. The dim, cool dining room felt welcoming after the oppressive heat and burning sunlight outside. Twelve booths and three tables filled the dining area. The counter provided room for another six diners. Each table had one of those little wire affairs that held a stack of napkins, salt and pepper shakers, and a little card inserted into the wire loop at the top, with today's specials printed on one side and a dessert menu on the other side. The evening rush, if there was ever one here, had yet to arrive. The sign at the register said to please seat yourself.

Nadia was ravenous. The last time she'd eaten was the previous day's lunch. She found a booth in the back corner and sat facing the front window, where she could see anyone else who came in. Right after she parked her bag underneath the table, the waitress approached, a glass of water in her hand. She was a slight, worn woman in her thirties with straight, dishwater blonde hair pulled back in a ponytail, and a tired but cheerful expression on her face. With weathered hands, she hauled a beaten old notebook from a pocket in her apron and said, "Can I get y'all somethin' to drink, hon?"

Nadia ordered a cola. The waitress, whose nametag said, "Phoebe," placed a menu on the table and spun around to fetch the drink.

Nadia fished a small pouch from her bag and took a quick inventory. She'd felt like a heel for walking out with the cash Irving had given them, but she didn't want Jon to have the means to come looking for her. Besides, if she was going to get back home, she'd need all the help she could get. It was getting to be painfully clear that one couldn't trust all humans. She counted the remaining bills. If she was careful with her spending, she could still make it to the west coast. What to do after that? At this point, she was not sure. But she had to do something. Eventually, they would find her again, and what would happen then, she couldn't bear to think.

Phoebe came back to get Nadia's order, and started getting tables ready for the dinner crowd.

A middle-aged man in jeans and a flannel shirt sat at the orange Formica-topped counter, working on a steak and baked potato. A young man and woman entered with a four-or-five year old girl in tow, and sat at another booth. Phoebe dropped what she was doing to get their drink orders and refill the steak man's iced tea, then went back to preparing for the increase of traffic that would be coming in any minute now.

Nadia noticed a short phrase printed with a script-style font on the napkins in the wire holder. She took one out and read it. There was a cryptic-looking abbreviation after the quote, followed by two sets of numbers separated by a colon. She read the quote but couldn't figure out the last part, and her curiosity was piqued. When it looked like Phoebe had a moment, Nadia got her attention and asked about the quote on the napkin.

"Oh, that's from the Bible," she answered, brightly. "It says that God loves everyone so much that he sent his only son Jesus to die, to save us from ourselves."

Nadia smiled. "Okay, so how does that work?"

"You mean you've never heard about Jesus, hon?"

"Let's just pretend for the sake of argument that I never have."

"Hey, Vern, I'm on break for a few minutes!" Phoebe shouted to the kitchen. Vern shouted something back, but Nadia was unable to make it out. Phoebe wiped her hands on her apron and sat at the table across from Nadia. "Well, it's like this: We, that is, me and Vern and a whole lotta other folks, we believe the Bible is the whole Word of God, and it says in there that a man's heart is always headin' for wickedness, even in spite of ourselves. Like, we do wrong things without even havin' to try, know what I mean?"

Nadia knew wickedness; she'd seen enough of it already. She nodded and waited for Phoebe to go on. "It also says that God is gonna punish the wrong things that we do one day. Jesus took the punishment for our wickedness so when we die our souls could stay forever with God."

"And that's everyone?"

Phoebe leaned back and tilted her head. "Well, of course. Since we're all made by God, we all have to answer to him for how we live our lives."

"Okay, then, what about people who weren't made by God?"

Phoebe blinked, and her jaw worked for a moment. "What do you mean?"

"What about clones?" Nadia hoped she wouldn't have to get too specific. But she had to know.

Phoebe looked at Nadia for a few seconds, and then closed her eyes. Her lips moved as if she were trying to think through her mouth. Then she opened her eyes again and took a deep breath before answering. "We believe that God puts something in a human that he doesn't put in any other living thing, and that's a spirit that returns to God when we die. The Bible says that God created man in his own image, with three parts: a body, a mind, and a soul. Only God can give a soul, man can't. So, I wonder if a cloned person would even be able to be saved. It's not like they have that eternal part that comes from God."

"So what happens to a clone when they die?"

"I guess they just die," said Phoebe slowly. "They have no part in heaven or hell. That's kind of sad, ain't it? Not havin' any hope of somethin' after you die?"

Nadia looked out the window, watching the traffic roll along the frontage road outside. "Yes, I suppose so."

Phoebe seemed to sense the desolation in Nadia's response. Her eyes opened wide, and a hand rose to her mouth. "Honey, are you all right? I don't mean to offend or anything—"

"No, it's all right," said Nadia distantly. "I'm all right. I just have a lot of things to think through."

"Can I pray for you, dear?"

Nadia looked straight into Phoebe's eyes. "No. I'm afraid it would only be a waste of your time."

"Order up, Phebes!" called Vern from the kitchen, interrupting the uncomfortable silence that followed.

"Okay, Vern, I'm comin'!" Phoebe stood and turned back to Nadia, smiling. "I'd like to talk some more with you later, if I could. Would that be okay?"

"We'll see." Nadia looked out the window again, signaling the end of the conversation.

* * * *

Phoebe had intended to talk more with this sad stranger, after giving her time to digest her dinner and the subject of their discussion. But no sooner had she set the woman's plate on the table when the dinner rush began, and she found herself up to her elbows in drink orders, hot plates, surly patrons and toddlers' spills. Beverly, the evening waitress, was late coming in, and when she did, the two of them kept Vern hopping for the next two hours. When the smoke cleared, the woman was already gone, and Phoebe never got to speak to her again.

That night at home, she and Vern sat on the sofa and Vern rubbed her aching feet, a regular evening ritual they shared. She cried to her husband about not being able to finish what she had begun with the stranger in the booth. "Vern, she was lost in so many ways, and she wouldn't even let me pray with her!" She ran a hand through her hair. "There was just so much *pain* in her."

Vern grabbed the bottle of lotion and went to work on her other foot. "Quit beatin' yourself up, babe. She's at least thinkin' about it. Maybe that's all God wanted from you tonight."

189

"I wish I believed that, Vernie." But Phoebe knew he was right. He usually was. She woke up later, and as was her wont, she prayed until she fell asleep again. She prayed for a woman who was at that moment thinking about it.

Chapter Fifty-Two

Nadia checked into a fleabag motel not far from the strip mall. The door creaked open to reveal stained, worn carpet. When she turned the lights on, something brown scurried underneath the air conditioning unit. The TV on the table had an old manual tuner, and probably didn't work anyway. Not that it mattered. She threw her duffel on a chair and flopped down into the lumpy bed. Lying on her back, she stared at the ceiling and spent the evening hours thinking about what she'd heard. There was something in what the waitress had said that sounded familiar, in a disturbing way. Could Alicia have been a believer in the same way as Phoebe?

She expected at any time the sudden rush, the dizzying flash of recollection that seemed to happen every time something came back from Alicia's memory into her own. *Her own.* She gave a derisive laugh. What *was* her own? The only thing that belonged to Nadia Velasquez was the duffel she carried on her shoulder. This mind was stolen from someone else and somehow implanted into her brain. Without that, she was just a hollow, dead shell. This body wasn't even her own. She was *property*, not even a real person.

She tried to shrink into herself, to contact that part of her that was still Alicia, to try to understand what was real. She wanted to remember what Alicia believed. She wanted to know whether she still had any part of Alicia that *meant* something. She wanted to be something more than manufactured flesh and blood, living only to kill.

Phoebe had seemed so sincere about her beliefs, and so concerned for Nadia's welfare. Nadia had wanted to spend more time talking with her, but the time didn't seem right. Moreover, there was no way she was going to tell Phoebe the truth about where she'd really come from.

She got up, checked her face in the mirror, and found with relief that the bruises and swelling from the attack had all but disappeared. She pulled the Band-Aid loose and found that the small cut was gone, too. *Good.* She wouldn't have to worry about standing out with an oddly colored wound on her face anymore.

She found a bible on the nightstand next to the bed. Phoebe had said the phrase about God loving everyone was in here. She opened it and scanned a few pages, looking at how the writing was structured, with each phrase being numbered like an outline.

She had no idea where to start reading, so she closed her eyes, opened it to somewhere in the middle, and stabbed her finger down on a page. She opened her eyes and read, "My frame was not hidden from you when I was made in the secret place." She thought about that for a moment. It would seem logical that if there was a God, and that if God knew everything the way she'd heard, that he or she or it would know about her.

Taking out a crumpled napkin from the restaurant, she flattened it out on the bed next to her, and read the words again. Opening the Bible to the front, she reviewed the table of contents. There it was: the Gospel According to John. She flipped to that section and began to read. "Flesh gives birth to flesh, but the Spirit gives birth to spirit." There was more, including the phrase that she had first read earlier in the day, but most of it didn't seem to make any sense to her. This man was talking in riddles, and it seemed he was skirting the issues that the other was asking him about.

Phoebe had said she saw something in that statement that spoke to something deep inside her. Flesh gives birth to flesh. Spirit gives birth to spirit. Did she even *have* a spirit? *Is a spirit the same as a soul? If I do have one, I have someone else's and not my own. What could that mean?*

She read the rest of John's account of the man Jesus and wondered if there was something there for her. No, Nadia answered herself. Alicia was dead, and whatever God had given her had already returned to where it came from. She, Nadia, was a recording, a program, and that was all. She was wasting her time trying to attach anything more to herself.

There was a gulf between what she was created to be and what she wanted to be, and there was no way to bridge across it. On one side of the gulf was the woman whose life still echoed in her mind, who had brought forth life and love. On the other side was the weapon, creator of death. She could escape neither, nor reconcile them to each other. There could be no way to walk in the middle between two such extreme beings.

Nadia closed the book and looked at the clock: 3:30 AM. She was lost, plain and simple, in more ways than even God could understand. She listened to the night traffic on the outskirts of Denver, Colorado— all those people going somewhere. *No matter where they're going, at least they all know where they're going. They all at least have a home to go back to. Even homeless people have somewhere to go, eventually. Sooner or later, they all go back to God. I can't even do that.*

There were no tears, just a languid helplessness and an aching in her breast that told her, *you have no one now. No one to help you, nowhere to turn, and no hope for your future. You would have been better off going to Tehran.*

Nadia felt more alone than she ever had before. She turned the light off, rolled over, and closed her eyes, but she did not sleep. She had to know what to do now, how to end this.

She could keep running. Jon was safe now. He was out of this, just as he needed to be. No one would be chasing him down if all they wanted was her. They wouldn't waste their time on him anymore, would they? However, he knew. They had to know that Jon knew about her. Would the fact that he knew too much forfeit Jon's life? What about Donna? Nadia had already been the cause of four deaths: Dr. Alverson and Bunny, and by extension, Roger and the man who had been with him. How many more would have to die, and how many more would find out the truth before they caught up with her and ended it all? There was also the cash: it would run out, and soon. With no source of income, she would be unable to run any more. As long as she drew breath, they would be after her. Sooner or later, she'd slow down or make a mistake, and they would catch her. It was only a matter of time.

She could bargain with them, whoever they were. She could contact Hamund and Spielberg, appeal to their respect for life. They were doctors, right? Weren't they supposed to take some kind of oath to protect life? She could bargain, her life for Jon and Donna. That should be worth something to them, anyway. She could use herself as a bargaining chip. Then what? Would she be reprogrammed and sent out again? Or would they simply kill her and start over with something even more horrible?

Nadia had another option: she could end this on *her* terms, in *her* way. She could bring this war home to whomever was behind Petr Hamund and his ilk. She would have to get back to Twin Oaks. What then? She thought for a long time, but nothing came to her. Her mind was fogged with fatigue. Oh, well: the "how" could come later. One step at a time.

By the time pastel shades of dawn colored the backsides of the drapes, she had made her decision. She set the alarm for ten, rolled over, and went to sleep. When it went off, she arose, showered, checked out, and was back on the road. For the first time in her life, she felt clarity of purpose.

Chapter Fifty-Three

Kit Carson County Airport had a runway barely big enough for a G-IV, and no tower. The pilot had to get approach clearance from Denver Air Traffic Control. When they pulled up at the fixed base operator's parking ramp, no one was around. The pilots shut down the engines, and Steven descended the air stair with his duffel slung over his shoulder and his cell to his ear. "Miss Preston? Mr. Olsen, here. We just touched down. Is my rental car ready? The blue Suburban? I see it, thank you. What about hotel reservations? You're kidding! Whatever they pay you, it's not enough. Thank you." He hung up. "Hey, Vince, Dean! I'll bring the car up."

Steven strolled across the ramp to the waiting SUV. *Man, I could get used to this team lead thing real easy. Now to catch up with Daniels.*

Chapter Fifty-Four

Steven woke early the next day, and called Karl Swope and Ben Patterson, his new team members, in their rooms. They met for breakfast and hit the road at seven. Steven had a list of every hotel and motel in the area, and they went to each in turn. At the seventh hotel, Steven walked in alone while Karl and Ben waited outside. He approached the desk and brought out a couple of pictures. "Excuse me, but have you seen these people?"

The desk attendant, a dumpy, middle-aged woman with dyed red hair, glanced at the photos suspiciously. "I'm not sure if I'm allowed to say," she said. "Can I call my manager first?"

"It's very important that I find this man. The young lady could be in danger."

"Are you a cop or something?"

"Or something. I'm a private investigator."

"Like Rockford?" she asked, brightening up.

Steven sighed and pulled a bankroll. He peeled off two fifty-dollar bills and laid them face-up on the counter. "Ma'am, have you seen these people?"

"Yeah, they were here a couple days ago. You said she could be in danger?"

"Can you tell me when they left? Were they still together then?"

She folded her hands on the counter. "Well, as a matter of fact, they were together when they got here. He left by himself, yesterday."

Steven got out a small notebook and prepared to write. "What was he driving? Can you tell me?"

The attendant looked through a small card file. "Here it is. Hm-m-m. I don't have a vehicle on here, but I know he left in a brand new Hummer. I saw him load it up when he checked out."

"Is there a Hummer dealership in town?"

"That'd probably be the GM dealer down on the frontage road."

"Thank you," said Steven as he turned for the door. "You may have saved a life."

Ten minutes later, he was talking to the manager at the Hummer dealership. When he got back in the Suburban, he smiled. "Karl, we need a helicopter. Take us back to the hotel. Let's have some lunch, and I need to make some calls."

"S'up, Chief?" asked Karl, a stocky man of about fifty with silver, flat-cut hair and a scar-pocked face.

"Well, it seems our Mr. Daniels bought himself a brand-new Hummer with cash. I got his VIN." Steven grinned. "GM's come standard with a satellite tracking service. We can have him nailed down today."

"Right on," crooned Ben. "What's the call?

"I think we need to have a talk with him. Let's convince him to come back to Twin Oaks. We need to find out what he knows, and if we need to talk to anyone else. And we have to find out what he did with Nadia."

"Who's this Nadia?"

"Right now, let's just say she's vital to the Pinnacle's vision, okay? The rest is classified, as far as you two are concerned. Someone else will make the call about what else you need to know. Let's roll out."

Steven was beginning to sense the end of the hunt looming nearer, and the feeling was good. With just a little luck, they could keep this from leaking out, and the Pinnacle would remain safe.

Chapter Fifty-Five

Jon got off the interstate in Casper, Wyoming and headed West on US-26, figuring the shortcut would save time. It would be a hard push to get to Pocatello by nightfall. He had to make sure he got to Twin Oaks before Nadia.

Coming through the Wind River Reservation, the view from the road took his breath away. Rugged grandeur filled the senses in every direction. It was a clear day in the high country and traffic was sparse. He'd stopped to fuel in Riverton and was making good time coming up toward the Continental Divide. From there on, it was literally downhill the rest of the way.

Somebody was assassinating world leaders, someone with a boatload of cash and a lot of clout. They controlled at least one news outlet, so they could twist information however they wanted to make it fit, to cover up their schemes. They were making living bombs in mysterious laboratories, using other people's minds and sending them out to kill. Now all he had to do was gather his evidence legally, and the bureau could shut down the whole thing. Soon, it would be time to bring his investigation out into the open.

However, Nadia would need to be left out of it all, somehow. He at least owed that to the memory of Alicia Burgess.

Maybe that was why she left. Maybe she just wanted to live some kind of normal life. Maybe she wouldn't show up at Twin Oaks after all.

The thought of never seeing Nadia again brought mixed feelings. Yes, he'd loved Alicia. He had no right to; he knew it. She was already married when they'd met, and he saw what she and Phillip had together. He knew they were good for each other, and so he'd never said anything, even as his feelings for Alicia grew with the time they'd spent together as partners in the bureau.

Phil was a great guy: handsome, an excellent dad, and one of the best federal attorneys the country could have. Alli was tall, dark, and gorgeous. Her parents came to the United States from Uganda, and typical of that population, her skin was a rich, smooth ebony color. She had straight hair that she kept in a little pixie cut off her shoulders, and she was the type who never went out of her way to look good; it just came naturally. Whenever she laughed, it sent a thrill through Jon's heart. He couldn't help but love her. She was sensitive, caring, outgoing, and affectionate to everyone around her.

Chicago changed everything. Chicago was the biggest damned mistake, and the best thing that had ever happened to him.

It was his suggestion to go out after work. They were investigating a racketeering case with a team from the bureau's Chicago office. The hour was late, and they were both famished. Jon had asked one of the Windy City agents about the best place to go for a casual steak, and got an address on Michigan Avenue, just down from the Art Institute.

The place was no disappointment. They brewed their own beer, and even had their own wine label. The porterhouse cut was a full inch thick, and done to a perfect turn, medium-rare. The decor was hand-detailed wood paneling, not just cheap veneer, but real mahogany paneling. The wait staff was pleasant, polite, and exactly on the spot for refills of a delightful cabernet sauvignon.

Jon and Alicia ate, talked, and took their time with each other. Jon felt truly happy, sitting across the small table from this woman. She had on a smart business suit that somehow, on her, looked like a designer concept ensemble. Her hair was pulled back from her face, highlighting her brown eyes and those perfect ears. The more they ate, the more they drank, the looser the conversation became. Sometime near the end of the bottle of wine, he made some lame joke about Chicago politics. He couldn't even remember exactly what he'd said, but Alli found it so funny, she almost choked on her food, which made the situation even more ridiculous, and they laughed until Jon's sides ached and the customers at the surrounding tables began to look uncomfortably at them.

Alli, still grinning, reached across the table and almost spilled his glass as she gave his shoulder a good-natured shove. He intercepted her hand, clasping it in his own, and looked her straight in the eyes.

Suddenly, it wasn't as funny as it had been. His breath left him, and his heart slammed in his chest. She looked back, her face turning a darker shade. Was she blushing? He knew he needed to let go, but somehow, the softness of her hand in his, the aroma of her perfume, the headiness of the wine all ganged up on him, making it impossible to do the right thing.

She hadn't taken her hand away. Not immediately, anyway. Jon let go only reluctantly. There was a long, uncomfortable silence, until Jon asked for the check and they stood to go.

The taxi ride back to the hotel was quiet, too. Jon felt all his emotions colliding, and the struggle escalated in his mind. He slid over next to her as they rode, their thighs touching just barely. She didn't seem to notice.

He stopped outside her room at the hotel to say good night, and held out his hand. She took it, and instead of just a shake, he found himself drawing her closer, and suddenly their lips met. Then they were wrapped around each other, and it all had gone downhill from there.

Of course, he knew she'd cried as she lay in his arms. He'd done a terrible thing and made her a part of something that changed their relationship forever. But then, she'd felt the same way about him, hadn't she? Both of them knew she'd never leave Phillip, and they could never have together what he wanted. Nevertheless, didn't she love him, too?

He remembered when she told him she was leaving for California. The office in 'Frisco had accepted her application for transfer, and the paperwork was all but complete. Phillip never asked why, and she'd never told him. Jon knew why. It was the best thing for them both, she'd said, and Jon knew it to be true, even though it tore his heart out.

Neither of them could afford the consequences of being together any longer. They would get over each other, move on. And so she did. But Jon Daniels couldn't move on. Even after she was gone, he found himself going to their favorite coffee shop on Lexington, just to sit and think about her while he watched the traffic go by outside.

It was after Christmas that next year that he heard about the accident out west. The Burgesses were traveling for the holidays, and while going through Oregon, the car spun out in an icy patch and went through a guardrail, falling fifty feet before crashing into a grove of trees. Just like that, the entire family was gone. Jon was shocked. He refused to go to the funeral. It was almost a year before he stopped choking up whenever he thought of her.

Then Alli turned up again, impossibly, in another woman's body. In a way, he had her back, even if just for a moment. In a way, he was glad to have another chance at being with her. In another way, she reminded him that he was the same flaming train wreck of emotions he'd always been.

Now that he thought about it, this person wasn't Alicia at all, even though she was using Alli's personality and even some of her memories. She was becoming someone entirely new through all this. For one thing, Jon couldn't remember Alli being quite this feisty.

Maybe he should be glad. Maybe it was finally time to let Alli go. *Let her go? Hell, she never was yours to let go of, from the beginning. Dammit, Jon, you wrecked something precious, didn't you? You could still have had her for a friend. She would never have transferred. She's dead because of you.*

Tears rose in the corners of his eyes and he had to pull over to the shoulder of the road to let it all out. He let his mind reach out and touch her memory one last time, the bittersweet night in Chicago when she was his, only for the briefest blink of an eye. "God, Baby, I'm so sorry," he cried.

Jon was so wrapped up in his grief he never heard the approach of the helicopter echoing off the sides of the cliffs. When it zoomed over the Hummer, he jumped. He rubbed his eyes clear and looked out his windshield as it swooped up and swung around, a huge dragonfly buzzing back down the roadbed cut through the badlands. His heart slammed inside his chest like a hammer as he jerked the Hummer into gear and took off.

The helicopter zoomed over and came at him again, the rotor blades seeming to come within inches of the cliff on his right. Lower and lower it came. A burst of gunfire erupted from the right side. Jon caught the image of a man leaning out the side door with an automatic weapon. The stream of bullets from the fusillade struck the pavement in front of him as he swung the Hummer closer to the base of the cliff. He goosed the accelerator, looking for some way off the road as the chopper slipped by overhead. Glancing to his left, he saw only a drop-off to the bottom of a rocky chasm. The cliff base on his right rolled up in a sheer climb of fifty feet and more. There was nowhere to go.

A movement in his rearview mirror told him the helicopter was coming back again. He could hear the roar of the rotors as it swooped down yet once more, heard the shots from the gunner in the side door as pieces of asphalt pinged off the side of his vehicle. On he raced, swerving and dodging in the narrow track of roadway.

There, on the right, an opening! The cliff wall dropped down to a low, sloping berm about five feet high. Jon stomped on the brake, swung the wheel to the right, and then back left, counter-steering to control the sideways skid. Then he goosed the pedal hard, heading up over the bank and off into the Badlands. He hoped he could lose his pursuers in a canyon or draw. He took the first turn he came to and led the chase up into the hills as fast as he could drive. The chopper stayed with him all the way. Bullets panged off the rock wall next to the Hummer, spraying chips against the passenger side of the vehicle. Jon stayed as close to the wall as he could, trying to limit the helicopter's avenues of approach.

He ducked into a narrow canyon just as it flew by yet another time. The Hummer went over the rim of the canyon at over fifty miles per hour, sailing out and down the slope. It landed hard halfway down and bounced twice, nearly toppling before settling back in, driving between the stone walls of the Wyoming Badlands. He had to slow down to negotiate the larger rocks strewn about the sandy floor.

The helicopter passed overhead again, but instead of homing directly in on him like before, it passed as a blur across the top of the canyon several hundred meters in front of him.

The stone walls closed in yet again, and the canyon became a ravine with overhanging cliffs on both sides that often overlapped above the Hummer, obscuring Jon's view of the sky.

He doubled back under one of the deeper overhangs and stopped the vehicle. His hands shook as he waited with his window rolled down, straining to hear the sound of the rotors. He heard the chopper pass over twice more, each pass farther away until it faded into silence.

Jon got out and opened the back door. He reached into the back seat and pulled out his weapons, strapping on the pistol and loading magazines for the carbine. He carefully loaded and checked each before scurrying farther back under cover of the rocky overhang.

The air was thin at that altitude, and his breathing was labored as he tried to calm his pounding heart. He waited several more minutes, hearing nothing but the wind blowing down the ravine, so he rose and walked out to the edge of the shadows, ears straining.

A small sound came from above and a pebble dropped into the sand under the edge of the overhang. He looked up as he approached the edge of the shadow, and that was when he heard a small *pop* from his left. He

202

snapped his head around just as the sting in his neck registered in his mind, and he saw the man holding the small rifle advance toward him.

Jon tried to bring the carbine to bear, but it was too heavy to lift. He dropped it and reached for the pistol, but his arm seemed weighed down by an immense burden. His fingers fumbled with the holster, but kept missing the clasp. Images in his vision began to dance in erratic, shifting patterns and he fell. Blackness swarmed over his mind as he heard a man talking and an answer crackled back on a radio.

* * * *

When Jon opened his eyes again, he was strapped to a gurney in a helicopter. The metallic, copper taste of adrenaline mixed with the salty warm flavor of blood in his mouth. He must have hit the ground pretty hard when he fell. His abdomen felt like someone had worked him over with a baseball bat. He tried to move his arms but they were strapped down, too. He heard voices above the beat of the helicopter's blades and the whine of the turbine engine, but could understand nothing. He tried to speak. A needle slipped into his neck, and a warm, sluggish feeling washed over his brain. He heard someone say, "Dude, like you didn't have to zap him again, he's tied down." The light began to fade.

Nadia, don't let them take you. The blackness closed back around him.

Chapter Fifty-Six

With all the stops, layovers and transfers, the bus trip from Denver to Klamath Falls, Oregon took almost two days.

Nadia climbed down from the bus amid the rumble of idling diesel engines echoing from every structure around, and walked in small circles on the parking ramp, stretching her legs.

The driver descended from the huge vehicle and opened the luggage doors on the lower side of the bus. Nadia waited while he sorted through the bags in the hold, tossing the ones whose journeys ended here on the ground behind him. She bent down to pick up her bag and a cramp shot through her back. She was sore from sitting, and road-weary. She hadn't slept for three days now, and felt like she would fall over. Although she was almost at the end of her journey, she would find one more night's rest before her final steps. She had to go into this with an alert mind, even if she would never do another thing again.

She looked in her fanny pack for what money she had left. Just enough for a hotel, laundromat, and a couple of meals. She would make a point of enjoying those.

Out in the streets of Klamath Falls, she began to remember things from her recent past. She'd come by this place on her way to the airport the last time she'd been in town. She recognized that hardware store by its name.

She breathed deep of the keen mountain air. Stark peaks rose above the tree lines on slopes all around the valley that cradled the sleepy little town. The main street cut straight through town, flanked by mom-and-pop stores and diners, interspersed with a few branch stores and franchises of more familiar, national brands. Here and there along the thoroughfare stood a small tavern or inn where small groups of adults congregated in the early autumn evening. There were few buildings taller than five stories, most notably a couple of banks, a sprinkling of apartment buildings, and a hospital.

Now if she could only remember how to get back to Twin Oaks. It had been almost two years since she was last here, and then only briefly. She walked along the main drag until she found a small motel next to a diner on the north end of town, and checked in. Although she was tired to the bone, she went next door and had a huge order of biscuits and gravy before turning in. Somehow, a full stomach helped her feel better about what she had to do.

While she prepared for a shower, her mind began to wander over her short life. She felt badly about leaving Jon behind, but he would never understand why she had to do this. He'd try to stop her, she knew. But why? She could never get him to admit that he'd loved Alicia, although he'd come close a few times. Nadia still wasn't sure if he'd said that he loved her. Then again, she'd never told Jon she loved him, either. It would be just as wrong now as it had been in Chicago.

For one thing, was it Nadia Velasquez or Alicia Burgess who loved Jon Daniels this way? Could it have been both? It was hard to say. She just knew that she loved him, but couldn't be with him. She wanted more nights like in Virginia, to be in his arms, held and loved. At the same time, she was a danger to herself and to anyone near to her, and there was nothing she could do about it, no way to disarm the weapon inside her.

She adjusted the shower and climbed in, washing off the grime from the road and cherishing the feel of the warm water as it massaged her skin. Nadia sighed, thinking of the warmth of his body, the feel, and smell of him. They had gone as far as they could, and now it was over. Too bad she couldn't convince her heart. She didn't want to leave with anything unfinished like this, but it couldn't be helped, not now or ever. The only thing she could do was give herself one last, good cry to say goodbye. And so, she did.

When the hot water started to run out, she finished her shower and climbed into bed. Her mind still raced with what had to be done tomorrow. The lab that made her could be, at that very moment, making more like her. They had to be stopped. Jon was trying, and although it had gotten them as far as Denver, they couldn't hope to do it within the bounds of the legal system. The people behind her creation were too stealthy, too powerful, to let that happen. So now, it was up to her.

Lying in bed, she steeled herself to what had to be. She would become what they made her to be. She remembered reading something in that bible she'd picked up in Denver: "For whatsoever ye sow, that ye shall reap." Someone had a helluva crop coming due, and it was harvest time. She closed her eyes, she supposed for the last time, and drifted into an uneasy, exhausted sleep.

* * * *

The next morning was overcast. Rain was in the offing, and the breeze wafting through the valley picked up into a stiff wind by nine o'clock. Nadia made her way to the little diner after checking out, and ordered steak and eggs with coffee, sharing the morning rush with the loggers and miners of the morning shifts. She savored every last bite of breakfast and let the waitress fill her cup four times before she laid her money on the table and grabbed her bag.

The waitress reminded her of Phoebe. Nadia tipped her with the last of her cash, and on the way out found herself wondering how Phoebe was doing. She thought back to the brief conversation they'd shared. Phoebe had said something about it being a shame that a clone could have no hope of anything to look forward to after its death. *Phoebe, you missed it. I'm already dead.*

The first time she came into town, the day she left the resort, there was a road with an unusual name. What was it? *Lunks...no, it was Hank's Lumber Road. That was it!* After asking for directions at one of the stores downtown, she was on her way. Stopping at a waste bin on the way out of town, Nadia fished around in her duffel bag until she found a gray fleece hoodie and slipped it on against the rising wind. She took one other item from the bag, the little bible from the hotel nightstand in Denver, and tucked it in her pocket. Then she picked up the duffel and stuffed it into the bin, one less load to slow her down.

She walked north out of town on Hank's Lumber Road, skirting the upper lake on a narrow, winding road that led up into the mountains around Klamath Falls. She breathed deeply of the mountain air, refreshing her lungs as she stepped out, hands jammed in her pockets. The aroma was clean, the air rich with life. She heard birds in the trees all around. A bear snorted and shuffled across the road ahead, hardly giving her a second glance. A gentle rain began to fall, and it wasn't long before Nadia began to feel the chill in her bones.

As she walked along, she wondered if the people who lived here appreciated the beauty that surrounded them. She wondered if they woke up and simply went on with their lives, not living each day to its fullest. How many people never heard the birdsongs in the trees, never saw the sky painted with so many beautifully sad shades of watercolor gray? They would call this dismal. They would write today off as dreary and depressing, and never bother to look out their windows to see the beautiful, clear raindrops gathering like a million tiny, silver-gilt diamonds on the leaves of the trees all around them. They wouldn't bother to smell the clean scent of the air, feel the coolness in their lungs. How many never really tasted the food they ate, or smelled the scent of the morning air in the mountains? How many people never really felt the other people in their lives, never appreciated the love that could be theirs? Deaf, numb, and blind, they existed only to exist. She took an extra deep breath of cool, moist air and felt it cleanse her being. *Breathing. They could start by being thankful they could breathe, and enjoy every breath because it meant one more that they could take.* How many more breaths would she be able to call hers?

Here, even so close to the end, she was thankful. Thankful for the few real friends with whom she'd shared time and laughs, thankful for this short time that she'd been given. At least she'd known friendship; she'd known love.

A car came by the other way, headed for town, throwing a fine mist from its tires as it passed. Nadia was so lost in her own thoughts she never heard it turn around and pull up behind her. She jumped when a familiar voice rang in her ears, and she started to run, but held up short when she heard a desperate shout. "No, Nadia! Please don't run away!"

Nadia turned around. Becca Mitchell was out of her car running toward her. Nadia held her ground. She stood on the shoulder and waited as Becca approached.

Becca stopped a few paces away and held her arms out, breathless. "Please, let me talk with you. Just you and me, and no one else, okay?"

"*Now* you want to talk?"

Becca's face was tight, her voice confused: "I've always wanted to talk. Nothing's changed."

"Everything's changed, Dr. Mitchell! I'm not who I thought I was, and you're a part of this whole mess. Why should I trust you?"

"I'm sorry, Nadia. Look, I'm just as confused about all this as you are. I want to understand. Will you help me?"

Nadia looked into Becca's eyes. Either Becca Mitchell was a better liar than Nadia ever dreamed, or she was dumber than a box of rocks.

She remembered when this whole mess began to blow up. Becca was anything but stupid. She was also the worst liar in history. That left only one other option, and that was the most frightening of the three. She followed the doctor back to her car and slid into the passenger's seat.

The car was warm and dry. The windshield wipers beat a gentle cadence as Becca put the car in gear and pulled out onto the road. The women spoke little as Becca headed down the highway toward town. "So you decided to come home after all?"

"After a fashion," Nadia mumbled, shivering in spite of the warmth from the car's heater. The rain had soaked her clean through to the skin, and she was losing body heat. Becca seemed to notice, for she reached over and turned the heater up to full so Nadia could warm her hands. "I know what I am now." She looked at Becca, waiting for some kind of response. She got none. "I'd like to know why."

"Why what?"

"Why did you make me like this? Why am I a bomb?"

Becca brought the car to a stop on the shoulder. "What are you talking about?"

"You people made me and put another woman in my head. And you put a bomb inside me. I was sent to kill the president of Iran. I want to know why."

"Are you okay, dear?" asked Becca. "You're talking strangely now—"

"Stop it, Becca! You were there when I came alive, on that first day! You were lying to me along with all the rest of them!"

"What are you talking about?" Becca's eyes were wide, and her face paled.

"You all told me I was caught in an assassination! You told me about all those surgeries—"

"Dr. Hamund said you needed care—"

"Who was Alicia Burgess, Becca?"

Becca slumped in her seat and looked straight ahead. Her trembling hands clamped to the wheel, her knuckles white from the tension. "Mrs. Burgess was an accident victim." She looked down at her feet. "You were in a persistent vegetative state after you came back from Nigeria—" Nadia lashed out and slapped her across the face. Becca stared at her, eyes wide, slack-jawed with shock. "Wh-why—?"

"Quit lying, Becca." Nadia brought her hand up again.

"Please," Becca cried, holding her hands up. "Why did you hit me? Please—"

"Tell me the truth! What really happened?"

"Please believe me, Nadia, I'm telling you all I know," Becca sobbed. "Please listen! Your brain was empty. You flat-lined six times on the plane —"

Nadia slapped her again, harder.

Becca held her hands out, pleading. "No! Please!"

"Tell me. Tell me everything, and don't lie to me again."

Becca gathered herself and wiped her eyes. While she continued, she watched Nadia out of one corner of her eye. "Dr. Hamund called me after your last surgery and told me how badly you were injured. He said they had a way to restore your higher brain functions so you could have a shot at a normal life."

"So where did Alicia Burgess come in?"

"Mrs. Burgess and her family were in an auto wreck on the mountain. She was the only one still alive when the ambulance arrived at Twin Oaks' trauma center, and she wasn't going to make it more than another hour or two—"

"What?" asked Nadia. Her head began to swim. She grabbed Becca's shoulders and clenched her fingers until Becca groaned in pain. "Who was killed?"

Becca's voice was tender, sympathetic. "The entire family, Nadia. Two adults and three children. No one survived...please...let go...."

"Deena, Wil, Maxie...." The names suddenly came to her from the shadows cloaking her mind.

She felt the familiar rush of dizziness, and she could almost hear them calling to her. The interior of Rebecca Mitchell's car faded, replaced by a darkness that wasn't quite total. She felt snow falling on her face, heard a child crying pitifully in the near distance. She was broken, a rag doll cast rudely aside. She was helpless to go, unable to rise. Her babies were dying, and there was nothing she could do.

The dark scene faded. Nadia's mind came back into the car. It was daylight again, but the loss of that night still throbbed in her heart; the rush of dizziness lingered.

She let go of Becca's shoulders. "Phil…." She felt a lump rise in her throat. It hit, harder than ever before: her children, her husband, all gone. She felt the confines of the car; the rush hit her mind in a silent wave of chaos. *No!* she scolded herself, *Hang on, you can't lose it now.* She looked at Becca, and through the fog clouding her mind she could see the doctor sitting in her seat, watching. A tentative hand reached out. Nadia grabbed at it and missed as her vision closed to a tunnel. *Deena. Wil. Max. Gone.*

The rush left Nadia's head, and she felt coherent again, but light-headed. She became aware of Becca speaking in low, soothing tones. "I said, 'Are you all right,' Nadia?" Nadia felt Becca's hand on her shoulder, and she felt hot tears on her cheeks. "Do you need a doctor…?"

"No!" snapped Nadia, "I do not need a doctor." She took a deep, hard breath, trying to clear her head more. A lingering malaise remained, but all else was clear. She fought off the wave of grief and despair over her children. "Becca, tell me all you can. Please, it's important."

"Drs. Hamund and Spielberg recorded the Burgess woman's brain and saved her personality," continued Becca. "They told me they could save you if they could transfer the data into your brain. I told them it would be too traumatic for you to retain any memories of that previous life and still be Nadia Velasquez. They assured me that long-term memory wasn't an issue. They wanted me to make sure you were stable, as Nadia Velasquez and not Alicia Burgess. All we wanted was to give you your life back. We tried, Nadia. We all tried to do what was best for you."

"Is that all they told you?" Nadia watched Becca's eyes, looking for signs of a lie, any untruth.

Becca looked back and there were tears in her eyes. Her left cheek bore angry, red welts. Her hair was a mess. And, her eyes were still sincere. "That's all, Nadia, I swear to God. That's all I know. I tried, honey, I'm so sorry I failed you."

Nadia looked around the inside of the car. Becca jumped in fear as Nadia's hand shot out and ripped the rearview mirror from the inside of the windshield. Nadia slammed it on the dashboard three times before it broke. Digging a shard out with a fingernail, she brandished it before her face.

Becca drew back, terrified, and reached for the door handle. Before she could get the door open, Nadia brought up her other hand and stabbed herself in the palm with the broken piece of mirror. As she held her hand up, palm out to Becca, white blood began to pour from the wound while Becca stared in horror. "They forgot to tell you something, didn't they?" said Nadia.

Rebecca Mitchell slumped back in her seat, eyes rolled up.

When she came back around, Nadia was holding her head in her lap, crying softly to herself. "I thought I could handle this, Becca. I thought I could get through this as long as I could say I was saving my babies. I wanted to save something of Alicia's, to do something for her in turn for what she gave me. But I can't."

Nadia sighed and leaned back in her seat with Becca's head still in her lap, gently stroking her temples as she listened to the rain falling on the roof. A log truck rolled by, throwing spray against the car, and it rocked with the draft. "I can't. It's my turn to apologize, Becca." She helped Becca sit back up. "I thought you knew."

"I don't know what to say," mumbled Becca. "This is so weird."

"You don't know the half of it."

"So, what are you, really?"

"I'm the reason President Bello is dead," said Nadia. She explained what she saw on the video file Bunny stole from KBGX.

Becca said nothing until she finished. "What are you doing back here?"

Nadia looked out the window again. *Why is it so hard to say?* The decision had been made; she thought it was set in her mind. Only an hour before she would easily have blurted out her purpose, but now it wasn't quite as clear as it had been. It wasn't as if there was any other way. She watched the rain fall and said nothing.

"Nadia, can you explain?"

Nadia shook her head. "I wish I could, but I haven't quite caught up with it myself."

Becca pulled the car back out onto the road. "Hold that thought, honey, I want to know some more about this. Let's go back to my place and you can get some dry clothes on, okay?"

Chapter Fifty-Seven

Donna paced back and forth in the small office, knitting her fingers. "Bunny, try to get some of these people connected somehow. All I see is a mish-mash of names that don't have any connection, other that the fact they were there at one time or another." They hadn't heard from Nadia or Jon in three days and they had no idea what was going on. Howard and Charles were expecting results and she simply had none to give. What good was a secure server when there was no communication to be secured? She began to feel like this whole mess was over her head. The trouble was, besides Bunny Kalinsky and Irving Ratzinger, she simply couldn't trust anyone.

She'd seen both Howard Standish's and Charles Gutenberg's names on billing lists from Twin Oaks Resort, along with fifty or more names of powerful and influential people, movie stars, and industrialists. Try as they might, though, a list of directors or administrators of the resort itself was elusive. The spa had no website; no advertisements appeared in the media. It was as though the place didn't even exist, apart from occasional vague references in the AMA listings. Only twelve doctors were listed as being on staff there, and none of those had a stated specialty in genetics or cloning research.

Bunny was scouring the billing center, trying to find another network connection when Donna stopped him. "Wait a minute. Look at that TV station's network again, the one she worked for."

"We gotta be careful there, Doc," said Bunny, grabbing another Twinkie and stuffing it nervously into his mouth. "We're messin' with bad juju here," he muffled around the mouthful of cake. "I think they know I was there."

"All the more reason to go back in. You said that they have an excellent watchdog program. They're hiding a lot more than one video of a woman blowing up. Do you have the equipment to do it?"

"Yeah, but I'm slower these days. I still have trouble typing. I can't feel my fingertips real good yet."

"Can you use the same route you used before?"

"Maybe, maybe not. Depends on if they found out how I got in before."

"Bunny, we have to start somewhere. So far the only way in seems to be through that station's system. Dig around some and see what you can find. If you get caught, back out as quickly as you can and we'll take things from there, okay?"

"Well, okay, Doc, it's your show." He began to type again. "What do we do once we're in?"

"We follow the money," Donna said.

"Okay, Boss Lady. But don't go blamin' me if they come along and pull our plugs."

Chapter Fifty-Eight

Jon woke up with a screaming headache and a taste in his mouth as if he'd eaten cobwebs for breakfast. He couldn't count how many times they'd drugged him on the way to...wherever this was. His body felt like he'd been dragged backward through a knothole.

It was dark. He lay on a thin mattress, on a hard, flat surface of some sort. He tried to rise and found he was strapped down.

He heard an odd, distant noise: a keening thrum, pulsating rapidly in a pitch almost above his hearing. Then he noticed another noise, an approaching thump-thump accompanied by the squeak of rubber on tile, and a door opened close by. Light spilled in through the open door, momentarily silhouetting a single figure. Area lights came on. He blinked in the bright light, taking in the green tile walls, medical equipment scattered about, and the huge swing-arm light over what he now knew to be an operating table.

Standing just inside the door was a woman supported on a pair of crutches. She was petite, about the same height and size as Nadia, only more curvaceous, with a rounder face and a small, delicate nose that turned up just a bit at the end. A pink cast on her left leg stretched from just above her knee down to her toes. She wore jeans with one leg cut off for the cast, and a Grateful Dead T-shirt. Her hair was straight and chestnut-colored, cut just off her shoulders and flipped under, and Jon could see in spite of his grogginess that she was very eye-catching. He had a strange feeling he'd seen her before, but couldn't quite place where.

She hobbled up to the table on which he was restrained and smiled down at him. "Hi. Glad to see you're awake. Steven's going to want to know."

"Who's Steven?" he croaked.

"I'll let him handle his own introduction. Want some water?" He nodded, and she hobbled over to a table-tray in a corner where she filled a Styrofoam cup from a pitcher and stuck a straw into it. She brought it back over with some difficulty and stuck the end of the straw in Jon's mouth. "It's okay, it's just ice water. Slow, now, okay? Not too much at once or you'll get sick." He sipped carefully and released the straw. "Other than thirsty, how are you feeling?"

"Like I've been worked over, drugged, and kidnapped."

"Yeah," she said, "Sorry about that." To Jon, she sounded sincere. He wasn't sure exactly how to take that.

"Who are you?"

"I'm Jenna." A playful smile appeared on her face. She leaned close to him and whispered conspiratorially, "I'm the carrot." She kissed him, flush on the mouth, a long, lingering kiss that ended in a gentle, teasing nibble on his lower lip. His brain screamed for him not to enjoy it, but his hormones simply were not listening. A subtle raspberry flavor lingered on his lips and her sensual, musky scent remained in his nostrils.

Jenna straightened back up and smiled again, giving him a wink just before she turned away. "Nice to meet you, Jon. Let me know if I can do anything more for you. Or even if you just want to talk." The door slid closed behind her and she disappeared, leaving the lights on.

"God, I am officially in trouble," said Jon to the empty room.

Some time later, the door opened again and a man entered, a huge, blonde young man in his twenties with savage, Nordic features. He drew a stool from a corner by some anesthetic equipment and parked it next to Jon. "Hi, Jon. I'm Steven. I see you've already met Jenna."

"Yeah," muttered Jon. "The carrot. So who's the stick?"

Steven smiled. "Hopefully, there won't be one. It's important that we have a talk, Jon. We seem to have a mutual friend, and she could be in some serious trouble even as we speak. Now, her welfare is of grave international concern. Do you know what I mean, Jon?"

So, this was it: "good-cop-bad-cop," only without the cops. Well, he may as well see how far they were willing to go. "If you mean that the world is safer without her in your hands, I believe I do."

Before Jon could flinch, Steven's fist shot out, and he heard a sharp *crack* against his jaw, right at the hinge. The pain made Jon moan in spite of himself.

"Respect is a big thing for me, Jon. We have to respect each other if this is going to go well."

Steven got up and left, coming back with a camcorder and a tripod. In a trice, he had the system set up and a small, red indicator came on over the lens of the camcorder. Steven then came back to his stool and sat down. Jon could see that Steven sat so the camcorder would have a constant, clear shot at the operating table. "Okay," he said into the lens, "this is Jon Daniels, Take One." He turned to Jon and asked, "Jon, where is Nadia Velasquez?"

Jon turned his head away from the camera. "I don't know." He felt another punch, this time to the back of his head. His head rolled sharply from the blow, and the bones in his neck popped.

"Jon, turning away like that is surely disrespectful, and I can't stand disrespect. Now, look at me. Good. Thank you. Now tell me, where is Nadia Velasquez?"

"I don't know. She left me in Colorado and I haven't seen her since."

Steven dug into his pockets and pulled out a pair of black, leather gloves. "Who hacked the server at KBGX?"

"I don't know."

Steven shook his head as he pulled the gloves on, meticulously adjusting the fit. "Jon, that was not the answer I was expecting." He stood up and hit a button on the camcorder. The red light extinguished and Steven turned back around and set himself.

The beating was bad, worse than anything Jon had ever experienced. Steven knew where and how to hit to cause maximum pain effect. He stayed away from Jon's face, but he worked everything else over thoroughly and, after what seemed an eternity, he backed off and removed the gloves. Panting, he sat down. "Now, that didn't need to happen, did it?"

Jon said nothing. He hovered on the edge of consciousness. He was barely aware of Steven walking out and closing the door behind him as he left.

Chapter Fifty-Nine

Nadia had coffee at Becca's house outside of Klamath Falls. Becca's living room had no furniture, just several dozen large, comfortable cushions arranged neatly around the room. Becca sat in a casual, lotus-style position, leaning up against a wall while Nadia lounged against a stack of cushions, holding her coffee cup on her stomach. Her cut hand sported a fresh, figure-eight dressing.

"So what would make you come back here?" asked Becca.

"Are you officially in psychiatrist mode?"

Becca's mouth turned up into an amused smile. "Which 'mode' would you prefer, Nadia?"

"I think I'd prefer a friend who can keep a secret."

Becca took another sip of coffee and smiled. "I think I can handle that."

Nadia explained everything she'd found out, from the memory flash in the grocery store to meeting Jon, to the fire and the fight at the cabin. She left out the details about her personal relationship with Jon. Becca asked few questions while the story was being told, and several minutes of silence followed after Nadia concluded her account with their reunion on the mountain.

Becca warmed their cups from an insulated carafe. "So what *did* you hope to accomplish by coming back here?"

"Nobody else should go through this. No person should be treated as less than human."

"But you're not human, are you?"

"My body may not be human, but my mind—"

"Is a recorded copy of a dead woman's personality," interrupted Becca, firmly but not unkindly.

"But I'm alive, Becca!" Nadia sat up, her eyes burning with passion. "I'm alive, I have feelings, I feel…." Her voice failed. She swallowed back a lump in her throat. "I am. I know…." Tears burned in her eyes.

Becca leaned back against her cushion and recited, "'I think, therefore I am.'"

"Huh?"

"René Descartes. He was a French philosopher. Short story: If I can have thought, if I can experience, then I exist. Okay, you exist. But are you truly alive? The biologist would say that, because by design you are incapable of reproducing, because you were actually fabricated rather than born naturally, then technically you can't be *alive*. You're a machine, a recording."

Anger rose in Nadia's breast. "I could care less what some jackass, cold-hearted scientist would say. I know better. Recording or not, I still *am*."

"But what part of you is Nadia, or Alicia? Obviously you are you, but *who* are you?"

"Hey, I'm not your run-of-the-mill schizoid, here." Nadia dried her cheek with the back of her hand. "I am *me*." She patted her chest with her open palm. "That's all I want to be."

"The woman or the weapon? What do you *want* to be?"

"What I want doesn't seem to matter. I was made to be a weapon, so I guess that's what I am."

"I'm asking you who you want to be, not what you are. You don't seem to see that you have a choice."

"No, Becca, I don't. I can't just decide not to be a bomb. All the thinking and wishing in the world isn't going to make me not explode if I'm triggered. I can't be a real woman, not for…." Nadia's voice faded, leaving the thought unfinished. She looked off somewhere distant, beyond the little room.

Becca swirled her coffee cup a few times before she spoke. "For what? Or better yet, for whom? For Jon?"

Nadia tensed. Her gaze snapped back to Becca and for just a moment, she wanted to cross the room and bash that smug face in. How *dare* she! How could she *know*? Then, she saw the look in Becca's eyes, that look Becca always got whenever she knew Nadia was hiding something from her. The anger subsided. Or was it shame that she felt? What she had with Jon was real, wasn't it? Was it so wrong to love him?

Nadia slumped and set her cup on the carpet. "Dammit, I hate when you do that."

"Do what?"

"Look right through people. I *hate* when you do that."

"So do I, sometimes." Becca took another sip. "So what was your plan? You *did* have a plan once you got into the facility, didn't you?"

"I was going to find Petr Hamund and make sure that he couldn't ever do this to another person."

Becca waited. Nadia said nothing more. Becca took a deep breath and let it go before speaking. "Were you going to kill yourself, Nadia?"

"I'm already dead, aren't I? I mean, if I'm not *alive*—"

"So can you kill someone who's already dead?"

"They were going to kill me, weren't they? Me and a lot of other innocent people, too," said Nadia, feeling her anger rise again.

"So you were going to kill yourself, then?"

"What do you think, Doctor? Did you think I was going to let them—"

"Were you going to kill yourself?"

"Why do you keep asking me that?"

"Because you keep refusing to answer it. Were you going to—"

"Yes! Yes, dammit! I'm going to go in there and kill myself! Is that what you wanted to hear? I'm going to find out how to set myself off, and go in there and kill them all!"

"Why?" Becca sat in her lotus position, her expression unreadable.

"Because there's nothing left for me to do! I can't be what I want to be, so I may as well be what they made me! But I'm damned well going to see to it they don't ever get a chance to do it again!"

"But what *do* you want to be?"

"Will you quit asking me that?"

"No, not until you give me the answer. What do you want to be?"

"Somebody besides me!" A fresh swell of tears blurred her vision.

"But what do you *want* to be?"

"I want to be left alone!"

"Okay." Becca took another sip of coffee. "But what do you *want* to *be*?"

"Alive! I want to be alive!" She slumped back against the pile of cushions and sobbed. "I just want to be *alive*—"

"Good," said Becca, "you're alive. Then live." She set down her cup and got up from the floor, crossed to where Nadia lay weeping and fell to her knees. Taking Nadia's head in her arms, she rocked slowly back and forth, stroking her hair and holding her close to her breast. "You're alive, honey," she whispered. "My God, Petr, what have we done?"

Chapter Sixty

"Gotcha, you knuckle-draggin' ape!" shouted Bunny.

"What is it?" Donna jumped from her stupor and almost knocked over the cot. She had grown drowsy while Bunny tapped at keys for what seemed hours. She heard an occasional slurp as he mouthed his can of soda, and now and then a wicked little chuckle came from his throat and he muttered at the computer. Bunny turned away from the screen and grinned at her. He was wearing a T-shirt that said "LOG OFF" in huge letters across the front.

"I finally tamed the dragon," Bunny announced, triumphant. "I was able to create my own password and access key so I can get in anytime I want. Better yet, their IS department won't even know I exist. In effect, I now *own* them!" He spun around in his chair, pointing at the screen. "Who's da man now, ya gutter-crawlin' maggots!"

She rubbed her eyes the rest of the way open. "Okay, Bunny, let's get back to work. I want to know the top leadership of that television station— their affiliations, charitable donations, which bathrooms they use, everything, okay? And I want it by tomorrow. Jon's and Nadia's lives may depend on it."

"Hey, give me two hours and I'll give you the world, doll." Bunny, resumed his frenetic tapping. "Stinkin' fingers…shoot me, ya helium-suckin' crab-sniffers, I come back on you like a bowl of bad chili."

"Hey, Doc," he said suddenly. "You get the report on her karyotype?"

"How does a computer hack know about karyotypes?"

Bunny shrugged. "Hey, a guy picks up a thing or two here and there. Anyway, did you get it?"

"Well, yes, as a matter of fact I did see it. Weird."

"Yes, and…?"

"A human karyotype would have twenty-three pairs laid out in order, with the X chromosome for females or Y chromosome for males at the far right. Nadia has four hundred and seventy-three pairs of chromosomes, with six Y chromosomes."

"Whoa, baby! Are you sure they ran the test right?"

"My assistant ran it three times. We only have so much material to work with, you know. Holli was pretty freaked out."

"So how'd you cover that up?" asked Bunny.

"I haven't, yet. I have to come up with a good lie."

"Maybe you could say you got a friend who's a marine biologist. There's some pretty ganky stuff swimmin' around down there no one's ever seen yet."

"Good idea, Bunny." Donna brightened. "That should work just fine. Thank you."

"Hey, Doc," said Bunny after another few minutes of tapping. "You ever hear of the Global Unification Alliance?"

"The what?" Donna leaned forward, looking over his shoulder.

"The big guys at the network give a wagon load of money to the Global Unification Alliance every month. Look at these figures."

Donna couldn't whistle; she'd never learned. And even if she could have, the numbers that she saw would have made it impossible to do so. "Bunny, see if these people have a website. No, wait. Check those names again and see which clients at the Twin Oaks Resort are members or contributors to the Global Unification Alliance. I have to make a phone call."

Chapter Sixty-One

"Are you sure you want to do this? You don't have to," said Nadia as they pulled off the side of the road a couple of miles from the main gate.

Becca slapped the Volvo into park and looked directly at Nadia. "We all have choices, Nadia. This is my choice. I want to help you end this peacefully. Besides, someone has to make sure you don't do something stupid."

"Don't you think we're already doing something stupid?"

"Good point. Let's go, before I chicken out." Becca got out and opened the trunk for Nadia, who crawled in and situated herself around the spare tire. Then Becca slammed the lid and got back in, started the engine and pulled back onto the road.

She flashed her pass card at the gate guard, who motioned her through with a casual wave, then found a parking space under an ancient red oak tree. Its spreading branches were heavy laden with flame-red leaves that blocked the camera in the corner of the lot from seeing the car. She got out and looked both ways before opening the trunk. "My heart feels like it's going to explode," she whispered as the two women made their way to the nearest entrance to the Twin Oaks Medical and Trauma Center.

Both of them wore business suits. Nadia was smaller than Becca, so she had to pin up the hems on her borrowed slacks and blouse. They hid the looseness of the clothes under one of Becca's lab coats, and Nadia's curly blonde hair was hidden beneath a scarf wrapped around her head in the style of a Muslim woman.

Once inside, they strode past the reception desk and made it to the elevators without anyone questioning their presence. Becca pressed the button for the fifth floor, and the doors slid shut. They picked up another doctor on the second floor. On the fourth floor, the doors opened again. And there was Red Hicks.

He stepped in and greeted Becca, barely glancing at the other doctor in the elevator. But when his eyes met Nadia's, she could tell it was pointless to try and fake her way out of this. He said nothing, but recognition was there. She felt her face flush, and her chest felt thick with fear. She could only imagine what was going through Becca's head right now. When the doors opened on Floor Five, the other doctor walked out, but Red called Nadia and Becca aside. "Doctors, a word with you, please?" He indicated an empty office just off to the side. His other hand clutched something in his pocket. What could they do?

He steered them through the door, coming in behind them. As soon as Nadia heard the door close, she spun around, throwing a backfist at his midsection, but Red jumped clear. She followed up with a jab to his face, and his hand flew from his pocket, dropping the pistol he'd been holding.

Red bounced off the door before landing on his feet, and brought his hands up quick enough to block her next punch. He grabbed her wrist and held it against his body, trying to spin back around and break her arm, but she brought up a knee to block his spin and hit him in the side of the head twice with her free hand. He let go and sidestepped out of range, knocking Becca to the floor.

Nadia tried to get to the door, but Red stepped back over to block her and threw a series of roundhouses and jabs that she had to work frantically to block. She finally saw an opening and aimed a kick at his torso, which he easily evaded. She backed off and shucked out of the lab coat, then took a ready stance. If she couldn't end this quickly, things would not go well.

"This time, I'm ready, Blondie," Red said, stepping in with another series of jabs at her body and face. A couple of blows got through her blocks and she felt a smashing blow to her midsection and one to the side of her head that sent lights flashing in her brain. She gave ground as Red chased her across the office, and she soon found her back against the desk.

Red planted a foot and spun a haymaker of a kick at her head. She ducked under it and rolled away to her right.

Coming out of the roll, she kicked herself into a standing position just as Red came at her again. This time, however, she knew what he was going to do. When the first punch came, she caught his wrist in a lock and kicked him three times in the side of his head. He dropped and rolled away to clear his head, but when he came up a floor lamp met him halfway. It knocked him sideways against the desk, and Nadia heard a sharp, sickening *crack* as his neck snapped. He hit the floor and lay still, his head dangling at an awkward angle. Becca stood, panting, the lamp still in her shaking hands.

She put the dented lamp-stand back down on the floor and crouched over him to check his pulse.

Nadia grabbed her arm and tugged. "Let's get him into the closet, over here. We've no time, now."

"My God, Nadia, I think he's dead," said Becca, horrified.

"Believe me, it was either him or us." Nadia helped her friend pack Red's body in the coat closet and close the door. Then she led Becca back out into the hall.

Chapter Sixty-Two

The closet was cramped. Even though the louvers allowed plenty of air and a limited view of Petr Hamund's office, Nadia felt like she was suffocating. She could just see where Becca Mitchell sat waiting in the chair in front of his desk. Although she sat quietly, Nadia knew that Becca must be just as terrified as she was.

Precisely at five-oh-five PM, the door opened, and Petr Hamund walked through. He stopped for a moment, his mouth open in surprise. "Why, good evening, Dr. Mitchell. How are you today?"

"Just fine, thank you."

He walked around his desk, removed his lab coat, and hung it on a corner coat rack before sitting down. Nadia caught a whiff of his cologne as he passed by her hiding place behind his desk. The great leather-upholstered chair creaked as his weight settled in. "You look distressed. Would you care for some water?"

"No, thank you, Petr."

There was an uncomfortable silence. Petr poured himself a glass from a pitcher on the desk and sipped. "So what brings you here to grace my office today?"

Becca stared down at her lap. "Petr, tell me about Nadia Velasquez."

Petr's voice brightened, as though he was hearing news of an old friend. "What about Nadia? Have you heard from her, then?"

In the closet, Nadia fought back the urge to leap out and strangle him. The rich baritone that used to comfort her as a patient, now repulsed her.

Becca gazed straight into Petr's eyes. "Tell me again how it was that she came to be here."

"You know full well, Doctor," said Petr. "There was an assassination attempt in Nigeria while she was interviewing President Bello. We barely were able to keep her alive to get her here, but her brain was damaged so. Your help in her adjustment was greatly appreciated."

"But what happened, Petr? Why would she go off the grid like this?"

"The mysteries of the human mind. Who can fathom them completely?" He threw up his hands. "Ach, Doctor Mitchell, that would be your area of expertise, and not mine."

"She said she found out some things about herself."

"So you have heard from her, then? Where is she? Is she all right?"

"She's all right. And I heard from her, earlier today. She's…different, now."

"Yes, I suppose wandering about the country on one's own has a way of revealing one's character—"

Becca's eyes raised, looking square at Dr. Hamund's. "Petr, is Nadia Velasquez an artificial person?"

Petr heaved a sigh and leaned back in his chair. If he was surprised, he didn't show it. "How did you come across that bit of information?

Becca said nothing. She didn't have to. Nadia opened the closet door and stepped out. Dr. Hamund turned around at the sound, and she saw the recognition on his face: recognition and a touch of fear. "Hello, Dr. Hamund. Let's talk, shall we?"

Petr's hands dropped to his lap. His expression returned to the same old, friendly grin that Nadia first knew. "Nadia, where have you been? We've all been so worried—"

Nadia walked around the desk, keeping her eye on him. "Knock it off, Doctor. If you were worried, it was only because you might have been found out. Well, you have. And I have some questions."

"Please ask them, my dear."

Nadia stood behind Becca, her arms crossed. "Let's start with where I really came from. What am I?"

Petr leaned back in his chair and looked steadily at the women for several seconds before he spoke. "Nadia, have you ever heard of the term 'transhuman'? No, I thought not." He spoke as though he were speaking of Plato to a litter of puppies. "A transhuman transcends evolution through technology. One example, as pitiful as it is, would be a bionic person, enhanced with technological advancements that would give them an edge, so to speak, either in speed, or strength, or in data-gathering and processing capability.

"You have no such primitive work-arounds. You are a totally new and special being, created to be the next step in human evolution. You, my dear, are a marvelous instrument of world peace…." He grinned in a way that Nadia did not like. "And a work of art, if I may say so myself. My masterpiece."

"Peace?" snorted Nadia. "What peace? You put a bomb inside me."

Hamund held up his hand, shaking his head. "No, my dear. The weapon is not inside you. The weapon *is* you."

Nadia came closer to the doctor's desk. "What exactly is that supposed to mean?"

"Do you know why we named you?" He was beaming, waiting for her to ask.

"I'm listening."

"NADIA is what you are—Nano-triggered, Antimatter, Demolition / Interdiction Apparatus. And," he added, "It was my beautiful first wife's name. She was the donor of your original DNA."

"Willing?" asked Nadia. "Or did you kill her to get it?"

Petr laughed easily, shook his head, and gave a supercilious shrug. "Would it have made a difference? Now, if you please, I have a question for you. What is it that you want?"

"Leave Jon Daniels alone."

"Who is this?"

"Jon Daniels, the…." Nadia's voice caught. *If I tell him Jon's a federal agent, Petr will never let him live.* "The man I was traveling with. Leave him alone. And leave me alone."

Petr's face might just as well have been carved from granite. He remained silent, his eyes boring holes in Nadia's very being. She felt her will dissolve, like a sparrow before a snake. The anger melted away, and all she had left was fear. Fear for herself, fear for Jon. If only she could make sure Jon was safe. "I won't go to the police, I won't tell anyone. Please, Petr. Just let us be and I promise no one will ever find out about me."

"I wonder how you could possibly keep that promise, NADIA." There was no longer any pretense of friendship, or of caring. Petr still spoke politely, but his voice was as flat and cold as a shark. "Ladies, I think we need another associate present before our discussion continues. May I?" he asked, reaching for his phone.

But the move was a distraction. While the women watched his left hand reach for the phone, his right came up suddenly from behind the desk with a pistol, and before either woman could react, he pointed it at Becca Mitchell's head and fired.

A weak *cough* and a tiny spout of flame erupted from the muzzle, and Becca's head snapped backward, spraying blood into the air as she fell. Nadia dove at Petr, but wasn't quick enough. The silenced pistol swung toward her and coughed again, twice. She felt the bullets smash into her midsection, knocking her aside as Petr stood and backed away. Nadia fell to the floor, gasping for breath. She landed on her side and pain shot through her body.

She saw Becca lying on the floor next to her, blood pouring from a hole in her face. Her eyes glassed over as Nadia watched, unable to move.

Nadia's vision closed around her. She couldn't seem to take a breath. In her mind, she was screaming Becca's name, but all that came out was a whisper. She coughed, and white blood sprayed from her mouth onto the carpet. Stars blinked in and out in her eyes as she tried to stand. All she could manage to do was twitch an ankle. Nadia heard Petr call for a trauma team as she faded back into the darkness.

Chapter Sixty-Three

Jon woke to the sound of the door opening. Jenna entered the room in a wheelchair similar to ones seen in shopping centers. Affixed across the front was a small basket containing a covered tray and fresh water pitcher. The door slid shut behind her and she wheeled herself over to the table.

"Hi," she said quietly, almost shy, which Jon found odd after their first meeting. "Jon, I'm so sorry. I didn't know he was going to do that."

Jon turned his face back up to the ceiling. "Yeah, I'm sure."

She wheeled closer, her eyes moist with tears. "Please, believe me. I don't want to see you get hurt anymore; you've been hurt enough."

Jon stared at the ceiling and said nothing.

"You need to move around to prevent thrombosis, so I'm going to let you up for a while. You have to promise me you won't try to get out, okay?"

Jon made no pretense of hiding his bitterness. He wasn't going to fall for this act; he himself was better at it than most. "Oh, gee, why should I do that?"

"Because you haven't heard the whole story behind Nadia. You don't know the good she could do for all of us, for the whole world. Please just give us some time and listen. I promise you, I'll report Steven and he'll be dealt with. But for your own good, just stay here and eat some dinner. I'll stay with you and we can talk."

Jon thought about waiting until the restraints were off, and then knocking her down and running for it, but he thought twice about that. It was plain they weren't going to let him get out of here alive if he did try to escape. It was a pretty sure bet they weren't going to let him out of here alive at all. His conscience nagged him about the thought of knocking over a person in a wheelchair. *But if I have to do it to get out of here....* But would these people be stupid enough to send her in here without having some side of beef with a machine pistol stand guard outside? *Probably not.*

He also knew the right time had to present itself. He knew nothing about being a prisoner, but he had plenty of experience in interviews, and if he went along with them, he could keep from being beaten to death while he waited for his opportunity to escape. Maybe he could also milk some information out of them and get something he could use in court without having Nadia come into the equation. Then he could get out and contact the bureau.

He could only imagine what would happen to Nadia if the government got hold of her. Her life wouldn't be worth a plug nickel. There was no way they could let her live and feel safe about it. "Okay, Jenna. I'll stay here."

He could hear the smile in her voice. "Great! I hope you're not a vegetarian, because I ordered roast beef for you."

She kept making small talk while she undid the straps and helped Jon sit up. His limbs ached at first and he had to shake some life back into them after being restrained for...how long was it? Hours? Days? He didn't know. Jenna invited him to sit in a chair. He sat down and pulled the tray table closer.

Working from the wheelchair, Jenna got some bandages, alcohol, and antiseptic ointment from a roll-around tool chest in a corner of the room while he ate, and arranged the supplies on a metal tray. When he finished, she treated his cuts, cleaning them carefully and applying the antibiotic. Then she applied dressings and tape as necessary. "There," she said as she washed her hands. "Not too shabby, if I say so myself. How was dinner?"

"Not too bad. How about we talk about Nadia for a while? You said I don't know the whole story."

"I don't think I can explain it to you in a way you could understand."

He narrowed his eyes. "Try me."

She rolled her eyes and sighed, then leaned back in her chair. "Okay. Try to understand. You know how dependent the United States is on foreign oil? Have you ever wondered why Congress won't let the oil companies drill more on U.S. soil?"

"I always thought it was the environmentalist movement blocking construction or drilling."

"Well, yes, that's part of it. But don't you think that someone with enough pull or enough money could bypass the environmentalists and make the drilling happen anyway?"

Jon sat silent, listening carefully. Maybe this was going somewhere after all. He let her continue.

"We need to stay dependent on foreign oil, because it's such a precious commodity. It's one way we try to keep peace. By helping countries depend on one another, we begin to realize that the countries *need* each other, and that makes them more eager to seek peace."

"So someone wants the world to be dependent for a critical commodity on a group of nations who want the rest of us dead?"

"We're working on that angle, Jon. We're working on leadership in troubled areas right now, and those attitudes will change, with a little patience and some hard work."

"Patience, hard work, and the threat of annihilation?" asked Jon pointedly.

She frowned, and it sounded to Jon like she was sincerely disappointed. "I knew you wouldn't understand." She stood on her good leg and moistened a cotton ball with alcohol. "It looks like I missed a cut, there…."

"Look, Jenna, I'm trying to understand, I really am. But you keep talking about peace, all the while your organization builds living bombs and sends them out to murder innocent people, and throw foreign governments into chaos. You kidnap federal agents and hold them against their will…ow!" He grimaced as she applied the alcohol to a cut on his head. Either this cut was worse than the others, or she was deliberately rough.

"Sorry," she said quickly, "But I did warn you first." She was leaning over while she applied skin glue to the cut. Her scent wafted into Jon's nostrils; sweet, subtle, and very feminine. She wore a green, low-cut top that showed off her curves. In any other situation, she would have been irresistible. As it was, Jon had to force himself not to look down her top. She caught him once, and a mischievous grin crossed her face for only an instant.

She finished with a satisfied grunt and sat back in her wheelchair. "Okay, now, can I try again?"

"I wish you would."

"No governments are being 'thrown into chaos.' We're working within the bounds of each nation's constitutions and laws to affect change where it's needed. We're a group dedicated to peace, not war."

"So why assassinate President Bello?"

"That wasn't my call. I don't get told everything. But it had to be done to fit the Plan."

"What 'Plan'?"

"World peace, Jon. That's what it's all about, and that's all we want. Most people talk about peace, and that's as far as it goes— just talk. Well, we're actually doing something about it. We're working through diplomatic and economic channels to bring it about. Only when those means fail is the decision made to go farther."

"You mean assassination?"

"I mean rearranging leadership. Now get up. I have some exercises for you, to prevent thrombosis." She backed up the wheelchair to give him room.

Jon stood, slowed by the ache from bruised and stiff muscles. "So I'm to be brainwashed? Is that why you're telling me all this?"

"I said I just wanted you to understand a little more of the big picture. Let's start with stretches." She gave him some instructions and he ran through some stretches and calisthenics. "We need you to tell us who else knows about Nadia, Jon. She has to stay a secret. There are international implications at stake that none of us could possibly fathom. Do you really want to see the kind of arms race she would start?"

"If I tell you who else knows, my life, Nadia's life, and how many more are forfeit? I understand you have a job, Jenna, and you're obviously sincere. But have you considered the possibility that somehow you've been misguided?"

Jenna crossed her arms defensively. "I know what side my bread's buttered on, Jon. I'm doing the right thing. Are you?"

She led him through a couple more stretching exercises, and then motioned at the operating table. "It's time for me to go. I'm sorry, but I need you to lie back down on the table."

"And what if I don't want to be tied back up?"

"Let's just say you'd rather I do it than someone else. Besides," she added with a sly grin, "you never know; it could be fun."

233

"I could just walk right past you, you know."

"Jon, for one thing you'd never make the door. I'm not as helpless as I seem. Why do you think I don't have anyone else here with me? For another, you don't know your way around here. You'd be lost, wandering the halls of the place, and end up in more trouble than you bargained for. Getting out of the building unescorted isn't something I'd bet on, either. So please, just get on the table for me."

"Let me help you clean up first." He sauntered over to the tray table and replaced the lid over the plate, keeping his body between her and what he was doing. He picked up the tray and placed it in the basket on the front of her wheelchair. He took a step toward the table, then switched and dashed for the door.

He never saw how she did it, but she got the chair tangled up in his legs, and they both spilled onto the floor amid dirty dishes and spinning wheels. He tried to get up, but Jenna was around him from the back with her arms and her good leg before he could get into position to rise, clapping a hold on him that constricted his breathing almost to the point of cutting it off completely.

"Okay, then," he rasped through the chokehold. "I think I'll lie down for a while."

"This is all a joke to you, isn't it?" Jenna growled into his ear as he continued to wheeze. "Do you have any idea of the number of lives at stake if we fail? Do you?" She let go and rolled Jon away from her with a shove. He choked a couple times, trying to get air into his lungs.

When she spoke again, she was smiling in a friendly manner. "Get my chair back on its wheels, please?"

Jon stood, shaking, and did as he was asked. The light in the room looked dim. Or was his brain still starving for oxygen? He helped Jenna up and back into her chair. "Sorry," he whispered through his aching throat. "I had to try."

"I understand." Jenna settled herself in the chair. "Now...." She motioned to the table again.

As Jon got up onto the table, he noted that she didn't look even winded from the scuffle. Nevertheless, she wore an expression that betrayed the pain in her broken leg. He lay down and let her refasten the straps and restraints that held him down. "But," he added as she finished, "what if I have to…you know…?"

"I think you know how to use this," she said, tossing a urinal onto the table so it landed between his knees. With no further word, Jenna turned the chair and wheeled herself back out of the room. The door closed and all was silent.

Jon lay still until he knew she was out of earshot. Looking around, he scanned the corners and walls for any cameras. He almost felt bad about tackling her, but man, she was *quick!* He hoped no one else would hear that he'd just had his butt handed to him by a girl with broken leg in a wheelchair. He'd never live that one down.

Deciding that the coast was clear, he worked the fingers of his right hand up under his buttocks and pulled out what he'd managed to sneak away with during the scuffle. He turned the dinner knife around and began to work on the strap. He wished it were a steak knife, but at least it had serrations on one section of the blade. It would work for what it was needed, as long as they gave him some time.

Chapter Sixty-Four

The car's rear end swung wide around the turn in the road, but Phillip recovered easily and slowed down as he apologized. "Sorry about that, hon, I didn't see the ice there. Now, the resort is supposed to be just over the next ridge. We should be there in another ten minutes."

She consulted the map with a penlight to confirm Phillip's claim. That was when they felt the bang from the rear, and the minivan went into a spin. She caught a glimpse of the guardrail just before the van flipped over it and into the air. The kids were screaming, terrified, as the van went tumbling down the embankment.

There was a sickening crunch the first time they hit, and she found herself flying through the air, away from the van and her family. She bounced and rolled, hit against a tree and felt her spine snap like a string of pearls. Her wind left her in a rush and she could no longer breathe. However, she could still hear the horrible crash of the minivan's last collision with the mountainside. In the silence that followed, she could still hear her baby, a weak bawl, fading away into silence. She tried to get up, but couldn't move anything other than her eyelids. The snow was still falling. Flakes settled on her face and melted, mingling with her tears. The sky, the trees, the mountain, all faded away....

Nadia woke up lying on her back. The mountain was gone. She was somewhere soft and warm, and she heard someone crying, a soul mourning an unbearable loss. A second later, she realized that it was she. She felt the hot tracks of her tears as they made their mournful way down the sides of her head to the pillow, where they faded away, leaving only the moist little memories of her sadness. *My babies. Oh, God.*

She opened her eyes on a view she never hoped to see again. It was the inside of a hospital room. The equipment buzzed, hummed, beeped, and ticked all around her again in its familiar singsong rhythm. It was silent otherwise; there was no one else nearby. She took in the sight of all the equipment, the tubes and wires that were attached once again to her body. This was the same windowless room she awoke in, the day she first opened her eyes.

The right side of her torso was afire with pain. Nadia tried to move but found herself unable to do more than flex her arms and bring her left knee up. With a grunt, she grabbed the side rail of the bed and tried to sit up. A restraint jacket held her down. Nadia flopped back in the bed, perspiring and panting from her futile effort.

She remembered the last thing she saw: Becca's face as she lay dying next to her in Petr Hamund's office. "Becca," she cried, and her chest heaved with sobs. The pain in her side flared with every breath. "Becca!"

A voice from the doorway startled her. "I'm sorry, my dear. We did all we could, but Dr. Mitchell didn't make it." Nadia knew the voice. She didn't have to look at him to know exactly who was speaking. Her grief was momentarily displaced by a cold, horrible anger.

"You bastard. You killed her," she croaked through dry lips.

"No, Nadia. You did." The mirth she remembered was gone now, the accented lilt replaced by a somber, matter-of-fact drone. "If you hadn't told her, she would still be alive."

"You murdered her." The effort of just talking was taking a lot out of her. Every breath wracked her body with burning pain. "Why did you save me?"

"Because, Nadia, you are critical to us. You are an important part of world history. Besides, if you expire, your stabilizers shut down and you go critical."

"My…what…?"

"You must not have figured that part out. It's all quite technical, but I believe you can understand. You are a system, an antimatter weapon. You have forty-eight grams of pure antimatter locked in stasis in your skeleton. It is held in a metastable state called Positronium by nanobotic power conversion. There's up to two megatons' yield if it gets released at once."

"N-Nigeria—" she started, but a spasm stopped her before she could go on.

"Yes, Nigeria. No doubt, it was you or someone you know who accessed the original file. That was your predecessor, Nadia. That model was only capable of about five hundred tons' yield. You, my dear, are the ultimate peacemaker."

"B-but…" She struggled with every word, trying to communicate through the wall of pain. "But I was born…Texas—"

"Oh, yes, that," he said, as if someone had just reminded him to pick up milk. "That young lady was…borrowed, just for you. Anyone who would interview a national leader would have to go through a thorough background check, you see. When the unfortunate Miss Velasquez died on her way out to California, it was an opportunity we could not pass up, saving her name like that. All we had to do was fix a few minor details in the public record."

He must have noticed the level of discomfort she was in, for he paused and stared at her for a few seconds. "I can see you need some rest, now. I have something for your pain." He reached into his pocket and produced a syringe, which he uncapped and plunged into a plug in one of the lines inserted into her hand. A few seconds later she felt a cold, burning sensation work its way up her arm, and she fell back into the darkness from whence she came.

Chapter Sixty-Five

Donna sat in Howard Standish's office, watching silently as he leafed through the pages of her latest report. He paused here and there, letting out a low whistle as he took in what he was reading. Finally, he put the pile back in its envelope, stamped it "FOR EYES ONLY" and "TOP SECRET" and placed it in a safe sitting in a corner of the office. He came back and sat down, taking a drink of water before he spoke. "Are you sure the karyotype was accurate?"

"I double-checked it myself, Howard. She's probably loaded with so many engineering adjustments and work-arounds, it takes that many chromosomes just to make her work."

"What about the other nanobot types in her blood?"

Donna consulted the file. "It looks like she has a different immune system than we do, a completely different mechanism for fighting biological threats. She may very well be immune to bio-warfare agents that would kill a human."

"Could these nanobots be inserted in a human to make him or her immune to these agents, too?"

"Probably not. Her body manufactures them the same way that ours make white blood cells and other immune system components. It's hard to say whether the nanobots would survive in a human system, or even work in a way that would benefit a human. For all we know, they would attack any human system they were introduced into, and kill it."

Howard leaned forward, knitting his fingers on the desktop. "Donna? Have we collected anything that could be used in court on these people yet? Whatever your team brings to the surface has to be admissible evidence or I can't know about it."

Donna took another sip of her coffee. "I wish I could say yes, Howard, but right now all we have is what my team has managed to glean on its own, and you don't want to know about it, trust me."

"I already know more than I want to. Keep working and get us something we can use. I want these people, and I want them before another world leader has an 'interview.'"

Donna put the medical file back into her briefcase. "Has anything turned up on the two dead suspects?"

Howard heaved a sigh and leaned back in his chair. "Nothing we could define as a common point of interest."

"What about any ties to an organization called the Global Unification Alliance?"

"The what?"

"The Global Unification Alliance. It seems to be some type of benevolent organization on the surface, but it ties together some names with possible connections to this situation."

Howard did a quick Google search, and a minute later, the site came up. His brows knitted as he read the home page contents. "Sounds like one of those 'one-world-village, Kumbaya' type groups started by a bunch of ex-hippies who listened to John Lennon one too many times. Why would they be interested in political assassinations and ultra-tech, living weapons systems?"

"Just gathering data right now," said Donna. "But if these two men have a connection with the GUA, this group could lead us to the Pinnacle."

Howard teepeed his hands in front of his face and wrinkled his brow in silent thought for several seconds. "I think you could be right. I'll assign it to Edwards and Shields. Give me the list you have and they'll gather more information on the names."

"Howard, with all due respect, I have a man who can find out more on those people in ten minutes than Bill Edwards could in ten years, and Jack Shields couldn't even do a background check on himself. Plus, if any of our targets finds out they're being looked at too closely, the whole operation may go underground even further and we won't hear about them again until the next antimatter bomb goes off."

"Very well, then, Doctor Hermsen. What's next?"

"I'm going to take a couple of weeks away from the lab. I have some items I want to follow up on."

"Fine. I'll pass this information on to Vice President Gutenberg. Just keep me in the loop." Howard stood, indicating the meeting was over, and Donna left.

Her mind continued to race all the way down to the lab area. She had to check in with Holli Hushido, the tech who ran the karyotype on Nadia's blood. Four hundred and seventy-three pairs of chromosomes! Six X chromosomes? So was Nadia male or female? *God, what a stupid question. You saw for yourself she's neither—she just looks female. More importantly, what makes the weapon work? What makes her go off? How can she be made inert, if at all?*

Holli was waiting for her when she got to her office. She looked ready to explode with excitement as Donna entered. "Donna, this is incredible! Where did you say the plasma sample came from?"

Donna always liked Holli. She was one of the most colorful characters in the lab, and one of the most intelligent young women with whom Donna had had the pleasure to work. Today she was wearing neon blue and pink striped hose, matching blouse, and a short black skirt probably fashioned after one of her favorite anime characters. Her short black hair sprayed out in twenty or thirty pink-painted, manga-styled spikes. However, right now, if there was one thing Donna didn't like about this little Japanese ball of pure energy, it was her explosive curiosity. Donna had to remember the lie she'd told her before and hope it would satisfy Holli enough to get her to just shut up and go back to work.

"Woods Hole," Donna said. "It's from a marine specimen."

"Come on, Donna." Holli stepped a little closer, a hopeful grin splayed on her face. She held up a folder and waved it in front of her for emphasis. "This is something from a land-based creature." She held her other hand up, her index finger hovering over her thumb. "Something *this close* to human, but not quite. You can tell me." Her voice lowered conspiratorially, even though it was only the two of them in the office. "You've found Bigfoot haven't you?"

Donna almost fainted with relief. The less anyone knew about Nadia, the better she liked it. The last thing she needed to hear was that Holli was trying to decode the DNA sequence from the blood sample. "Well, you got me, Holli. We have a sasquatch hidden in the evidence room." She hoped that would end it. It didn't.

"Really? Can I see it? Is it dead? I have to see it! This is *so* cool!"

"No more sugar for you, Hushi," said Donna, using her nickname. "And no, you can't see it. It's in cold storage." She changed the subject, hoping she could keep Hushi sidetracked long enough to get away without having to answer any more uncomfortable questions. "What do you have on Case 022?"

"Oh, that," said Hushi, deflated. "The DNA on the bedspread doesn't match the guy they're holding in Vegas. It's from a white guy with diabetes."

"Is there any evidence of more DNA in the room that could match the subject in Vegas?"

"All I can vouch for is that I've analyzed every sample that was submitted, and none of them match this guy."

"Hushi, you're something else. Why don't you call Vegas and let them know? I'll let you have the whole case, okay?"

"Awesome!" squealed Holli, "Do I get my own desk?"

"As soon as I can order you one. Now get on the phone, okay? We have to let an innocent man off the hook."

Holli flew out of the office and Donna sighed. Keeping this on the low-down wasn't going to be easy at all.

Chapter Sixty-Six

The light came on, and in the few seconds it took for Jon's eyes to adjust, Steven charged across the floor and cuffed him across the mouth. Stars popped into his vision, and the room did flip-flops.

Steven's voice betrayed an undercurrent of anger. "Trust is another thing we value around here, Jon. She trusted you not to bolt, buddy."

It took all he had for Jon to hold his tongue. He'd have to wait and bide his time. This was critical.

Steven set up the camera and turned it on, then pulled the stool up and sat next to Jon's head. He spoke first to the camera. "This is Jon Daniels, Take Number Two." Then he turned to Jon. "I'd like to pick up where we left off, Jon. Who hacked the server at the station?"

Jon worked a cramp in his jaw loose. "It doesn't matter. Your people killed him."

"Oh? How was he killed?"

"It was a Barrett fifty-cal." Jon stared at the ceiling. He kept an eye on Steven, watching for any sudden movements.

Steven leaned back, nodded, and pursed his lips with his arms across his chest. "Well, it looks like we're getting somewhere, Jon." He even smiled. Jon wanted to rip that smile from Steven's face with his teeth. "I sense respect and trust. That means a lot to me. I'd like to know his name, please."

Jon choked up with grief and rage for the little man who'd helped him. "Kalinsky. It was Bunny Kalinsky." *And it's my fault. He's dead because I dragged him into this.*

Steven seemed to read his mind. "You know, Jon, he's dead because of you. You said our people killed him. How do you know this?"

"He was killed by the same gun that killed my uncle." *Uncle Mike, this is gonna be for you.*

"And what happened to the 'people,' Jon?" Steven scooted just a little closer. Jon waited. He was only going to get one good shot. The timing had to be right. "How did you know it was a Barrett, and not a Browning?"

"I didn't know Browning made a sniper rifle."

"What happened to the sniper, Jon?"

"I don't know."

"Jon, I'm beginning to feel a little less respect," said Steven as he pulled his leather gloves from his pocket.

"I'm telling you, I don't know. You have to believe me!" Jon gripped the edge of the table, as if getting ready for the blow. Steven pulled the first glove on, adjusting each finger meticulously.

Jon waited until Steven had his attention on the second glove and knew the time had come. He let go of the table edge, slipped his hand through the cut strap and slammed his fist into Steven's head, knocking him off the stool. He then swung his legs over and sprung up off the table.

Steven rolled away toward the door. Jon charged him before he could get up and kicked at his head. Steven grabbed Jon's foot and shoved. Jon bounced off the huge man and Steven came up at him, wrapping his arms around him, and hoisting him up and back. They slammed into the wall and Jon's wind left him for a moment, enough for Steven to start working at Jon's face with his fists. Jon put up his arms in a boxer's cover and managed to block a couple of the haymakers the bigger man threw, but enough blows got through to rock Jon's head and body like a hailstorm of cinder blocks. In desperation, he stepped up and threw his knee into Steven's groin.

Steven backed off, groaning, and Jon waded in, throwing punch after punch into Steven's midsection and head. Style and technique were out the window now; this was sheer survival.

Something smashed into the side of Jon's head and stars glimmered in his vision. He caught a glimpse of the operating lamp swinging past from Steven's hand as he flew back over the table and crashed onto the floor.

Steven was on top of him in a flash, his hands around Jon's throat. Jon kicked futilely at the air and pulled with both hands, but Steven was stronger and the grip only tightened, cutting off Jon's air. His lungs burned. His vision began to fade, and he knew he wouldn't last much longer unless.... He grabbed Steven's right pinkie finger with both hands and bent it back until he heard the *snap* of bone. Steven howled and pulled back. Jon clocked him in the ear, and the big man rolled away, holding his head.

Jon rolled over and lashed out with his feet, landing three hard kicks before struggling to his feet. Steven started up also, but Jon found an IV stand, grabbed it, and swung it like a baseball bat. It caught Steven across his chest as he stood and he fell backward, crashed into a rolling tool chest and collapsed like a puppet. The tool chest toppled away, spilling bandages, syringes, and paper-wrapped suture kits all over.

Steven lay, heaving and trembling, in a bloody heap on the floor of the operating room. A dark red pool spread around his head. Jon heard a bubbling, gurgling sound coming from Steven's chest with each breath, and crimson bubbles formed at his lips. His mouth moved, but all he could get out were a couple of empty, wet grunts. A rib must have broken through one of his lungs.

Jon stood swaying and panting, and suddenly the strength left him. He collapsed into numb unconsciousness.

* * * *

When the room spun back into reality, he felt like he'd been hit by a truck and backed over a few times for good measure. Breathing was painful and stiff, but manageable. He struggled to his feet and looked around. There was a pool of coagulated blood on the floor where he'd lain.

Steven lay still in the middle of the floor. A wide blood trail led a few feet from the spot where he'd fallen. He must have crawled a few feet before he died.

Jon stooped and rifled through Steven's pockets, finding a wallet and keys. Dammit, those were *his* keys! His Hummer must be parked outside somewhere. He pocketed the keys and took the cash from the wallet. In Steven's left front pocket, Jon found a small black cylinder similar to a mini-flashlight. There was a charging port at the rear, and the lens was convex, capable of throwing an intense beam. Five small buttons lined up along the side, similar to the cipher lock on his Hummer. A sixth, red button was just behind the bezel of the light. When he pressed it, an intense series of bright strobes erupted out through the lens. Then he remembered: Nadia had told him Steven was her cameraman! This must be the triggering device that was used in Nigeria.

He finally had his case! Kidnapping and assault of a federal agent was just enough to crack into the case. This implement could…what? Without knowing what it was used on, so far all he had was kidnapping and assault.

Nigeria was one. Nadia was two. He was willing to bet there was at least one more living weapon under construction somewhere, if he could only find it. Right now, though, it was out of the question. He was in no shape to conduct a search. He just had to get out and return with a team and a search warrant to shut this place down for good. He searched Steven's body for anything he could use as a weapon and found only an empty shoulder holster. *Oh, well*. What he had would have to do.

A stab of pain in his nose made him wince. He put a hand to his face and pulled it away. It was covered in blood. A metal tray lay nearby, and he used it as a mirror. What he saw shocked him. Numerous cuts and bruises slashed his face. He had a split lip, and one eye was almost swollen shut. He dragged himself over to the crash cart and used what he could to stop the bleeding from his wounds. It was a clumsy but effective job, and took a lot out of him.

How much time did he have before Jenna came by and finished him off? He had no idea. After a short rest, Jon fought back to his feet and staggered through the door of the operating room into a long, dark hallway. There was no sound to betray any other living soul nearby. The only light shone from the room he had just left. There was an unfinished look about everything, as though this was not an area open to the public. Pipes and conduits ran the length of the ceiling as far as he could see, disappearing in both directions. He picked a direction and followed along the wall, leaning against it every few steps to rest. The rough cinder blocks felt cool to his hand.

His head throbbed with every heartbeat. His lips felt like inner tubes. He was sure he was missing at least one tooth, and his mouth was filled with the taste of blood. After ten yards or so, he had to stop to throw up. The pain from heaving nearly made him pass out again. This was not good. He'd never get far like this.

A high-pitched, pulsating hum irritated his ears. It seemed to come from everywhere, filling his head with a sick, cottony feeling.

He passed several wooden doors on both sides of the hall, all closed and locked. The smooth concrete floor under his feet echoed with every shuffling step he took. After reaching the end of the hall, he stopped and examined the wall. It looked blank in the dimness. The pipes and conduits disappeared beyond it. He started back up the hall toward the other end, but he stopped at a sound that came from the other side of the wall, footsteps of a person walking past. Then he noticed the dim glow underneath the wall and around where the pipes went through. That was when he saw the handle over on one side of the end wall, about halfway up. He took hold of it and turned, and the wall swung away on silent hinges. He limped through.

He found himself in a finished hallway. The lights were dimmed. It must be night. The tiles in the floor were inlaid with colored lines, each with a label indicting to which department it led. The red line read, "Emergency/Trauma;" the orange line read, "Laboratory." There were more, six in all. But Jon had seen enough to know he was in a hospital.

The door closed silently behind him. He heard the click too late to find something with which to block the latch, but at least he knew where it was. Moreover, it was nothing that would stop a police ram. The high-pitched, throbbing whine became more muffled as the door swung to, although it persisted in the background of the life-beat of the building.

A service door appeared in the gloom on his left, a garage-door affair with a man-door next to it. A deadbolt on the smaller door was the only security; no alarm would sound when he opened it, or so he hoped. He pushed it open. No sound other than the outside noise of the mountains at night reached his ears.

He found himself on a concrete loading dock illuminated by two security lights. A recent rain left the pavement slick and wet. The service drive led from the dock off into the night and disappeared around a corner of the brick hospital building. Scud clouds soared silently across the sky, making the moon wink intermittently down on Jon from its night-throne.

A broom leaned against the wall next to the door. Jon managed to unscrew the handle and, using it as a support, set off down the drive. The parking lot should be around the other side of the building. As long as he didn't run into any security personnel, he should be able to find a ride out of here and come back with a warrant. He pulled the keys from his pocket and clutched them in his fist.

The lot was sparsely populated with autos and SUV's of various makes, but there was only one Hummer, and Jon made his way to it, watching for any guards. As he pulled the driver's door open, the dome light revealed what he'd feared: they'd taken the guns and gear away. No matter, he had higher priorities right now.

The engine started with ease, and he put the Hummer in drive. Every turn of the steering wheel made lightning bolts of pain shoot across his chest, and the spasms that resulted nearly made him faint again. *Breathe, Jon— slow, easy breaths.* He drove down a one-lane road through thick mountain forest, and the lights of the hospital faded behind him as he made his escape.

A mile or so from the facility stood a guard shack next to a sliding chain-link gate. A light was on and Jon could see a lone, sleepy-eyed guard seated at a small desk. As he neared the gate, the man barely turned his head. His job was to keep people out, not in. At Jon's approach, the gate started to slide open. He was halfway through when the guard looked right at him. For an instant, there was no reaction. Then the confusion suddenly cleared as the guard saw Jon's face and the hastily applied dressings.

Jon goosed the accelerator as the guard slammed his hand down on a red button built into the desk and stood, unslinging his automatic rifle. Jon was already a hundred meters down the road before the first shots spanged off the Hummer's backside. A second burst shattered the rear window and the bullets flew like angry bees past Jon's head. Spiderweb cracks *spacked* across the windshield. Jon grabbed the broom handle and knocked the pieces out of his way. He kept the pedal floored even around the first turn and only slowed when the lights disappeared and the shooting stopped.

His pulse pounded in his head like a bass drum, and his vision narrowed to a tunnel. Shock was setting in. Jon was no medical expert, but he knew he was in bad shape. If he didn't get help soon, he might not make it off this mountain.

His vision closed farther. He heard gravel showering the bottom of the Hummer, but when he tried to hit the brake his leg refused to move. He didn't remember missing the turn, nor the first three times the Hummer rolled before it hit the water.

* * * *

Jon came to when icy water touched his head. He was upside down, held in place by his seat belt. The sound of rushing water surrounded him. Releasing the belt, he fell into the water coursing through the shattered passenger cabin. The driver's window was no longer in its place; he took a deep breath and ducked down, squeezing through the hole.

The current slammed him against a huge rock, knocking his wind from him with a whoosh. Coughing and gagging, he tried to reach his feet, but twice more he was swept away downstream, before he managed to crawl up onto a sand bar and collapse into unconsciousness.

Chapter Sixty-Seven

Nadia took another breath, grateful she still could. The flash of pain that shot through her side as she inhaled reminded her of what had put her back here, and she mourned again for Becca. If there was a better place, Becca would surely be there. She herself knew there could be no better place for her. Her only redemption could come from making sure that there could be no other of her kind.

She struggled feebly against the restraint jacket again, but a fresh twinge hit her and she sank back. There had to be a way out of here, some way to warn everyone else. She couldn't just give up and let them roll over her like they did everyone else who got in their way. And she wasn't going to just give up and die; if she was going down, she'd go down fighting with everything she had.

She reached across her body to feel the dressing over the wound, but her hand stopped short, held up by a strap. So, they restrained her arms as well. She could get her right hand to her side, if she strained. It was still tender, but the level of pain was more tolerable than before. When she moved her head, she felt resistance from several points. Her scalp itched, and she heard wires dragging across the pillow. She lay her head back down.

Aside from the humming of the equipment, the hospital was silent. There was no casual muttering of nurses and staff, none of the normal business of a medical center. There was, however, one sound that stood out from the background; a high-pitched, throbbing whine. She couldn't identify it or guess where it came from.

She was alone.

She was still in shock over the sudden violence displayed by Petr Hamund. She couldn't believe that the man who had poured so much concern into her own treatment and rehabilitation could shoot an associate to death with no remorse. *Then again, this is the same man who created a person in a laboratory, imbedded two megatons' explosive power into her bones, and sent her out to kill and die, unaware of the danger to herself.* For what reason? She may never find out.

The question now was what to do about it. She'd witnessed a murder. *Well, Jon, is this enough to open a case?*

Jon. Where was he? He must know she was here, but she couldn't count on him to come riding over the ridge on a white charger, especially after leaving him the way she did. She got herself into this mess; she would have to get herself out of it.

Petr (she couldn't bear to call him "doctor" anymore) had said she was critical, an important part of world history. What good was she to them now? She was positive she wouldn't willingly carry out her mission for them, whoever "them" was.

The door opened and the man she had so highly respected walked in, accompanied by Anna Spielberg. Nadia looked away in revulsion as they entered.

"Good day, Nadia." She met his cheerful greeting with stiff silence.

Petr pulled on a pair of exam gloves and stepped closer to the bed. *If that bastard so much as touches me again, I swear….*

"Dr. Spielberg, please check the placement of the probes before we begin. Are you sure we can salvage it?"

"We've never had to do this before, so I can't answer that," said Anna in a nervous voice. "If it goes wrong, we could lose her."

"As long as it remains stable, we shall be safe." He turned to Nadia. "My dear, we have to try something radical to save what we can of you."

"Save? Why?"

He seemed surprised that she should even ask such a question. "Why, so you can fulfill your purpose, of course. You know you're no good to anyone as long as you're corrupted. Dr. Spielberg will record your responses while we talk, and then try to find a way to fix your memory."

Nadia turned to look Petr in the eye. "Then you won't mind answering a few questions yourself, will you, Petr?"

Petr raised an eyebrow to Anna in silent consultation. She nodded, and he turned back to face Nadia. "I suppose that's a fair exchange. What would you like to know?"

"Who am I? Why was I made?"

Petr seemed to be waiting for someone to ask that question— as if it were a secret he had been dying to share. His voice brightened even more and his movements became animated as he answered. "You, my dear, are a product of cutting-edge cloning and genetic engineering technologies. I used some of my own Nadia's DNA to start with, and we refined the process to create cellular systems that could grow around a preconstructed frame.

"Your main systems are all based on the processes used by living organisms. We 'taught' proteins to grow in certain patterns, create organs and systems for you. We streamlined the process, of course, to leave out functions and systems unnecessary for your primary purpose. But, basically, you and your sisters were grown very carefully and wonderfully in our laboratory here."

"Sisters?" Nadia asked anxiously, "What sisters?"

"You are the fifth NADIA. Nigeria was the fourth. There were three others before her. But, for what it's worth, you are the best so far."

"So that's your hobby? Build girls and have them blow stuff up? Wow, Petr, you really need to get a life."

Petr's face wrinkled in rebuke. "No, no, you don't understand at all. You are part of a vision of global peace and unity."

Nadia tried to sit up, fighting against the restraint vest. She fell back as another painful spasm slashed her chest. "Peace? Peace through murder?"

"Peace through the lowering of walls. The fulfillment of a vision without conquest, without war. Do you know what a sniper does, Nadia?"

"Cold-blooded murder. Pure and simple."

He bent down close to her face. "No! *Not* murder! How many people died during the D-Day Invasions? Of course, you wouldn't know. I will answer you, Nadia. Nearly seven thousand Allied troops and the same in German boys and men killed. Over twenty thousand wounded. Twenty-four warships destroyed and sent to the bottom of the sea, where they still seep poisonous oil into the ocean's waters.

"Even more, the Battle of the Catalonian Fields left over three hundred thousand dead in one day's fighting. Three hundred thousand brothers, sons, and fathers whose blood turned a small stream into a raging torrent! Do you have any idea how many lives could have been saved if the leaders of those warring tribes would never have been able to send forth their killing machines? Do you?"

He sat on a nearby stool. His voice lowered, but he still spoke with a passion that told Nadia how much he believed what he was saying. "How does one negotiate with another Adolph Hitler or Josef Stalin? Can you stop Attila the Hun with words? They were evil, sick people, Nadia.

"Because of Attila's twisted mind, pyramids of human skulls twenty feet high adorned the fields surrounding smoking ruins that were peaceful cities weeks before. Because of Stalin's demented vision of peace, twenty-five million innocent people were dragged from their houses and their blood spilled in the streets as their families watched. Because of Adolph Hitler, six million Jews were gassed in the death camps and their bodies incinerated in ovens. And," he added, his eyes moist. "And I never got to see my father again. He was one of those Germans at the Atlantic wall who never came home to see his little boy grow up.

"This should never happen again!" Petr hissed. "Now, listen closely, Nadia. What if one soldier with a weapon could get close enough to stop Hitler from conquering Europe? Would it be murder to save six million lives at the cost of one?

"Let me tell you how Attila died, my dear. He had a drunken nosebleed on his wedding night and drowned in his own blood. He had married a Roman woman. His armies had raped, murdered, and pillaged their way down the Italian peninsula. This woman's people were his victims. Now, do you think maybe that nosebleed might have had a little help getting started? How many innocent lives were saved by one little nosebleed?

"Now, what do you think of the value of a sniper? The sniper's job is to save many lives at the cost of one. You, Nadia, are the ultimate sniper. You need no weapon. You *are* the weapon."

"Then why did you give me Alicia Burgess' mind?"

"Ah, that," he said, shaking a finger at nothing in particular. "In order to get a NADIA in its proper place, it has to appear as a real person. We grew the body, but the brain, the mind...alas! Man is no God. The first two units failed to become aware. The third was as an infant and never matured. NADIA IV was our first personality transfer, and our first successful NADIA.

"Dr. Spielberg perfected what William Bainbridge pioneered— Neurostructural Personality Transfer. She recorded the personality of a woman who was dying of cancer. The data was saved and downloaded into NADIA IV with great success. Nevertheless, we knew we could do better.

253

"Mrs. Burgess was dying when she came in here to the trauma center. There was nothing anyone could do to save her. So, just before the body expired, we recorded her complete personality and gave it to you. And so, in a way, she was saved, after all.

"Unfortunately, you received more than what was intended. I'm so sorry, NADIA, that you received all these horrible memories. You seemed so happy just to be yourself before you malfunctioned...."

"So I'm a mistake? Is that what you're saying?"

Anna, busy making adjustments and taking measurements behind Nadia's head, broke in. "Goodness no, dear, we just...." she stopped when Petr gave her a sharp look, and nodded at the console that was wired to Nadia's head.

Petr put on a pair of spectacles and consulted a chart before speaking. "Nadia, I want you to remember for me the first thing you said when you became aware. You asked about a man named...?" He stopped, leaving the answer blank.

"Phillip," Nadia whispered. She had involuntarily called up Phillip's face before her mind's eye, the blur of his memory a small comfort.

Anna said, "Got it." A beep registered in Nadia's ears, and a slick, warm feeling entered her mind, sliding subtly over Phillip's face like a slimy, black veil. It sank away into dimness and dissolved before her. She could no longer remember what she was thinking. "What happened?" she asked, sleepy.

Petr's voice seemed to be coming from the end of a long pipe. "Just a minor adjustment, Nadia. Who is Phillip?"

"I...I don't know who you're talking about. What are you doing to me?" Nadia didn't know why she was suddenly frightened. The slick, drowsy feeling in her mind persisted for several more seconds and then slowly faded.

"We're helping you come back to yourself. Now I want you to think of your mother, Alicia."

"What...." Nadia heard another beep, and that strange, wet tickle entered her brain again. "Stop...please...." She suddenly felt a terrible sensation of a loss, something that was very important, but was there no more. A very small part of her mind saw what was happening, but she found herself unable to resist. Her stomach felt heavy. Her scalp began to feel a burning sensation where the wires were attached.

Petr's voice echoed down the tube again. "How many children do you have, Alicia?" The tiny part of her mind that was aware screamed at her not to remember, but their faces hovered in her mind, only for seconds. The beep sounded again, and again.

"Wil?" she called distantly. "Willy, Mama's here…." Nadia saw little Wil Burgess flash in her memory as he slipped away, leaving a gaping hole in her mind and her heart. She began to weep bitterly. The slick feeling grew stronger in her head, and she was engulfed in a dizziness that nearly overshadowed the mysterious grief that wracked her body with heavy sobs. She couldn't remember why she was crying, but it was…someone important….

Petr persisted. "What about the others, Alicia? What other children?"

Nadia's mind was a buzz of static. Images in her mind began to scramble. Memories flooded over her in a hot, sickening rush, and she gagged. She could no longer see beyond the hallucinations that danced tauntingly before her, images that ranged from the merely bizarre to the obscene. She fought against the invasion of images, tried to keep her memories coherent. Murder scenes mixed with birthday parties; Roger Glass tumbled through the air at her wedding to Jon…*no, who*—

"Focus, Alicia!" Petr barked. "Focus on your children!"

Nadia's tongue grew sluggish. She tried to raise her arms, and came up against the restraints again. She couldn't break free. Something icy slithered up her arm; Petr had just put something in the IV. She felt too weak to move. A strange buzzing started in the muscles of her arms and legs. A wave of heat swept over her head.

She heard distant voices, desperate and terse. "Dammit, Petr, we have to stop, she's seizing." Nadia felt her body begin to stiffen and twitch. She tasted copper.

Peter called out, "Dilantin, quickly! Three hundred milligrams!"

"Channel Fourteen's triggering at a thousand microvolts! Oh, God…."

Becca sat cross-legged before Nadia, saying, "I think; I am God." Darkness opened its maw and swallowed Alicia Burgess/Nadia Velasquez in one hot, steaming gulp.

Chapter Sixty-Eight

The little underground room in the Shenandoah valley was getting more and more comfortable with each visit she paid to Irving Ratzinger's little cabin. A regular computer desk had replaced the wooden crate where Bunny's computer originally sat, and a comfortable, ultramodern office chair was parked at it. Bunny's bedroom was now down the hall, with a regular twin bed and dresser that he had managed to obtain somewhere.

Another room in the underground complex had been cleared out for Donna and now housed a small medical facility, thrown together from Mike Alverson's office in Front Royal and some items she'd liberated from her own lab in DC.

Bunny even had satellite TV and a game system. Whenever Donna pressed him, he always answered, "Don't worry, Doc, it's bought and paid for," and refused to elaborate any further. She noticed he had a new T-shirt that said, "RAM it."

At this particular moment, she sat in Bunny's office, in a recliner, the source of which she knew better than to ask. She knitted her fingers while Bunny typed and clicked furiously, trying to find some more information on a group of people who called themselves "The Pinnacle."

"Bunny, we have to do something! I feel so damned helpless."

"Don't sweat it, Doc. Jon got out of Burlington all right."

Donna sat up. A sickening dread rose in her abdomen. "What did you do? Wait, I don't think I want to know the answer to that. Just tell me if he's all right now."

"Have no idea, myself, Doc. I just know he left Burlington in a brand new Hummer. Hey," he said in response to Donna's sharp look, "It's just a matter of puttin' two an' two together."

Donna's eyes squinted in suspicion. "And just how did Jon manage to acquire a brand-new Hummer?"

"Maybe he came into an inheritance or somethin'. Look, Doc, you asked me to help. I helped."

"I didn't ask you to do anything illegal!"

Bunny turned in his chair, and through his thick eyeglasses, Donna saw a different look in his eyes from the first time she'd seen him. While he used to avoid eye contact when he spoke with someone, now he looked her straight in the eye, and he spoke with the passion of a man on a real mission. His voice was even, but held an edge of defiance. "Show me a law that says I can't give someone a little help."

"I could start with forgery."

"Sorry, I don't own a press."

"You know exactly what I'm talking about, Mr. Kalinsky! And deal or no deal, we aren't helping those two at all if you can't stay within the bounds of the law."

Bunny turned back to his keyboard. "Don't worry 'bout me, Doc. You'll never hear about anything illegal bein' done on this machine."

"Why is it that I don't find that especially reassuring?" Donna was beginning to wonder if turning him loose like she had wasn't a huge mistake. "Just keep the funding straight up and on the level, okay? We don't want to start another recession." She sat back, defeated for now, and watched as he pecked away.

When Bunny wasn't stuffing junk food into his mouth or swilling Mountain Dew, he was chewing gum, and she began to know him well enough by now to see that the faster he chewed, the more extreme the action. Right now, he was chewing so intently, she would have laughed if she weren't so frustrated. It had been almost a week since she'd heard anything from Jon, and all attempts to contact him via Mike's computer had been fruitless. The room was silent except for the buzzing of Bunny's fingers on the keyboard while she sat and fretted.

Irving brought a picnic basket and set it up on a small table in a corner of the office. In a trice, he hauled out two plates and loaded them down with brisket of venison, homemade stuffing, fresh-steamed vegetables, and honey rolls made from scratch. Donna was glad for the distraction and thanked him profusely. "Irving, you are so bad for my waistline, and I thank you."

"Okay," laughed the little man with the twinkling eyes. "Now, tell me something." His expression grew somber. "The time for secrets is past. I know Jonny's in trouble, and I can help."

Bunny stopped typing and looked around. Donna saw the look in the old man's eyes, and there was no doubt he believed what he said.

She stood and took her plate. "Let me take this upstairs and we'll talk, Irving. You're going to need a place to sit before I'm done. Bunny, give me a shout as soon as you find anything, okay?" Bunny nodded and parked his gum on the edge of his plate before shoveling a mouthful of venison into his mouth without looking away from the screen.

Donna followed Irving up the steps, and they had their dinner together in the kitchen. She explained what she knew, from the time she first came out to Mike's cabin up to when they lost contact with Jon.

He listened patiently, albeit with a shocked expression that remained long after she was finished speaking. His hand shook as he reached for his wine glass and took a deep swallow. That seemed to loosen his tongue. He muttered in German for several seconds, then sat silently with his head down and his eyes closed. Donna was going to say something, but when she saw his lips moving in silent prayer, she held her tongue. When he finished and looked up, he had tears in his eyes. And fear.

"A golem," he whispered. "They have built a golem."

"What's that?"

"In Jewish legend, a man is built from clay and a certain word is spoken to make him alive. A brute with no self-will or soul, a weapon at the command of its maker. When that word is spoken again, the golem dies and turns back into clay."

He slapped an angry hand down onto the table. "These people have created an abomination to God!" He stood and paced the room, a stream of German pouring from his mouth so fast, Donna couldn't separate one syllable from another.

"I'm sorry, Irving, but I can't understand a word—"

"The abomination that causes desolation!" he shouted. "The Prophet Daniel spoke of it. *No*, I will *not* accept it!" He walked over to his cupboard and pulled out a bottle of brandy and two glasses. With shaking hands he poured, and set one glass down in front of Donna.

"What's this for?"

"It's so I am not drinking alone." He tossed his back, setting the empty glass on the table. "I have to slow down and think clearly." He poured himself another, not noticing that Donna hadn't even touched her own, and took a sip from his second. He closed his eyes and took a deep breath. "There was a conversation we had, on the riverbank." He pulled up the sleeve on his left arm and traced a finger along the length of his tattoo. "I was such a fool. I thought she was a person."

"We all thought she was a person," said Donna. "Worst of all, *she* thought she was a person. Imagine being in her place, Irving. Imagine *being* that 'abomination.'" She touched his tattoo with a fingertip. "Somehow, I think you know. Ask God what's going on in *her* mind right now."

Irving stared at his arm. *Abomination*. That's what they'd said about him at one time: him, and several million others like him. But they were God's chosen people, were they not? They were people. They were real, flesh and blood *people*. Gassed, burned like rats. Buried in mass graves, thousands at a time. Emaciated, hollow-eyed corpses, stacked like so much cordwood. *Father and Mother*. He closed his eyes and prayed again, his voice soft. His hands still trembled when he opened his eyes. A tear rolled down his cheek.

"That poor girl," he moaned. "She has no hope. She has no soul. Man has built another Tower of Babel, and it is doomed to fall. But how many must die for this?"

"Irving, we're trying to save her and Jon, but we have to find them first. The people who made Nadia may have them, but we don't know. If we knew where they were, we could help them, but right now there's nothing we can do."

"So you heard from Jonny where?"

"Burlington, Colorado. He said Nadia had left him there."

"I would assume they're going back to Oregon, then. I have some friends out there I can contact."

"Please, Irving, no one else can know about Nadia," Donna begged. "If word got out, there'd be a panic. They'd chase her down...." She stopped, and took a sip of her brandy. Putting the snifter back on the table, she slowly turned it by the stem, watching the light from the window play through the glass. "They'll kill her."

Irving patted her hand to reassure her. "Not to worry, child, we can omit that small detail. I believe my friends can help in a small way, but they need to know for sure if Jonny and Nadia are really in there."

"What kind of friends are you talking about?" asked Donna nervously. "I showed you my cards, now you can show me yours."

Irving sighed and smiled. "I only speak of someone who could meet them and maybe provide shelter. What were you thinking?"

At that moment, Bunny called out from the shed, "I found 'em, Doc! We gotta be quick. Holy cow!"

Donna ran to the shed, and followed Bunny down the steps. When they got into Bunny's office, he sat in his chair and pulled a sheet from his printer. "I put a sniffer on the station's server, and I caught this email from a Dr. Hamund to the TV station's owner. They had both Jon and Nadia at Twin Oaks, but it looks like Jon escaped. He killed some guy named Steven and disappeared. Nadia is being held in 'Section A,' wherever that is."

"This can't be good," said Donna.

"No, Doc, it's great! We know where they are, and now I think I can use the address information to hack the hidden server at Twin Oaks! This is wicked awesome! Oh, crap!" he quickly opened a new screen.

"What?" asked Donna.

"I gotta fry that laptop before anyone tries to access it. If they got Jon, then they have Mike's computer." A few minutes of breathless silence later, and he relaxed, if only for a bare second before refocusing on his current projects. "There, I just sent it a surprise. It's already programmed to connect to the web using its satellite modem on startup. As soon as it does, it'll commit hara-kiri. Now, about that server...." He printed a page and started to put it in a manila envelope when his eyes flew wide. "Doc, you got a problem."

Donna came around behind him and pulled the sheet from his shaking hand. The email from Petr Hamund was sent to John Bowman, the CEO of Bowman Communications. Reading it, she didn't notice anything other than what Bunny had already told her. Then she looked again, and saw that a blind carbon copy of the message had been sent to someone inside the FBI!

Bunny's voice broke the shocked silence. "You recognize the name, Doc?"

She shook her head. "No, I have no idea who this is. But I'm pretty sure I can find out."

Bunny took the sheet back and filed it. "They know about you, you know."

"I know. But now we know about them, too."

"I got a few tricks for this mook."

Good. That should give him something to do other than make my blood pressure go up. "Okay, Bunny, do what you can. I think I have to make some calls. I'll be right back, and when I do, I want to arrange a trip out west." She headed up the stairs, pulling out her cellphone.

Chapter Sixty-Nine

When Jon next opened his eyes, it was daytime, possibly after noon. He was inside. Warm sunlight shone through a window, and birds sang back and forth in the summer heat. It was cool where he was. A soft whisper of air conditioning caressed his ears. He lay flat on his back, in bed, and above him stretched a white, drop ceiling. A hollow voice over a PA system paged Doctor Brooks.

An IV hooked up to his left hand dripped a constant supply of clear liquid into his arm, and an additional injector pump added either a painkiller or antibiotic to the cocktail. When he looked down, he saw that he was dressed in one of those stupid, backless gowns. When he raised his head, a wave of dizziness washed over him and, bringing his hands to his head to stop the room from spinning, he found a mass of bandages over his face. He concentrated on the ceiling until the motion stopped. A hospital. But *which* hospital? Where was he?

He had no idea how far the river had taken him from the crashed Hummer. Obviously, someone had found him and brought him in here.

He lifted his other hand before his face and found a plastic band on his left wrist that identified him as a John Doe patient…in Twin Oaks Medical and Trauma Center! He'd been found and brought back! An icy lump grew in his stomach and he closed his eyes. *Damn.*

He opened his eyes again and looked around again. A call button clipped to his side rail trailed away to a jack in the wall. Dare he try it? The longer he stayed here, the greater the chance he'd be found out. Unless they already knew. If he hit the button, would Jenna walk through the door and tell him it was all a joke before she killed him?

Probably not, he decided. If nothing else, his captors, with one singular exception, didn't come across as cruel. Misguided, maybe. Deluded, definitely, but not cruel. Besides, he had to find out where his clothes and effects were, especially the triggering device.

He already had enough for a case. He knew where the secret wall hid the lab area. He could just take off, save himself, and forget about Nadia. He had no idea if she was even here. He could only assume that this was where she was headed. That is, if she didn't panic and run off somewhere entirely different.

She'd already written him off. Could he do the same thing to her? Two weeks ago, he could have said yes, but now he wasn't so sure. He'd said goodbye to Alicia, and let her go. Nadia was someone else in so many ways now.

He'd seen differences in more than her physical appearance. He had known Alicia Burgess, and could readily see aspects of her personality in Nadia. That was what raised his curiosity to begin with. However, since they had begun this voyage together, he'd also seen glimpses of someone entirely different. Alicia was a very no-nonsense girl, down to earth and practical, laid-back and casual. Nadia had a more impulsive side that peeked around the corners of the Alicia imprint, a fiery and energetic temperament that, if anything, made her even more beautiful. In so many ways, she had become a living dichotomy, a contradiction of herself.

Then there were Roger Glass's last words: "She likes daisies." For one thing, why would he waste his last breath talking about flowers? Could it be that he had more than a professional interest in her? For another, Alicia's favorite flowers were carnations. *No, I can't walk out and leave her if she's here.* He would have to find out one way or the other for sure. With any luck, the legitimate hospital that operated here was so far removed from what was going on in the basement, no one here would recognize him. Then again, with his face wrapped in bandages, he could pass himself off as anyone he wanted to be, couldn't he?

He pushed the call button, and less than a minute later, a plump, freckled young woman in scrubs strode in. "Hey, good morning! You're finally awake! How are you feeling today?"

"Like ten miles of bad road. How did I get here?" It was the question he was afraid to ask. If *they* found him and brought him back, he was as good as dead.

"A hunter found you on a sand bar in the river and brought you in."

He hoped she didn't notice the sigh of relief that escaped unbidden from his chest.

"How long was I out?" He winced. His head felt like it was going to explode from the vibration of talking.

"Two days." She stepped up and wrapped a blood pressure cuff onto his upper arm. "You were a real mess when you came up here." She squeezed the bulb, bled off the pressure with a hiss as she watched the dial. Then she dropped her stethoscope back around her neck. "What happened, anyway? Do you remember what caused the wreck?" Putting a finger to his wrist, she looked at her wristwatch for a few seconds, and wrote on his file.

"I don't remember what exactly happened."

"Don't feel too bad. It happens a lot in accident cases." She pulled up a stool and sat down. "I have to get some information if I can, is that okay?" He nodded and she went on. "Can you tell me your name?"

"Wasn't my wallet on me?" he asked, feigning surprise.

"No, there was no ID anywhere, hon. Can you tell me your name?"

"Uh, yeah," He remembered an identity he'd used in a previous undercover assignment. "I'm Dan…Dan Stilwell." He provided Dan Stilwell's Social Security number, address, and insurance information.

The nurse filled out the form while he provided the information. Then she stood up and folded the file's cover back in place. "My name's Beth, and I'm your day shift nurse. Your doctor is Doctor Liston. She'll be glad to know you're awake. Is there anything I can do for you before I leave?"

"Yeah, some breakfast maybe. Got any hash browns?"

Beth laughed lightly. "I'll see what I can do about that. Anything else?"

"When can I get up?" he croaked. He really didn't feel like getting up, but time now could be of the essence. If Nadia was back in their hands, there was no telling what they might do to her. He had to push himself.

Beth looked in the chart. "Dr. Liston wants you up and around as quickly as you can tolerate it. So do you want to sit up for a while?" She raised the head of the bed and helped him to sit.

His head spun for several seconds and he thought he would vomit, but he had nothing in his stomach to throw up, so all he could manage were a couple of dry heaves.

Beth stood by while he got his bearings again, and then helped him get situated comfortably. "We'll get you up out of bed after Physical Therapy gets a chance to evaluate you later today." The last thing she did was hand him a TV remote control before she left to tend to her next patient. "I'll come back in a few minutes to see how you're doing, okay? If you need anything, the yellow button on your remote is the call button. Don't get up by yourself." He nodded, and she closed the door behind her.

Jon sat for a few minutes and then dropped the side rail. Fighting to a sitting position on the edge of the bed, he eased off onto his feet and tried a few steps on his own. His legs felt like rubber and his head swam, but he managed well enough, as long as he held onto the IV stand. He circled the room a couple times and got back into bed after the dizziness became severe.

Beth came back as she said she would, bringing a set of scrub pants and some slipper socks for him to wear while walking around. With her was a small, attractive woman in her thirties with red, curly hair that came just down to her shoulders. She introduced herself as Belinda Liston. She examined Jon's head and eyes, helped Beth change his dressings, and sat back with a grunt.

Jon smiled inwardly. *What is it with the grunt? Is that something they teach you in med school or something?*

Dr. Liston looked at Jon's chart for a few seconds. "Mr. Stilwell, let's get to the point: You have two broken ribs, a blunt head trauma, and the obvious cuts and contusions that accompany either a car accident, or a street fight. Unless there was another cause for your injuries, of course. Can you remember anything else that happened?"

"I only remember driving up the mountain," said Jon, dutifully sticking to his lie.

"What were you doing on the mountain?"

"I might have been trying to get to a hiking trail," he suggested.

"You don't remember, then?"

"No." He felt like she was fishing for something, trying to get him to trip up. But he was having none of it. *Just answer the question. Don't volunteer anything.*

Dr. Liston took an otoscope from a bracket on the wall and selected a cone from the rack. She fit the cone to the end of the scope and examined each eye in turn. When she was done, all Jon could see was a single, blue-white orb dancing around in his vision. He was feeling the beginnings of quite a headache, and said so.

"Mr. Stilwell, I'd like to keep you here a couple more nights just to observe your head, if that's all right with you. Is there anyone we can call for you?"

"Actually, Doctor, there is a call I need to make, but I'll make it myself. How do I get an outside line?"

"Beth can show you. I'll check back tonight, okay?" She scribbled a scrip for a painkiller into his chart and breezed out.

Beth showed him the phone, and how to use it. When he asked her, she told him his personal effects were in the closet there in the room. His clothes, she said, were so full of blood they were destroyed. Maybe a friend or family member could bring him some clean clothes for the morning? Then she, too, left.

Jon pulled the scrub pants on and crawled back into bed. He could afford to play this game for a few hours, but he would have to get some clothes and start searching for Nadia by the end of the day. And he knew just where to start. *First, that phone call.*

Chapter Seventy

Howard picked up the phone on the second ring. "Director Standish."

"I'm sorry," slurred the weak voice on the other end. "I was trying to get my section chief, but someone sent me to you—"

"Agent Daniels? Jon, my God, man, where are you? Are you all right?" Howard waved frantically at his secretary, and motioned for her to close the door.

Jon still sounded confused. "Ah, yeah, but I think there's been some mistake."

"No, there's been no mistake. I left instructions with your section supervisor to patch you directly to me."

"Mr. Standish, I know I've been out of the loop for a while—"

Howard cut him off before he could continue. "Yes, we know some details already, but we needed to hear from you to move forward. This is big, and it's complex. Can you give me anything that would get us a warrant to search the place?"

"We can start with abduction, assault of a federal agent," said Jon, "and maybe throw in strong-armed robbery, unlawful confinement, and first-degree murder."

That last one got Howard's attention. "Who was the murder victim?"

"Mike Alverson, for one. Bunny Kalinsky, for another. Oh, and there was the political assassination of President Bello of Nigeria."

"Are you sure you can tie all this together, Agent Daniels?"

"Believe me, Mr. Standish, we can get this to stick. I was in the secret lab area where they made…the bombs."

"'Bombs'? You mean there's more than one NADIA?"

"I don't know about right now, sir, but I was confined in a very sophisticated operating room in a hidden basement of the hospital. I didn't have time to explore any further."

"Where are you right now, Jon?"

Jon told him.

"Are you *insane*? Get out, right now. I can have some special agents meet you in Klamath Falls."

"I'm okay, Howard. They think I left after I escaped. They're not expecting me to stay around here. I'm probably safer right here than wandering around in the woods, where I hope they're looking. My face is messed up enough so that no one's going to recognize me, and I gave them my Dan Stilwell information."

"Good. Is there anything else you need right now?"

"Actually, I could use some clothes. It seems mine were too messy to keep."

"You got it, Jon. Listen, call my direct line with anything else. I'm supervising this case directly. Don't discuss this with anyone, do you understand? I'm sending a team out there as soon as we get done with this call. Get better and I'll see you immediately after you get back to DC. Good luck."

* * * *

Howard hung up his phone, not noticing that the line wasn't yet dead. He didn't hear the extra little *click* that strained out of his earpiece just before the handset hit the cradle. Three floors below him, in a small cubicle in the IS department, another phone hung up and a recorder stopped. Nervous hands typed out an email and sent it out to an address far away.

Chapter Seventy-One

Petr Hamund's voice rang like a death knell in the twilight that was Nadia's mind. "Nadia? What are you thinking of now?"

"I don't...." She began to answer as the waves stopped rolling. Becca Mitchell's memory faded away into the depths of the Sea of Forgetfulness and disappeared altogether as Nadia's conscious mind cried helplessly, and then forgot why her heart was broken.

She was so sleepy. She just wanted to rest, but they wouldn't shut up, they wouldn't leave her alone.

"Nadia? Can you hear me?" Petr asked again. She heard him, but couldn't make her mouth form the words. All she could do was listen while Petr and Anna spoke of her like just another piece of hardware to be used and discarded in their despicable plan. "This is going too slowly. Is there a way to make the process go faster?"

"Depends," said Anna. "Do you want her operational, or would you rather just fly her over the target and drop her like another Hiroshima?"

Petr grunted. "How thorough is the process? Are you getting everything?"

"We thought we got everything last time, Petr. There's just too much we don't know about the brain yet. She may have such strong emotional bonds to certain people and events we may *never* get them all."

"What about just wiping the long-term memory center? Can it be overwritten then?"

"Petr, we're running on the ragged edge here as it is. Why not just write this one off and start over?"

"Because our employer wants this one to be ready *now*. We don't have enough time to get another one operational. Plus," he added, "this is good troubleshooting experience. What if the next NADIA deviates from its programming? We have to prove the technology is stable in order to continue studying it. Besides, what do we do with forty-eight grams of unstable antimatter once the container is non-operational?"

Nadia heard all of this, but at this point, she was beyond caring. The warm, slick waves that had been washing her mind clear all day had taken a terrible toll on her, physically as well as mentally. She could barely lift her hands to the limits of their restraining straps. She couldn't remember how long she'd been here, couldn't even remember what it was that she couldn't remember. Shock and confusion wrapped themselves around her brain like the tentacles of some cold, wet thing from the depths of a nightmare. She drifted in and out of the Nothing. Nausea wrenched her stomach, but she no longer had the strength to retch. She lay in delirium, sweating as if in a dreadful fever.

Anna set her machines to standby mode. Petr looked at her questioningly. "You said you want her operational, Petr. You need to grow some patience or see this one turn into another vegetable."

Petr looked at his watch. "It's almost five o'clock. We could use a break, anyway. All right, then. We meet back here in two hours and go back to work."

Nadia heard them leave, and some corner of her mind gained small comfort from the knowledge. However, she knew they would be back. They would be back, and then she wouldn't be *her* anymore.

Chapter Seventy-Two

When Beth came through on rounds later that afternoon, her face was pale. Her hands shook as she took Jon's vital signs.

"Is something wrong?" he asked.

She stepped over to the door and closed it before coming back to the bed. "Please, tell me something," she whispered. "Who are you really?"

"I told you—"

"Look, your personal information doesn't jibe. The Dan Stilwell with your Social Security number died in 2005. Besides, some of your injuries are older, by hours or even days...." She paused, narrowing her eyes. "Are you that guy they're looking for?"

Jon saw no reason to keep up the charade. "Beth, you have to trust me. My name is Jon Daniels, and I'm a federal agent. There's some foul play going on at this hospital. I was investigating when I wound up in your emergency room. Now, where are they looking for me?"

"There were some guys walking around in the woods outside. But, now they're going from room to room."

"How many? Have they started on this floor yet?"

"There's five of them. They're at the other end, around from the nurse's station. Are you really a cop?"

"Can you take this damned tube out of my arm?"

"Yes, now look at me. Are you really a cop?"

Jon couldn't tell whether she was involved in the conspiracy here or not. But he could tell she was frightened out of her wits. He didn't blame her.

"Beth, I *am* a special agent for the FBI out of New York. I'm following a...murder investigation, and the killers are from this area. We need to get out of here, because if those people find us they're liable to kill you just for having spoken to me. Now get this damned tube out of my arm and let me out of here. And whatever you do, don't talk to them, do you understand me?"

"I understand." An eternity later, she said, "God, I don't know why, but I believe you." Beth got a small gauze dressing from the supply cabinet in the room and had the IV removed in a trice. Jon got up, shaking from the exertion, and found a plastic bag with his few belongings in the lower shelf of the closet. He rifled through it, and was relieved to see that he hadn't lost the triggering device. Together, they crept from the room.

Halfway down the hall, Beth waved her pass card in front of a sensor and opened the door next to it. They entered, and she dug out a scrub shirt for Jon. After he shrugged out of the hospital gown, she unwrapped his face. She winced and shook her head before tossing the bandages in the trash. Then she helped him put the shirt on, and a bouffant cap. The final touch was a pair of shoe covers. "The elevator is around the corner to the right," she said. "Take the B elevator down to the main floor, and the hospital entrance is to the left. Follow the blue line."

Jon shook his head. "I have to get to the basement, Beth. I have a friend who may be down there, and if she is, I have to save her, too."

"Maybe you better call for help. You're a wreck."

"I already made the call, but it's going to be some time before they get here. My friend may not have that time. I have to get down there before it's too late."

"Well, I can't babysit you. I have patients here that need my help."

Jon took her by the arm. "If you don't help me get to the basement and find my friend, you may not have to worry about your other patients." He waited for that statement to register before giving her the coup-de-grace. "I'm a federal agent. I could conscript you as part of an official investigation."

He winced as his breath caught. "Beth, you're right— I am a wreck. I can't do this by myself. If you don't help me, a lot of people could die. Please help."

Beth stood slack-jawed while the full impact of the situation sank in. Finally, Jon saw her expression change. Backing up, she opened the linen room door a crack and peeked out. "Two men and a woman just went into the room next to yours," she whispered.

"Can you see the other two?"

"No. Let's get out of here and walk toward the elevator. Your back'll be toward them, so they should think we're a couple of scrub nurses." She dug another bouffant cap out of supplies and quickly tucked her short, brown hair up into it.

"Here goes," she whispered breathlessly, and together they stalked back out into the hall.

Jon walked as casually as he could, but by the time they got to the elevators he was struggling along from shooting pain in his ribs. The doors were sliding closed when they heard urgent voices and quick steps coming down the hall in their direction.

The hum of the elevator's power system was the only sound for a space of time. Jon looked at Beth. She was shifting from foot to foot, looking at the ceiling.

"What made you believe me?" he asked.

"I can tell when someone's lying. It's kind of a gift."

"Why couldn't you tell I was lying before?"

"People come in traumatized and confused. I give them the benefit of the doubt for a while. Besides," she added, "I'm a nurse, not a cop. If someone lies to me, what can I do about it?"

"Ever thought about becoming a cop?"

Beth smiled, but her fear still showed. Her jaw trembled as she spoke, and her eyes darted around the ceiling. "When I was younger, maybe. I think I do more good as a nurse."

"Right now, I'd have to agree," said Jon, slumping against the handrail in the elevator. "Thanks for your help."

"It's not like you gave me much of a choice."

"I wouldn't have really conscripted you."

"I know. But it beats obstruction, don't it?" She reached out nervously and took his free hand. Her fingers trembled, and her palm was sweating. When he looked at her face, he saw she was biting her lip and staring at the numbers above the door as they counted down to the basement level.

The doors opened on a darkened corridor. Jon couldn't remember having been this way before. At his instruction, Beth led him to the hallway just behind the emergency department and he began to backtrack, trying to find the secret door to the lab area.

Halfway there, the sound of running feet echoed down a side hall. Jon grabbed Beth around the waist and dragged her into a utility closet as the footsteps rounded the corner and stopped right outside the door. A few hasty whispers later, they set off again. Jon listened to the echoes fade away before he peeked through the door. Satisfied that the coast was indeed clear, they slipped back out into the hall and continued on their way.

Eventually the two came to the wall through which Jon had staggered two days previously.

"Are you sure this is it?" asked Beth.

"I believe so." He held his hand up next to one of the pipes where it came out through the wall in the corner. He felt a slight breeze. "Yeah, this is it."

"How do you know your friend is back there?"

"If she *is* here, I think it's the only place here where they would dare keep her, at least for now. How to get in is the question."

"I think I have the answer," said Beth, trotting off down one of the halls. "Come on!"

Jon tried to jog to keep up, but after a few steps, all he could manage was a walk.

* * * *

The secret door under the Twin Oaks Resort was built for concealment, not strength. Its designers assumed that no one would try to force an empty wall in a basement, and they were right, up to a point. Now that Jon knew where the door was, and where the latch was, it was only a matter of the proper application of sufficient force in the right place. In this case, a wheeled hospital bed pushed by two people at a running speed provided just the right amount of force. With Jon guiding and pulling at the front and Beth pushing from the back, the bed slammed into the wall and through it, knocking it off its hinges as it did.

Jon doubled over for a moment in the hall, trying to catch his breath. His head felt like it would explode at any minute. He could hear every heartbeat in his ears like a cannon round. He felt Beth take his hand in a gentle grip and let her lead him in. He noticed that she was still quaking, so he gave her hand a reassuring squeeze as they made their way down the darkened passageway. The hall remained quiet. Several seconds passed while Jon listened. Nothing but silence greeted his ears.

"The bad guys must be watching the exit doors," he panted. "Gonna play hell getting out of here."

They hadn't gone far when Jon heard a weak cry from beyond one of the doors on the right side of the hall. He tried the door, but it was locked. "Nadia! Nadia, can you hear me?"

Her voice was strangely weak, but she managed a reply. "Hello? Help me, please."

Jon tried kicking the door in, but he was too weak. The impact ran straight up his leg into his head and he staggered against the opposite wall, sliding down to the floor with a moan.

"Smooth move, Ex-Lax," muttered Beth. Jon glowered at her.

"Okay, hang on." Beth ran back to their erstwhile battering ram and fiddled for a few seconds before she managed to remove one of the side rails. She brought it back and began to beat at the door with it, swinging it at the doorknob like a medieval ram. On the fourth try, the door burst in. They found Nadia still strapped in, entwined in a multicolored, latex and copper jungle of wires and tubes.

She looked toward the door as they came in, and Jon expected recognition and relief in her eyes. There was neither. Jon staggered over to her bedside and took her face in both his hands. "Nadia? Nadia, honey, it's me. It's Jon. Can you walk?"

"Jon?" she asked, her face a jumble of confusion. An instant later, the light came on in her eyes, and she wept. She tried to reach up, but her hands came up short against the straps. "Jon, please help. They're taking things, they're taking *me!*"

"Beth, help me get her out!" Together they got her disconnected, unstrapped, and extricated from the IVs. Jon found some scrubs in a closet and they began to help her to get dressed. He saw the large dressing on her right torso and a wave of anger rose in his chest. "What did they do to you?"

"Later, Jon," said Beth breathlessly. "Let's get you two out of here first, and then we can all catch up."

"Point taken. Let's go, Nadia." They finished getting her dressed and helped her to her feet. Her first few steps were so off balance and uncoordinated, Jon and Beth each took an arm, helping her back down the hall. They got back past the entrance to the secret lab and Jon led them over to a corner out of the way.

"I'll be right back," he said. "If anyone comes, you scream." He staggered back past the door. Entering the room again, he took the bedrail

275

that Beth had used as a ram, and smashed every piece of equipment in the room. The work didn't take long, but by the time he was finished, sweat poured from every pore in his body, and he shook with the pain and effort of walking. The women were still waiting right where he'd left them. They took off together, making the best speed they could. Jon prayed that they wouldn't have to run any time soon.

Beth trotted ahead and came back with a wheelchair as they neared the emergency department. "Can I ask something? What the hell were they doing in there, and who was doing it?" Then, to Nadia: "Park it here, hon. You're going out of here in style."

"Like you said," said Jon as he helped Nadia sit in the chair, "later. Are there any goons in the ER?"

"I didn't see any. Does anyone know where we're going after we get you out of here?"

"Hopefully, the cavalry is on the way. Here, let me push, I need the support anyway."

Beth led the way to an elevator that took them to the ground level, and then to a side door to the outside. They rolled out into the parking lot and almost reached the first row of cars when a call from behind them stopped them up short.

"Not good at all," said Beth. "Look."

Three figures advanced purposefully toward them from their right. The one in the middle was an older man, stocky with a full head of gray hair and a power suit. The two who flanked him were well-built, rough-looking men in jeans and flannel shirts with ski vests. One was shaved bald, with a goatee. The other had long red hair tied back, and a cruel look about him. Their right hands were stuck inside their vests. As they drew near, they fanned out to cut off any possible escape. The older man's expression was open, almost friendly. His companions' weren't.

Chapter Seventy-Three

Bunny punched in the last few keystrokes needed to confirm the flight reservation. "Okay, Doc. Your flight leaves at four-forty-five. First class from Dulles to San Fran, then a transfer to Eugene, and a commuter flight to Klamath Falls. Best I could do on short notice."

"Excellent, Bunny," said Donna. "Now, add one more seat to that flight."

Bunny leaned back in his chair and raised his hands, palms toward Donna. "Sorry, Doc. I been safer down here than anywhere else I've been. This Bunny ain't leavin' his hole, okay?"

"I don't mean you, Bunny. As much as I adore your company, I need someone with expertise in genetics and physiology, and I know exactly who I want. She's already packing." She gave Bunny the name, and he quickly made the arrangements.

"Bunny, can I ask you something?"

"Not unless you want the answer, Doc," said Bunny flatly. He turned and looked at her. Today's T-shirt said "SAVE THE FILES."

"Bunny, where's all this money coming from? You didn't hack the Fed again, did you?"

"Far from it, Doc," said Bunny reassuringly. "Look—for your comfort, I happen to own some software patents under a few different names. I just couldn't collect on the royalties without a computer at my disposal before. Okay?"

Donna looked at him hard for several seconds.

"Th-that's the 'mom' look. Don't give me the 'mom' look, I can't handle the 'mom' look." Bunny looked away uncomfortably.

"Okay. If you're telling me the truth, I'm fine with that." Donna rose and pulled the e-ticket sheets from the printer. On her way out she said over her shoulder, "Thanks, Bunny. You're a great help to me."

Bunny went back to work after he heard her ascending the stairs to the surface. "What she don't know won't kill me," he muttered as he added a few more keystrokes. Someone else was due for an "inheritance."

He finished that business, and then paid another visit to the FBI's server. What he found there confirmed his last suspicions: someone in Information Technology had sniffers and keyholes on everyone's email accounts, and had set up keywords that seemed to be entirely too coincidental not to be significant. One quick file upload later, and four CPUs in Washington DC crashed and belched smoke as their hard drives committed hara-kiri. Bunny leaned back and took another swig from a green and yellow soda can. He smiled and belched. "Happy freakin' birthday, ya knuckle-dragger," he muttered. He powered his machine down and disconnected the input cable from the back of his server before he turned on his game console.

Chapter Seventy-Four

"Jon," said the older man, "Agent Daniels? We need to talk. Would you follow me, please?"

Jon, Nadia, and Beth stayed planted where they were. "What if I politely refused?" asked Jon.

"I would hate for there to be a scene, Jon. We really need to go inside now."

"Who are you?" asked Nadia. The man said nothing.

"The lady asked you a question," said Jon. The two men in jeans spread wider apart. Jon pulled the chair back a few paces, preventing them from being outflanked.

"Jon, you know as well as I that *that*," the older man said with a scornful gesture at Nadia, "is no 'lady.' I deal with people, not *those*."

Jon felt a prickle on the back of his neck, as his anger rose and mingled with the shame that he felt, knowing he had once treated Nadia the same way. "Okay," said Jon, "I'm asking now. Who are you?"

The man stepped closer and smiled. "I'm Alan Whitfield, of Whitfield, Campbell, and Moore, Attorneys at Law. And you, young man, have something that belongs to me. I'd like it back, please." He turned to one of the men who were with him, the bald one. "Mr. Hammersmith, please notify the rest of the team that we have the merchandise and have them come out to the parking lot. Mr. Billings, please watch the merchandise."

Hammersmith took his hand from his vest and pulled a radio from his belt. It got halfway to his head when a dry, soft voice croaked from the woods at the edge of the lot. "Hey, stupid—drop the radio."

An old man dressed in deer-hunter's camo stepped out of the woods with an ancient combat rifle held ready at his hip. He was wiry and gaunt, with short-cropped silver hair and steel gray eyes. A shadow hovered over his face, one that whispered of a thousand horrors in a long-ago lifetime, and the death of boyhood innocence in a far-away land.

The two thugs accompanying Whitfield stopped. Billings began to pull his hand out of his vest.

The old man swung the rifle over to cover him. "Next idiot takes a notion, gets a new hole! I wanna see fingers!"

Billings and Hammersmith looked at each other and began to back slowly toward Whitfield. A sharp *boom* echoed across the lot from the old man's Garand and chunks of pavement kicked up between Billings and the first row of cars in the lot. The ricochet whined past Jon and the women, smacking into the trunk of a tree at the other end of the lot. Pieces of bark flew off and rained down onto the tarmac.

As the echoes died, the old man's voice floated across the space between them. "I still got four rounds. You're tryin' my patience, boys."

Hammersmith and Billings froze, their hands in the air.

"Jon," said Whitfield, "we really need to have that talk, and this," he said, waving at the parking lot, "is not the place for it."

The lot began to fill with staff from the hospital who had heard the shot and came out looking for the excitement. Several people pulled out cellphones, and Jon could hear at least one person say, "Call the Sheriff out here."

"Wait!" Whitfield held out a hand to the crowd as he cried out to them. "Don't call anyone. There's just been an accidental discharge. No one's been hurt. Please go back to your duties." A few people went back in, but most stayed put on the sidewalk outside the building.

"Looks like a perfectly fine place to have our little chat, Mr. Whitfield," said Jon. "If it'll help, come on over here and we can have a little privacy."

Whitfield stepped a little closer. "Jon, this is highly irregular."

"Whitfield, let me tell you what's irregular," said Jon in a loud voice. "How about we start with murder? Conspiracy? Abduction? Hey, what about that *killer* erector set you got in your basement here? Oh, speaking of killers, let's talk about living weapons and assassination plots, shall we?" He looked over at the crowd who still stood at the edge of the lot by the hospital building. He was sure they heard; several people started to mutter amongst themselves about murder. "Get that sheriff up here," said one voice above the others.

"Jon, please, not so loudly…." Whitfield glanced from the crowd in front of the building, to the old man at the outer edge of the parking lot, who still had his finger wrapped around the trigger of his old rifle and a tense, hard expression on his face.

Jon looked at the old man, too. He had no idea where the hell he came from, but he was glad he showed up. As long as things stayed the way they were right now, Jon had the upper hand. "Then why don't you bring your happy little rump over here and let's talk, Al, because as of right now, it doesn't look like anyone's going anywhere."

"Jon," whispered Beth, "could you tell me what in God's name all this is about?"

"Where's your car, Beth?" he whispered back. "We need it. And please tell me it's got more than two seats."

Beth's voice quivered. "If I, like, move, is someone going to shoot me?" Whitfield was edging closer. He was almost close enough to hear them whisper to each other.

Jon looked at Beth. She was shaking horribly, and a tear was tracing its way down her cheek. He winked, and turned back to Whitfield. "Hey, Al, Miss, ah...."

"N-Nelson," stammered Beth.

"Miss Nelson is going to go get her car while we're talking, and bring it up here."

Beth sounded close to panic. "My keys are in my purse. Back on the floor. I...I have to get my keys."

Jon whispered as he stared at Whitfield. "Beth, listen very closely. If you don't bring your car up here, we're all going to die. I have to make you understand that. They will kill me and Nadia, and come after you, only because you talked to me. These people don't care. Do you understand me?" Beth nodded. "Now, please go get your car and bring it here. How much time do you need?"

"About ten minutes."

"I'll give you five."

"I doubt that will be necessary," said Whitfield, stepping up close. "Nobody's going anywhere."

Jon stepped between Beth and Whitfield. "On the contrary, Mr. Whitfield." He pointed at the hospital doors. "Miss Nelson is going because the last thing you want is for her to know what you're really about in your little laboratory downstairs. If the news got out about that, then your whole organization isn't worth a tinker's damn and your investment goes up in smoke. Then I still get to arrest you for conspiracy and murder, which will put you away for a long, long time. That is, unless Audie Murphy over there caps you in the head first." Jon eyed the old man in the camo's. *I have no idea who he is, but 'the enemy of my enemy is my friend.'*

"Name's DeBartolo," said the old man. "Call me Jimmy."

Jon wondered why that sounded familiar, but before he could make any connection, Whitfield spoke again. "Mr. Hammersmith, take the lady to get her car."

"No!" barked Jon, holding up a hand toward the men. "She goes alone. Hammersmith, you take one step and it'll be the last one you take!"

Whitfield looked around and sighed. "You drive a hard bargain, Jon. All right, she goes." Jon nodded at Beth and she took a few shaky steps toward the hospital. When nothing happened, she started running, and disappeared through the door after the crowd parted to let her through.

"Whitfield, if she isn't back here in five minutes, I give a signal and Jim here goes to town." He looked at the old man, who nodded back, his face tight with determination.

"There's no need for threats, Jon. I'm a man of my word. Now, let's chat about my stray property."

"Okay, let's talk. What's with the assassination of President Bello?"

"Jon, our organization's vision is about achieving world peace in our time."

"Funny definition of peace you have there, Al."

"Are we going to have a conversation or not?" asked Whitfield impatiently. "You seem to already have all the answers you want, Jon. Does that justify theft?"

"Okay, I'm listening." Jon felt his jaw tightening in anger at the continued reference to Nadia as property. He glanced down at her, to see how she was reacting to all this. She was still sitting in the wheelchair with her hands on the armrests of the chair. A second look showed him the wheel locks were engaged, and her knuckles were white, her fingers clenching the frame. Her eyes were wide open, her lips pursed. The last time she'd looked that way, he'd felt the slap for the rest of the day. While Whitfield talked, Jon slowly reached out and touched her arm, hoping she'd read his thoughts. *Wait. Just wait a bit.*

"Jon, what I'm talking about is the saving of countless lives. Bello was a corrupt little megalomaniac who cared for nothing more than what he could extort, twist, and steal from his own people. Millions suffered under horrific poverty while he lived in luxury in a fifty-room palace in Abuja. His replacement is a much gentler man who's vowed to do away with corruption in his country's government. The world is a much better place without Bello, don't you agree?"

"So, Javad was supposed to be next? Who decides who leads which country, Whitfield? Is that what you're about? Empire-building?"

Whitfield chuckled, a dry, humorless laugh. "Come, now, Jon, which is better—to *become* a king, or to *make* a king? The Pinnacle's vision is not to rule, but to place our support behind just, kind rulers who can help lead the world into a future of peace and justice."

"And those who don't fit your qualifications?"

"We exhaust every diplomatic means before we resort to force. Now, I want my property back."

"What about law, Whitfield? I thought you wanted justice."

Whitfield's smile was haughty and smug. "Rules are for followers, Jon. We lead. We're above rules."

"So how much yield?" asked Jon. "What capability does she really have?"

"That's none of your business, I'm afraid," said Whitfield. "I'll take it back, now."

"And what happens to her then?"

"We'll finish reprogramming it. A simple repair to get it back on line."

"And what about the rest of us?"

"You can go right back to your lives and forget this whole mess ever happened," said Whitfield, smiling. "You can just walk away and forget the whole thing. I can see to that."

"So let me get this straight," said Jon. "You take the artificial person that you created, erase her brain, and try another download. Then send her out to kill a hundred, a thousand, or a million other innocent people. And, since I know about her, and maybe someone else knows about her, you send your goons out to wipe us all from the face of the earth. Am I right?"

Whitfield's smile faded, and his face took on a menacing cast. "Who else knows about NADIA?"

Jon threw Whitfield's words back at him. "That's none of your business, I'm afraid. Now, since United States federal law prohibits the ownership of people, I'm going to leave with Miss Velasquez, and you're going to prison."

Whitfield laughed, pointing at Nadia. "You think *that* is a *person*? I think you need a refresher lesson in biology, Jon—"

"Define 'person,' Al."

Whitfield's face turned serious. "We seem to be at an impasse here, and I'm running low on patience, Mr. Daniels." He looked down at Nadia, still sitting in the wheelchair, and held out his hand. "Come."

"No," said Nadia. "I won't."

"Have it your way," he said, and Jon's eyes picked up a faint glimmer. It was almost as if Whitfield's diamond tie tack had reflected some of the sun's rays at them. It shimmered and flashed eerily for a few seconds and then went dark.

"Oh, God, no," Nadia moaned softly.

"What is it, hon?" asked Jon.

"Jon, the difference between me and you right now," said Alan Whitfield as he turned, "is that twenty minutes from now, I'll be a safe distance from here. Goodbye, Agent Daniels."

He took two steps toward his bodyguards and then Nadia gathered herself, lunged out of the wheelchair, and wrapped him up in a half nelson. Her feet dangled from the ground as he tried vainly to shake her off.

Hammersmith and Billings drew their weapons. Hammersmith fired off-balance. Jon ducked as the round buzzed past his head.

Jimmy swung his rifle and, firing from the hip, shot Hammersmith in the belly. Billings returned fire, and the old man crumpled to the ground. Then the thug turned his pistol toward Nadia and Whitfield.

"Don't shoot, you fool! It's going critical!" Whitfield shouted hoarsely, still trying to pry Nadia's arm loose from his neck. In response, she yanked up on the wrist she had pinned behind his back, and he bent backward. She dragged him down onto the ground and pulled her elbow up tight into his throat, grunting with the exertion.

Nadia growled into Alan Whitfield's ear as she held him pinned to the ground. "Make the goon disappear." He said nothing. She yanked up on his wrist again and he groaned.

"The lady made a request, Al," said Jon. "Or, don't you address—"

"Please!" grunted Whitfield. "In thirty minutes there's going to be a crater a half-mile wide—"

"Then turn me off!" said Nadia desperately. "Make it stop!" She began to tremble.

"I…I can't," he replied weakly. "The codelite is a single use—"

"Looks like we have a problem then," said Jon, "Because you're not going anywhere."

"Call it off!" screamed Whitfield. "Billings! Get this thing—"

"Looks like Billings has something better to do," said Jon, watching as the man ran around the corner of the building on his way out of there. He turned to the bystanders standing at the hospital entrance. "Look, everyone! I'm a federal agent. There's a bomb in the area! You have to get as many people out of here as you can in the next twenty minutes! Take any means you can. Go!"

Nadia shuddered like someone punched her in the gut, and she grunted in pain. "I'm going to die, Whitfield, and you're going to die with me! I may not go to heaven, but I know where you're going!"

Chapter Seventy-Five

Donna and Hushi sat next to each other on the 707. Donna almost wished it were otherwise. Holli Hushido seemed to have an incredible talent for talking without inhaling, or even saying anything for that matter. Donna let it go for about twenty minutes after the plane took off, and then she held up her hand. "Hushi, I need about fifteen minutes of your time, okay?"

"So we're actually going to see a Sasquatch?" Hushi whispered excitedly. "This is so cool!"

"Hushi, please just shut up and listen for a few minutes, would you? We're not investigating Bigfoot. This is something much more serious than that. Now, you've been working on your own to decode the traits of the... creature the white blood came from, haven't you?"

Hushi's face flushed. "Oh, you knew about that? I hope that wasn't out of line, it's just that it's so unique—"

Donna held up her hand again, cutting her off. "This means a life, Hushi, maybe millions of lives. I need you to concentrate. What I need from you is your medical training and a lesson in what makes Nadia, Nadia."

Hushi froze in her seat, her face screwed up in confusion as she chewed on her gum. After a breath, she found more words. "Okay. What's a Nadia?"

In hushed tones, Donna told her. Hushi became silent for the second time in ten minutes, a minor miracle by some accounts. Then with shaking fingers, she opened her briefcase. "I was wondering why you wanted me to take this file along. Do you think she'll be all right? Does she speak, like, English, or does she have her own...." She saw the look Donna was giving her, and settled down again, pulling out a stapled report she'd compiled over the last couple of days.

"Well, first of all," began Hushi, "she's got a dynamite immune system...oh, pardon me..." She looked concernedly at her senior companion, who just nodded acknowledgement, ignoring the unintentional pun, and then continued. "I get blonde hair, brown eyes, about five feet tall. Am I right?"

"That's why I have you along right now. Keep going."

"She probably will never get sick from anything that we would, although I don't know if there is a pathogen that would affect her.

"With the oxygen content and makeup of her blood, she's probably capable of healing at a much faster rate than you and me. Blood, incompatible with human blood. Those little machines would pretty much eat one of us alive. Our blood wouldn't be able to carry enough oxygen for her body, so that would rule out any kind of transfusion, if it came to that. There's a bunch of information I can't quite decipher—"

"She's a weapon, Hushi. That's probably the part you can't read. Some of that is probably code for maintaining the containment cells for the antimatter. I just really need to know if we can treat her using basic first aid if it comes down to it. You know," Donna mused, "we're trying to be combination doctors and bomb squad. If she dies, her body will most likely shut down. It would be very bad."

Hushi's eyes grew wide. "What the hell is happening, here?"

"She's being held, Hushi. I have no idea what they're going to try to do. We may be the only medical people she has."

"What was that yield number again?" asked Hushi as she pulled out a pocket calculator.

"Two megatons."

Hushi's fingers paused over the keypad of the calculator. "You said what?" Donna repeated it, low enough for only the two of them to hear. If any of the flight crew heard them talking about nuclear yield....

"Okay," said Hushi, punching numbers and functions. "We're looking at a crater almost a half-mile wide. Anything inside that radius will never know what happened. Total destruction— out to three and a half miles. Donna, I don't need to add any more to know that if this chick goes ballistic, that could be a bad day for Oregon. What about radioactivity?"

Donna recounted from memory, "Antimatter reactions throw out an incredible amount of gamma radiation, but mainly just a short burst. Very little or no residual radiation remains after the fact. That's what tipped off the OSI team in Nigeria that the bomb used there was an antimatter weapon."

"Donna? Do you, like, really hate me or something?" moaned Hushi.

"Why?"

"Are we going to get ourselves vaporized out there?"

"God, Hushi, I hope not. I really need you there because of your knowledge in genetics and biology. Plus, among us, you've at least been to med school." Donna pulled out a medical journal and began to read.

Holli Hushido was quiet for the next five minutes. When she spoke again, Donna heard a plaintive tone she'd never dreamed of associating with her. "This is the first time I've ever flown anywhere. Can you promise me it won't be the last?"

"No, Hushi, I can't."

Holli looked out the window. "Guess I better enjoy the view then." She was silent for the rest of the trip.

Chapter Seventy-Six

Nadia's grip on Whitfield was beginning to loosen. She felt weaker by the minute. All the same, Whitfield was unable to break the hold she had on him. "No, wait! It can be disarmed! We need another codelite!" Whitfield tried to get up, but Nadia ground her arm harder into his neck. He grunted and choked.

"Another codelite like this one?" asked Jon as he produced the one from his plastic bag and showed it to Whitfield, who stretched out a hand toward Jon.

"Give it to me, quickly!"

"How do you use it?" Nadia pulled back again. Whitfield choked. "What's the code?" she demanded again, grinding her elbow in so hard his neck popped.

Medical teams from the hospital had collected Hammersmith and Jimmy DeBartolo and dragged them into the trauma center. Ambulances began to line up at the front entrance to carry patients away down the mountain. Those who could walk were packed into private cars until even the trunks were filled.

A sound behind Jon separated itself from the tumult, rising even above the sirens of the outbound ambulances. Beth Nelson pulled up in a run-down Toyota that was older than she was and got out, leaving the engine running.

"Sorry, Beth, there's been a change," said Jon as she ran to his side. "I need you to make sure all your patients get down the mountain to Klamath Falls. We have a situation that could end very badly."

Beth looked at Whitfield where he sprawled on the ground with Nadia wrapped around him in her hold. Her hands still shook, but she held her ground.

"Then you're going to need a nurse, aren't you?" Beth said to Jon.

Jon glanced at her. Somewhere along the way, she had found some resolve. She was still trembling, but no longer seemed so prone to panic.

"Beth, you don't understand. We could all die very soon. You can save yourself."

"Who's going to save you?" she countered. "I'm staying right here."

Nadia groaned and shifted. "I can feel—"

Jon gently pried Nadia loose and yanked Alan Whitfield to his feet. He was too weak and terrified to try anything. Jon sat him down on the pavement with his wrists locked behind his back in a police hold. Nadia sat panting next to him, her color beginning to pale.

Beth knelt beside Nadia and felt her head. "She's burning up, Jon. What's wrong?"

"No time to explain. Keep her comfortable for me while Mr. Whitfield and I have a discussion, okay?" He bent closer to Alan Whitfield's ear. Jon could see him pouring sweat, feel him trembling in fear. "Better give her the code, Al. She's not in a real good mood right now, and we're running out of time. Which, coincidentally, applies to you, too. This is simple, Al. She lives, you live. She dies…you get the picture."

"Six-four-four-seven," Whitfield rattled off. "Then press the red button. Now, please, let me up."

Jon pointed at two large orderlies. "You, and you—come over here and hold this man for me. I don't want him going anywhere. Hurry up!" After they had Whitfield pinned securely, he pulled out the black cylinder. The five buttons along the side were marked each with two digits, so that all ten basic digits were represented. He punched in the code and pulled Nadia's right eye open. He hit the red button on the device and saw the series of pulses reflected in her pupil. When he let go she collapsed over onto the ground.

"How do we know it worked, Alan?" he demanded.

Whitfield's voice quavered. "We'll know in about ten more minutes."

Jon advanced closer, his voice raising. He wanted to make sure the crowd heard every word. "We'll know what, Mr. Whitfield? Whether the artificial person you created to be a bomb goes off and kills us all?"

"It has to work! I don't want to die!" shouted Whitfield.

"Neither did she!" Jon shot back. "How is she, Beth?"

"Not good. I don't know…."

Jon nodded to the two men holding Whitfield. "Bring him with us, inside. Tie him to something. Then help continue the evacuation. Beth, help me. Let's get Nadia inside."

A weak gasp brought his attention to Nadia. She lay on the ground, deathly pale and shaking all over. "Jon?"

He sat down and pulled her head into his lap. "I'm right here, honey."

"J-Jon, you have to leave." She was having trouble keeping her eyes open.

"I'm not going anywhere, babe. We're staying right here."

"Jon? I can't help it, I'm sorry," she cried, and her eyes closed. She stopped shaking.

"Nadia? Nadia!" shouted Jon. She was a limp rag in his lap. He picked her up, pushing through his own pain, and carried her toward the Trauma Center entrance. He was halfway there when the first wave of seizures hit Nadia.

Chapter Seventy-Seven

Donna and Hushi arrived at Twin Oaks in a cab, amid a cacophony of police cars and television cameras. They flashed their FBI credentials at the door to the trauma center and followed a beefy sheriff's deputy back to a bed that had been curtained off in a corner of the treatment area.

They passed three other beds along the way. On two of them lay still, silent figures. One had a sheet over its face, the other lay ashen and lifeless, but a heart rate monitor attached to his finger reassured Donna that there was still life in his body. An older man in a business suit who looked like he'd been wrestling in the parking lot occupied the third bed. He had numerous small scrapes and cuts on his hands and face. His suit was worn through in spots, stained with dirt. He lay in a restraining harness surrounded by Oregon State Police and local FBI agents. He, too, remained silent.

The deputy stopped and pointed at the curtained area. Donna pulled it aside, and she and Hushi walked through. Next to the fourth bed sat a bedraggled, battered man in scrubs. It took Donna several seconds to realize the man was Jon Daniels. His face was beaten and cut, swollen on one side. He sat silent, weeping. A nurse on the other side of the bed worked to treat a still and pale Nadia. She pushed a small syringe into a rubber lock on Nadia's IV bag. Hushi drew the curtain closed behind them and stood at the foot of the bed.

"Hold on, please," said Donna. "What's in that syringe?"

"Dilantin," said the nurse. "It seemed to help control the seizures. I gave her three hundred milligrams an hour ago, and now I'm pushing two hundred more. She's had eleven hundred total."

"Go ahead. Where are the doctors?"

"They all went to Klamath Falls with the rest of the patients. There was a bomb scare."

"The hell you say," said Donna. "I'm Doctor Hermsen, and this is Dr. Hushido."

"Beth Nelson, RN. Look, I know she's…I'm trying the best I can. Jon told me not to say anything to the police…." Her voice began to waver. "I just don't know what else to do—"

"That's all right, Beth. We can take over. But we may need your help, too, all right?"

"Y-yeah, sure."

"What's the story on the others?"

Beth sat in a second chair crowded into the curtained area. Fatigue and stress showed in her face. "Bed Five is gone. Gunshot wound, lower abdomen. It hit his descending aorta, and he bled right out. Bed Two is another GSW, upper thorax. Through and through. Nicked a lung and out through the scapula. A helicopter's on its way to take him to Klamath Falls. There was a team here long enough to stabilize him, and he's been holding his own." She shook her head. "Stubborn old codger. I have no idea where he came from, but I think he saved our lives."

Donna couldn't suppress a sudden smile. "Irving, you and I need to have a talk when I get back," she muttered.

"What?" asked Hushi.

"Nothing, dear. Beth, please take care of him, he's a good friend." She sat by Nadia's bed in the chair Beth had vacated. When she spoke, it was in a whisper, loud enough only for the two of them. "Jon, talk to me. What happened?" After Jon filled her in, she asked, "How long was she in an active state?"

"About fifteen minutes. Whitfield told us she needed thirty to reach critical and collapse. When we got her in here, she started having seizures and then blacked out. Beth gave her Dilantin, and that seemed to help the seizures, so we've been using that, but she hasn't come back around. I don't know if we were too late—"

"How long ago did you deactivate her?"

Jon ran his fingers through his hair and grunted in pain as he shifted in the chair. "It's been about four hours. Her pulse has been getting faster and weaker, and her breathing is getting weak. I don't know—"

Holli stepped up. "What's her blood oxygen saturation?"

"Beth took the sensor off because she thought it was defective. She hasn't gotten a new one yet."

"Beth!" Donna called. "We need an O_2 saturation reading right now!"

"The equipment's broke, Doctor."

"It's all right. We need the reading now."

Beth sighed and came over. After clipping the sensor on Nadia's fingertip, she placed the blood pressure cuff on her upper arm, then initialized the screen. The numbers for oxygen, pulse, blood pressure, and temperature appeared over their respective scan lines, and the display beeped with every beat of her heart. The oxygen level read one hundred and fifty per cent. Her pressure was low, pulse weak and rapid, a hundred and thirty-six beats per minute.

Donna thanked Beth and fished around until she found a stethoscope. "Jon, I'm going to ask you to leave. I'll let you know when you can come back in."

"I'm not going anywhere." His mouth was set in a firm line, his eyes glared grim determination.

Donna touched his arm. "I need to remove her gown for a bit. Look, if she turns for the worst, none of us will know what hit us. If she wakes up, I'll send Beth out right away. Right now, get out. Go for a walk or something. Take some aspirin, for crying out loud. Just get out. While you're at it," she added, "you might want to have everyone out there get the hell away from here unless they've already made out their last wills."

She pushed him out of the treatment area, then returned to Nadia's bedside and helped Hushi get her gown off. She gave an exclamation when she saw the dressing still on Nadia's right side, and lifted it off. The fresh scar underneath seeped with Nadia's pale blood. The wound itself was swollen, and purple streaks ran from the area in angry smears. Donna heard two gasps— one from Hushi, and the other from Beth. "Make sure no one else comes in here!" Donna barked. "Hushi, come here. I think she may be bleeding internally. Are we going to have to go in?"

Hushi sidled up to Donna and looked up into her eyes. "Med school and a six-month, flunked internship don't make me a surgeon, but it looks like this incision isn't healing," she whispered. "The signs on the wall unit are telling me the same thing. She's bleeding out."

"How was your cadaver practice?"

"Pretty good." Hushi's eyes widened as the realization hit her. "Oh, my God, are you telling me we have to perform unlicensed surgery on an antimatter *bomb?*"

"Well," said Donna, "Think of it this way. We don't need a license to operate, because she's not a human or an animal. As for the bomb part, well, that's just the bonus. If we live through this, you can submit an article to the Journal of the American Medical Association, or Popular Mechanics, take your choice. Beth, how are you in an OR?"

"I had the training when I first hired on here. Helped out a couple of times; everybody in nursing had to, at least twice— Did I hear you right? *She's* the bomb?"

"Give that girl a kewpie doll," said Donna, sardonically. "Beth, I wish I could give you the option to run away like everyone else, but unfortunately, neither of us is a medical doctor, and we really need someone here to help us save her life." She pulled the covers back over Nadia's body and removed the sensor clip from her finger.

Beth spoke over her shoulder as she pulled the curtain aside. "I'm not going anywhere. Let me get her ready to move, and we can roll right in."

Chapter Seventy-Eight

The operating room was dark, except for the light from the swing-arm lamp overhead and the screens that showed Nadia's life signs. Beth served as anesthesiologist and scrub nurse. Hushi performed the work, and Donna assisted, providing a second set of eyes. Jon guarded the door, making sure no one entered.

"There's another bleeder, Hushi."

"Yeah, I see it. Can you pull that open a little wider? How's she doing, Beth? Give us some numbers."

"O_2 is holding steady at a hundred sixty percent. Pulse is weak and one-forty, BP ninety-two over forty. Respiration twelve. Is that good? For her, I mean?"

"I wish I knew more," said Hushi. "We don't have any real set of baseline numbers to go by, but I think it's good as long as she's stable. There's another one. I need more silk. Beth, do we have any more Oxycyte?"

"The last bag is ready to go. Do you need it?"

"If her pulse drops below sixty, put it in; otherwise, we'll wait."

"So, what happened?" asked Beth. "I thought you said she had like, super healing powers or something."

"I think something happened when she was triggered," said Donna. "Here, Hushi. Right there. You want some suction?"

"No, just a lap sponge. She's lost enough blood; I just want to remove enough fluid to see. The edges of the tissue are weak. I'll have to be careful I don't tear through when I sew it shut."

"Anyway," continued Donna, "when Whitfield flashed her the first time, some of her systems probably started shutting down right away. I think the blue nanobots convert power for her stabilizers using oxygen and standard nutrients. They also supply energy for the other nanobots. She has three types in all, and they have different functions. Some of this tissue looks like it actually began to break down instead of healing. Almost like her nanobots were consuming her own tissue in order to keep powering her stabilizing system, like a timed fuse."

"To let the person with the trigger get far enough away," suggested Beth.

"Yes, that's right," said Donna. "Then when Jon coded her again, the systems kind of turned back on, but the damage was already done. How are we doing here, Hushi?"

"One more. Do you see any more, chief?"

"No, it looks like that's got it. Let's get ready to close. Beth, have you ever—"

"Doctor," Beth interrupted, "We have a problem. Her BP's dropping like a rock; pulse is fading and erratic…. Dammit, she's going!"

As if to punctuate the statement, the machine that monitored Nadia's vital signs began to beep faster and the display numbers started to flash red. An alarm began to sound, a desperate buzz filling the background. Then the display line for Nadia's heart stumbled and went into an erratic, rhythmless pattern. "V-fib!" called Beth.

"Pump in that last bag, Beth! Get it going, now," ordered Donna. "Have you ever hooked up a heart-lung machine?"

"No, and it's too late for that now." Beth brought out the last bag of artificial blood, connected it to the tube going into Nadia, and gave it a squeeze, forcing a good flow to start. Nadia's pulse line became weaker. "Look, ladies, we have to defibrillate like, right now, or we lose her for good."

Donna's voice was tense. "Beth, if we shock her we may set her off, and that would ruin Christmas for everyone within ten miles of this place. Get over here and start CPR."

"But you said those little robots need power," Beth objected. "If we hit her maybe they'll charge back up—"

"Shut up and get over here! Keep her blood flowing so we can finish—"

"Dammit, all you doctors are the same!" shouted Beth. "She's dying, and if she dies, we all die anyway. I may be only a nurse, but I do know when a shock is indicated, and we need one RIGHT NOW!"

Hushi and Donna looked at each other for some kind of support. Donna could only see the same kind of fear in Hushi's eyes that she was feeling. She turned to Beth. "God, help us all. Okay, Beth, tell us what to do."

Beth got the paddles ready and set the dial. "Just stand back when I yell 'clear,' or this thing'll knock you right through that wall."

Donna heard Hushi muttering something under her breath. "What?" she asked.

"I'm...praying," said Hushi breathlessly.

"I thought you were an atheist."

Hushi blushed behind her mask. "Didn't want to be wrong. You know, just in case."

Beth placed the paddles on either side of Nadia's chest and watched the dial on the defibrillator. "Charging... and...clear!"

Hushi and Donna stepped back as Beth hit the trigger. Nadia's body jumped as the shock snapped through her, and then she went limp again. The women looked at the display screen while the rising whine of the unit's power supply filled the background of the operating room. The lines still trembled on the monitor screen, but no rhythm appeared.

Beth's voice rang sharply. "Charging...clear!" Again, Nadia's body arched and fell back. "Good pulse," Beth announced, watching the screen. "BP coming back up. I think we have her back."

Donna didn't realize until now that she'd stopped breathing. She took a deep breath, and it came out with a sob. "Oh, God, honey, I'm so sorry—"

"Okay, then," sighed Hushi. "Let's close. I just hope we don't get sued for malpractice."

Chapter Seventy-Nine

It was dark. She remembered a sick, sinking feeling. Slowly, she became aware of a discomfort on her right side. She moaned and tried to sit up, but was unable to do more than move her arms.

As her consciousness began to absorb her surroundings, she heard voices—whispers and quiet, thoughtful phrases. A spasm of pain ripped her side, and she moaned again. Sounds became louder, as if she were emerging from water. Something was stuck on her face, blowing a cool breeze into her nostrils.

She felt someone take her hand, and she struggled to open her eyes. Her lids were stiff, sticky. She caught a glimpse of scrubs and a mask, felt a mass of wires attached to her head. A tube ran into her arm from an IV bag.

A wave of panic arose. She tried to scream, but the pain in her ribs caught the breath in her lungs, and all she could manage was an excruciated grunt. "Jon! Jon, help me! Don't let them—"

The figure stood and pushed her shoulders back onto the bed. "Wait! Nadia, it's me. I'm right here. Honey, it's me, it's Jon!"

She stopped struggling, but couldn't stop trembling. The figure pulled down its mask to reveal the face: bruised and scarred, but recognizable. She looked at him, glassy-eyed and delirious. Sweat matted her hair.

He reached out to brush a stray lock out of her eyes.

"Oh God, Jon, they were going to…." She broke into tears, and he bent down and held her. She clung to him and wept. "They were going to take everything away," she cried. "They wanted to take *me*…the wires—"

"It's okay now, it's over," he crooned into her ear and held on until she calmed down. She heard someone mumble something in the background. A heavy door opened and closed. "They're doing an EEG, looking at your brain. Donna just wants to make sure you don't have epilepsy."

Nadia felt fear washing away in the scent of Jon. "You didn't run away. Why did you stay?" she asked.

"Because it was the right thing. Because you needed me. And because," he said, bending low over her and taking her face in his hands, "I love you." Gently, he kissed her forehead.

She tried to shrink back, but her pillow stopped her head. "But you can't, Jon. We went over that—"

He shushed her. "*You* went over that, Nadia. You never gave me a chance to tell you my side."

He sat back in the chair and drew the mask back over his face. "By the way, you're supposed to be highly contagious. This is an isolation room. It's the only way we could limit access to you until you could leave."

"Limit access?"

She could see Jon's eyes laughing behind his mask. "Yeah. Hushi and Beth came up with this story to get you out of there, in a way that no one asked questions about who you really are. You have a rare, highly contagious virus. You should have seen all the people in the astronaut suits handling you with kid gloves. Beth laid it on so thick, they were all terrified of touching you."

A glimmer of hope, then? "S-so maybe they don't know—?"

"No, babe, they don't. No one knows. You're perfectly safe, here."

"Where am I?"

"Johns Hopkins Medical Center. You're in DC."

"Was I in another coma?"

His eyes moistened. "You were out for five days. I thought I was going to lose you. I can't lose you again."

"Jon—"

"I brought you daisies." He held up a small vase that sprayed a half dozen little green stems like rocket trails, each topped with a bright yellow firework. He handed her the vase, and she took it. It felt heavy in her hands. "Nadia, I've thought about you ever since you walked out in Colorado. I thought I wanted to be with you because of who you used to be—"

"Jon, look what you'd be giving up—"

"Hold on," he said, holding up a hand. "Wait a minute, let me finish. I had to say goodbye to Alli, and I did. I let go, finally. She's gone. But you're still here, Nadia; you're still in my heart, and I know who you are now. You're *you*, and I love you for it."

She reached out, grasped his hand, and smiled tearfully. "I just can't get out of this, can I?"

"Not on your life, babe," he said, and kissed her again. This time she kissed him back.

Chapter Eighty

The hand holding the phone in the mahogany-trimmed office trembled ever so slightly. It would do no good to demonstrate a lack of composure. The other hand reached into his pocket for the handkerchief that was always so impeccably folded, and withdrew it to wipe the sweat from his brow. "Miss Paine," he said, straining to sound calm, "I empathize with the loss of your team. However, I'm afraid your work is just beginning…. Yes, we'll have to take some time and regroup. That is to be expected.

"What is your analysis of Mr. Whitfield?…Yes, I agree. Do you think you can take care of that for us? Yes, thank you. There will be a bonus…no, no, you deserve much more than that, I assure you.

"There will be a ring….Yes, that's the one. Please don't forget it. I'll send a messenger to pick it up. In addition, he has a book we need…you know the one.

"Miss Paine, I don't think I have to tell you how important this is, do I? Thank you. Goodbye."

He placed the handset back in its cradle and put his face in his hands. The gold ring on his finger felt so heavy now. He rubbed his eyes and put his left hand on the desk before him. The blood-red ruby with the mystic inscription stared back at him like a malevolent eye, a dire prophecy of what could happen if this situation ran away from him. *So much work, so much research. So much blood, sweat, tears, and faith poured into one basket of eggs so easily dropped.* However, it was too late to give up on this phase of the Vision. They had to press on. In spite of the vote from the rest of the Council, he knew it would work, and it would only take one more success to secure unanimous approval. Wilkes and Bowman had assured him they could get the votes to make it final.

Moreover, one more up-and-coming member of the Faith, shaken and broken like Judas. He just hoped Whitfield wouldn't say anything before Jenna's visit.

He stood and turned out the lights before closing the office for the night. There was hope yet.

Chapter Eighty-One

Irving Ratzinger's cabin windows glowed with rustic warmth in the early evening gloom of a late November as Jon parked the Range Rover back up the drive. There were already several vehicles parked in the woods outside the little man's cabin. Nadia looked questioningly at him. She was uncomfortable around crowds these days. Odd for a woman who, just a year ago, was in the limelight of a promising television career.

"Don't worry, honey, you'll have a great time. Irving fixed a special dinner just for you. Trust me." He got out, walked around, and opened her door, helping her swing her legs out before he picked her up and carried her to the steps. "I'll come back out for the chair if you want to go for a walk later, okay?"

He tapped on the door a couple of times with a foot, and Irving opened it with a cry of joy. Jon carried her in, set her carefully in Irving's old, comfortable recliner while the old man got her a brandy. She noticed that Irving wore a strange grin, and when she pressed him, he refused to say anything.

When Jon straightened back up, she asked, "Where's everyone else?"

"Close your eyes," said Jon. "When I tell you, you can open them." She did, and heard several people enter the little living room amid whispers and the occasional chuckle. Then there was silence. "Okay, Nadia, open your eyes and meet your team."

"My God—Bunny!" she exclaimed as the skinny little man stepped forward and gave her a hug. She cried and clung to him. "God, I am so sorry!"

"Come on, Kalinsky, you're making me jealous here," joked Jon. Everyone laughed, and Bunny stepped back, blushing.

"What's this about a team?" Nadia asked, wiping her eyes. Then she looked around as Jon introduced everyone there: Beth Nelson and Holli Hushido were her medical specialists. Bunny was her logistical specialist. In addition, Donna was the team leader, and Jon was lead agent. Irving and Jimmy were there because it was Irving's house.

"Let me explain," said Donna, pulling up a chair in front of Nadia and sitting down. "We shut down the Twin Oaks lab. Jon destroyed the equipment so our own defense department can't reverse-engineer the technology they saw there, thank God. Alan Whitfield is up on a series of charges from conspiracy to murder, to abduction of a federal agent...well, let's just say there's a list.

"But guys, he's just the tip of the iceberg. There's a group who call themselves The Pinnacle behind this whole operation. Whitfield was part of it, but he was a lower-end stooge, not in the big leadership. I'm afraid our work is only beginning.

"This Doctor, Petr Hamund, disappeared along with Anna Spielberg. We can't find them anywhere. They could be going back to the drawing board on the NADIA system—"

"Wait a minute," cut in Nadia. "I thought Jon broke up their equipment?"

"There's an old adage in design, Nadia," said Donna. "'You can build two as cheaply as you can build one.' They must have another lab, somewhere."

Donna took a deep breath and let it out. "Our operation is totally black. You all report to me, I report to someone else. They don't know who most of you are, and you sure as hell don't want to know who they are, but take my word, they're the good guys. It stays that way so we can keep The Pinnacle from knowing who we are, or where we are."

"Okay, Donna, where are we operating from?" asked Nadia.

"Why, right here, of course," said Irving, smiling. "You, young lady, are staying with me as long as you like. That reminds me, I need to check on dinner." He disappeared into the kitchen, humming a tune as he went.

"Now, for the news," smiled Donna. "First, a mixed blessing." She put a clipping from the *Eugene Chronicle* in Nadia's hands and briefed her as she read. "The bomb scare at the Twin Oaks Resort turned out to be a prank called in by a mischievous teenager. No mention anywhere of Doctor Hamund's little project or the investigation which, by the way, will probably yield no charges against anyone but Whitfield. After all, you're our only real evidence, and we're not about to bring you forward, for your own safety. Second, I saw this article on the cover of everyone's favorite grocery store magazine, and immediately thought of you." Donna grinned as she handed Nadia the issue.

The photo on the cover was the man who'd tried to rape her in Colorado, shown screaming in terror behind a thick dressing on his face. The headline read, "ALIENS TRIED TO EAT MAN'S FACE!" Nadia laughed out loud and threw the magazine back at Donna.

"Now, moving on," said Donna after everyone recomposed themselves, "how are you feeling? Stronger yet?"

"A little, but I don't understand why it's taking so long. The cut I got on my face healed in a matter of hours. It's been two months and I still can't walk, or even feel my legs. In Oregon, I could still use them—"

"I think I can answer that one," said Hushi. "First of all, you have to remember that neural tissue damage is, by reputation, nearly impossible to heal. When Whitfield set your trigger, your nanobots kind of rebelled. Some tried to eat you, and most of the others died or bled out on you when you shut down. On top of that, your nerves appear to be more than just nerves, Nadia. They're also the circuits that set off the antimatter device inside you. Many of those nerves fried out, mainly in your lower torso.

"By all rights, you should be dead, and so should we. But Miss Nelson's quick thinking and downright bitchiness saved us all." Hushi paused to allow the laughter to settle before continuing.

"Your body is making more nanobots, and your neural tissue is actually rebuilding, but more slowly than the soft tissue in your face and abdomen. Plus, we still want you to take it easy until we know you're not going to tear open again. You scared the hell out of us once. I'll pass on another time. Tonight I'll take a blood sample and do a 'bot count. We'll know more then."

"Tonight?" asked Nadia. "What lab is open on Thanksgiving?"

"Show her after dinner!" shouted Irving from the kitchen. "For goodness' sake, people, let's eat!"

They gathered in the little living room at Irving's, all of them, and bowed their heads while Irving situated his yarmulke and sang the blessing over the feast. Then Jon placed a full plate on Nadia's lap, and they all dug into turkey with all the trimmings: dressing, cranberry sauce, mashed potatoes and gravy, and pumpkin bread piled high. She inhaled the aromas and laughed.

Nadia looked around, taking in all the smiling faces, surrounded by the memories lining the walls of Irving Ratzinger's cabin, and she was nearly overcome. Now, finally, she could start making her own memories. She whispered a prayer of thanks before digging in. *It's good to be alive.*

Chapter Eighty-Two

Howard looked up when he heard his office door open. Walter Brady stepped through and closed the door behind him. Howard suppressed the sigh that tried to escape from his chest. *'Tis an ill wind that blows no one good.* He forced a smile anyway.

"Morning, Howard."

Why does he always look like he slept in that suit? "Good Morning, Congressman. This is a pleasant surprise. I'll have Marie bring in some coffee. Cream, right?"

"No, that won't be necessary. Thanks, anyway." Brady crossed the carpet and flumped into the visitor's chair. "Howard, do you remember the resort I took you and Danielle to last year? In Oregon?" Howard nodded, but kept silent. Walter went on, "The place was invaded, vandalized."

Howard tried to sound surprised. He didn't care whether he succeeded. "Imagine that, Walter."

"The administrator said the FBI caused a significant amount of damage to some valuable equipment."

"They said *my* guys did that? Now, what reason would they have for damaging this equipment? Maybe you could have them send me a detailed list—"

An agitated grimace crossed Walter's face. His voice rose a level. "Howard, this is serious. We can't have rogue agents running around like jack-booted thugs, initiating bomb scares and breaking up hospitals. You should be thankful that charges weren't pressed against your agents."

"With all due respect, Congressman, *you* should be thankful our people were there. It's my understanding that many lives were saved as a result of their actions out there."

"Speaking of 'your people,'" said Walter, "I have a concern for one agent, a rogue by the name of Daniels…." He paused, choosing his words carefully. His face turned red, betraying the seething fury behind the controlled manner. "He's been cited for violating procedure numerous times. I've been up here before on his account, if you recall."

306

Howard leaned back and teepeed his fingers. "What do you want, Congressman?"

Walter leaned forward and slammed his hand down on the desk. "*I want this man's badge, Howard!* He kidnapped a woman, hid her away, did God knows what to brainwash her. He was out there, and you know it! He's not fit to carry that badge!"

"Very well," said Howard, not even flinching. "He's gone. What else can I do for you, Congressman?" If he told Walter that Jon Daniels had already turned in his badge to make way for higher clearances and greater authority, Walter would have had a stroke right there. *That's right. Keep your friends close, and your enemies closer.*

Walter Brady sputtered, nonplussed. It was obvious he was expecting some kind of confrontation, and when he didn't get it, he was taken completely off-guard. But he recovered quickly. "You have a Donna Hermsen, an agent in your lab—"

"Can't help you there, Congressman. Doctor Hermsen is the only one qualified to run that operation in an efficient manner, and she stays."

"Well, then. I'm going to trust you to make sure she stays in her place, and doesn't meddle where she's not needed." The congressman stood. Somewhere in the process, his suit picked up yet one more set of wrinkles. "One more thing, Howard. I want to know everything that went on out west."

Howard didn't stand. "You'll have my report in the morning, sir."

Walter adjusted his tie, and the sun through the window caught a glittering red jewel set in the ring on his finger. Howard flinched at the sudden stab of light. "The committee may call you to testify. I can't guarantee whether you'll still have a job, after this fiasco." He started for the door.

"Congressman?" said Howard. Walter turned. "You may want to be careful yourself. There are rumors floating around about some of your lobby groups, and the activities they are involved in. Some of those rumors may lead to further investigations."

Walter stood with his hand on the doorknob. "There's a saying I want you to remember, Howard— 'Meddle not in the affairs of dragons.'"

"Is that a threat, Congressman?"

"Let's just say I'm watching out for your best interests, Howard." The congressman left the office, closing the door quietly behind him.

Howard Standish looked at the safe in the corner of his office and considered the files that he had secreted there. "I'm getting too old for this," he muttered.

Chapter Eighty-Three

Give a man a job he loves, and he'll never have to work a day in his life. Anton "Tony" Pugachev was proof of the truth of Jefferson's adage. He loved washing windows on Madison Avenue. His friends all thought he was wasting himself. He had a bachelor's degree from the University of Minsk in Applied Mathematics, and he could have been so much more than a window washer in New York. But Tony just loved doing windows. He loved the solitude. He loved the view from fifty stories up, and he loved the way the buildings looked with whole walls of perfectly clean windows, and especially he loved the fact that he could choose to be a window washer.

He was fifteen when the Soviet Union fell. His father died the year before the Wall in Berlin came down. He'd worked himself to death in a job he'd hated, trying to support Tony's mother and all four brothers. He'd never had the chance to choose what he'd wanted to do; the State chose for him. When Tony first came to America, he stood on the sidewalk downtown and watched the window cleaners plying their trade on the scaffolds for hours, fascinated by the ease with which they worked, each window spotless from just a couple quick swipes with a squeegee. Call him crazy, he just decided that that was what he wanted to do.

Twenty-five years later, he still loved windows just as much as he did that first day. He knew every business on the other side of those windows. It was his standing joke that he could make himself invisible just by washing windows and pretending not to notice anything that went on inside those offices. After applying himself to reading lips, he knew more than anyone could ever want him to about how things really worked on Madison Avenue. That was another thing that made this job so great.

The law offices of Whitfield, Campbell, and Moore occupied the entire thirtieth floor of the 800 Block of Madison Avenue. Tony was out early this Monday morning; he wanted to see the sunrise coming up behind Lady Liberty, a view that never ceased to take his breath away, which was why he saved it for special occasions. Like his twentieth anniversary as an American citizen.

He came across the hole in the fourteenth window of the row. Bullet holes were fairly common down lower, but up this high? He pulled out a notepad and jotted down the location of the window to report to the building's owners. Then he taped it to keep it from breaking any farther. That was when he noticed the hand on the floor, peeking out from behind the huge, curly-maple desk in the plush office on the other side of the pane.

A white-hot flush splashed Tony's face. He quickly wrapped his hand with a towel and covered his face while he smashed the window with his squeegee. Climbing inside the office, he found a man lying on the floor with a neat hole in the right side of his head, the left half blown to jelly. Then he saw the pistol in the man's hand. He'd been dead for some time; the blood on the carpet had congealed and dried. Tony recognized him right away; he was one of the main partners of the firm, a Mr. Whitfield.

Tony picked up the phone and dialed 9-1-1. While the phone rang on the other end, he noticed the note by the phone: *I can't live like this anymore....* Tony stopped reading there. The police could sort out the rest when they got there. They wouldn't see, though, that the glass from the window had been blown in and not out. Tony's own footprints covered up the set of smaller footprints pressed into the deep-pile carpet from the only other visitor to that office in the last twenty-four hours. They would never find any trace of evidence that would lead them to believe that this was anything but straight and simple suicide.

Tony Pugachev never thought he could be guilty of covering up a murder, but when he first saw Alan Whitfield lying in his own blood he only thought of helping.

As the place crawled with New York Police taping around the body, checking for fingerprints on the gun, testing for powder marks on Whitfield's hand, checking his handwriting on other file documents against that note on the desk, and taping off the room, Tony found himself answering questions from a police investigator.

Why did he break the window? "I thought the man might still be alive." Did he write the note? "No." Did he kill Alan Whitfield? "No." Is this the phone he used? "Yes." They lifted his fingerprints from the handset. They measured his bloody footprints on the floor. When they finished they took down Tony's phone number and address, and warned him sternly not to leave town. And then, they just walked away and filed it as another useless suicide.

"Such a shame, to work so hard and to come to this end," Tony told them, more than once. He thought again of his father. "Such a shame, to be so rich, and yet so lost."

Tony found himself still shaken hours later, back out on the scaffold. *Such a waste. Give me windows any day.*

Chapter Eighty-Four

"Are you sure you want to do this?" asked Jon. The Range Rover sat idling in the crisp morning, the heater on low against the cold outside. The threat of a winter rain hung low in the steel-gray sky.

"By now I feel like I owe it to her. There's so much to say," she sighed. "Let's go."

Jon got out first to help her down. The forearm crutches were ungainly on the soft ground at first, but she adjusted her steps and managed slow progress as he walked slowly beside her.

Nadia was healing: slow for her, but phenomenally fast for a human. There was still a long way to go, but she was getting there. Patiently, determined as an emerging butterfly, she was healing.

The stones were arranged in neat little rows on the manicured lawn. A huge marble statue of Jesus stood on benevolent watch over the garden around the base of the sculpture.

Ten minutes' searching yielded the stones they were looking for. They were in magnificent, black granite, deeply and simply carved with names and dates. Alicia and Phillip Burgess rested together next to three smaller stones for the children. There were flowers and toys neatly arranged around the stones in an impromptu memoriam.

Nadia stood and read each stone, coming in closer to touch each in turn. She spoke each name as she brushed a gentle fingertip across the top of each stone, finishing with the children: "Wil, Deena, Max...." When she spoke the last name, her voice caught, and she brought a hand up to her mouth. Her knees trembled. Something struggled to come back from the blackness of her mind: a stirring, a boiling of dark swirls roiled in her brain. But she couldn't *remember*. A nauseous feeling rose in her abdomen and she swallowed hard. Then, just as suddenly as the feeling rose up inside her it passed away, leaving faint echoes of a loss too terrible to bear.

Jon stepped up and took hold of her, and she turned and wrapped her arms around him, burying her face in his chest, and crying. "She gave me so much. I just wanted to say... Did I do okay? Am I someone she would have —?"

"It's okay, babe. I think she would have approved."

She brushed a tear away. "I can't remember them anymore. I don't even dream about them. There's a hole. I feel like I lost something so precious—"

He held her close until she steadied and looked up into his eyes. "Me too, babe. But I think it's going to be okay now."

"People don't appreciate what they have," she said.

"What's that, honey?"

"You have life. You have day after day, given to you to live in, and I see people going about day in and day out, just surviving; doing the same thing and hoping for a different result. And then they end up here. I don't want to just survive. I want to live."

"Good idea. I think I'll join you," he said as they turned and headed back for the car.

"I'd love to have you, Jon Daniels," she said, smiling as she wiped her eyes against a shoulder.

It started to rain then, a steady, gentle shower. Jon pulled her along a little faster, but she held back, stopping as she turned her face up, eyes closed. "Wait a minute. I want to feel it on my skin. It reminds me of someone." She had a strange, distant smile on her face as she stood soaking in the rain.

"Who?" he asked, puzzled.

She smiled. "I don't know, but it feels like they were a good friend."

Jon took her face in his hands and looked her square in the eyes. She liked it when he did that. "You, Nadia, are a one-of-a-kind."

She pulled him close. "God, I hope so."

About the Author

Born and raised in Northern Indiana, I grew up learning how to camp and fish with my scoutmaster dad, who instilled in me a love for the outdoors and nature.

A proud U.S Air Force veteran, I've worked a wild variety of jobs. In addition, I played bass with the best rock-punk band that never launched a record, invented the best board game that never sold a copy, and with a friend developed a role-playing game that to this day gathers dust in a Rhode Island closet.

I live in Michigan with my wife, four kids, and half the whitetail population of North America.

* * * *

Did you enjoy Becoming NADIA? If so, please help us spread the word about Cyrus Keith and MuseItUp Publishing. It's as easy as:

•Recommend the book to your family and friends
•Post a review
•Tweet and Facebook about it

Thank you
MuseItUp Publishing

CPSIA information can be obtained at www.ICGtesting.com
Printed in the USA
LVOW080853090213

319279LV00001B/109/P

9 781771 271813